Freedom's Choice

A Novel by D.J. Lambert

Freedom's Choice

First Edition

Printed in the United States of America
May 2013

All scripture is from the King James Version of the Bible

(Public Domain)

This is a work of fiction. Names, characters, places, and incidents are the products of the author's imagination. Events, locales, or persons, living or dead, are fictitious.

ISBN-10: 0615784607
ISBN-13: 978-0-615-78460-1

DEDICATION

This book is in dedication to the memory of:

Dolores Johnson Broyhill Greer

An encouragement to all who knew her...

The best Sister ever!

ACKNOWLEDGMENTS

Numerous individuals have contributed to the reality of this first book in the Freedom Series. Without the support and encouragement from my family and my friends, this book may still be a dream rather than a reality.

Of special note, I want to give a warm and loving thank you to my husband of forty years. He is my biggest fan. He always encourages me to share my God-given talents. His keen insight for readability is an invaluable trait.

I wish to thank our daughters, who also gave their encouragement and assistance for this project. Both daughters opened my mind to varying aspects of presenting situational conflicts.

My dear departed sister, Dolores, was the inspiration for one of my characters. Dolores continually gave me that little extra push and encouragement for completing my writing.

Thank you to Donna, a special friend who took the time to critique the content of my writing.

Finally, gratitude goes to the following professionals who either coached me or edited my work; Sheryl M., Hope F. and my Son-In-Law, Travis.

"Therefore, my brothers and sisters, I want you to know that through Jesus, the forgiveness of sins is proclaimed to you. [39] Through him everyone who believes is set free from every sin, a justification you were not able to obtain under the Law of Moses.

Acts 13:38-39

Chapter 1

Jodie's Prison

Jodie felt the warm early-morning light as it filtered through the cloudy jail cell window. The sun reached for her tired, aching body, its rays baking into her bones. She hesitated to move because it seemed to relieve some of her pain. However, she was hungry and confused; still wondering how she ended up in this cold place. All she could remember was being at the Country Club for Johnny Ricks' celebration party.

"Is this real? Oh Lord, what happened for me to be in a jail cell? Were we too loud at the party? But how could that land me in jail? I have tried to remember what might have taken place. Am I the only one in jail? Where are the others from the party? Where are all my friends who were so willing to help me give the party for Johnny? Connections really do pay off, but what about now? What am I going to do? Surely, I can make a call, but who will I call? I know I have the right to make a call! Everyone has that opportunity, right?"

"What am I doing here?" Jodie finally yelled in desperation.

Jodie's head was already spinning with questions as it ached relentlessly. Now, it felt as if a dozen hammers were playing a symphony in her head.

"Dear God," Jodie cried. "My head is killing me!"

Suddenly, Jodie was brought back to her senses by the turning of the lock. A big, burly woman stepped into the light with a tray of food that smelled rank. Any other time, Jodie would have been ready to eat. She was not sure now if she was hungry or not. The headache and all the many questions running through her mind made her think she might hurl at any minute.

The woman mumbled a good morning as Jodie noticed the name tag she wore. The tag read - Frank, Guard. "Oh great, a woman named Frank, if you could call her a woman." Frank slammed the tray down on a tiny table in the corner and in a gruff voice; Jodie could hear Frank talking as though someone else was in the cell with her other than the two of them. Jodie had not seen anyone, so she could not help but ask.

"I'm sorry, are you talking to me?" Jodie asked.

"I'm a talkin' to myself young lady!" Frank replied.

"Sorry! I didn't know."

"Well, look at you anyways, Miss High and Mighty." Yo' sho' nough looks like a Councilman's daughter! All jumbled up clothes and her hair all twisted...!" Frank turned and stared at Jodie. "You better be eating this here food young lady. You gonna' need yo' strength for what you got facing you!" said Frank.

"Wait," cried Jodie, as Frank turned and locked the cell behind her. "How do you know my Father?" It was all Jodie could do to keep calm. Jodie's mind raced as she ran to the door.

Beating on the jail cell door, Jodie cried. "Come back, please come back!"

Despair loomed its dark, ominous cloud over Jodie's head. "Even if the woman does know who my Father is, I still do not know what I have done to merit this wonderful suite in jail!" The nausea she was feeling became even more intense as her head continued to pound.

"Look at this food. Yuck! I wish I could eat, but I feel so sick, and I am not sure what is on this tray." Jodie played with the food on the tray. She stirred the fried eggs and what appeared to be oatmeal -"I really need to concentrate on why I am here."

Determined to keep her strength and presence of mind, Jodie decided to try the food. She took a spoonful of the oatmeal. She rolled the pasty, lukewarm cereal around on her tongue until she knew she would vomit if she swallowed. Suddenly, Jodie spewed the oatmeal from her mouth across the floor. Disgust and anger began to swell up inside her being.

"Where is everyone? Why has no one been to tell me what is going on? Frank could have said more before she so rudely slammed the cell door." Jodie began pacing the floor. "I need answers!"

Jodie tried looking through the tiny window in the cell door. It appeared she was at the end of a long hallway. There was a big steel door at the end of the hall with a red light above the lock. The light kept a steady rate of blinking. "So, this must be where they keep their dangerous criminals! It looks like I am in a secure area or a red-light district! I know I make my mistakes, but seriously! Oh my gracious, that light is certainly bright."

Jodie turned from the light, as she did; she immediately felt a wave of nausea sweep from her feet through the top of her head. Then almost instantly, Jodie had an excruciating pain behind her eyes.

"Oh God, what is happening to me?" A sweet and sour smell filled Jodie's nostrils as she began to heave. The room started spinning and she felt herself falling...falling, until at last there was no more pain.

"Who in heaven's name keeps calling my cell phone?" Johnson Scever exclaimed. Johnson, President of Metro-Council, was in the middle of a heated debate over the City's contract with Sky Development. "This is not the time to be answering my cell phone, especially since I am the one who arranged this weekend meeting and kept everyone from their families." Johnson looked quickly at the number calling his phone. The number was not one he recognized. Johnson shut his phone off as he turned his attention back to the meeting. "Sugar Falls desperately needs the additional businesses and parking for upcoming community events and for the recent increase in Tourism. Metro-Council entrusted this contract with your company gentlemen, to have our project complete within one year and in time for the holidays. We are very pleased with the Visitor's Center. We already have tenants waiting to stock and decorate their shops. The Bistro is almost ready for customers. Gentlemen, we need parking. We are not going to be able to attract business when patrons are not capable of finding parking!"

The CEO of Sky Development stood and asked permission to present an extension option to the Parking Garage contract that he felt would be agreeable to everyone on the Council.

Jack Renault, another member of Metro-Council, countered, "Sir, we appreciate the willingness on your behalf to offer other options, however; our Council prefers to present a counter-offer for extending the contract. If you turn your attention to the packets in the center of the table, you will find a packet for each of your team members. Your company will be given an additional 30 days, including extra costs along with a Ten Percent across the board rate reduction for the entire contract. Metro-Council agrees the project could have been completed within the time frame allotted. Sugar Falls may lose an unprecedented amount of revenue without ample parking for the upcoming holiday season. The Community Theatre is getting ready to be in full operation. The Holiday Shopping season will be bringing lots of traffic to the area, not to mention the religious services and holiday parties. We realize the rainfall has interfered somewhat with the project."

Johnson was listening intently, as the door opened and Johnson's secretary passed him a note. She whispered to him, "Sir; I apologize for interrupting, but this note is urgent."

Johnson read the note. "Your daughter, Jodie, is a patient at Saint's Hospital in Johnsonville. Her condition is serious. Please come." - Matilda.

Johnson's demeanor immediately changed. Jack Renault broke the silence.

"What is it Johnson?"

"I apologize but it seems I have a family emergency. Gentlemen, please excuse me for a moment. Jack, will you continue until I determine the extent of this situation?"

Johnson excused himself from the meeting. He questioned his secretary who could only tell him that Matilda had a sense of urgency in her voice.

Johnson sighed, "Why on earth does Matilda feel a need to call me. She has always handled everything with Jodie."

Johnson gave his secretary instructions to have Jack extend his apologies, bring the meeting to a satisfactory close and re-schedule another session with Sky Development for the end of the week. The current contract did not expire for another fifteen days, so they had a little time to complete the legalities once he determined what was happening with his daughter. He also told his secretary to go on home. He hated to ask her to come in on a Sunday, and now he felt even worse that he was leaving. Johnson then took time to call his wife. Her cell phone went straight to voice mail so Johnson left her this message.

"Susan, it appears I am needed in Johnsonville for Jodie. It has something to do with an accident and Jodie being in the hospital. I don't know how serious this is, but as soon as I know details, I will call you."

The autumn air was crisp, and the sky was a perfect blue! This was just the kind of weather Sugar Falls needed right now, if only the weather holds out to see the completion of the parking garage before the end of November. Johnson started the engine of his Cadillac and pulled into the traffic. "This day is too gorgeous for bad news to come my way." Johnson liked to feel in control of his circumstances, but this news gave him quite an unexpected jolt. He realized Matilda would not have called him unless it was truly urgent. Johnson really couldn't remember the last time she had called him. It would take him at least two hours to drive to Johnsonville in the afternoon traffic. There was little time to waste.

Johnson began reminiscing about his family. "How have I allowed my relationship with my children to become so severed? I guess Jodie being with us this past summer caused me to realize how much I have missed out on, but I can only be angry with myself. It was I who left them."

Even though Jodie's time with him was rewarding, he felt the animosity from Jodie almost daily. Johnson knew deep inside that he had never stopped loving or caring for his children. There was even the nagging question in his conscience of how much feeling he still carried for Matilda.

"Susan can never find out that I continue to hold feelings for Matilda. She is not capable of understanding the relationship

Matilda, and I had since she is totally opposite of Matilda. No, it will never do for Susan to know."

Johnson was a master of hiding his emotions, a business trait he had learned over the years. One should never let the other party know what you were feeling. "Oh what a charade I have played out. I have allowed my mistakes to make me a hard person."

Johnson pulled into the driveway of his elegant home in Sugar Falls. He almost ran as he went inside to pack an overnight bag. Who knew what he would find when he arrived at Saint's Hospital?

Jodie's Mother, Matilda, and the Pastor from Matilda's church, sat in the conference room listening in shock as the Neurosurgeon explained Jodie's situation.

"Jodie was transported to the hospital from the county jail. The information given is that Jodie was involved in an automobile accident. Due to the questionable circumstances, she was held at the jail. When she became ill, they immediately transferred Jodie to the hospital."

"Ms. Scever, your daughter Jodie suffered a head injury from the accident. She has a vessel that is leaking into the brain. It is imperative that we repair this vessel and stop the bleeding as quickly as possible. Our staff is prepping Jodie as we speak for the needed surgery. I expect we will have Jodie in surgery within the next thirty minutes."

"Will she be okay Doctor? How serious is this injury?" Matilda questioned.

"It is always serious anytime the brain is injured. However, we are certain we can stop the bleeding vessel in time. We plan to take good care of Jodie for you. One of the nurses will be out momentarily to obtain your permission for the surgery. It is really urgent that I attend to your daughter now. Do you have any further questions?"

Matilda's mind was reeling from all the unfolding news. The doctor mentioned Jodie being in an accident and then being transported to the hospital from the county jail. This was almost more than Matilda could think about right now.

"No, not at the moment doctor, please take care of Jodie. I will sign whatever I need to sign, just bring her back to us."

Matilda turned to her pastor. "I still do not understand what Jodie was doing at the County Jail so early in the morning. Perhaps the person who caused the accident was at fault, and Jodie thought she had to go to rescue them. Jodie is always trying to make peace or fix the hurt. Why else would she be at a jail?"

A gentleman appeared in the doorway. "Is Ms. Scever in the room?"

"Yes, over here," responded Pastor Rayford as he stood to intervene for Matilda.

"Hello, I am Thomas Wiley. I am an Intern in the Neurology Department assigned to Dr. Smith. It is my pleasure to meet you Ms. Scever. I am available to you and your family anytime you have questions or concerns for your daughter."

"Thank you so much. That is good to know."

"I will be assisting Dr. Smith with the surgery. We will begin shortly. Dr. Smith explained to you that we needed your signature to proceed with the surgery. I have the paperwork here and will go over it with you."

"Oh! Dr. Smith said a nurse would come for my signature."

"We all have to assist. The nurses are busy with Jodie."

"I understand," replied Matilda weakly.

"Let's look at the Consent for Procedure together."

Thomas Wiley explained the procedure; and what happens during surgery. Matilda listened intently with worry written all over her face.

"Do you have any questions Mrs. Scever?" Thomas asked.

"No, I don't think so."

"If you will sign here then, and again on the back, we will be able to get started."

Matilda signed the consent and watched the young intern leave the room. She felt such heaviness in her heart and soul. With all she and Jodie had been through; she could not stand the thoughts of losing her. Matilda thought about the intern's last words to her as he left, "I look forward to seeing you soon with good news!"

"Good news is what I need to hear."

Jodie's sister suddenly appeared in the surgical waiting room. "Mother, tell me this is not true. It is all over the news this morning about Jodie's accident."

The voice of Edee was normally a welcomed voice, but the obvious hysteria in Edee's voice was very disconcerting to Matilda; and what was this about the morning news?

"Edee, I do not know what you are talking about. Will you please sit down, try to calm yourself, and explain what you are talking about?"

Edee, the oldest of the family had always felt the burden of taking care of her siblings. Edee had taken care of Jodie as if she was her own child after her parent's divorce. There were also two brothers, Shelton and Henry, who were in between Edee and Jodie. Jodie was the baby girl, and had been doted on since the day she was born.

Edee began in an almost breathless voice, "Apparently; Jodie was involved in a single car crash last night. Johnny Ricks, you remember him, was in the car with her. The whole thing is under investigation because it appears Johnny had a gunshot wound. The police feel the gunshot was the actual cause of death. It was stated that the Coroner would determine if Johnny died from the wound or from trauma caused by the accident. Jodie was taken to jail because she is a prime suspect!" Edee explained.

"Oh no Edee, I had no idea. Heavenly Father, what will we do?" Matilda moaned in a worried tone. Matilda got up from her chair and began pacing back and forth.

"Jodie, in trouble and considered a murderer? This is impossible and entirely too much to consider."

"I know Mother. I am sorry to break the news so suddenly, but I thought you knew."

"That's okay Edee. I had to find out somehow. It is better for you to tell me than a stranger."

Edee felt the need to embrace her Mother. As she stood to walk toward Matilda, Edee heard Matilda mumbling as she lay her head in her hands. "Oh gracious, I feel so very weak and sick."

Matilda began sinking to the floor.

Edee rushed forward to embrace her mother before she completely fell to the floor. With her arms around her mother's waist, Edee gladly accepted Pastor Rayford's assistance in getting Matilda back into a chair. Edee kneeled beside her mother to assist her as Pastor Rayford looked on trying to discern what action he needed to take.

"Mother," called Edee, "wake up Mother. You fainted. Mother, are you okay?"

Edee was ready to send Pastor Rayford for a nurse when someone knocked on the door.

"Please come in," Edee called out.

"Hello, I am Kathy, the volunteer for the waiting room… oh my, is this lady sick? Do you need me to get help?"

Edee replied affirmatively.

As Kathy left for help, the closing of the door caused Matilda to stir.

"Goodness, what happened?" whispered Matilda.

"You fainted, Mother. Now just sit still, we have sent someone for help."

"No Edee! Please don't let them take me from here. I have to know what is going on with Jodie!"

"Calm down mom, we only want to be sure you are going to be okay. I will not let them take you unless it is necessary."

"You will not let them take me Edee! I will not leave this room!"

"As you wish, 'Mom!'" replied Edee with a look of concern on her face.

Pastor Rayford stepped in to diffuse the situation. "Mrs. Matilda, do not worry, everything is going to be fine. You just fainted. I am sure one of the staff here will be willing to assist you according to your wishes."

"Mother, I should have waited to say anything. I was so upset and confused. Let's focus on Jodie's survival since I really do not know any details. When you feel ready, you or pastor can fill me in on everything that is going on with Jodie's surgery."

Matilda held onto Edee's hand. "Thanks for helping me. I would have been a sight lying out here on the floor!"

Someone knocked on the door again. Pastor Rayford opened the door and made way for the volunteer. Kathy came into the room with a nurse. Kathy introduced Nurse David.

"Mrs. Scever, I understand you are feeling sick and had an episode of fainting."

Edee noticed her mother starring at David. "Mother, the nurse is talking to you. Do you hear him?"

"I do." replied Matilda as she continued to gaze.

"Ms. Scever, again my name is David. I am one of the nurses on the Critical Care Unit. Kathy found me to take a look at you. Do you want to tell me what happened?"

Ms. Matilda continued to stare at David. Edee became frustrated with her mother.

"Mom, are you going to speak or what?"

"Well, it is just that I've never seen a male nurse!"

"MOM!" Edee exclaimed.

"Well, have you?" Matilda asked.

David laughed. "Ms. Scever, I get that reaction often. You will find several male nurses in our hospital. Hopefully, you will be comfortable with me. If not, I will be glad to get our charge nurse, Mandy, to take a look at you."

"No, I am fine with you helping me. You just took me by surprise. It seems I am having lots of surprises today! Please forgive me."

"You are forgiven already! Now let's see what is going on with you."

David seemed very competent to Edee. He examined Matilda as thoroughly as he could under the circumstances. David's direction to Matilda was firm.

"Ms. Scever, I believe you are dehydrated and most likely exhausted with worry. You need to drink plenty of water and remain as calm as possible. I will let our charge nurse know what has happened. We may be able to order some medication to help you relax."

"I do not want to be asleep or out of my mind David. I need to know what is happening with my daughter."

David patted Matilda's hand. "I understand completely. This is a medicine which will take the edge off and calm your nerves. I promise it will not put you to sleep."

Edee spoke up. "David, I think that is an excellent idea. I am sure mother does too; she just needs a few minutes to process the information."

"Very well then, I will see what we can do. In the meantime, I will have Kathy help you find a more comfortable area to wait. We have some nice sofas and chairs in the waiting area, much better than these conference room chairs."

Kathy came and did just as David mentioned. After everyone was settled and Matilda was comfortable, the conversation again turned to Jodie and the reasons behind this present ordeal.

"Mother, do you feel like telling me what the doctor said?"

"I believe I can now. Let me think. According to Dr. Smith, the Neurosurgeon, there is a lot to be thankful for, Edee. He states that given the worst-case scenario, Jodie has a ninety percent chance of a full recovery. Dr. Smith states Jodie has a leaking blood vessel in the brain as a result of the accident. It is imperative that the bleeding is stopped before the vessel is weakened any further. The surgery prognosis is good, however;

the recovery outlook could be long-term. There is the possibility of Infection, Pneumonia, Seizures, Depression, Memory Loss and Speech Impairment. Is that all he said, Pastor? So much has taken place."

The intercom sounded, "Scever family." Pastor Rayford responded to the front desk as a representative for the family. He returned with the news that Jodie's surgery had just begun.

"Mother, you and I might need to go find something to eat. We should have time before another update from the doctor. You probably need some nourishment, especially since they gave you the shot. I don't want you to get sick from not eating."

"That sounds like a good idea to me." expressed Pastor Rayford. "I have no reason to leave and plan to stay with you until we know Jodie's surgery is over. Take as much time as you need, Edee. I do however; think it wise for you to find a wheelchair to take Matilda, so she is not weakened any further. I'm sure you do not want her to pass out on you if the shot is stronger than we were told."

Although Matilda protested, Edee managed to get her into a wheelchair. Edee felt as though the walk to the cafeteria was ten miles long as she and Matilda made their way in silence - the seriousness of the situation heavy on their hearts. Edee could not help but wonder how Jodie ended up here.

"I know you don't know the entire story mother, but why wasn't Jodie checked out thoroughly after the accident? Why did the authorities not notify us sooner?"

"I know Edee; I have been wondering the same." Matilda replied.

"I just talked to Jodie two days ago. She called to tell me about the party plans for Johnny. The party was to be a celebration for Johnny Ricks and his accomplishments. Now, Johnny Ricks is dead. I pray Jodie is not at fault for whatever happened last night."

Although she could not fathom the idea that Jodie was capable of killing someone, Edee wondered about the contributing factors and why Jodie was a suspect. Jodie, an honor student in her final year at Johnsonville University was set for a life of endless opportunities. Jodie already had offers from several companies, including the large retail chain, Eagles Dress Factory, based in Cherry Hill. Jodie had worked for Eagles Dress Factory in the Advertising Department during High School and continued there during the summer months after she left for college.

"Mother, as much as I want to find out what is going on with Jodie, I imagine we need to put all this behind us until Jodie is stable. I will be here for you and try not to cause you anymore distress. After all, Jodie is clinging to life; her future hanging in the balance accused of a murder. Jodie needs my support and love, not a million questions."

"Thank you Edee. I agree with your thoughts. I really appreciate your being here."

Chapter 2

Unplanned Reunion

Johnson found a parking spot near the entrance to Saint's Hospital. As he stepped out of the Cadillac, he verbalized his immediate reaction.

"It has been at least twenty years since I have been in Johnsonville. This is the same hospital where Jodie was born. We lived in Johnsonville until shortly after Jodie's birth."

Johnson recalled earning his Real Estate License while they lived in Johnsonville. He had the opportunity to open a realty company in the neighboring town of Cherry Hill. This opportunity came along at a time when he and Matilda were dealing with some family issues, so it was a welcome change for Johnson. He took advantage of the opportunity to start over in a different town. Thinking back, this is certainly a strange coincidence. Here we are at the hospital facility that gave Jodie her start into this world, only now to save her life and keep her alive.

"I wonder if Jodie knows just how much I love her. I need to be certain to let her know at the first opportunity. Lord, please give me the chance."

Johnson made his way quickly into the hospital, and as he rounded the corner to the information desk, he practically ran all over Pastor Rayford.

"Johnson! It has been a long time. I am certainly sorry about Jodie and even sorrier that we have to meet under these circumstances. Ms. Matilda called as soon as she received the news. My wife drove us here to the hospital."

"I am glad Matilda has someone with her." Johnson replied.

"Jodie is in surgery and the family is in the Surgical Waiting Room. I need to go make a few calls, and I will be back shortly."

"Thank you. Which way do I go to the waiting room?"

Pastor Rayford quickly gave Johnson directions to find his family and went on his way. Johnson suddenly felt overwhelmed. Here he was on his way to find out why his youngest child's life was in a critical state. The uncertainty of Jodie's condition, the return to Saints Hospital, and now running into Pastor Rayford were all too overwhelming. Johnson felt very awkward being in the presence of the man of God who knew all the family secrets! Pastor Rayford and his wife had been there for Matilda and Jodie after the divorce. Johnson always wondered if Matilda would have survived had it not been for Pastor Rayford, his wife and the church family. Matilda's life was almost consumed by her church work, her devotion to God and to the church itself. Johnson felt that he was second to the church in Matilda's affection. In all honesty, Johnson knew this was not entirely true, but it certainly made it easier to cope with his guilt. Now he was unsure if he could handle being in the company of all Matilda's church family even though it had been ten years.

Johnson found the waiting room. He inquired of the person at the desk. "I am looking for the Scever family. My daughter is in surgery, Jodie Scever."

"Yes sir, we do have your daughter in surgery at this time. The family is in the back left corner of the waiting room."

Johnson stepped into the waiting room to see Matilda, Edee, and Mrs. Rayford in the back corner, just as he had been told. He stayed in the background until the present conversation ended. Even though he was hesitant for a moment, he forced himself to move forward feeling all his confidence waning.

As soon as the Edee noticed Johnson, she stepped forward to embrace her Father. She held onto Johnson for a lengthy embrace.

"Dad, it is so good to see you! We are all here now. Jodie has been in surgery a little over an hour. We are so concerned for her!"

"I understand Edee. I am too."

"Come over here Dad and sit with us."

Edee led Johnson to the small area where they were waiting, and for just a moment it seemed as though all the past was erased. Edee's embrace seemed to take away some of the disturbing emotions Johnson was feeling. Then, he found himself face to face with Matilda.

"Hello, John," greeted Matilda as she stood and took his hand. "I'm glad you made it here. I knew you would want to know about Jodie."

Johnson held Matilda's hand casually and mumbled a thank you for calling. He started to take a seat beside Edee just when he noticed his sons, Shelton and Henry, sitting on the back side of the room. Being here with Matilda and the children was going to be more difficult than he expected. A sick feeling rose in the pit of his stomach as he allowed the circumstances to sink into his mind. He knew he had to muster all the strength possible to endure the situation. It no longer mattered what had happened between he and Matilda; the real issue now became Jodie's fight for life.

The family came together as they talked about the events surrounding Jodie's accident. Johnson asked numerous questions. Edee kept him calm as she assured her Dad that everyone had acted as quickly as possible in Jodie's best interest.

Each time someone opened the waiting room door or the telephone rang; they stopped talking. Their sentences went unfinished hanging like a mist in the air. It had been almost four hours since Johnson arrived. By his calculation, Jodie's surgery was at least into hour five.

After what seemed like an eternity, the young intern named Thomas Wiley returned to the Surgical Waiting room. Thomas was of medium height with a confident presence about him.

"Scever family, I have an update for you. Is everyone here family?" Thomas inquired.

"Yes, we are." Edee answered. "This is our Dad, Johnson Scever, our brothers, Shelton and Henry, and I believe you already met our Pastor."

"It is a pleasure to see each of you, perhaps not under these circumstances though." He took a seat beside Matilda and began to explain what was happening with Jodie.

"Thus far, Dr. Smith has been able to stop the bleeding. It appears Jodie took a severe blow to the head most likely from the auto accident. Luckily, the damage was contained to one area of the brain. Jodie seems to be a healthy young lady. Other than the amount of time between the accident and her arrival here, Jodie is blessed with a positive prognosis."

"How much time lapse was there before Jodie arrived here?" Johnson inquired.

Thomas quickly responded, "Perhaps five hours. It is hard to say exactly. However, she should recover nicely."

Thomas continued, "Although we have a positive outlook for your daughter Sir, she did have a few complications during surgery. Jodie began to have seizures during surgery, which increased the amount of time for the procedure. It is not uncommon for someone with head trauma to experience seizures. The main issue will now be to keep Jodie calm and her body at rest in order to reduce the brain swelling and hopefully stop the seizure activity."

"Goodness," exclaimed Matilda, "How could you do anything if Jodie was having seizures?"

"I'm sorry to alarm you Ma'am. We have Jodie on various monitors to show us her heart activity, blood pressure, and her brain activity. The anesthesia kept Jodie from having body tremors, yet we could see the activity on her monitor. As I said, this is not uncommon, and we are praying Jodie will not continue to have the seizures."

"Oh I certainly hope she doesn't." Matilda replied in a frightened voice.

Johnson interrupted with more questions. "How long do you expect Jodie to be in the present condition of possible seizures and the swelling of her brain?"

"Good question. We can control the seizures with medication. As long as Jodie responds to this medication, you may not see any further seizures. As for the swelling, Dr. Smith plans to keep Jodie in a semi-induced coma to allow her body to rest and heal properly. This and certain medication will be used to reduce the swelling. It could only be a few days or it could be a few weeks."

Thomas waited giving everyone a chance to absorb the information. He then began again, "Dr. Smith was beginning to close the surgery site when I left to come find you. Jodie will be moved to recovery and will remain there at least an hour, possibly longer. When we are comfortable moving her, Jodie will be going to the Neurological Critical Care Unit. There, Jodie will have her own nurse to keep an eye on her around the clock."

"Will we be able to see Jodie?" Edee asked.

"Yes, we will give you some time with her when she is settled. The nurses will let you know how often you may visit. Normally, you are allowed to check on your family member as often as you like unless the nurse sends word otherwise. Please do not expect changes overnight. Jodie is still critical although I believe with the right combination of medical care and prayer; you will see Jodie improve soon. If your family believes in prayer, it is my experience you will find peace and understanding. One of our staff will call you and let you know Jodie's room number. After you are notified, you are welcome to make your way to the waiting area for Jodie's room number."

Thomas took a moment to shake hands with Ms. Matilda and with Johnson. He then disappeared through the doorway leaving the family to digest all he had explained.

"He is certainly a nice young man!" Matilda exclaimed. "That was very thoughtful of him. I am pleasantly surprised that he mentioned prayer. That makes me feel so much better knowing he believes in prayer!"

Johnson replied before he thought, "Yes, and now you probably think he is the best intern around."

Edee gave her Father a stern look and tried to smooth the tension quickly. "You know we need to pray for the doctors as well to make the right decisions for Jodie. It is unusual to find a doctor willing to admit to prayer."

Johnson immediately felt the sting of Edee's words.

"Hey Dad, will you walk with me to my car? I need to gather my overnight bag since I am planning to stay here through the night. I may need some help."

Johnson nodded as he knew he had messed up. He had no choice but to comply. He followed Edee, prepared to hear her words of advice.

Chapter 3

Reminiscing

Mabry Allen rolled over and looked at her clock. "What a headache! I don't remember one this bad in quite a while."

Mabry managed to get up and partially open the window blinds. Thinking back, she had stayed at the Johnsonville Police Department most of the day Monday filling out papers that could condemn Jodie for events of the past week. Mabry's conscience gave her a fit in trying to control the lies she was telling, but it became easier and easier to cover up the truth. The voices in Mabry's head seemed to be in a constant battle against her conscience. More often than not, the voices won.

Mabry made her way into the Living Room hoping to hear the latest news on the local TV station. The story was still being aired. It always amazed her how the news media could find so many angles on one story! It appeared the authorities were still considering Jodie Scever as the prime suspect. Mabry knew she should be feeling good about Jodie being investigated; but somehow it did not ease the guilt she was carrying. She sat on the sofa listening to the news and soon found herself reminiscing over the past three years.

"Jodie, do you remember the Sorority gathering at the beginning of our freshman year at Johnsonville University? I knew you immediately from class and from that idiotic smile you always wore. All you ever do is smile. How a person can manage to smile all the time is beyond me even during those boring lectures? I believe the oddest thing is when you introduced yourself to me as the one who sat near me in accounting class. You did not even realize we had more than one class together! That night was the beginning of a tumultuous journey for us, don't you agree?"

Tired of hearing the news, Mabry went into the Kitchen to pour another cup of coffee. With the pouring of the liquid in the cup, Mabry could see visions of the time she and Jodie spent as roommates.

"I guess we did become good friends and roommates while it lasted. You just know entirely too much about me and my family. I remember you always encouraged me to stay strong though. You supported me when the issues seemed to be too much to handle, but I need to stop thinking about you, Jodie Scever. This will drive me crazy. If only my father were still alive! Perhaps, my life would be different and we would not be in this situation!"

Home life was difficult for Mabry, especially where her Stepfather was concerned. Mabry always wished she could have known her birth father, and things might have been different for her. Her Father died in a factory accident when she was a toddler. Mabry had very little memory of her father and always enjoyed when her mother spoke of him. This only happened whenever Mr. Allen was not around. Mabry's mother had met Mr. Allen about a year after her father's death. It was not long until they were married. Mr. Allen adopted Mabry as his own child.

With hot coffee in hand, Mabry stood in thought by the kitchen counter. She let her mind wander to last spring - the end of their junior year.

"Jodie, we were so excited about our futures. I was to become Mrs. Johnny Ricks! You were busy looking for a place to intern. It seems like you always got what you wanted! Trouble seems to brew around every turn for me. That should have been the happiest time of my life!"

Mabry finished her coffee and considered another cup, but changed her mind. Instead, she went back to the sofa to see if the news was reporting anything different than she already knew. Mabry was still day dreaming when the news Anchor commented that the police department might have more than one suspect in the Johnny Rick's murder. Mabry immediately came back to her senses as she spoke directly to the TV screen.

"What did you say?"

Mabry tried switching channels but did not find any further information concerning the case. She could not believe what she just heard. The ever-persistent voices chimed in immediately, "You are in trouble now young lady!"

Mabry covered her ears and shook her head. "Stop," she cried. She felt tears touch her cheek as they slowly cascaded down her face. She had to control the voices, or else she would go crazy. This must stop. Mabry fell back onto the sofa in tears. She soon fell asleep from exhaustion, but even in her sleep, she could not shake the memories of Johnny and the tangled mess she was in.

Mabry sank ever so slowly into the arms of her dreams. She dreamed of the visit she and Johnny made to her home and how Johnny went out of his way to please her parents. Johnny was an immediate hit with Mrs. Allen, which was more than could be said concerning Mr. Allen. Her stepfather was quite a different character, and Johnny was constantly asking Mabry questions that she did not want to answer. All the events of that week left Mabry confused and afraid. She never wanted Johnny to find out the truth, especially the way it happened.

Something caused Mabry to stir on the sofa, but she quickly fell into her dream. Suddenly, they were back on campus and Mabry kept seeing Johnny and Jodie together in the local coffee shop sharing what appeared to be intimate moments. Mabry could see Jodie's face. It appeared as though she were laughing at Mabry. Again, Mabry stirred on the sofa in her sleep.

Inside the hospital room of Jodie Scever, she too was dreaming of recent events. Jodie wanted to wake up so badly. She could hear voices around her. She seemed to recognize her Mother's voice; her sister Edee's voice and what sounded like her Father's voice. Where am I; Jodie thought? Why am I not able to open my eyes? I want to see who is talking to me! Jodie sensed a warm feeling going through her body as she fell back into the dark hole she was trying to climb out of. She was soon in another time and another place.

Jodie was on summer break. She and Johnny were making plans for their summers at home after a very troubling semester in which Jodie, Johnny and Mabry had many arguments. Jodie welcomed the summer, although she dreaded being back home with all the expectations her Mother placed upon her. "I wish I could spend this summer somewhere else; far removed from anyone who knows me!" She especially needed the break from Mabry, who had become almost obsessed with tormenting her. Mabry accused her of stealing Johnny's affections and alienating him from her. Jodie had listened to Mabry for six weeks now and was ready to get away from her, the university, and all the accusing stares.

"Hey Johnny, don't you live in Sugar Falls? I think my father has a Summer Internship arranged for me at the local TV station there. We could spend some time together if you want."

Jodie dreamed of her Father's downstairs apartment. He let her use it for the summer. The apartment is almost as big as Mother's home in Cherry Hill.

"This is such a wonderful opportunity for me to fine tune my advertising skills and for father and I to re-connect. After all, he seems so sincere in his apology to me for becoming entangled in his new life and losing touch with his own children. I will enjoy every minute of this apartment and maybe even spending Daddy's money!"

Jodie stirred in her being again. What was this dark hole she was in? She continued to dream of the summer months that went by entirely too quickly. She and Johnny grew closer over the short time they were away from Johnsonville. Each knew they had a challenge before them when they returned to the university. The break-up with Mabry turned ugly. Johnny had continually met with Mabry to try to smooth things over. Jodie could hear them arguing.

"Mabry, listen to me. I do still love you, but I am not comfortable with your stepfather. I do not know how to handle him or this new information."

"If you love me, stand like a man and think of a way to face this head-on without backing down!" Mabry cried.

Jodie remembered the look on Johnny's face. It was as if Mabry had actually slapped him across the face.

"Mabry, you just don't understand." He replied.

"Oh yes I do! You are using this as an excuse to leave me and get close to that sorry roommate of mine! I am not an idiot Johnny!"

Jodie's dream then turned to the new apartment she moved to with an old friend of hers, Debbie Michael. Mabry practically pushed Jodie out along with her belongings. Suddenly, right in the middle of Jodie's dream, a younger face of her Mother appeared. Matilda seemed to be warning Jodie of consequences of pretending to be someone else.

"Jodie, you have an unhealthy behavior. I fear you are becoming addicted to this way of treating people and locking your emotions inside."

Jodie tried her best not to listen. She was becoming restless again. How could her Mother ever know her true feelings and how it had hurt her to the core when her father walked out of their lives? Jodie could remember the pain of her Father leaving as if it was happening all over again each day of her life.

Jodie heard herself make the awful reply that day to her mother.

"I lock my emotions inside because no one cares, including you! I never plan to allow any kind of heart-wrenching pain in my life again regardless of what I have to do to ensure happiness!"

The walls of Jodie's prison were being built stronger and firmer.

Matilda stood at her daughter's bed with tears streaming down her face. It was becoming so difficult to watch Jodie struggle. She prayed without ceasing since hearing of Jodie's accident and arriving in the hospital. All she and the others could do was to pray and wait. It seemed that each time they thought Jodie would be able to come out of the sedation; she became so agitated that Dr. Smith continued the sedation. Now when Jodie began the tugging, pulling and crying, the nurses immediately allowed the full sedative back into her system.

"Jodie, we are all here for you honey. Rest and get well soon," Matilda said as she leaned into Jodie's ear.

Jodie could hear her mother calling her name. She tried to answer, but she could not seem to get out of the deep dark hole that had her trapped. She felt a presence with her Mother's voice yet she was spending time with her Father. She was living life to the fullest, and although she was spending quite a bit of money, it was about time her Father made things up to her. Jodie was enjoying this newfound freedom her Father had given her. She really did not care if it was his guilt or his love for her as a daughter that caused him to welcome her. She planned to have the time of her life this year.

"Jodie, I hope you know how much we all love you. Regardless of what you think or feel, I would be lost without you."

Thomas Wiley appeared at the doorway, "How are you this morning, Ms. Matilda?"

"Very well Thomas, just wishing to see Jodie open her eyes."

"I understand. That will come soon enough. She is getting the rest her body needs. Perhaps you should take some time to get away for a little while. You could probably use a good night's sleep and a home-cooked meal."

Thomas was becoming a blessing in disguise to Matilda. He now came by two and three times a day to check on Jodie and would spend time with Matilda, reassuring her and encouraging her to keep praying. Matilda found herself thanking God for Thomas Wiley and secretly wishing Jodie had someone like Thomas in her life.

"I'm sure I could use the rest. It is just so hard to leave, but maybe I will talk to Edee about going home for at least one night."

"Well, that is all one can ask. Just don't let yourself get down."

Jodie stirred. Thomas felt her arms. He listened to her heartbeat and studied her monitors. Matilda watched intently. Jodie heard a different voice this time. It sounded like a man's voice. She did not recognize this person. She listened for the voice again but could not find it. Thomas gave Ms. Matilda a pat upon the back. "Jodie is doing fine. She is exactly where we want her in her condition. I will see you later. Promise me to consider resting."

"I will try. Edee should arrive soon. I may take a short nap while she is here."

Jodie shook off the voices coming from the distance. She now found herself in the middle of planning a party for Johnny, who recently signed a contract with the Dallas Bullhorns as an Assistant Trainer. She knew her Mother would not approve, so it would be best if they just stayed out of her life. Suddenly, there was another voice. It sounded like her sister this time! Why did she keep hearing all these voices?

"Jodie, this is Edee. I am here if you need me. You look like you are not comfortable. Do I need to get the nurse for you? Jodie, do you hear me? We can move you around if you want."

Jodie turned her head from side to side trying to find the voice. She wanted to shake off the voice of her sister and

44

continue living her dream. Her dream kept her from being surrounded by the darkness.

The weeks flew by, and it was Homecoming Weekend at Johnsonville University. Friday was a scheduled day off for the University in order to promote the Homecoming activities. A Parade was being held Friday afternoon in downtown Johnsonville, with the Mayor, Local Officials, Johnsonville University's conference winning Football Team, Cheerleaders, the Band, and so many floats it was hard to remember them all. Jodie first thought the Homecoming Parades were old-fashioned, but now she had come to love the revelry and celebration along with the rest of Johnsonville. It was a big event every year. The citizens of Johnsonville were proud of the University that had finally given Johnsonville recognition in the State.

Jodie heard one of her friends warning her to watch out for Mabry. Jodie laughed it all off. She was not afraid of Mabry! Even if Mabry still carried a grudge, she would never do anything. Besides, there were too many events and people around to be worried about Mabry.

"Jodie, I really wish you had listened to me and thought twice about this party you gave for Johnny. Maybe he would still be alive, and you would not be here."

Jodie felt the darkness enveloping her again as she thought, "where is Edee's voice coming from?"

Matilda returned to Jodie's room after taking a few minutes for herself. She knew she could not leave Jodie, as long as she

45

could maintain the pace. The staff was being so kind to her. Each visit, she was allowed to stay much longer than the allotted time. It had been three days now since the surgery. Matilda refused to leave the hospital. Edee tried to get her to leave, but Matilda argued and won. The only rest Matilda agreed to take were some short naps while some of the family was there with her.

The rest of the family returned home. Johnson returned to Sugar Falls but had intentions to be back over the weekend. Edee left to take care of some things at home and so Matilda continued her vigil. Edee was not sure how much more her Mother's heart could handle. As long as Jodie was in an induced comatose state, there was very little anyone could do. Edee and her mother agreed to pray often at specified times for Jodie to be stable enough to be taken off the many medications. It seemed at times Jodie wanted to speak so badly. Watching her struggle like this made it all the more difficult for Edee to leave her side.

Matilda stroked Jodie's cheek. "Jodie, you look like you are resting better now than earlier today. Edee and I have been so concerned for you. It is really hard to see you sick like this. The last time Edee talked to you, you were so excited about the party you had planned for Johnny. I know it is hard for you to hear, but I can't help wondering how things would be different if you had never had that party!"

Jodie continued resting oblivious to all around her.

"You are my baby girl. I thought I taught you all the right things. I guess what your Father did damaged your heart more than any of us ever realized. Maybe if we had known, we could have kept you from going down a reckless path over the last few months."

Matilda recalled all the times she tried to talk to Jodie but as always, their conversations would end in arguments. Edee and Matilda both knew Jodie was using Johnson as a pawn for permission to the behaviors that had become so addictive in her life. Matilda felt faint as she thought about all the events leading up to this moment. Jodie would most likely still be in jail had it not been for the brain trauma she suffered due to the accident. She was also concerned that as soon as Jodie was well enough she would be returned to the County Jail.

"The news media reported all weekend the murder story of Johnny Ricks and how he was found in a wrecked Mustang. They are saying very little about you Jodie, except the Mustang is registered in your name."

Matilda laid her head on the side of Jodie's bed and wept silently until sleep enveloped her body.

On her way home, Edee decided to stop at one of the local gas stations to see if any newspapers might have Jodie's story. As she pulled into a parking space, there in the news stand starring back at her was the Johnsonville Herald with a picture of Jodie as the top headliner. The caption read, "University Student Suspected in Murder of Johnny Ricks."

As Edee stepped out of the car, she wished she had stopped before she was this close to home. She knew she wanted to read the newspaper. What if someone she knew was in the store? She might have to answer questions.

"Why Jodie, why, what have you done?"

Edee's heart almost jumped out of her body as someone tapped her on the shoulder. She turned her head slowly and saw Pastor Rayford standing there. He had a concerned look on his face. Edee sighed with relief.

"Edee, are you okay? We are on our way back to the hospital and stopped for gas. I could not help but notice you seem distraught."

"Yes, I guess. Well, maybe not either. I wanted to stop for a newspaper, but when I thought about Jodie being in the paper, I became sick to my stomach."

"I see," said Pastor Rayford. "Why don't I get you a soda and a pack of crackers? It might help settle your stomach. I can also get a newspaper for you although it might be best if you wait until you are home to read the paper."

"Thank you; that would be very kind of you. I think a soda might help, and I really would like a newspaper."

"It is done then. You get back in the car and I will get that for you."

Edee thanked God repeatedly on her drive home for sending Pastor Rayford to help her. As soon as she pulled into the carport at her home, she grabbed the paper and almost ran into the house. She thought to herself that everything else could wait. She had to read the article now, or she would be crazy thinking about it.

According to the article, Jodie was found by a motorist passing by the old abandoned high school on River Road. The motorist called "911."

The 911 operator cited the motorist's words. "I need to report an accident on River Road just past the old high school. There appears to be someone in the car. There is also a young lady acting strangely, pacing up and down the highway close to the wreck. It is a Mustang lying upon its side."

According to the article, "The motorist would not approach the vehicle due to the erratic behavior of the young lady. When the emergency vehicles arrived at the scene, Jodie Scever was found pacing frantically just as the motorist described in his call. Paramedics on the scene gave Miss Scever a quick examination to determine any injuries. She appeared to be shaken up and in shock. Miss Scever was given a sedative but refused further treatment. Jodie Scever was then turned over to one of the Officers."

The article continued to describe in detail. "The emergency personnel examined the overturned Mustang. The car was lying with the driver's side up in the air. With rapid motion, the workers were able to reach the young man who appeared to be lifeless in the front passenger seat. Paramedics worked to find a pulse. Soon the young man was placed gently on a breakaway stretcher and moved from the vehicle. After much effort to revive him, Johnny Ricks was pronounced dead at the scene. Authorities have determined that Johnny was involved in some form of foul play. Powder burns were found on Johnny's shirt from an apparent gunshot wound. Jodie Scever was questioned at the scene. Miss Scever admitted to being the driver of the car. Miss Scever was taken into custody."

The paper continued to elaborate on the two lives, stating what a tragedy it was to cut short the promising career of Johnny Ricks, who was in his senior year at Johnsonville University.

Edee threw the paper aside. "Oh Jodie, I believe I have seen enough! There is no way I can let mother read this story even though I know Mother will keep asking for a paper. I will deal with mother later; right now I have to have some rest."

Edee lay down on the sofa. She did not resist the releasing of her body into the caressing arms of the sofa as it pulled her deeper and deeper into its gentle hold.

Chapter 4

Detectives

Detective Wilson sat inside his office overlooking the University walking trail. The view was one of the nicest in the building, and he was reminded of that quite often by the Chief. It was 7:00 am Friday morning. Wilson was not sleeping much lately thinking about the young Jodie Scever lying in the hospital with no recollection of the events surrounding her or of the present day. Wilson continually reviewed Jodie's case which was now assigned to Homicide Detectives Wilson and Minton. Wilson worked the night of Johnny's apparent murder and had been called to the accident scene. The gunshot wound entered Johnny's body just under the rib cage. Detective Wilson received the Autopsy report and the pictures taken at the accident scene. There were also reports filed by one Mabry Allen accusing Jodie of stealing a pistol from Mabry's apartment along with statements of bizarre behavior by Jodie recently. The stolen pistol matched the bullet from the ballistics report. Mabry filed the stolen weapon report Saturday afternoon at exactly five fifteen.

On Monday morning, at exactly nine sharp, Mabry arrived at the Sheriff's Department to file reports of harassment by

Jodie against Mabry. Mabry stated that in light of the weekend's events involving Jodie, she wanted to be certain the department knew of the accusations and threats Jodie had recently made against Mabry. Further research revealed a Restraining Order on file from August 2nd of this year stating that Jodie could not be within fifty feet of Mabry unless it was in a supervised setting such as a common classroom where avoidance was impossible. Wilson considered the events as he sipped his fifth, or maybe it was his sixth cup of coffee. He sat the coffee cup down as he heard someone entering his office.

"Hey Boss," said Detective Minton as he entered. Minton enjoyed working under Wilson, who was a veteran detective. Minton had been in the department for eight years now. Wilson and Minton became unlikely buddies given their age difference and interests in life. However, both men were tops in their field when it came to solving the most disturbing of murders.

"Let's see what you've got on this Jodie Scever," Minton said as he pulled a chair up to the small work table beside Wilson's desk.

Detective Wilson slid a wire basket toward Minton that had pictures, the accident report, complaints filed by Mabry and other pertinent data Wilson had collected in the past week. As Minton studied the information he commented; "I remember this family. They used to live in Johnsonville. Johnson Scever was a successful businessman who owned the local Dry Cleaners. Johnson knew how to hold his own against any business in town when it came to turning a profit."

"He sounds like an interesting man," interjected Wilson.

Minton continued to explain to Wilson his recollection of the Scever family.

"Johnson attended Clevenger Business College in Johnsonville with my Dad. Our two families even attended church together."

"Johnson Scever also ran for office in the County's commissioner race. My Dad was actively involved with the Johnson County Democrats, who were strong supporters of Johnson Scever. There was only one seat available at the time, and it became a long heated battle. I recall it being the months prior to the election that Jodie was born to Johnson and Matilda Scever. This is crazy that his daughter from that time is now involved in a murder."

"So, what happened in the election?" Wilson asked.

"Well, Johnson was a town favorite, but in the end he lost by a narrow margin to a younger man who boasted of higher education and quality experience in governmental business."

"The best I remember, Johnson never quite recovered from the loss. It seems it was not long after his loss that Johnson became involved with Susan Harrison. Susan mostly kept to herself except for work and being involved in her children's activities. Johnson hired Susan to work for him at the Dry Cleaners and to help Matilda out at home. It was Susan who became the object of Johnson's affection following his loss in the Commissioner's race. Johnson's ego hit an all-time low and word around town was Susan was just what Johnson needed."

"Very interesting, it helps to have someone around who has lived here a while! What else do you remember about this family? Perhaps if you keep digging into that memory of yours, you'll come up with something beneficial." Wilson remarked.

"Hey, I pay attention to details, okay? Am I boring you?"

"No, keep going. This is quite a story."

"Anyway, Johnson spent a lot of time talking to my Dad. I remember Johnson struggling with the election loss. I overheard a conversation between Dad and Johnson one evening. Johnson complained that Matilda no longer had time for him. She seemed to be too busy taking care of the family and now the new baby."

"I imagine by that age; Matilda may have had some problems." Wilson submitted.

"Yea, we heard the pregnancy had been hard for Matilda. I think Johnson had a difficult time dealing with Matilda's health when he was in an emotional crisis himself. Matilda's church friends filled in the gap of caring for Matilda and soon found out about Johnson's affair. My Dad also happened to be on the Church Council committee that confronted Johnson."

"It sounds like your Dad gets around too!"

"Hmmm, I will put that remark aside for later!"

"The next thing we knew, Johnson put the Dry Cleaners up for sale. After the sale, he relocated to Cherry Hill with Matilda and the children. Even with the distance, the word around town had it that Johnson continued seeing Susan on weekends.

Rumors were that Johnson knew Susan from earlier in his life. Folks suspected he and Susan were picking up where they left off. Matilda finally discovered his unfaithfulness. He and Matilda divorced. Johnson re-married Susan and moved to Sugar Falls. That is the last I knew of them until now."

"Somehow, I am not surprised that Jodie Scever ended up in Johnsonville." Wilson answered.

"This is certainly going to be a challenging case considering all the history surrounding Jodie and the family connections to Johnsonville. Do you know if Jodie Scever has any relatives living in Johnsonville?"

"If I am not mistaken, Johnson has brothers and sisters living in town and one of the brothers was a prominent minister in the northern part of the county at one time."

"That is just great to hear, a murder and a minister! It sounds like our fun is only beginning Detective Minton. We had better strap in for the fun!"

Chapter 5

Waiting

Dr. Smith stopped by the Nurse's station to check Jodie's overnight chart. Thomas was already there waiting for him. "Good Morning Thomas, it is a beautiful fall morning. Have you checked on our patient yet this morning?"

"I have sir. It appears Miss Scever has had an impressive twenty-four hours."

"Great," replied Dr. Smith. "Let's take a look and see if we can help Miss Scever make some progress. It is one-week today since the surgery."

Dr. Smith and Thomas made their way to Jodie's room where they found Matilda resting. Thomas, in his caring manner, lightly touched Matilda's hand to make her aware of their presence in the room.

"Good Morning," Matilda, I certainly hope you rested well last night" Thomas remarked.

"Oh yes, I did, thank you for asking. Jodie had a good night as well. She rested so much better last night."

Dr. Smith moved closer to Jodie's bed to observe. He moved her feet first and then picked up her legs. Jodie did not fight this time as she had before. Her vital signs were the most stable during the night since the surgery. He continued his examination of Jodie while Thomas and Matilda discussed how Jodie had seemed to be more at peace than the previous nights.

When Dr. Smith completed the examination, he motioned to Thomas. "Thomas, will you dress Miss Scever's surgery site while I write some new orders?"

"New orders; is this good news?" Matilda questioned.

"Yes, this is good news! The last twenty-four hours have been the best for Jodie since her arrival here last Sunday. There have been no further episodes of seizure activity. She is breathing on her own and no longer struggling as before. We will begin reducing the medications and allow her to wake up slowly," explained Dr. Smith.

Forgetting herself, Matilda immediately stood up and hugged both Dr. Smith and Thomas. Tears filled her eyes as she tried to control her emotions. She tried hard to find words to express her gratitude to the doctors through the tears flowing relentlessly down her cheeks.

Thomas again in his gentle manner offered; "Matilda, you deserve a good cry, and you may use my shoulder if needed."

Matilda managed to let out a slight giggle at Thomas' offer.

Dr. Smith continued, "We will request Jodie be moved to the Intermediate Care Unit. There, you may come and go as you please. Jodie should be awake enough by nightfall to carry on a very limited and simple conversation."

"This is the best news I've heard in quite a while. Thank you so much for taking good care of my baby girl!" Matilda graciously replied.

Dr. Smith acknowledged Matilda's gratitude. "I am a mere instrument in Jodie's healing. I believe that prayer, the family's support and Jodie's determination to survive have and will continue to make my part in Jodie's care much easier. However, let me caution you and the family again about depression and short-term memory loss. It is entirely possible Jodie will not remember anything that happened."

As he finished giving Matilda the details of today's plan for Jodie, Matilda made a request of him that few people ever asked.

"Will you have a prayer for Jodie before you leave?" Matilda asked. "You are a wonderful Doctor and it is evident you are a Christian man. It would mean a lot if you would pray for her. I am confident God will heal Jodie physically. It is her future and what is to become of the charges against her that worry me most."

There, she finally voiced her heart's concern. She had all the faith in the world that God would heal Jodie, but right now she needed a little extra assurance for the coming events.

"I will be more than honored to pray for Jodie." Dr. Smith said as he saw Thomas coming back into the room.

The three formed a small circle, and Dr. Smith led them in prayer for Jodie. "Our Father who art in Heaven, we believe in your divine power. We claim that power for Ms. Jodie Scever and welcome Your hand in Miss Scever's complete recovery. We ask for Miss Scever's strength as she faces the days ahead. Allow her to remember and come to terms with any role she may have played in last weekend's tragedy. Cover Matilda with Your strength and mercy, so she may remain strong for the coming days. We claim this in Your Holy Son's name, Amen!"

"Amen!" they heard a voice behind them echoing the same. Thomas turned and recognized Jodie's Father, Johnson Scever, who from the tears in his eyes had apparently been a silent partner in the prayer. Standing beside Johnson was a younger woman with jet-black hair who appeared to be quite uncomfortable. Johnson introduced her as his wife, Susan. Thomas' keen sense of insight told him to stay with Matilda. For some reason, he sensed Matilda's uneasiness. Dr. Smith must have sensed it too.

"Mr. Scever, it is good to see you again. Let's step outside and I will update you on Jodie's condition."

After they left the room, Dr. Smith began by detailing to Johnson the ups and downs of the week since the surgery. He explained that Jodie had improved quite a bit, and the family should begin to see a noticeable improvement soon. The plan is still to be taking things slowly, but the prognosis was very optimistic.

Johnson asked several questions which Dr. Smith answered to Johnson's satisfaction. Johnson thanked Dr. Smith for all his expertise in caring for Jodie.

"As I was telling Ms. Matilda, Jodie may not remember much of what happened. It is important to keep Jodie from any undue stress or excitement. We do not want her to become agitated or upset."

"I understand." Johnson replied.

"One other thing if you will allow me, Ms. Matilda has not left the hospital. I have a suspicion that she has some health issues. She needs family support and some relief from the hospital."

Susan immediately chimed in, "Well, I would be happy to help if Ms. Matilda can handle my being here!"

Johnson gently nudged Susan but not discreetly enough to keep Dr. Smith from noticing the motion.

Dr. Smith replied quickly, "Matilda is a remarkable woman. She has been by Jodie's side without any thought for herself. I am sure she will be most appreciative of the offer. Now if you will excuse me, I'll leave you to visit with Jodie. Perhaps you should discuss arrangements to help Matilda in the days ahead."

After Dr. Smith was out of sight, Susan remarked, "Well, he is certainly arrogant and snippy! I will be happy to help if Matilda is agreeable."

Johnson knew it was going to be a long ordeal, so he just patted Susan on the back then taking her arm, the two walked back toward Jodie's room.

Chapter 6

Funeral

Mabry Allen hoped to slip quietly in, and out of the church where Johnny Rick's body lie in state awaiting the farewells. The funeral was being held at Johnny's home church in Sugar Falls. Mabry had awakened at 3am Sunday morning, so she would have time to make the drive and arrive before the family, and friends came to pay their respects. Even with all the confusion, anger, and hatred in her soul, she still loved Johnny. That part would never change.

Mabry pulled into the parking lot of the First Baptist Church in record time. She was hoping no one would question her because she did not trust what she might say. She entered the church from a side door she discovered to be unlocked, and then tried to find her way to the Sanctuary without being noticed. Mabry had attended another such memorial service a couple of years ago and was trying to remember exactly how everything was laid out.

"Good! It looks like I took the correct door."

To her pleasant surprise, Mabry realized she was in the correct part of the church. From the hallway she could see through an open door. There in a room off the Pulpit area she saw a casket and lots of flowers. She slowly and cautiously made her way further down the hallway that led into the room.

"Churches give me goose bumps. It is almost like I don't belong in one."

"Ha! Mabry belongs in church? That's the last place she should be. No one wants Mabry in their church!" the voices chimed unexpectedly.

"What? Go away. This is not the time or place for you to bother me today!" Mabry put her hands over her ears in an attempt to stop the voices.

"We're still here!" they rang with laughter.

Mabry focused her attention on finding the casket. If she ignored the voices, they usually went away. Thus far, today was only the second time she had ever been inside a church. She had to be on her guard anyway to keep from making any mistakes. Mabry made her way to the casket. She stopped just long enough to catch her breath before she peered into the casket at Johnny's cold body. So this was it, Johnny was truly dead. He looked so vulnerable and pitiful lying there in the casket. Mabry remembered how powerless and surprised Johnny was that night at the party. She had wanted to stop what was happening but....

"Hello, Miss. May I help you?" a male voice sounded from behind her.

Mabry turned to look into the face of a gentleman dressed in a funeral suit, as she had referred to them once before to Jodie. Mabry wondered how long the man had been watching her.

"Oh hello," replied Mabry. "I should not be long. I am a friend of the family. They knew I could not be here for the regular services, so I was given permission to come by at my convenience this morning." Mabry was quite nervous as she spoke. She prayed within herself that the man would not notice.

The gentleman gave Mabry a puzzled look as he said, "Well Miss, you have just missed the family. They were here moments ago to have their quiet time with Johnny before the afternoon services. Perhaps I should contact them for you."

"Oh no," replied Mabry, "I could not bear to trouble them. I know how difficult this time is for them. I will just pay my respects in private and leave."

"That will be fine, Miss. I will be at the door waiting for you when you finish. We will need to secure Mr. Ricks' body until after the church holds their normal Sunday services. I do not mean to rush you, but just as soon as you have your time, I will assist you to the exit."

"Now, see what you have done," hissed the angry voices inside her. "What if the family had caught you here? Then just what would you have said? What do you plan to tell Stephen if he finds out? You were a fool to come. Now hurry before anyone else sees you here and starts asking questions!"

"Oh, Shut-up you idiots and leave me alone. I am so sick of hearing from you!" Mabry whispered under her breath. She could tell that she must hurry before she blew her cover. She walked back to Johnny's casket and in a split second held her fingers to her lips then back to Johnny's.

"Sleep well, Johnny. I will love you forever! I am so sorry this had to happen." Mabry laid her hand on Johnny's as she cried. She and Johnny should be planning a wedding. Why did I ever listen? Just in that moment Mabry felt an overwhelming nausea and thought she might faint. She held onto the casket to steady herself.

The voices started mocking her again. "Ms. Mabry is sick. If she passes out here, she will be arrested."

Mabry stood up straight and shook off the queasiness. She leaned into the casket and kissed Johnny's forehead. She then left as quickly and mysteriously as she came.

All the way back to Johnsonville, Mabry relived her time with Johnny Ricks.

Chapter 7

Instability

Wilson arrived at the Police Department bright and early
Monday morning. It was a whirlwind of a weekend for him. He
made the rounds with the wife to all the grandchildren's
activities, soccer, football, a birthday party and a family dinner
on Sunday. If Wilson had his choice, he would have been down at
the office pouring over Jodie Scever and Johnny Ricks'
information along with interviewing persons of interest.
However, he knew from experience that if they were patient
enough, someone would make a mistake or say something to the
wrong person. So what were a couple more days in the equation,
with Jodie still hospitalized and Johnny barely in the grave?

Wilson started the coffee pot he kept in his office. The glass
pot was stained from all the strong coffee made daily. The aroma
of the coffee began to awake Wilson's senses as he warmed a
bagel in the microwave and pulled out a container of strawberry
cream cheese from the small refrigerator. Wilson's wife had
often mentioned that all he needed was a bed in his office, and
she would probably never see him again. Of course, she
understood the importance of Wilson's job and how dedicated he

was to his work. Wilson was passionate about his work, just as he was passionate for life and his family.

With a coffee cup in one hand and his bagel in the other, Wilson moved toward the table where all the documents and pictures were spread out. Everything was basically untouched except for a few notes Minton had made on Saturday.

Wilson gently set the coffee on the table. "Let me see. Where is my list? The first order of business is to fine-tune the list of persons we need to question."

Looking over the notes he and Minton made together, Jodie's sister, Edee had been interviewed with little or no new information. The sisters were too close for Edee to compromise anything she said in detriment to Jodie. The brothers and other family members would come later if necessary. The motorist who called "911" had already been interviewed, and his statements were verified with the transcript of the intake call.

Minton made a few contacts at the University and had some names of persons who were close with or knew Johnny Ricks well. Then, there was Mabry Allen, whom Minton found very interesting, according to the remarks he had written under her name. Obviously, Mabry and Jodie had some problems that needed a little more explanation for Minton's satisfaction.

"Minton may be onto something with this love triangle as he calls it. I may let him go with his instinct and see what turns up." No sooner than Wilson spoke, he heard a sound outside his office door. Wilson turned as he heard his door open. Minton stood inside the doorway with a pistol in his hand.

"Look what turned up last night," Minton said as he held the pistol out for Wilson's observation. It was a 25 caliber semi-automatic pistol. "A ground's worker from the Country Club found it late yesterday afternoon in a ditch near the building where all their mowing equipment is stored."

"It looks pretty rough. A 25 pistol does match the autopsy report." Wilson commented. Has it been dusted yet?"

"Yes, I just picked it up from the lab." replied Minton. "They will send the report up as soon as it is ready."

"Do you remember the report Mabry Allen filed concerning a pistol being taken from her apartment?" inquired Wilson.

Both Minton and Wilson recalled that a 25 caliber semi-automatic pistol was reported stolen a week ago Saturday by a Mabry Allen. Miss Allen actually accused Jodie Scever of the theft. Wilson held the pistol in his hands moving it back and forth in his palms as he spoke instructions, "I believe we need to bring this Mabry Allen in for some coffee and questioning. She is becoming more and more interesting to me. See if you can find her for us. Take whatever you need, but bring her in today."

"Will do Boss," replied Minton as he picked up his coat and left the office.

Minton drove straight to the university. This would be his starting point in trying to locate Miss Allen. The morning air was crisp, and the university campus was active as it was now beginning a new week. Most of the student body had left town for Fall Break last Wednesday so it was good to see the hustle and bustle in Johnsonville again. Minton knew the university had brought life back into the town that otherwise would have been just a tiny speck on a map. He made his way to the administration building carrying the necessary paperwork in hand. There he would present the order to the Dean of Student Services for all and any information they had on Mabry Allen. Once he had what he needed from the university, he would watch and wait for Miss Allen.

Jodie was awake. She moved her eyes searching about the room. "Where am I?" She saw she was hooked up to monitors and had tubes going everywhere in her body. "I need to move so badly! My back hurts, my head is pounding! First, I wake up in a jail and now what looks like a hospital room."

The only thing Jodie could remember was being in that awful jail cell where she had awakened not knowing how or why she got there. So here again, Jodie was in the same situation, wondering where in the world she was and why?

Jodie began to drift back into the dark hole she had just climbed out of when there was a knock on her door. A young man in a white doctor's jacket appeared in the doorway, hands in his pockets, looking Jodie in the eyes with a smile that should cheer up any woman. Jodie tried to speak but found that words were not accessible to her. She became frustrated and the young man must have noticed, because he came over to her bedside and placed his hand on her arm. The touch of his hand sent chills through her body! What was it about his touch that made her feel so uncomfortable? Was it because he was a stranger to her?

Why did his touch feel so inviting yet so awkward? Why can I not talk?

The young man spoke in gentle tones as he introduced himself. "Good Morning, Miss Scever. My name is Thomas Wiley. I am an intern in the Neurology Department studying under Dr. Landon Smith, your primary doctor. You have been a very sick young lady. It is good to see you awake this morning."

Jodie was trying to process all the information this Thomas was giving her. "I am sick? What happened and what is wrong with me?"

Thomas continued, "You were brought in a week ago Sunday with head trauma and a bleed on your brain. Dr. Smith skillfully stopped the bleed, and you have been recovering nicely for the past week. In case you are wondering today is Monday, November 2nd. Your family has been keeping vigil waiting for you to wake up."

Jodie wanted to speak. "Why is my family here? Where am I? Is Johnny nearby?" She felt the words in her spirit and wanted to scream them to the nice calm doctor who kept talking while her body was almost in a rage!

Thomas sensed that Jodie was becoming agitated so he tried to calm her and told her he would be back in a few hours to check on her.

"If you need anything at all, use this panel of buttons. I will put it here by your hand. The largest button will call the nurse."

Thomas made his way to the door, "Oh, and by the way; your Father is here. He just stepped out for some breakfast. He should be back soon."

Thomas closed the door behind him leaving Jodie alone with her questions. Her mind was racing with the new information she had been given. She could not imagine why her Father was there given his busy schedule with his position on the, on the... oh my! Jodie could not think! What is it that my Dad does for a living? Why, oh why, can I not remember? She tried harder to recall but failed. The young intern said I have been very ill, so that must be it. I am tired because of being so sick. Jodie turned her head away from the door and waited for sleep to find her again.

Johnson talked Matilda into leaving the hospital for some much-needed rest. He called his brother, Dean, and asked if Matilda could spend the night at his home. Johnson and Susan drove Matilda to Dean's home just a short distance away in the northern part of Johnson County. Dean lived in a little community called Sandy Creek. The drive was awkward, but Susan did her best to keep things civil. Johnson actually thought Susan handled herself well. He made a mental note to compliment Susan at the appropriate time.

Johnson and Susan were finishing breakfast in the hospital cafeteria, when Johnson suddenly felt an urgency to return to Jodie's room.

"Susan, please hurry; I am ready to go. I would like to be in the room if Jodie wakes up. Matilda would never forgive me if Jodie wakes up, and no one is with her."

With that, Susan slammed her hand on the table and caused Johnson's coffee to spill over into the saucer.

"Just when did you start caring if Matilda forgave you for anything? You would think after this many years, it would not matter. Why is it that you always worry about what Matilda thinks or how Matilda would handle this and that? One would think you were still married to her and not to me!"

Susan picked up her purse in a hasty jerking motion and told Johnson she was going to the ladies' room.

"You can wait or take yourself on back to Jodie's room without me. I really do not care and can find a way home if you prefer I not be here."

Johnson stared into the coffee cup with tears in his eyes as Susan walked away. How in the world did his life evolve into such a crazy triangle? Like it or not, he had no choice but to make the best of the world he had created. He would try to smooth everything over with Susan later. He certainly did not need any more conflict in his life. Johnson paid the waitress, picked up his hat and newspaper, as he waited patiently for Susan.

Johnson and Susan's short walk back to the hospital room was a quiet one. They returned to find Jodie sitting up in bed. She appeared to be sleeping, but the movement caused her to look around. Johnson's emotions overwhelmed him when he saw her look at him; however, his inner resolve kept him in check. He wanted to give Jodie a big hug but given the earlier circumstances at breakfast; Johnson chose to remain aloof.

To Johnson's surprise, Susan hurried to the bedside and gave Jodie a hug even suggesting Johnson call Matilda to give her the news that Jodie was awake.

"Johnson, look; Jodie is awake. We are so happy to see you alert Jodie. This is wonderful. I know your Mother would want to know. Johnson, go ahead and call Matilda. She must know her sweet baby is awake!"

Johnson almost made a hateful remark to Susan for her seemingly caring words. He knew that was a remark Susan made to cut at him. Rather than create more friction, he took out his cell phone and dialed Edee's number.

"Hello Dad, I just picked up Mother, and we are leaving Sandy Creek on our way to the hospital. Is everything okay?"

"Yes, all is well. As a matter of fact, you will be surprised! Jodie is awake and is trying to talk," replied Johnson. "Be careful and drive safely. I just wanted to let you know the good news."

"We will be there as quickly as possible Dad. This is such wonderful news! I am so anxious to hear Jodie's voice again; it seemed as though we had lost her. I am glad you called. Mother will be so excited!"

Edee finished the conversation with her Dad and gave Matilda the good news. Edee knew the car beside them at the stoplight was probably wondering why they were hugging and crying, but Edee felt such a sweet presence in the car she truly did not care who was looking on. She reveled in her soul at how powerful her God is.

Shortly before noon, Edee pulled into the parking lot at Saints Hospital. She and Matilda quickly gathered their things and almost ran into the hospital. As they made their way to the floor of Jodie's room, Matilda stopped long enough to catch her breath.

"Mother, I am sorry to make you rush. I am so excited to see Jodie and now you are out of breath. Let's rest a minute."

"Yes, let's do. I am anxious to see Jodie too." Matilda said between breaths.

Edee took a magazine she had in hand and fanned her Mother gently to stir the air around her.

"Edee, I am okay. I just became a little winded. Why don't you lead us in a prayer for Jodie while I rest a minute?"

"I will be happy too."

There in the middle of the hallway of Saints Hospital, Edee prayed the sweetest prayer for Jodie and the situation surrounding their family. Matilda felt a renewed strength from taking time to pray and she was now ready to see her baby girl.

"Thank you Edee. That was special. Now let's go on to Jodie's room."

Jodie sat propped up in the bed with pillows around her. She looked at Edee and Matilda as they entered the room. A big smile came across her face as she tried to motion them over to the bed. The stiffness and tenderness in her body was something she was not used to. The three women embraced together for what seemed like an eternity to Susan, who stood in the corner looking on.

"Goodness!" Edee exclaimed, "It is so good to see you alert and smiling. We have all been so worried about you!"

Jodie mumbled something that sounded like thank you for worrying, but Edee could not be sure, so she just kept talking to relieve the uneasiness they were all feeling.

Jodie sat watching them all, her big Sister, who had been more like a second mother to her; her Father and his wife; and last, her precious Mother, Matilda. It was amazing to Jodie that these people could be in the same room together and be civil to each other. "God must be working overtime up there today to keep this gathering peaceful," thought Jodie with a smothered giggle.

Everyone turned their attention back to Jodie as they heard the slight sound. Jodie was grinning at them all. Jodie struggled inside to bring her thoughts into words that would make sense. Finally, Jodie managed to say, "Good...see you...words...not come!"

Each of them starred at Jodie. Susan was the first to speak. "There, there," said Susan. "We have plenty of time for talking; we just want you to rest and get well."

Matilda felt her body stiffen. She quickly prayed a soft prayer for strength lest she speak words she could not take back.

"Yes, we all want you well Jodie. It is good to have support, love and prayers from all our family. We will be here with you whenever you are up to talking."

"Good here," said Jodie. She added very slowly, "Can…tell me why sick?"

"Of course, she wonders why she is sick! Here we are blabbering on about her being awake and she doesn't even realize why she is here!" remarked Susan.

Johnson could feel the tension in the room. He also felt Susan was speaking unnecessarily. So, without hesitation, Johnson took Susan by the hand and led her to Jodie's bedside.

"Jodie, Susan and I are going to take a short walk since your Mother is here. That will give you time to catch up and let Matilda explain what is going on. Don't worry, we will be back." Johnson patted Jodie's hand and with a slight nudge moved Susan toward the door.

Matilda watched as Johnson led Susan out of the room. She looked back at Jodie, who had tears in her eyes. Edee saw the tears at the same time and took a Kleenex to wipe them away. "Jodie, we can't change what our Father has done, but we can all support you and help you get well. I hope you know that Dad loves you very much. Let's focus on that and know he is doing the best he can under the circumstances."

Jodie nodded her head in agreement and held onto Edee's hand.

"Do you feel like hearing about your sickness and why you are here?" Matilda asked. Again, Jodie nodded her head affirmatively as she squeezed Edee's hand. "Mother, do you feel like explaining or do you need me to tell her?"

"I believe I can tell her. If I miss anything, you can help."

"Jodie, you were in a car accident the night of your party," began Matilda. "Evidently, you were in shock and did not know what to do. A passerby called "911." Eventually, you were brought into the hospital and had major surgery to relieve a bleed on your brain. You have been here since last Sunday."

Jodie was gazing toward the window with no emotion showing on her face. Matilda felt that was enough information for Jodie to digest for now.

"Anyone with… me?" Jodie questioned. Matilda and Edee glanced at each other. Edee was squeezing Jodie's hand harder than she realized.

"Stop!" cried Jodie. "Hand sore. Tell me?"

"Jodie, you and Johnny were both in the accident." replied Edee.

"Johnny…okay?" asked Jodie.

"He was injured also." Edee replied. Jodie was becoming agitated. A few tears streamed down her checks. She was trying to say something else but could not get the words to come. She finally just closed her eyes and turned her head away from her family. After a few minutes she thought… why was I in jail? She turned back and started to reach for her Mother when her arm began trembling. She tried to hold her arm still but soon lost control of both arms.

Jodie's eyes flew open wide, and she began grasping for breath as the sick feeling returned. She tried again to reach for her Mother with a trembling hand. The darkness seemed to appear from out of nowhere. Jodie felt herself sinking as she began the descent into that dark black hole again!

Matilda was so startled she almost fell as she tried to move closer to Jodie. "Honey, what is wrong? Are you hurting? Let us help you, tell me what to do." Matilda cried. No sooner than Matilda asked, Jodie began shaking violently. Edee could not believe her eyes!

Johnson and Susan had just returned and were standing at the door. Susan cried out, "What is happening?"

In an instant Jodie's nurse, along with two other nurses came running almost knocking Johnson and Susan out of the way. Matilda and Edee moved away from the bed, so they could have access to Jodie. Jodie's nurse had a needle and began putting whatever was in the needle into the IV tubes. The other nurses were checking Jodie's vitals and were helping to stabilize her in the bed. Jodie calmed just as quickly as the tremors began.

In a tearful voice, Matilda asked, "Was that a seizure?"

"Yes, Ms. Matilda. That was a seizure. It is the first one she has had since surgery. We gave her medicines to stop the seizure and some sedation to keep her calm. Jodie will not feel up to talking for several hours, in fact, she may sleep for hours. I'm sorry to ask, but it would be best if all but one person left the room until later."

Edee and her Mother looked at each other with questions evident in their eyes. She turned to Johnson; "Dad, let me walk with you and Susan out to your car. I am sure you need to get back home soon."

In spite of the turmoil going on inside Johnson's head and heart, he understood the gesture. He walked over and gently placed his hand on Matilda's shoulder. "Matilda, Jodie will be okay. You have to take care of yourself too."

He then placed a kiss on Jodie's cheek before he left the room. He could feel the animosity from Susan. It would definitely be a long ride back home.

Chapter 8

Finding Mabry

The afternoon sun was very warm on Minton's back as he sat on a bench outside the Science building. He had decided to enjoy the beautiful November day while he waited for Mabry Allen. Miss Allen's last class would be over at one-thirty this afternoon. The Dean's office had been most accommodating in their sharing of information on Miss Allen. They also gave him a schedule of her classes for every day throughout the week. As he sat on the bench, he studied Mabry's schedule and decided he would grab a bite of lunch from the cafeteria since Miss Allen had one more class before she was through for the day. It had been noted that Miss Allen was very conscientious and rarely missed any classes so Minton felt comfortable in giving her the extra time. It might prove to be beneficial to him anyway if he could pick up a tidbit or two of information from any student willing to talk.

Minton made his way to the cafeteria and moved slowly among the students, asking each one he met what food they suggested. He stated he had never eaten in the cafeteria before in an attempt to lead someone into conversation. Finally, he came across a young man very willing to talk. Roger introduced himself to Minton as a senior at Johnsonville.

"It is good to meet you Roger. Thanks for the suggestion of food, say, has anything interesting had been going on at the university lately."

"The hottest news going around is the murder of Johnny Ricks and the suspicions of everyone as to which one of the girls killed him."

"You had a murder on campus?"

"Surely you have heard. It has been in the papers and on T.V. Do you live under a rock or something man?" Roger asked Minton.

"Well no, I guess it seems that way. I actually have been out of town for a few weeks and just returned. I am visiting the university today in consideration of advancing my career in Criminal Justice."

"In that case," replied Roger, "you need to have lunch with me and let me fill you in on the murder case. Maybe you have some knowledge about the system and can clear up some questions I have about this ordeal."

Minton felt satisfied with himself. He had a person willing to divulge information!

Without hesitation, Roger starting spilling everything he knew and some of what he did not know. Minton was enjoying every moment of this conversation as Roger played right into his hands. He was making mental notes of what seemed most important.

"Say you know this Mabry Allen personally?"

"Oh yes, you could say we are becoming close friends!" Roger replied.

Minton was surprised that Roger's so-called closeness did not keep him from offering quite a bit of information. Roger kept singing like a bird!

Minton realized the time. "Roger, it is a pleasure, but I must move on. I need to finish my business on campus."

"Hey, if you need some more help with your Criminal Justice program, just look me up."

Minton chuckled to himself as he left the cafeteria and Roger behind. Minton made his way to a bench between the buildings and the parking lot. He watched patiently, and soon saw the doors to the Science Building begin to open and students exiting the building. That is when he caught a glimpse of Miss Mabry Allen. She was taller than he expected, she had dark-brown hair that fell on her shoulders. In the sunlight, she was quite attractive.

Minton waited for Mabry to walk by him, and then he began the chase. He could have stopped her at any moment but there was an adrenaline rush every time he pursued a suspect, and he thrilled at the high it gave him. That rush sensation was one of the reasons he remained a detective, although he could have a desk job anytime he wanted it.

Mabry approached her car. Minton knew he should stop the little game he was playing even though he was enjoying the view.

Minton could not help but be drawn to the almost perfect outline of the body he was chasing.

He closed the gap between them and called out her name. "Miss Allen, may I speak with you a moment?"

Mabry turned and looked at him with hesitation. Minton had his badge ready in his hand, and he flashed it where she could see he was legitimate. He introduced himself as Detective Minton with the Johnsonville Police Department. He handed her a legal looking document that stated she was being taken into custody for questioning in the case of Johnny Ricks.

Minton motioned Mabry to the unmarked car parked directly behind her car. Without a word, Mabry turned toward the car and took the seat offered to her in the back on the passenger's side. The short ride to the police department did not end too soon for Mabry. The voices were trying to break through in her conscience, and she was doing all she could to stifle them. Minton led Mabry into the building and down the hallway to a glass-enclosed room. He asked her to be seated and gave her a glass of water. He left the room and waited outside for Detective Wilson.

"Now, what will our Mabry do?"

"Don't start on me now! This is not a good place for you to interfere." Mabry replied.

"Ah, but you know you need our help."

"Leave me alone you crazy idiots. If I ever get rid of you, it will not be too soon!"

Mabry heard the turn of the doorknob. She sat up and focused her attention to whoever was entering the room. Both Minton and Wilson entered, each with a coffee cup in their hand. They took a seat and relaxed. They appeared to Mabry to be getting ready to have a leisurely conversation.

Wilson studied Mabry Allen. The silence within the room was almost unbearable to Mabry as she continued to stifle the voices. She seemed collected and at ease but inside, she was becoming quite uncomfortable at the silence.

"So, are you here to question me, or to study me for a painting?"

"Young lady, you will be here as long as we determine the need to keep you. I am sure you have an interesting story you would like to tell us." Wilson replied.

"I have nothing of interest to you." Mabry answered. She noticed a slight grin on Minton's face at her statement. Quickly, she looked away before her fear took over.

Wilson began, "In that case, let me ask you some questions to see if we can jog your memory."

As Wilson asked a round of questions, he could not help but notice how Mabry turned her head to the side at each question before she responded. It was almost like she was talking to someone beside her although it was not audible. Mabry turned the questioning back to the detectives when she asked why they had not informed her of her rights. She then refused any further questioning without the presence of an attorney.

"Excuse me! What rights do you think a murder suspect has?" Wilson replied.

"You know very well. Now, you may let me go or I will file a lawsuit."

Wilson was angry enough to punch a hole through the wall. After Mabry was released to return to her car, Wilson let Minton have a few choice words for not taking care of the details.

Another officer escorted Mabry to an unmarked vehicle. She was taken back to the university parking lot where her car was parked. Once back on campus, Mabry breathed a sigh of relief. Almost immediately, the voices began tormenting her again.

"Gracious, what a day! We really showed those detectives, didn't we? Miss Mabry caught them off guard when she told them they had failed to inform her of her rights!"

"Well of course we did!" sounded a voice that was not immediately recognizable. Mabry was surprised at the voice and stopped to take note as the voice continued. "I taught Mabry Allen everything she knows and without me, she knows she would be nothing but trash!"

"STOP!" yelled Mabry, as she then looked around and realized she was in the middle of the university parking lot with people all around. Some fellow students looked her way to determine if she was having a problem. Mabry waved at them and smiled so they could be content in their concern that she was fine. She quickly unlocked her car and slid into the driver's seat. She had to get back to her apartment where she could find solace. She did not fear the voices when locked inside her apartment.

Mabry drove faster than usual, but as she pulled onto her street in the apartment complex, she immediately recognized the silver sports car parked in the space reserved for her apartment. She had no desire to have a confrontation with him today after all she had just been through. Maybe he did not see her turn down the street. She would take her chances and turn around quickly.

From there, Mabry was not sure what she was going to do, but she knew going home tonight was not an option.

Chapter 9

Untimely News

Debbie Michael, Jodie's new roommate, returned to the apartment she and Jodie shared. She had been out of the country for a mission trip with the Baptist Student Union when Jodie and Johnny had their accident. Debbie and Edee had both tried to talk Jodie into joining the group for the mission trip, but Jodie was not about to miss the Homecoming celebrations to go wipe snotty-nosed kids in outer Zooloo, as she so adamantly proclaimed.

Edee had always wanted to do mission work and was really upset with Jodie for not taking advantage of the opportunity. Rather than create conflict between them, Edee let the subject drop. She spent her energy encouraging Debbie for the trip.

Debbie heard of the accident from a phone call home. She had only been able to find out bits and pieces of information concerning Jodie and Johnny while she was away. Debbie knew Johnny was dead, and that was about all the details she had. The first thing she planned to do was to visit Jodie at Saints Hospital to see what, if anything, she could do to help out. She was certain Jodie was devastated over the loss of Johnny.

Debbie arrived at Saints Hospital just after Edee and Matilda left for home to rest. Edee lived a shorter distance from the hospital than Matilda and since her husband was out of town, Edee would be alone. She and her Mother would have time to ponder all the events of the past several days not to mention the fact that they both needed time to share details that could not be discussed in front of Jodie, such as the pending charges. With the help of Jodie's Nurse, Nikki, they convinced Matilda to leave.

Debbie's uncanny timing for visiting also found Nikki to be at Supper. Debbie was made aware of this when she stopped at the Nurses' Station to inquire of Jodie and a possible visit.

"Nikki, Jodie's nurse has just gone on her supper break. It will be about an hour before she returns. Do you have time to wait?"

"Goodness, is there someone else that can give me permission? I have been out of the country for a mission trip. I am Jodie's roommate and am very anxious to check on Jodie."

"Just a moment please." The secretary returned with another nurse who gave Debbie permission to visit briefly. The nurse instructed Debbie not to excite Jodie and to refrain from trying to get Jodie to talk.

"Thank you so much. I will not be long."

Jodie was awake. She gave Debbie a big smile and made a motion for her to come in. Debbie tried not to stare, but her eyes automatically fell on Jodie's scalp where her head was shaved. She also could not help but notice the heavy dark circles under Jodie's eyes.

Debbie immediately began apologizing, "Jodie; I am so sorry for not being here for you."

Jodie shook her head as if to say to Debbie not to worry. Debbie was so taken aback at Jodie's appearance; she broke down in tears, and then had to apologize to Jodie for crying.

Jodie tried to comment, "...no tears!"

Debbie took a seat on the chair beside the bed. She was quiet for a few minutes as she regained her composure and tried desperately to think of ways to comfort Jodie. She told Jodie a little of her mission trip and promised pictures with a full-blown report when Jodie was well. Debbie continued the one-sided conversation until she was afraid she was overstaying her time.

Debbie rose to go and as she leaned over to give Jodie a hug, Debbie said, "Jodie, I am so sorry about Johnny's passing. I would have been here to help you if I could have. Don't worry though, I will be back, and you can talk all you want when you feel better." Debbie placed her cheek on Jodie's in a friendship hug then turned to leave.

Debbie left the hospital in a mix of emotions. It was very difficult to see Jodie the way she was. She purposed in her heart to pray harder than ever for Jodie.

Jodie lay in the stillness of the room listening to the "beeps" of all the equipment. What was it Debbie just said to her? What could she have meant about Johnny and a passing? Jodie was having a very difficult time understanding the meaning of their conversation. Surely, Debbie did not think Johnny was... gone...

dead even! He had to be alive. Why would Debbie even think that Johnny was dead?

"Where is everyone?"

She needed answers. Jodie tried to sit up, so she could see if any of her family was outside her door. She made it to an upright position and realized everyone was gone. Please, she thought to herself; someone please come tell me what is happening!

"Where is Johnny? Please, Johnny, please don't be dead!"

Jodie began to feel a warm tingling sensation that started at the tip of her toes. "Oh, she exclaimed loudly. Then suddenly, she began feeling sick as the sensation rose all the way through her body from her feet to the top of her head. She became dizzy and felt as though she was going to pass out sitting upon the bed! There it was again, the sweet and sour sensation in her nostrils. Jodie cried inside her soul, "please, don't let this be happening again."

One of the nurses thought she heard sounds from Jodie's room and was hurrying into her room just as Jodie's alarms began sounding. Jodie was having another seizure. Nikki was called back to the floor. She assisted with Jodie until they had her stable again although Jodie kept asking for "Johnny" repeatedly. Nikki decided she needed to alert the family.

Nikki immediately dialed Edee's cell phone and let it ring several times. Finally, on the second try, Edee answered in a sleepy voice.

"I'm sorry to disturb you Edee. This is Nikki, Jodie's nurse. Jodie had another seizure tonight and is resting for the moment.

However, she is very distraught and keeps asking for Johnny. I believe it best if you or your mother came back to the hospital. We have not been able to keep her calm."

Edee responded that they would be there very soon and hung up to go to wake her Mother. From the tone of Nikki's voice, Edee felt they would need to make it back as soon as possible.

It was a long night for Jodie, Matilda, and Edee. Matilda and Edee managed to calm Jodie down enough to share a few of the details of Johnny's fate. Jodie took the news a lot better than they anticipated, especially after being so upset at Debbie's untimely spilling of the news.

Jodie remarked how unfortunate that the accident had caused Johnny's death.

"Jodie? Do you understand what we told you?" Edee asked again after Jodie's remark.

Jodie showed no response. She soon fell asleep. Edee was actually quite concerned that Jodie seemed to have no remorse for Johnny's death. It was as if she had not grasped the seriousness of the situation or did not want to face the facts. Edee knew, however, that Jodie had a way of putting up a wall so it was hard to read her emotions. Matilda tried to ease Edee's concern, reminding her Jodie is more than likely hurting emotionally from the loss and is drawing within like she so often does.

"I am sure once Jodie has all her senses about her, she will be very saddened. That is when we must be strong for her."

"I hope you are right Mother."

Thomas Wiley made his way to Jodie's room bright and early Tuesday morning. He found Edee, Matilda and Jodie all sleeping soundly. Thomas had read Jodie's chart and was aware of what happened overnight. Nurse Nikki had made detailed notes before her shift ended. It was not any wonder he found them all sound asleep. He dared not disturb them, although he did linger in the doorway for another glimpse of Jodie. He was finding himself hopelessly attracted to Jodie Scever. He was not sure if it was her situation, or if it was her delicate features. Whatever it was; he knew he needed to get control of himself.

Thomas left the floor and made his way to find Dr. Smith. He found Dr. Smith in the conference room with another gentleman who had his back to the door. Thomas politely knocked, and Dr. Smith motioned at him to enter the room.

"Thomas, let me introduce you to Detective Wilson of the Johnsonville Police Department. We were just discussing Jodie Scever and when we might allow the department to question her."

"Good Morning,"

"Morning," replied Thomas as he offered Wilson a welcoming handshake. "I trust you understand the seriousness of Miss Scever's health at the moment," Thomas said with a demanding tone.

Dr. Smith gave Thomas with a questioning look. This was so unlike Thomas to speak in such a tone of voice. However; without any word to Thomas, Dr. Smith continued his conversation with Detective Wilson. Thomas immediately realized his quick reaction, excused himself, and quietly left the room.

Dr. Smith and Detective Wilson continued to discuss an appropriate time for questioning.

"Detective Wilson, I realize how important it is to the case to have information as soon as possible. However, Miss Scever has begun to have seizure activity, which seems to be brought on by stress. I am not sure I can allow this questioning without great concern for Miss Scever's health."

"I understand your position Dr. Smith. I will be certain to go easy on Miss Scever and try to limit our time with her."

Finally, Dr. Smith agreed that Jodie could be questioned as soon as she could go forty-eight hours without a seizure. Dr. Smith also stipulated that a nurse or other medical personnel be present. His original thought was for Thomas to be available, but after the sharp remark Thomas made, Dr. Smith would have to give it more consideration.

Dr. Smith went through his routine with plans to talk to Thomas before the day was over. He knew Thomas had taken Matilda under his wing. Dr. Smith hoped his less than professional comment was only out of concern for Matilda's health. All hospital staff knew the policy against becoming involved in a patient's life beyond what is needed for medical care and advice. However true Thomas had been to the policy; Dr. Smith had noticed the extra time Thomas was giving to Jodie's case.

Chapter 10

Scheming

Roger knocked on the bedroom door. He let Mabry crash at his apartment after coming to him in hysteria begging for a place to stay. For some reason, she was convinced there was a man waiting for her back at her apartment. She was afraid to go home. Roger tried to get more of an explanation, but Mabry insisted she had told him enough! Roger gave in and told her she could have the bedroom, and he would sleep on the couch. Mabry made him promise he would not attempt to open the apartment door for anyone in case the man followed her there.

Mabry responded to the knock at the door. "Good Morning Roger, I am awake."

Roger opened the door slightly, "I have an eight-o'clock class. Do you need anything?"

"No, I'm fine. I will be getting up soon and try to be on my way."

"You are welcome to stay here as long as you need. I hope you know that," Roger explained as he moved a little further into the bedroom still holding onto the door.

"Yes, I know that and I do appreciate your concern, but I need to be on my way too."

Roger turned loose of the door and began to move toward the bed. Mabry immediately put up a hand in a motion for Roger to stop. She pulled the covers up over her body.

"No problem Mabry. I was just going to give you a good-bye hug."

"I appreciate your thoughtfulness Roger. You better be going so you won't be late."

Roger reluctantly backed away and left Mabry alone. He was so angry with himself. He had a right to her affection after all the help he continued to give to her. He would try to be patient and wait his time. If he remained a true friend, then perhaps he could have more of Mabry than a thank you.

Mabry waited until she knew Roger was gone, and then she called Detective Minton. She asked him to meet her at Roger's address. Minton was hesitant, but finally agreed after she explained the reason for being at Roger's apartment.

Mabry walked out to her car to retrieve some necessary items. Even though she did not see the sports car anywhere, she had a feeling she was being watched. She would follow through with the plan, and then this would be the end. It was possible he was at her apartment to remind her of her part of the deal. Whatever, the reason, there would be no more deals or plans made between them.

Once back inside Roger's apartment, Mabry took the items from her backpack. She had been smart enough to let Roger look at the laptop she used for correspondence with Johnny. Roger's laptop had been in repair, so she conveniently allowed him to borrow her laptop to finish an assignment. She was sure it had his fingerprints all over it. The only thing Roger did not know about this laptop is how Mabry acquired it. She placed the laptop under some clothes lying on the floor of Roger's bedroom closet. She took the other items and placed them in specified locations in Roger's apartment. Once she was satisfied with the placement of each item, she started a pot of coffee and patiently waited for Detective Minton. It was up to Mabry to convince the Detective that Roger had motives to kill Johnny Ricks. Try she would, but Roger had been so kind to her. She willed within herself to have this be the last act she would do for "him."

"You will never be through Mabry. He owns you!" The voices mocked.

"Do not be concerned with what I will or will not do. Maybe I am doing this for Jodie! By the way, no one owns Mabry Allen! You can write that down." Mabry walked away from the kitchen hoping to leave the voices behind. She knew the consequences if this did not work out; however, she would no longer move at his beck and call. "He" could take over the plan himself. Mabry determined she was finished!

Roger sat in Dr. Rhodes class trying to absorb the lecture even though his mind was preoccupied with Mabry Allen. What was it about her that got under his skin? Mabry was definitely an attractive girl but there was something quite strange about her. Last night, when she came to him in distress, he would gladly have comforted her. A strange, sinister feeling seemed to fill the room. He noticed the same odd atmosphere over the past weeks without being able to determine the cause. Perhaps it was just Mabry's way to show him she was not interested in him other than for friendship. As difficult as it was to control his needs, he would be patient with Mabry's wishes in an attempt to prove his feelings for her.

Detective Minton was en route to the apartment address Mabry gave him. He thought it strange that Miss Allen would contact him so soon after their questioning session. He wondered what more Miss Allen needed to say, and why she wanted him to meet her at Roger's apartment. He ran the address before he left the department. He now knew it belonged to the young man who had freely offered information to him yesterday. Minton alerted the Department to have someone on standby just in case he needed assistance. He called Wilson personally. Wilson told him he would park across the street with his eyes on the apartment.

Minton got out of the car slowly, checked the area around the apartment, made contact with Wilson and then proceeded toward the door. There was no need to knock as Mabry had been watching for him. She already had the door open with tears in her eyes. She immediately fell into Minton's arms, much to his surprise. Minton managed to peel Mabry away from him and move her back a couple of inches inside the door.

"What is it Miss Allen? Why do you need our services?"

Mabry responded, "If you come inside with me, I can explain."

"I will not come inside. If you have more information you need to share with us, you may accompany me to the station."

Mabry realized her little tactic was not working so she began sobbing as she told Minton about fearing someone was at her apartment last night.

"I became scared last night and came here to Roger's apartment to get away. Roger is more than a friend; he is almost like a brother, but recently I discovered things about Roger that really bother me. After Roger left this morning, I was looking for a pair of shoes I believed I left here. That is when I came across my laptop in his closet!" Mabry added a few extra tears before she continued.

"Honestly, I never take my laptop out of my apartment. Why Roger has it is beyond me. Things about Roger are just not adding up lately."

Minton shifted his weight from side to side. He observed Mabry closely as she was giving her explanation. He had a feeling that Mabry's story was not altogether truthful.

"If you just come inside with me, I'll be happy to show you what I'm talking about." Mabry said with tears streaming down her face. She reached out and held onto Minton's shirt front to entice him inside.

Minton placed his hand on Mabry's removing it from his shirt. "Miss Allen, it would be wise for you to be certain of any information you are offering as well as your motives. Perhaps, you need to question Roger yourself concerning your laptop."

"But you don't understand. How could Roger have my laptop when it never leaves my apartment?"

"If you wish to file a report, please contact the department to complete the proper paperwork."

"Wait, please. I really am scared. Could you at least wait around until I finish up here and leave for class? You can have a seat on Roger's sofa. I promise I will hurry."

"Miss Allen, I will not enter the residence without you being in some imminent danger. All appears quiet and in order here. If you are truly in fear of someone harming you, this needs to also be addressed down at the Department through proper channels." With that remark, he bid Mabry good day and left.

Mabry slammed the door and moved toward the window to watch Minton leave. She was so angry with herself and the voices that kept telling her what to do. She knew she had not imagined the way Minton looked at her yesterday in the campus parking lot. Most men would have jumped at the chance to come inside an apartment alone with her. She had not imagined the car at her apartment last night either and she knew there would be a price to pay if she did not follow through just as "he" described.

"Has Mabry lost her touch? He is going to be angry when he finds out you could not do as he told you. You will pay now."

"You are making me insane!" Mabry covered her ears with both hands. "This has to stop. Leave me alone. Go back wherever you came from."

Mabry suddenly bent over in pain as the voices became louder. She was hearing heinous laughter filling the room. It sounded like a jungle full of monkeys calling to each other, almost in deafening proportions.

Mabry gathered her strength. She would not mess up again! She began to straighten her body back out, when she noticed through the window, a black Blazer pull onto the street directly behind Minton. The face looked so familiar. Who was that and where had she seen him? Had he been there watching the whole time?

Chapter 11

Uncertain Feelings

Thomas finished his patient reports for the day. He began packing up as he realized he had about an hour before his four-thirty meeting with Dr. Smith. Thomas was uncertain of the reason for the meeting. Dr. Smith usually just told him anything he needed to know. At any rate, he would find out soon enough. He noted that he had adequate time to go by Jodie's room to check on her once more.

Thomas found Jodie's door open. He entered to find Jodie sitting up in bed. It appeared to him that she was resting. She appealed to Thomas even with all the hospital equipment and the bald place on her scalp from surgery. Thomas managed to look past these obstacles into Jodie's inner beauty. He knew he had spent too much time on Jodie's case. He also knew the hospital policy on becoming involved with a patient; however, Thomas kept telling himself that he could handle the situation. Now he wondered if he may have truly allowed himself to become entangled in his patient's life. He had never before met someone who captivated him as Jodie Scever had captivated him. His comment this morning to the Detective in front of Dr. Smith was the first indication that he was not in control. He was now almost sure that Dr. Smith wanted to meet with him to discuss the matter.

Jodie stirred as she felt his presence within the room. "Good Afternoon Thom... Doctor! I was wondering if I would see you today."

"Hi Jodie, I could not go through the day without spending a little time with my favorite patient." Thomas replied.

"You are too sweet."

"I just had to wrap up some reports for Dr. Smith. I do need to talk to you seriously for just a minute though if you feel up to it."

"Sure, I am feeling so much better than I did this morning. Actually, Nurse Nikki tells me I have had a good day considering all that happened last night."

Thomas was surprised at how well Jodie was communicating today after all her trauma. He pulled a chair close to Jodie's bedside. The closeness gave him a warm feeling. He hung his head as he took a moment to compose himself.

"Jodie, there was a detective from the police department here today. Dr. Smith is cooperating in arranging a time for you to be questioned. I am sure he will give you the date so you will be prepared. I felt like you should know."

Jodie starred at the ceiling without any word. Thomas felt so drawn to her. She caught him looking at her and smiled.

"What is on your mind today, Miss Scever?"

"Actually, I was wishing I knew why I was in jail, and why the detectives want to question me? All I remember is being at a party with Johnny Ricks and the next thing I know I wake up in jail. Johnny's death is such a mystery to me as it is to everyone."

Thomas stood up and took hold of the bed rail to Jodie's bed. "Jodie, you are a very special person. You have been through a very traumatic time with the accident, and then finding out your friend has passed away. Somehow, there will be something to trigger your memory. You need to concentrate on getting well and allowing your body to heal. Let the detectives do their job so maybe they will determine you are no longer a suspect in the case."

"That would certainly be wonderful," replied Jodie.

"There is no reason to worry. The detectives are just doing what is necessary for the case. Be confident in yourself and pray about your answers."

"You are very reassuring Doctor. I will try not to worry."

"Professionally speaking, I would like you to know that you can call for me anytime you feel the need to talk. I may not have the answers, but if I can help your progress by assisting you emotionally and physically, I will be happy to do so."

Jodie looked at Thomas waiting for him to continue.

Thomas felt the uneasiness of the moment. He cleared his throat. "Perhaps you should try to sleep for a while before visiting hours."

"That is probably what I will do. Thank you for your concern, not just for my injury, but for my overall well-being."

"It is my pleasure," Thomas replied. Being afraid to say anything else that would expose his feelings, Thomas politely excused himself and made his way to Dr. Smith's office. He began feeling foolish for his comments to Miss Scever just now. He knew Dr. Smith would be able to read him like a map as soon as he saw him. There was little time to pull his act together. He tried to muster the strength necessary for this meeting, as he knew Dr. Smith was certainly waiting.

Thomas had barely left the room when Jodie heard her Mother's voice in her conscience. Matilda was scolding her for the thoughts she was having of Thomas. "Do you not realize Johnny has barely been buried? How can you so callously forget him and anything he remotely meant to you? You should not be flirting with feelings for anyone else when you should be mourning the death of a friend?"

Jodie did not want to hear her Mother's voice right now. She would just not think about that today. Jodie started singing to herself hoping it would drown out her Mother's voice. Soon she fell asleep to the sound of her own voice.

Thomas entered Dr. Smith's office exactly at four-thirty. The receptionist told Thomas to go on in that Dr. Smith was ready for him. Thomas inhaled deeply, prayed a simple prayer, and then opened the door for what lay ahead.

"Thomas, come in. Thank you for being on time. Have a seat. I hope your afternoon was not too hectic."

"No, it consisted mostly of just finishing paperwork. Things are fairly calm on the floor."

Dr. Smith cleared his throat, "I imagine you might be wondering why the formality of my asking you to my office."

"It has entered my mind Sir."

"Thomas, you are a fine young man. I can see you having an excellent career ahead of you in the medical profession. Your dedication, character and dependability surpass most interns."

"Thank you Sir." Thomas answered.

"There are just a couple of matters I think we need to discuss pertaining to your internship. First, I have given your second set of observation reports to the Dean of Neurology. You will be receiving a copy in your mailbox. There is no need to worry as the reports are above expectations as always."

Dr. Smith stood and made his way around the desk. He pulled up a chair and moved it closer to Thomas as he sat down.

"That brings me to my second point today. In light of our recent case concerning Miss Jodie Scever; I must give you a warning of becoming personally involved with your patient. I know you are aware of hospital policy. I also understand how the mind justifies our ways, in order to permit us the right to be excused from accountability."

"Sir, with all due respect, I already realize I may be pushing the edge."

"Interesting, I'm not sure I was expecting that comment. I have noticed that you do not seem to be yourself. Knowing your character, I sensed you could be struggling."

"Yes, I admit I am. Miss Scever has captivated my attention. I have not been able to understand my feelings, except to know that I must control them."

"Perhaps you need a few days to think through your situation. I do not doubt your sincerity and appreciate your honesty. I believe you are already off this Friday. Let me go ahead and give the permission for you to have Thursday as well. It might do you good to get away, maybe visit with your family, or just spend some time reflecting."

"Thank you Sir. I appreciate that offer. It may be just what I need."

Thomas stood and offered his hand to Dr. Smith. The two shook hands. Unexpectedly to Thomas, Dr. Smith pulled him close for a quick brotherly embrace.

"Son, I will be praying for your peace of mind."

Chapter 12

Interrogation

Jodie sat looking toward the window with the rays of sunshine peeking through the blinds. She watched the little specks of dust float inside each ray. Somehow, she could relate to the floating sensation. It would not be long before the detectives from the Johnsonville Police Department arrived. Dr. Smith explained to Jodie that the hospital had to cooperate in the matter of her questioning. He further explained that Detectives Wilson and Minton, who were veteran detectives with the department, would be at the hospital Thursday afternoon to question her. Fortunately, for the detectives, Jodie remained stable without any seizure activity since very early Tuesday morning.

"Look what I just happened to find in the refrigerator." Nikki said as she waved a Dr. Pepper at Jodie.

Jodie's nurse, Nikki, knew that Dr. Pepper was Jodie's favorite soft drink. She thought it might be good for Jodie to spend a few minutes chatting while she had the time to sit with Jodie. Maybe it would help ease any tension or nerves Jodie was feeling.

"Wonderful, I'm so glad someone thought of me. You are the best!"

"Of course, it is caffeine free."

"Just what the doctor ordered I guess!" Jodie replied.

Nikki pulled up a chair to Jodie's bedside. "Is there anything else you need before the detectives arrive?"

"I am fine, Nikki. It is just troubling that I do not recall how Johnny and I got in the car or how we wrecked. All I can vaguely remember is having a confrontation with Mabry at the party and then waking up in the local jail."

"Perhaps you are expecting too much from yourself Jodie. Your memory will come when it is time. You only need to worry about the memories you do have. That is all you can be responsible for until more is revealed."

"But what if I really did pull the trigger that took Johnny's life? If I can't remember happened, maybe I've blocked it from my mind."

Nikki sensed Jodie's apprehension. "Jodie, would you like for me to pray right now and ask God for your guidance?"

With tears in her eyes, Jodie said, "It would please me greatly if you prayed."

Nikki held Jodie's hand as she began. "Father, I am here with your child, Jodie Scever. We all know how much you must love her, because you spared her life. She has had major trauma not only physically, but emotionally and mentally. You have brought her through the shadow of death, and now we call upon You for Your grace and guidance through the questioning session this afternoon. We ask You to anoint Jodie with vivid memory and answers that will not be doubted. Give Jodie a peace that only You can give. I commit Jodie into Your hands. Amen."

Outside the doorway, Dr. Smith whispered "Amen" under his breath and walked away.

Johnson Scever looked at his watch again. It was almost time for Jodie's questioning. He tried all morning to pray for his baby girl. Susan even surprised him by bringing lunch and afterward allowing Johnson to lead them in a prayer for Jodie. His personal faith walk had never been one to boast about, but today he had a renewed feeling in his heart that he had never experienced before. Perhaps God could forgive him of all his failures after all.

Johnson was about to open the folder on a new project for downtown. The parking garage was almost complete and would open in time for the Christmas season. Suddenly, Johnson felt a strong urge to put everything on hold for the afternoon. Jodie's life was on hold. Johnson sat behind his desk thinking back on Jodie's life and all the memories he could never retrieve. Perhaps if he had been a better Father, even if he had been the husband he should have been, maybe the families involved would not be going through this hard time. He had always found it easy to blame Matilda; however much the fault may lie with him.

Johnson notified his secretary that he would be leaving for the afternoon. He turned the lights off and closed his office door. He could be reached at home if there was an emergency. Johnson's Cadillac was waiting for him at the curb thanks to his most efficient secretary. It was a relief to be in the car away from the telephones, questions and constant barrage of information. He was looking forward to making a fresh pot of coffee and sitting by the fireplace, for as long as he wanted. Perhaps he would look for the Bible that used to be so important to him and see if there was anything new and invigorating for him in the Word.

Detectives Wilson and Minton arrived at Saints Hospital. They brought along a clerk who would be recording Jodie's statements. They made their way to Dr. Smith's office where they were to meet with Dr. Smith prior to the session. Just outside Dr. Smith's office they saw Nurse Nikki.

"Good afternoon Gentlemen. I am Nikki Claremont, Jodie Scever's nurse. Dr. Smith is with Miss Scever and asked that I meet you. I suppose you are ready to begin your session with Miss Scever?"

Detective Wilson responded, "Yes, but we were hoping to meet with Dr. Smith prior to the questioning."

"Dr. Smith asked me to take you up to Miss Scever's room. He is waiting for you there. He wishes to brief you in the room so that Miss Scever hears the same information. I'm sure you may ask your questions of him at the same time."

"Very well, lead the way," replied Wilson.

Dr. Smith was waiting in Jodie's room as Nikki said. Detectives Wilson and Minton entered the room. They started to introduce the clerk when Dr. Smith asked them to close the door. Dr. Smith proceeded to lay out the instructions to be followed so that everyone was looking out for Jodie's best interest. He requested that Jodie not be coerced, or made to feel pressured in any way.

The detectives responded that they would refrain from incriminating remarks or comments that would lead Jodie into distress; and they would not use tactics to make Jodie feel she was at fault.

Wilson directed to Jodie, "Miss Scever, you do understand that without a lawyer present, you have the right to refuse to answer any question you are unsure of?"

"Yes Sir, I am aware. Dr. Smith gave me the papers you sent. I have read and signed them for you."

"Excellent, then shall we begin?"

"Whenever you are ready?" Dr. Smith answered.

Wilson and Minton exchanged humorous glances. Anyone could see they were astounded by the protection the hospital seemed to be providing Miss Scever. It was almost humorous how Dr. Smith had taken command of the session. There was really nothing at this point to prevent them from beginning since Dr. Smith had taken care of the preliminaries.

Wilson began the session. "Miss Scever, we need to inform you that this session is being recorded for playback on DVD to assist the investigation. If anyone has cause for objection, please inform us now."

The room remained silent as each one looked to the other in anticipation.

Wilson saw no response, so he continued, "For the record, please state your full name."

"Josephine Luella Scever," replied Jodie.

"Miss Scever, Is it true you were friends with Johnny Ricks?"

"Yes, we have been friends all during college."

"Are you aware that Johnny Ricks is dead?"

Jodie hesitated… "Yes."

"Miss Scever, is it a fact that you and Johnny Ricks had become more than friends over the last several months."

"Our friendship was special, if that is what you mean."

"Miss Scever, let me rephrase the question? Were you and Johnny Ricks lovers?"

Dr. Smith cleared his throat in an effort to ease the tension he could feel creeping about the room.

Jodie looked at Dr. Smith and gently nodded as to say; it is okay. She then continued with her answers.

"Johnny and I did become involved, but we were not lovers."

Minton cast a look of disbelief toward Wilson, who was showing similar signs of disbelief. Wilson then began probing into the months last summer that Jodie spent with her Father, Johnson Scever.

"Miss Scever, please tell us where you spent your summer?"

"I stayed with my Father and his wife in Sugar Falls."

"Is Sugar Falls also Johnny Rick's hometown?" continued Wilson.

"Yes, it is."

"Would you say that you and Johnny had the opportunity to see each other during the months you resided in Sugar Falls?"

"Yes."

"Miss Scever, the department has been made aware by one Mabry Allen that you became a threat to her after the break-up she had with her fiancé, Johnny Ricks. There is a restraining order on file to this effect. Are you aware of such an order?"

"Yes, I am."

"Miss Allen has also filed a report of theft for one 25 semi-automatic pistol. She claims this pistol was a gift from her Step-father to keep on hand for protection and that you, Miss Scever, had knowledge of such a pistol. Is this correct?"

"Yes."

"Did you ever use this pistol?"

Jodie had a look of shock as she replied, "No, I have never even picked the pistol up. I do not like guns!"

"So, are you saying then that you have no knowledge of the whereabouts of the said pistol?"

"That is correct."

"Miss Scever, will you take a few moments and explain to us how you and Johnny Ricks became friends, and how you both ended up at a party together on the Saturday night of your accident. Any other information you remember concerning this night will be of utmost importance in helping the JPD find Mr. Rick's murderer."

Jodie turned in the direction of Dr. Smith as she motioned for him to come to her bedside. Jodie whispered something in Dr. Smith's ear. Dr. Smith shook his head affirmatively then turned to Wilson.

"Miss Scever is in need of a short break."

Wilson started to object but realized before he spoke that it probably would not do any good. Minton and Wilson felt like puppets on Dr. Smith's hand. Never before had they encountered anyone quite like him. His reputation as the "Patients' Doctor and Confidant" now took on a different meaning. Wilson just hoped Dr. Smith was not trying to circumvent any evidence which could otherwise be collected. The detectives decided to walk to the unit's kitchen and have a quick cup of coffee while they waited.

Meanwhile, Jodie asked Dr. Smith if he could get her something to calm her nerves. Dr. Smith ordered the proper medication and had Nikki administer to Jodie. As soon as Jodie received the injection, Nikki escorted the detectives back into the room.

For the record, Detective Wilson stated; "this is the continuation of a questioning session with suspect Josephine Luella Scever in the death of Johnny Ricks. Now, Miss Scever if you will continue to share with us any further details of your relationship with Johnny Ricks. "

Jodie Scever finished telling the detectives everything she could remember that occurred during the time she knew Johnny Ricks. She continued to the point of their return from summer break to begin the Fall Semester at Johnsonville University.

Jodie seemed to be sincere in everything she said. Actually, if the detectives did not have conflicting evidence, they would have thought Miss Jodie Scever to be completely innocent. However; they had been in the business long enough to know one could not jump to conclusions so quickly. All the evidence, whether circumstantial or not had to be studied thoroughly.

"Detective Wilson, I really have told you all I remember at this point. I am feeling very tired. Could we stop for today?"

"I think that is a good idea gentlemen," Dr. Smith interjected.

"Yes, I believe we have enough to get us started. Thank you for cooperating Miss Scever and I certainly hope you feel better very soon." Detective Wilson replied.

Wilson and Minton packed their briefcases. They exchanged cordial good-byes as they made their way to the door.

"We will be in touch later." Wilson commented as they exited.

Once back at the department, Wilson told Minton he was going to stay late and go over the information while it was fresh in his mind. Minton agreed that he would like to stay as well. So, once again, Wilson started some coffee in the well-used coffee pot as Minton made a call to the local sub-shop for delivery.

Minton placed the recording in the DVD player and sat down beside Wilson. They both had their notes, a cup of coffee and plenty of time. Jodie began her story with some background into her relationship with Johnny Ricks.

"Johnny and I met when I was a freshman at Johnsonville University. We both had similar interests and became friends. There were lots of times that we would hang out together in groups at ball games, socials, and other events. Johnny would press me to see him as a couple, but I just was not interested.

When Mabry Allen and I became roommates, she and Johnny seemed to connect and began seeing each other regularly. They included me, but it was just not the same as before. Johnny and I even discussed that we were probably too close as friends to ever be anything more to each other."

"Mabry and Johnny's relationship began to develop, so I felt it best to keep my distance. I just tried to be the best friend I could to both of them. By the time of our junior year, Mabry and Johnny had become serious enough that they were discussing their future together. In December, Johnny asked Mabry to marry him and she answered affirmatively. They discussed a lot concerning their future but Johnny was not happy that Mabry had not told her parents. Johnny was finally able to talk Mabry into introducing him to her parents. This was a major accomplishment in their relationship."

Detective Wilson interrupted Jodie at this point and asked if Mabry had any specific reasons for not taking Johnny to meet her parents.

Jodie sighed and replied, "Yes, there is a reason. I had been home with Mabry on two occasions both of which could not end too soon for me. Mabry's stepfather is a domineering man and treated Mabry like his slave. He also treated Mabry's mother with great disrespect. I felt very uncomfortable in that home."

Detective Wilson stopped Jodie again stating that this seemed a flimsy excuse for not taking a fiancé home to meet the parents.

This time Jodie gave the Detective a stern look as she firmly said, "If you allow me to finish my story, then you may understand the reasons."

"My apologies, Miss Scever, please continue."

"Mabry agreed to take Johnny home with her over Spring Break to meet her parents. When they returned to campus, I could sense a tension between them that was more than just a little argument. Mabry would not talk to me. She just said that she realized while at home that it could never work out between she and Johnny. I was floored! Everyone was! We all thought Johnny and Mabry were soul mates. This is where I pick back up with our friendship."

Wilson looked frustrated as he once again interrupted Jodie.

"Miss Scever, I believe you were going to enlighten us as to why Mabry Allen did not want Johnny Ricks to meet her parents, along with how the relationship between you and Johnny Ricks unfolded. If you would be kind enough, we also need information leading up to and surrounding the night of Mr. Ricks' death."

"Yes," replied Jodie. "Again, you will get your answers."

Dr. Smith stood and faced Detective Wilson. "Please remember that Miss Scever is still a patient needing hospital care. She is not to be antagonized. I hope this is clear."

Detective Wilson nodded in response and motioned for Jodie to continue. She began again this time a little more worn and with sadness in her face.

"As I stated, Johnny and I were very close friends. When he and Mabry returned from the visit to her parents, it was obvious something very unfortunate had happened. Johnny seemed withdrawn from everyone, and Mabry would not go out even to class for several days. Mabry would not talk to me about the situation, so I began spending time with Johnny hoping to help the two of them work through their problems.

Unfortunately, it seemed that nothing anyone did helped either of them. Johnny began to confide more and more in me. I began to wonder if perhaps he and I really should have given ourselves a chance at having a relationship. I knew that he was still upset, and that I was more than likely just an emotional outlet for him. However; I chose to ignore the circumstances and decided to hang on to Johnny in case he and Mabry could not work things out. There were times I wondered if I was doing the right thing. It was as if I was running down an unexplored path with Johnny. The farther we ran, and the more distance we put to the past, the more our friendship took on different qualities. I wanted to stop running but I did not have the strength to do so."

Jodie hesitated for a moment. "Johnny and I discussed our summer plans. I arranged to spend the summer at my Father's home in Sugar Falls, which is Johnny's hometown. My father found a good opportunity for me to work in Advertising at the local TV station. I moved into Dad's downstairs apartment for the summer trying to convince myself it was for the work experience. It was during this time that Johnny and I grew closer."

Jodie stopped and looked directly into Wilson's eyes. "We may have been close, but he understood my choice to remain pure."

Jodie hesitated again for a few moments. Detective Wilson began patting the floor with his foot in apparent dismay. He dared not say anything or even look towards the direction of Dr. Smith. Soon Jodie returned her attention and focus back to the detectives and the clerk who was recording. The sound of an expectant sigh could be heard clearly on the DVD.

"Shortly before time to return to college for our senior year, Johnny finally broke down and confided in me the circumstances surrounding his visit to Mabry's parents. All was going well in the beginning. Johnny really liked Mabry's mother, but felt quite uneasy around Mabry's stepfather. He had overheard several arguments in which Mr. Allen verbally abused Mrs. Allen. On one such occasion, Mr. Allen was arguing with Mabry's mother that she needed to convince Mabry to stop seeing Johnny.

Unfortunately, it was during that argument that Johnny accidentally knocked a candle holder off the foyer table. Mr. Allen suspected Johnny of eavesdropping and was very cold to him the remainder of the visit.

What Mabry's stepfather did not know, was that Johnny overheard a sickening conversation between Mr. Allen and Mabry later that same evening. Johnny had been in Mabry's bedroom with her when they heard Mr. Allen coming up the stairs. They could tell he was in a drunken state. Mabry made Johnny hide in the closet before Mr. Allen managed to get her bedroom door open."

"Johnny heard Mr. Allen begin an onslaught of obscenities at Mabry. He said he heard the unmistakable sound of Mr. Allen slap Mabry's face."

Jodie stopped. It was obvious she was becoming agitated. "I'm sorry!" Jodie cried. "I just can't go on right now. This is more difficult than I expected it to be. I am very tired and feel very weak. Please, Dr. Smith, will you take over?"

"Gentlemen, you have a good two hours of recording to keep you busy for a while," responded Dr. Smith.

At that point, the DVD went black and fuzzy! How frustrating this is becoming thought Wilson! Wilson hung his head. In any other situation, the two would have probably been verbally demanding.

"Can you believe the nerve of that Doctor?" Wilson said in a questioning tone. "I guess we will have to wait until Miss Scever is out of the hospital, which hopefully will be soon."

Minton stood, then slowly walked to the window and quietly stared into the distance. Wilson was right. Dr. Smith acted as if he owned Jodie, the case and everything the department needed to do. Dr. Smith was lucky Wilson did not take the offensive. Minton knew very well what that was like.

Perhaps she could be discharged soon. Then they would have their chance at Miss Jodie Scever without any on-lookers or over-zealous protectors.

Chapter 13

Family

Thomas Wiley felt a sense of relief leaving Saints Hospital Thursday morning after making morning rounds. He had no interest in hanging around until the detectives arrived to question Jodie. He did not want to see Jodie upset, or to have to deal with his feelings over the matter of Jodie Scever.

"How have I allowed myself to become so involved in a patient's life?" he asked himself as he packed the last of his belongings in his car. The ride to Buck Valley would be welcomed. Maybe it would take his mind off the fact that today was Thursday; a day which could create more trauma for Jodie Scever.

There was something about Jodie; something that pricked a place inside his heart that had never before been touched. Thomas pulled out into the highway deep in thought concerning his situation. Before he realized it, he was moving along at a fast pace to the little community of Buck Valley where he grew up.

Thomas turned onto the dirt road that led to his parent's humble home. He knew his Mother would be waiting for him. He called her early Wednesday to tell her of his plan to come Thursday and stay through the weekend. She was ecstatic that he was coming! It had been over a month since Thomas had seen his family back home. His Mother, Nancy, was a strong, yet sensitive and caring person. Thomas had never heard his Mother say an unkind word to or about anyone. He desperately needed to talk to someone who would understand; someone who would not be critical of the emotional roller-coaster he was riding right now. It was going to be great to have some time for conversation with his mother.

Thomas first noticed the smoke rising from the chimney as he pulled into the driveway. The smoke appeared as a pair of hands wafting his way and then becoming wispy as they circled back toward the house as if to draw Thomas in that direction. Thomas thought, surely I am imagining things, or maybe my heart truly is so heavy that everything appears to be drawing me home.

Thomas spied Nancy as she came to the front door, which always stayed open at the Wiley home. She waved at Thomas, and waited to hold the door for him as he carried his things inside.

Nancy gave her son a great big hug. "It is so good to have you home. As usual, we will have a lot going on around here for you to get involved in if you wish, or you can just rest and talk to your momma!"

Thomas knew in that moment this was where he needed to be. The aroma from the kitchen filled his senses as he stepped inside. He knew immediately that a pot of blackberry dumplings must be waiting for him. With further investigation, Thomas found country ham, creamed corn, green beans, and his mother's homemade "Cat Head" biscuits, all just waiting to be enjoyed. She must have worked all afternoon. There was enough food to feed the community. Of course, there were five children, including Thomas. He could hardly wait for them all to be seated for supper even though he knew he might have to fight for the dumplings!

"Hey everyone, what is this... a family reunion?" Thomas heard as one of his brothers came in the front door.

Thomas could tell this was going to be a great evening. He was glad he had phoned in time for his Mother to gather everyone for the evening meal. Soon everyone was seated around the modest dining table. It was amazing how they all connected so quickly after the blessing was said.

"I hear you are getting to be a mighty fine doctor down there in Johnsonville," commented Thomas' Dad.

"I'm not sure about mighty fine, but I believe I am keeping up the pace and passing," answered Thomas.

Nancy added, "Thomas has always been at the top of his class. I doubt any less from him as a doctor. Why, it'll be nice to have a son for a doctor!"

Questions started coming at Thomas from each sibling all at once. He tried to answer each one without ignoring the other. Food bowls seemed to keep passing by Thomas as everyone shared. Once the bowls were empty, and the dumpling pot sufficiently scraped clean, Nancy offered to fix more. She declared matter-of-factly, "Gracious, that pot of dumplings sure got gone in a hurry!" Everyone just looked at each other and laughed. Thomas was enjoying this immensely.

Thomas' Dad was the first one to get up from the table. "That sure was a good meal there Momma. The young'uns can keep you company tonight. I believe I will round up the dogs and go Coon Hunting."

Thomas so wished his Dad would stay around. They never had time to talk. He would love to interact with his Dad, but he was soon gone for the evening. One by one, Thomas' siblings hugged Thomas and told him they would see him in the morning.

Thomas' Sister, whom they lovingly referred to as "Sissie," declared she was going to stay in tonight and help their Mother clean the kitchen. Sissie always admired Thomas' brotherly strength and wisdom. Sissie was almost as devoted to her brother, Thomas, as Nancy their mother was. Sissie wanted time to catch up with Thomas. She was concerned as to why he appeared at home so suddenly. She had a feeling something more was involved than just needing a good home-cooked meal.

It was a cool November evening. The warmth from the fireplace soothed Thomas spirit. He settled himself in his Dad's recliner and simply savored the moments of peace inside his parent's home. He could hear his Mother and sister talking and laughing as they washed the dishes. Sissies' laughter was infectious. It almost made Thomas want to be a part of the conversation.

"Sis, you two better not cut-up too much over there, I'm sitting over here all by myself."

"You just stay in your skin, young man. Me and Momma's a-talking about some really important stuff."

Thomas was glad Sissie had decided to stay. He knew she probably had plans with her fiancé, but he would be happy for her company this evening.

With the dishes put away, Sissie made her way to the family room in hopes of some revealing conversation with her brother.

"So, I'm here now. What do you want to talk about?"

"Oh, just any old thing, maybe an update on your Wedding plans or what our little sis has been doing?"

"I will go first if you promise to tell me all your secrets," laughed Sissie.

"Okay, I guess that's only fair. Go ahead!"

Sissie began. She updated Thomas on her plans for her upcoming Wedding. Her fiancé had found them a nice place they could buy for a starter home. It was near his parents. Sissie continued until she filled Thomas in on all the siblings and even some of their cousins' mishaps or good news.

The time was getting late. Thomas sighed and pushed the recliner back to stretch out. He closed his eyes and turned his head away from Sissie.

"Hey now brother; you promised me some secrets. You better not sit there and fall asleep."

"I'm not. I was just gathering my thoughts."

Thomas picked up the bible that their Mother consistently kept on the table beside the recliner. You could count on finding it there between where she sat upon the sofa and his Dad's recliner. He held it in his hands as he let the recliner slip back into an upright position.

Thomas stopped and looked at Sissie very seriously. "What?"

"I've been doing a lot of reading lately. Do you know what Genesis 2:24 and Proverbs 18:22 say concerning marriage and taking a wife? Sissie, I have met a lot of young ladies, but I have never found that one to consume my every thought, until maybe now."

Ah Ha, Sissie thought to herself. "Well Thomas, you need to tell me about her, and I'll decide if she is right for you or not!" Sissie replied laughingly.

Thomas grinned and began to tell the story of Jodie Scever. He tried to explain his feelings in the best way possible. It really did not take long to fill Sissie in on all the details.

"Well, she sounds quite interesting," said Nancy, as she entered the room. "I overheard most of your conversation. I hope you don't mind."

Thomas replied, "Not at all. I hope we're not keeping you up too late."

"Oh no, I still don't go to bed before eleven," answered Nancy.

Sissie studied her brother's face. "This Jodie, do you think she is guilty of murdering of that Johnny person?"

"It is hard for me to believe she is, or that she is capable of such an act. I have spent a lot of time on her case. I have taken the extra time to talk to Jodie when I was off-duty even though it was a risk to do so. She shared her family's story with me and a lot of what she has been involved in during her years at Johnsonville University. I just can't get her off my mind. There is something so innocent and genuine about Jodie. She has the most beautiful brown eyes. They seem to burn right through to my soul."

"Oh son, you barely know the girl. It sounds like you are falling hard for this one. I will never stop you from following your true love. If Jodie Scever is the one for you then I will support you. I just ask you to be cautious in giving your heart away too soon. You have barely met her and know so little of her true character."

"I know. That is one of the reasons I needed to get away for the weekend, to distance myself from Jodie and all that surrounds the situation."

"What do you mean; one of the reasons?" Sissie questioned.

"Jodie is the main reason, but there are some other things I'm dealing with spiritually. I knew if I could get back my roots, it would give me some perspective."

"Sounds serious" replied Sissie.

"Actually, it is Sissie. This decision could be life-changing; one of the most important choices I have made in a long time. I think I need to sleep on it tonight and maybe have a talk with momma in the morning."

Nancy gave Thomas a concerned look as she nodded affirmatively, "I'll be right here son."

"Well, I can tell when I'm not needed!" Sissie threw back at Thomas and grinned. She stood up, stretched and bent over to give Thomas a big hug.

"I believe I will go to bed. Some of this family has to work tomorrow. I will probably see you in the morning, goodnight."

Later that night, as Thomas listened to the familiar night sounds, he so often missed hearing; he felt a peace that he had not felt in a few weeks. He knew within his heart, he was falling for Jodie Scever. It just seemed to be in the plan somehow.

"Jodie Scever, I hope you feel the same way!"

Thomas let his mind wander some more. He knew the morning would hold some answers for him. His Mother always knew the right words to say to help him. He wasn't sure how his Dad would feel about him switching career paths after the comment at the supper table, but he knew within himself, there was something deeper and greater planned for his future.

Thomas yawned. "I am really tired." Sleep soon enveloped his body like the mist that covered the valley.

Chapter 14

Fatherly Concern

The early-morning drive from Sugar Falls to Johnsonville was uneventful and even pleasant. Johnson decided to drive up by himself to check on Jodie. Susan was attending church services with one of her daughters. If he waited for her to return, there would not be enough time to go over the things he wanted to discuss with Jodie and her Mother.

It had been three weeks today since Jodie's surgery. From all accounts, Jodie was improving daily. The seizures had stopped even though the possibility of having another still existed. There were no signs of depression or any major loss of memory as anticipated. The only problem Jodie seemed to be having was trouble remembering was the night of the accident. Dr. Smith remained confident that Jodie would be able to remember in time. Because Jodie was doing better than anticipated, Johnson knew that it would not be long until she would be released from the hospital. Johnson wanted to talk to Jodie about what could possibly be facing her on the outside.

Nurse Nikki was outside Jodie's room when Johnson arrived. They exchanged cordial greetings. Johnson asked how things were going for Jodie this morning.

Nikki answered in somewhat of a concerned voice. "Jodie is not her bubbly self this morning. She seems to be distant and is sleeping a little more than normal this morning. We all know she had a rough day Thursday with the questioning, but she seemed to handle the situation remarkably well."

"Thank you for letting me know," replied Johnson. "Is anyone else here with her today?"

"No one as of now, but Jodie did say one of her brothers is bringing Matilda in after church service, and then Edee is coming later to take Matilda back home," offered Nikki.

Johnson thanked Nikki and stepped down the hall to Jodie's room. He knocked lightly on Jodie's door and slowly opened it. He saw Jodie resting peacefully in the bed. Johnson tried not to make any noises to disturb her as he walked over to her bed. He sat down in the reclining chair that had been brought into the room for Matilda. The squeaking springs broke through the stillness in the room and caused Jodie to stir.

"Good Morning," said Johnson.

"Mornin', what time is it?"

"It is eleven o'clock sleepyhead. Did you not get any rest last night?"

"Hum, well I thought I slept but sometimes I wake up feeling just as tired as though I had never been to bed. Thomas told me that could be part of the trauma."

Johnson nodded in agreement and asked if Dr. Smith or Thomas had been by yet this morning.

"I have not seen them. I think I overheard one of the nurses say Dr. Smith was not coming by today, unless they needed him. She wasn't sure about Thomas."

"I'm sure they both need some time away from the hospital. Listen, I came on early today because I want to talk to you before your Mother comes about your plans. Are you up to listening?" asked Johnson.

"I guess so Dad, just please don't try to get me to explain anything." pleaded Jodie.

"No, I will not do that. That is not my intent at all. I am more concerned with how you are going to cope when you are released from the hospital and what choices you will make if you remain a suspect in Johnny Rick's murder."

Jodie started to stop her Dad, but he asked her to hear him out before she argued.

"I would like to offer my assistance with an attorney and whatever else you need. I know I have let you down as a Father and I wish to make it up to you somehow. I hope you will allow me. It would be in your best interest to consult with an attorney before you have any more dealings with those detectives."

"But Dad, I have done nothing wrong, and they need to know the truth!"

"Jodie, I understand and I believe you, but they do not have your best interest at heart. They are doing their job, and that job is to find the person who killed Johnny regardless of who it is or how they intimidate you," replied Johnson.

"Oh! And you do have my best interest at heart after all this time?" Jodie stormed at her dad in angry tones!

"Where were you when I was floundering, looking for someone to really love and care about me? I am not trying to be disrespectful Daddy, but you have no idea how my heart ached for a Father all those years. Do you know how many nights I cried myself to sleep because you were gone? Do you think you can just come waltzing in here now as if you care about me and have all the answers for my life? No, thank you! Mother and I have made it just fine without you, and we still can. All you really care about is your reputation."

"Jodie, you are not being fair."

"Dad, just leave. I appreciate your coming here today, but this is not the time."

"Jodie!"

"I am not up to this Dad! Please go!"

Johnson could hardly get up from the chair. Jodie's words stung as hot as fiery darts piercing through his heart into his very being. He wanted to make her listen and tell her that what she said was not true. All the hurt he had caused Jodie was more than he could have imagined.

Johnson left the hospital as quietly as he came. He did not even see Nurse Nikki of which he was thankful. As soon as he made it to his car and seated himself inside, he allowed built-up tears to flow.

The remainder of the day was uneventful for Jodie. She continued to be tired. Jodie's brother, Henry, brought Matilda to the hospital and stayed with them awhile. They had a good visit talking about all the places he and his wife had discovered on their recent travels from State to State. Jodie was amazed at all the places Henry had been to visit. She was even more amazed that they could just leave everything behind for a year and travel. Jodie admired their ability to put their lives on hold to fulfill a dream. She thought about her life being on hold but for different reasons. There were no tales to tell of beautiful canyons, trees that reached Heaven or of peaceful valleys. All Jodie could tell of was pain, hurt and confusion.

The conversation continued into the late afternoon as they reminisced about all the camping trips they made together when Jodie was younger. "Do you remember the time we thought a bear was eating our food?" Jodie asked her brother.

"Yep and I remember how scared you were too!"

"My favorite campsite was on the New River. I loved going there. I could go swimming, ride my bicycle and even fish when I had someone to help me," laughed Jodie.

"What do you mean when you had someone to help? That is all I did, was help you and the boys. My fishing pole almost drowned before I got to use it," replied Henry.

Ms. Matilda and Jodie began laughing at Henry.

"Oh, those were such fun trips. You have to promise to take me camping again sometime."

"Only if you learn how to fish before we go again," answered Henry.

The conversation helped improve Jodie's mood. It was wonderful to remember such happy times.

Edee soon arrived. It was not long until the afternoon visits were over and everyone began to leave. Jodie looked tired, which concerned Matilda. She worried that perhaps they overstayed their visit today.

"Jodie, you seem to be more tired today. Have we talked too long?" asked Matilda.

"No, I've enjoyed the visit and the reminiscing."

They kept Jodie in constant conversation. Although Jodie seemed engaged, Matilda felt she may have been trying to please them instead. At times, Jodie seemed to wander away from the present. Matilda had a strong feeling something was different.

Jodie kept to herself and did not tell Matilda about Johnson coming by that morning. If Jodie had her way, the visit by her dad today would soon be a vacant memory. She would figure out a way to deal with any future visits when the time came. As for now, she had been hurt enough. Jodie's inner cavern of brokenness continued to hold her captive, adding more barriers against the pain of heartbreak.

Chapter 15

Uneasiness

Monday morning came with the usual hustle and bustle on campus. Students were returning to class, parking lots full of cars and the town running over with the excitement of a new day with new opportunities. Everyone, that is except Roger Yaddinski and Mabry Allen.

Roger Yaddinski began his day at five in the morning with his normal morning routine of preparing to jog. As he left his apartment, he happened to see the same silver car parked on the street that he had noticed during the day Sunday. Roger felt it odd since he had never seen this car before. He knew all his neighbor's vehicles very well. Perhaps one of them had friends over. With an uneasy mind, Roger continued down the street on his way to the park where his run would take him by the river, past the field house at the University, and next back to Main St. to make his way home. This was his routine for almost two years now; jogging the same three miles every morning, and stopping afterwards for coffee and an occasional donut at the small shop one block from his apartment. Normally, the run took Roger an hour and he could shower in plenty of time for class.

A few short blocks away, Mabry spent the weekend barricaded inside her apartment. She was in fear of someone watching her. Mabry was a mental wreck all weekend. She spent her time arguing with the voices and keeping watch around the clock.

She woke up when her alarm clock sounded although it was so difficult to shake off the fuzzy feeling in her head. Mabry had a horrible feeling of dread this morning. She reluctantly got up and slowly gathered the needed items for a shower when she had a chilling shudder that raced up and down her spine. "What is happening to me," she thought out loud. Immediately, she turned as she felt someone was listening. No one was there, yet she sensed an eerie presence like those she had felt many times before. Afraid to leave the bedroom area, she went into the bathroom to take her shower. She locked the bathroom door behind her.

Classes began at Johnsonville University that Monday morning without Mabry Allen or Roger Yaddinski.

Jodie awoke feeling better physically than she had over the weekend. Mentally, and emotionally, she still could not shake off the feelings concerning Thomas Wiley. Thomas was nowhere to be seen since the day of her questioning. Jodie tried to be understanding, but not seeing him at all was eating away at her heart and soul. She knew she could not allow these feelings, or she would end up being hurt exactly like all the times before. She had only to think of Thomas as another pawn in her game of life.

She would enjoy his company whenever he came by and nothing more!

"I will not allow myself to be hurt again, even if he does have a strange effect on me. He seems to be genuine. When he looks at me, I can feel goose bumps all over."

Thomas treated Jodie with much gentleness and respect. If she looked into his eyes very long, she could feel herself melt.

"Oh mercy, I have got to stop thinking like this." Jodie chided herself harshly for her reaction. "He is just one of my doctors doing his duty, so what if he is nicer than most. It is probably because he is trying to earn some brownie points or an extra grade!"

She recalled when Thomas introduced himself. He told her she had been in an accident. He was very gentle as he explained what had taken place and why she was in the hospital. He touched her arm that day. It sent cold shivers up her spine. If she closed her eyes, she could still feel her heart's reaction to his hand on her arm. Jodie could hardly stand to think about how she might react if he were to appear in her room right at this very moment. Her emotions seemed to be running rampant.

In a whisper, Jodie sighed, "How silly of me to think my doctor could fall for his patient."

At that moment, a knock sounded on Jodie's door bringing her back to reality. It was Dr. Smith. He was later than usual in coming to check on her today.

"I apologize for being so late this morning. I've been tied up in an emergency. How are you feeling today?"

"I'm feeling well enough."

"Well enough for what? Your Mother seems to be concerned about you. She left me a note with the nurses."

Jodie tried to laugh it off. "My Mother is such a worrier! You should not listen to her," Jodie replied with a grin.

"Well Jodie, sometimes a mother's intuition says a lot. Perhaps I should take her advice and keep a close eye on you for the next twenty-four hours," replied Dr. Smith.

"Really, I promise I am doing fine. I know my Mother wants what is best, and I appreciate that, but how am I ever going to clear my name if I stay in the hospital?"

Dr. Smith stared toward the window and tapped the end of his pen on Jodie's chart.

"Jodie, you must understand that you have been through a very traumatic event physically. Unfortunately, you have not begun to scrape the surface of what may have happened to you emotionally and mentally. While you have made tremendous progress, we are not able to speculate what amount of stress may trigger another seizure. It could take up to six months for your brain function to stabilize."

"Dr. Smith, I understand and know I am facing a lot of uphill battles, but my intuition tells me things are going to be okay. Now, when can I go home?" Jodie said with a grin.

"My goodness, you are a determined young lady! I really do not think we can talk about that today. Let's see how you do the next couple of days and then we'll talk about a possible discharge at the end of the week. Even so, you will not be able to return to any of your normal activities at least until January."

Jodie thanked Dr. Smith and told him she understood. Then she hesitantly asked the question that was eating away at her. "I haven't seen Thomas around lately. Is he sick?"

"No, he took a few days off to spend time with his family." Dr. Smith replied as he continued to write on Jodie's chart.

"Well, Jodie Scever, I believe I am all finished here. I will see you sometime tomorrow. If you have any problems, Nurse Nikki will contact me as usual. Any walking you feel like doing around the floor today will be fine and will help your progress. I will leave a note for Nurse Nikki to make sure someone helps you."

"Thank you again Dr. Smith. If you will, when you see... oh well never mind... thanks once again."

Dr. Smith finished his patient rounds and returned to his office. He had concerns about Thomas as well. He had a distinct feeling that he knew what Jodie wanted to ask but thought it best to let the subject drop. As long as she was a patient, there could be no interaction. There were several messages on his desk, and he also noticed his private line was blinking to show he had a message. Dr. Smith put everything down so he could check the message. The only people who knew that number were his family and the hospital staff. Dr. Smith dialed into his voice mail.

"Dr. Smith, this is Thomas Wiley. I am back in town. I wondered if you could find some time to meet with me late this afternoon. I will be back at work tomorrow as planned, but I would like to discuss a few things before tomorrow. Call me please on my cell number. Thank you."

Dr. Smith checked his calendar and gave his Secretary a note to call Thomas with an appointment time of five-fifteen that afternoon.

He was just about to get started with his incoming patient visits when his private line rang. "Dr. Smith here," he answered.

His Secretary's voice announced that she was transferring Detective Wilson of the Johnsonville Police Department which stated he had a matter of urgent business. "Fine, put him through," answered Dr. Smith.

"Dr. Smith, this is Detective Wilson calling. I trust you are having a good day today. Let me cut straight to the reason I called. The report came across my desk just a few minutes ago concerning a Roger Yaddinski that you treated earlier today. Do you have a minute to discuss this with me?"

Dr. Smith wanted to answer no, but knew he would have to work this into his schedule today as well. He already knew in the back of his mind that it would be a matter of time until someone from the department called. Only he wasn't expecting Detective Wilson from Homicide.

"I was just getting ready to start my afternoon patient appointments. I could probably work you in around four-o'clock this afternoon if you don't mind waiting."

"That will be perfect. I will see you then." Detective Wilson hung up and left Dr. Smith holding the phone, wondering why Wilson wanted to talk to him about Roger Yaddinski.

Mabry Allen had taken four showers already since returning home this morning. She felt so dirty, used and worthless. How could she have allowed what had just happened? She was torturing herself with question after question. It did not help any that the voices chimed in agreement with all the accusations of guilt.

"It all happened so fast. Why; why does it have to be this way?" she cried aloud!

She thought she had enough resolve about her not to ever give in to his demands again. However, there he was staring at her as she was getting ready to get in the shower. All the doors were bolted tight, even the bathroom door. She had not heard any sound to let her know he was in the house. She shuddered as she thought back to the early morning. Had he been in the house all night? She was horrified with the thought. When she started to scream, he immediately stuffed her mouth, and tied both her arms to her sides. She fought with all she had, but lost the battle as she had so many times before. What he forced her to do afterwards chilled her to the bone! How would she ever be free of this devil-man and the pain he caused? She had so much hatred and confusion inside her.

She thought that once she moved away from home and started at the university things would change. Although, he did leave her alone for some time - he became so furious and jealous over her relationship with Johnny Ricks that he had threatened to kill her Mother. How could she ever have a meaningful, lasting relationship while he remained in her life?

"Somehow, things have to change, or I can't go on living like this! I hate you! You are the reason that Johnny and I could not be together. You are nothing but a big fat jerk. Do you hear me? I hate you?" Mabry cried.

However much she loved Johnny; she loved her mother more than anyone else. She knew within her heart that he would eventually take his rage out on her Mother if she did anything to jeopardize his lifestyle. As long as Mabry lived, she would not allow anything to happen to her mother. She honestly did not know how many more of these attacks she could handle. Here she was, caught up in the same situation she had left home over, only this time she had to come up with a way to end this game forever. After the events of this morning, Mabry determined she could not ever face him again.

"I have to be strong and make a change. I cannot let you continue to hurt me and my Mother."

Mabry thought as she walked the floor. Turmoil raged inside her soul. She was witness to enough pain at her stepfather's hand. She did not know how or when, but she had to see that it stopped.

Mabry walked over to her desk in the corner of the living area. She sat down and picked up pen and paper. She sat staring into space, as she pondered the possibilities of leaving this man behind. After some time of thought, she began to write to the only person she trusted.

Mom,

I was thinking it would be nice to get away for Thanksgiving together. Remember our shopping trips? I miss our talks and our spending time together. I want you to know that I love you very much, no matter what!"

Mabry

Mabry folded the letter, placed it inside an envelope and began to address it to her Mother's work address when the mocking voices began.

"What's wrong Mabry? Are you afraid to send the letter to your house?"

"Whatever! Think what you wish! It is time to be rid of you and your friends as well," said Mabry. "From this day forward I demand you to leave me alone!"

Mabry put a stamp on the envelope. She could decide later whether she would mail the letter or wait. As she picked up her purse to leave, she noticed a piece of paper that had slid under the edge of the sofa. Mabry picked the paper up. She was surprised to find Roger's name and address written on the paper. She tried to remember writing the note but could not remember. Even if she had written the note, it was very curious to her that she found it today, of all days!

Detective Wilson arrived at Saints Hospital early hoping to catch Dr. Smith, so he could be on his way. It was now four-twenty in the afternoon and Wilson was becoming agitated. Dr.

Smith's secretary explained that Dr. Smith had been called to the floor for a patient in distress. He would be back as soon as possible.

Five o' clock came, and Dr. Smith still had not returned. Wilson insisted that Dr. Smith be paged to find out how much longer he would have to wait. The secretary had no more than sent the page when Dr. Smith came through the door to his office complex. All the patients had re-scheduled their appointments so the only persons in the office were Wilson and Dr. Smith's secretary.

"My apologies, today has been one of those days! Dr. Smith lamented. "Kathy, will you stay until Thomas arrives? Ask him to be seated until I finish with Detective Wilson."

Dr. Smith then motioned for Wilson to enter his office. Once they exchanged the usual greetings, Wilson offered that Thomas was welcome to sit in on the conversation. Dr. Smith declined by explaining, "Thomas has been out-of-town since Thursday afternoon. He is not aware of anything involving Roger Yaddinski, so it would be best for this conversation to include only the two of us."

"Very well," replied Wilson, "then let me get straight to the point. It turns out that the victim of today's stabbing is a close friend of Mabry Allen. I do not know how much of the information surrounding Johnny Rick's death you are aware of other than we have reason to believe Jodie Scever may have been involved. Up to the last few days, Miss Scever was our only suspect. Certain events have caused us to look at another person of interest."

Wilson continued, "Mabry Allen was until this past August, a roommate and close confidant of Miss Jodie Scever. Miss Allen was romantically involved with Johnny Ricks prior to his fling with Jodie Scever. We learned recently that Mabry Allen had become romantically involved with Roger Yaddinski as well. Hopefully, you can see why we have an interest in Mr. Yaddinski. It is imperative that we obtain information concerning this morning's incident as soon as possible."

"Yes, I can understand. What is it you want me to do, Detective?"

Wilson replied that the department needed an opportunity to talk to Roger soon. He explained they only wanted to get a statement from Roger of what happened and hopefully an identity or description of the perpetrator. So far, there seemed to be no witnesses to the crime. There was only the Senior Citizen couple out for their morning walk when they came upon Roger's body in the edge of the trees along the river bank.

"As soon as Mr. Yaddinski is stable enough, I will contact you."

"In the meantime, JPD wishes to place extra patrol in the area since Saints Hospital is presently guest quarters for two high profile patients. We will be seen on and around your hospital grounds. We have already spoken with the Dean of the Hospital, but wanted you to be aware of our presence."

"Very well, I'm sure we can use the extra patrol in the area."

Wilson bade Dr. Smith a good evening and left to return to the police station. Wilson seemed to be spending a lot of extra time at the office these last few days.

As Wilson was leaving, he was greeted by Thomas Wiley, who was definitely more cordial than the last time they had seen each other. "Hello, Detective Wilson," said Thomas as he offered a friendly handshake. "It is good to see you again; I hope there is nothing else up involving Miss Scever."

"Not necessarily, but this might be related. It is good to see you also, now if you will excuse me I was just leaving."

"Certainly," replied Thomas.

Thomas wanted to ask Wilson specifics of why he was here again so soon after questioning Jodie Scever, but knew better than to ask. Thomas made his way into Dr. Smith's office where he would disclose the decision he had finally made concerning his career.

Dr. Smith acknowledged Thomas as he entered his office. "Thomas, it is good to see you are back where you belong. I will have to admit that I have missed you."

"Thank you, it is good to know I am missed," replied Thomas. "If you don't mind my asking, is everything going well with Miss Scever? I ran into Detective Wilson just now."

"Yes, she is progressing nicely. It seems we have another patient of interest to the detective, a young man by the name of Roger, who was stabbed this morning."

Without giving Thomas an opportunity to comment, Dr. Smith continued, "Now, you said you needed to talk with me concerning an important matter. I trust your family is well, and you did not receive any bad news while you were home."

"No bad news Dr. Smith," said Thomas. "I just did a lot of soul-searching and decision making."

"Is that what you need to discuss?" Dr. Smith asked of Thomas.

"Yes, it is. I should start by filling you in on my struggles with being on the right career path. You see Dr. Smith; I have always felt a call on my life to serve people. I sought a career in the medical field for that reason. However; the longer I work with patients, the more desire I feel within my soul to counsel them with their life issues. I imagine this trait is one I have always had if I am willing to be honest with myself. Up until recently, I was not sure how or what to do with this desire."

"So I take it that perhaps you have come to some sort of conclusion now?" Dr. Smith said in a questioning voice.

"I have. I feel strongly that my life is to be spent in Christian Ministry such as counseling and helping people through difficult times when they are not sure where to turn. I have tried to follow what everyone thought was the right path for me. I even believed this was for me until recently. When I really began searching for answers, God pointed out several opportunities He had placed before me. As I studied, I realized each situation was leading in the same direction. This yearning desire in my soul to show God's love and His counsel is more genuine than ever before." Thomas hesitated.

"Go on, I'm interested," encouraged Dr. Smith.

"Take Ms. Matilda, for example. She is such a sweet Christian Lady, but needs a little extra assistance right now emotionally. My heart's desire is to help people like that find peace in the midst of their problems. As a Doctor, I have certain opportunities, yet am constrained by the boundaries of the medical profession to attempt any appearance of practicing outside my field. In other words, I have a heavy burden to share God's word, to offer godly counseling, and yet I feel bound by my obligations as a doctor. I have been in quite a battle of late."

"It sounds as though you have given this quite a lot of sincere thought."

"Yes, I have Dr. Smith. Therefore, I will be submitting my withdrawal from the internship program effective December 31st."

"Well Thomas, I must say I am saddened to lose you. I can certainly understand your position in wanting to follow the call you feel you have on your life. We will be losing a fine Intern and for that I will be disappointed."

"One thing sir, I would like to let a few of the staff know my decision before it is public knowledge among the hospital."

Dr. Smith agreed and gave Thomas his best wishes along with an offer to assist him with any necessary documentation or references needed.

Chapter 16

Midnight Visitor

Jodie was sleeping soundly. She seemed to be more tired tonight than usual. She asked one of the nurses to turn all her lights out early. Jodie was in the midst of a dream with Mabry and Johnny. They were at a local restaurant that university students frequented. Suddenly, Mabry turned on Jodie and began accusing her of ruining everything for her and Johnny. Mabry even had a knife in her hand with which she held up as if she were going to thrust it at Jodie.

Jodie's scream resonated down the hallway! Several nurses came running to check on Jodie. Arriving in her room, they found Jodie sitting up in bed shaking and crying. The time passed slowly as one of the nurses stayed with Jodie. They had a long talk. Jodie was reassured she was only dreaming; however, it eventually took medication to calm Jodie down enough to fall asleep again.

The call came at approximately four o'clock Tuesday morning. Matilda awakened out of a deep sleep to hear Dr. Smith's voice on the other end. She immediately sat up in bed as she feared the worse when she heard his voice. Her Mother's intuition knew something was wrong from the minute Dr. Smith said hello. He apologized for waking her so early to which Matilda replied that it was not a problem. "Please Dr. Smith; just tell me why you are calling. What is wrong?"

"I am afraid Jodie has endured another seizure except this time she is not responding as quickly as we prefer. I have moved her back into the Critical Care Unit. I thought you would want to know."

"She has been doing so well. Do you know what happened?"

"I will talk to you later this morning. Will you and someone from the family meet me at my office around nine o'clock this morning. In the meantime, you may see Jodie as soon as you arrive."

"Yes, we will be there," replied Matilda.

Matilda slowly laid the phone back on the nightstand and stared toward the ceiling. Tears began to slip from her eyes.

She immediately began praying. Prayer was Matilda's source of strength. "Dear Lord, why has this happened when Jodie has been doing so well? She has even been up walking around the hallway near her hospital room and has shown improvement. Oh, listen at me Lord, as if You do not already know these things. Forgive me for my questions. Help me to see the work you are doing in Jodie's life."

The room fell silent.

Matilda finally managed to get up and start a pot of coffee. She would need to call Edee and the boys. She would also have to call Johnson. Matilda really dreaded making the call to Johnson after the visit he had with Jodie on Sunday. She would not have known about the visit if Nurse Nikki had not mentioned him being there, and that she noticed him leaving in a hurry. Someone else reported to Nikki that they had seen Johnson sitting in his car crying. At first, Matilda did not make much of the situation until she remembered Jodie's somber mood and the fact she seemed withdrawn on Sunday afternoon. Jodie did not mention her Father or the visit.

Matilda had taken the time to phone Johnson when she learned of his visit with Jodie. He explained to Matilda what happened with Jodie on Sunday. He had only wanted to help, but Jodie defiantly rejected his offer. He continued to explain that Jodie had some very harsh words for him; some he felt certain he deserved.

Matilda apologized for their daughter's behavior, even though she felt whatever Jodie said was coming from years of pain and truly meant no harm to Johnson.

So now, less than forty-eight hours later, Matilda dialed Johnson's number wondering how he would react. It was still early but if Johnson truly wanted to be involved in Jodie's life, he would need time to drive to Johnsonville for the nine o'clock meeting with Dr. Smith.

Susan stirred, looked at the clock, and exclaimed, "Who in the world could be calling at five-thirty in the morning!"

Johnson answered the phone. He knew it could not be good news when he heard Matilda's voice, especially this time of morning. Matilda filled him in on what was happening with

Jodie. He told her he would definitely be there for the meeting. When Johnson clicked the phone off, Susan immediately began a barrage of questions. It took him a while to calm Susan and get her to understand what he had to do. He had not told Susan of his visit with Jodie and knew that he should, but this was his concern right now and there was nothing Susan could do to help. Johnson quickly showered and headed for Johnsonville without Susan.

Thomas Wiley reported to the hospital early feeling on top of the world. His meeting with Dr. Smith had gone very well, actually much better than expected. Thomas was confident this time that God was leading him. He was happy to have Dr. Smith's blessing for this new pathway. Not only was Thomas excited about finally accepting the call into Christian Ministry, he was almost giddy thinking about Jodie. His Mother had advised him to follow his heart, especially since he would be resigning at the end of the semester. They all knew everyone would be stunned and have many questions, but that would not hinder Thomas today.

Thomas had a new zeal for life this morning! He was determined not to let Jodie Scever leave the hospital without making some connection with her on a personal level.

Thomas checked in on the Neurology floor and began updating himself on all the patients and their status. He read the reports on Roger Yaddinski and began looking for Jodie's chart, when Nurse Nikki came over and asked to speak with him privately.

"Thomas, this may not be my place…," she began. "However, we have all noticed how you act concerning Miss Scever. Anyway, Dr. Smith wanted you to know that she had a rough weekend. She had an encounter with her father on Sunday and then last night a situation took place which security is currently checking out. We all wanted you to know before you look at her chart."

Thomas was just a little stunned. First, that anyone considered him to have feelings for Jodie Scever. He had no idea that it was evident.

"Nikki, regardless of what people think, I need to know what is going on with my patients."

Nikki appeared slightly embarrassed. "I apologize for presuming, Thomas. Jodie had a Grand Mal seizure early this morning and has been moved back into the Critical Care Unit."

"What does this have to do with security?"

Thomas almost felt nauseated as Nikki explained the situation.

Thomas took Jodie's chart from Nikki and found a quiet place to look over everything. After reviewing the report of the last few days, Thomas put the chart back in its place and left the floor to find Dr. Smith. He knew he would be in his office having devotions as he always did before he started a day at the hospital. Thomas knocked lightly on the office door to which an inviting "enter" was replied. Thomas found Dr. Smith sitting in the arm chair facing the window. Dr. Smith acknowledged Thomas being in the room but never turned his gaze from the window.

"Thomas, I've practiced over twenty-five years now. I do not recall ever dealing with such twisted events surrounding any of my patients. This case with Jodie Scever is quite disturbing. I told Nikki to enlighten you on the episode from last night. At any rate, a doctor is to protect life. Our hospital is to be a safe zone for healing and re-entry into living. How can such a thing happen here?"

Thomas remained silent and waited.

"Early this morning, Miss Scever had a Grand Mal seizure, and she has not regained consciousness as of the last report. I have always cautioned you and my other understudies to be aware of personal feelings, yet to find out one of your patients is targeted brings to surface unlikely feelings."

"I don't think any of us can deny the way Jodie's personality attracts us like a magnet."

"That is true Thomas. At the core though, is our duty to our patients. What more could we have done to prevent what happened here last night?"

Thomas made his way to the window and joined Dr. Smith by sitting in the opposite chair. He waited until he felt it was an appropriate time to question Dr. Smith on last night's activity.

Thomas began, "Do we know how the person gained entry?"

"Security is working through these questions as we speak."

Thomas continued, "So what we know is the nurse first believed Jodie was dreaming. Later, it was reported by security that a young lady dressed in a heavy black overcoat was seen leaving Jodie's room at midnight?"

"Yes Thomas, that is correct. When we pull the video from the security cameras, we are not able to see the woman's face, but we could identify the car in which she left the hospital. Security is contacting Detective Wilson's office this morning."

"So do you have any idea what this person was doing?

"No, we just know that Jodie was very distraught afterwards and had trouble falling asleep. The night duty nurse gave Jodie sleeping pills and sat with her until she finally fell asleep around two-thirty this morning. The seizure occurred at three-fifteen."

Thomas told Dr. Smith that he could cover the floor or anything he needed him to do today since it sounded like his day was going to be overwhelming. Dr. Smith graciously accepted the offer and gave Thomas his instructions, one of which was to attend the nine-o'clock meeting with Jodie's family.

Chapter 17

Seeking Answers

Mabry Allen was exhausted! She felt so very tired mentally, physically and emotionally. She spent most of the night crying and wrestling with her anxieties, not to mention the voices.

"If I do not get some help soon, I am going to have a complete nervous breakdown. I am so tired of these voices! I feel ugly enough without them trying to convince me further."

It certainly did not help that she had given in once again.

"This time I am through. He can try whatever he wants, but this is the last deed I plan to do to cover his tracks."

She knew within her heart, she was only lying unless she could get some help. It appeared that as long as he lived, she would probably never be able to keep him at bay.

"It might be better for everyone involved if I end my own life now," Mabry whispered.

Mabry walked over to the kitchen cabinet to see what medications she might find. Perhaps she had some sleeping pills. At least she would be asleep and maybe there would not be any pain involved. As she contemplated what she might do to take her own life, she suddenly thought about Jodie Scever's sister.

"Edee! That's what I should do. I should call Edee. She always seemed interested in me. Perhaps Edee would have some answers," Mabry wondered aloud.

"She is such a religious fanatic though, I'm not sure. Maybe I need some religion to help me get out of this mess. Maybe Edee knows how to pray for me and get these voices to leave me alone, even if she will not assist me. I can at least clear my conscience before I no longer have a conscience to worry about. Then I can just end all this nonsense once and for all."

Mabry closed the kitchen cabinet, now wondering how she could arrange a meeting with Edee. No one could find out about this new plan, especially her stepfather. She picked up the telephone book to search for Edee's phone number. She stood at the kitchen window starring into the parking lot as she tried to remember Edee's last name.

"What a beautiful day it is going to be. It is a shame I feel so ugly!"

Mabry searched and searched the phone book becoming more anxious by the minute. Should she really try to contact Edee? "What if Edee wants nothing to do with me? Maybe she is really a goody two-shoes who thinks she is better than anyone. After all, most religious nuts have that kind of attitude!"

"How could you even think of calling that woman?" the voices chimed. "She will probably be glad to come and bring a police escort with her!"

Their heinous laughter made Mabry cover her ears.

"I'll show you stupid idiots. Edee will come! I will call her now just to spite you. She will come; you will see! She cares too much about Jodie not to come and at least find out what I have to say."

The room echoed a thousand voices laughing uncontrollably. It was all Mabry could do to stand long enough as she searched to find what she thought was Edee's name and then dial the number.

Johnson's drive to Saints Hospital was not the same pleasant drive he had last Sunday morning. This morning, his heart was heavy with the fresh sting of Jodie's words. Now he had to face the fact that Jodie was back in critical care again. He pulled into the parking lot and left his car with the attendant, so he could make it inside before the meeting started.

Edee was waiting for him at the elevator leading from Dr. Smith's office. They made their way to the Neurology unit conference room where everyone had settled and was ready for the meeting to begin.

Taking no time for pleasantries, Dr. Smith began by going over the events that had occurred since last Thursday, the day the detectives questioned Jodie. Dr. Smith explained the questioning session actually went well. It seemed Jodie handled the situation with much control under the circumstances.

"Sunday, the nurses and staff noticed Jodie was withdrawn and lacked her usual spark. Yesterday, however, she seemed back in good spirits and was urging me to let her go home soon." Dr. Smith laughed.

"Unfortunately, whatever happened around Midnight may have been the trigger that set off undue stress causing this last setback to Jodie's progress. We have security video that confirms, along with eyewitnesses that saw a young woman leaving Jodie's room at the mentioned time. The woman had on a heavy black overcoat keeping her head down and moving about as if she knew where the cameras were. She was only in Jodie's room a few minutes. We see on the video that she left in a late model, silver sports car, which appeared to be waiting for her. What we need to know is who she was, what she was doing in Jodie's room and why it upset Jodie so greatly."

Johnson immediately interrupted. "First, please tell me why no one investigated this stranger at the time of the incident rather than waiting until nine hours later?"

Dr. Smith acknowledged Johnson's concern. "The Hospital's Security team took every precaution necessary. They spoke with the Charge Nurse who reported there had not been any unusual activity on the floor or near Jodie's room."

Johnson stood up in a rage, "You have got to be kidding me! Jodie screams and there is video evidence. What if that woman had actually done more to harm Jodie, would that have made a difference? I thought you had a police officer on duty here!"

Matilda was wringing her hands in her lap. She never got used to Johnson's sudden outbursts of anger. It had been years since she had witnessed one, and this was almost more than she could handle right now. Thomas noticed Matilda's distress and spoke up.

"Mr. Scever, we understand your position. You must understand that we are a Hospital and not a Police Station. We have the best security officers and security equipment possible in order to maintain a safe environment; however, we are not equipped to do the work of police investigation. Our responsibility is to the patient and from what I have seen in the reports; we took that responsibility seriously last night."

Dr. Smith added, "Thomas is correct. As you mentioned, we do have extra patrol in the area, so we are hoping they might shed some light on the incident. The JPD is investigating as we speak. The matter at hand, and the reason we are gathered here is to discuss treatment options for Jodie."

Shelton apologized for his Father's outburst. He explained how upset Jodie had been with Johnson on Sunday and how she had forced him to leave. Johnson acknowledged his son's revelation.

"Forgive my outburst Dr. Smith. I only want what is best for Jodie, and I certainly want to feel she is safe in your hospital."

"I understand, Mr. Scever," replied Dr. Smith. "We are taking extra security measures now as we speak. Until the investigation on the stranger is complete, Jodie will remain in the Critical Care unit even when she improves. Visiting the unit is by secure access, and no one will be allowed entry into the unit without first being screened."

Dr. Smith continued to explain that Jodie could not be released anytime soon. Jodie's memory may again be affected, and she would be very tired. The family should limit their visits with Jodie for the next few days. In the meantime, Jodie was going to need as much rest as possible. Dr. Smith explained the trauma of this seizure was more extensive than before. Sufficient rest would be critical to assist the recovery process.

"If you have further questions, make a list, and I will address them. I must excuse myself now, in order to meet with our hospital Security Officer, and Detective Wilson. I will keep you informed of the progress made in identifying the person in our video."

Dr. Smith found Detective Wilson leaving the Security office where he had just picked up a copy of the security video. They discussed the events of the night. Dr. Smith expressed his concern with the silver sports car that waited for the woman. Whoever was driving the car had parked in a position where the license tag was not visible on camera according to the Security Officer.

Wilson agreed to come back and meet with Dr. Smith later. He then took the video and headed to JPD where he would add it to the mounting information in the case of Jodie Scever and Johnny Ricks. He and Minton would take time to go over the video today. Wilson's immediate thoughts were that he needed to interview Miss Mabry Allen again, and that it needed to be this morning.

Nurse Nikki and the other staff on the Neurology Unit took turns visiting the Critical Care Unit Waiting room to give their encouragement to Ms. Matilda. They all felt the same way about Jodie and Matilda. So it was not a surprise when Thomas found one of the nurses sitting with Matilda in what appeared to be a prayerful position. Rather than interrupt, Thomas made his way into the unit with the intention of only checking Jodie's chart for any changes.

Once Thomas walked into the unit, he could feel his heart tugging and pulling him closer to Jodie's room. He told himself; "this is not in the best interest of Jodie's immediate needs." Thomas suddenly found himself at her door. His heart ached as he looked at her lying so helplessly with the machines and medications that kept her stable.

Thomas stepped into the room, all the while his heart was pounding in his chest as if keeping rhythm with the constant sounds of the machines! He stopped at the foot of Jodie's bed and whispered a prayer.

"Dear God, I am in need of your strength. My feelings for Jodie Scever are greater than I am able to conquer. You alone are the only One who understands. Allow me to focus on her needs for life and health right now. Help me know the direction to take to assist with Jodie's care. Then and only then, may You allow time for our relationship to be more than patient and doctor. Thank you Father, Amen!"

Thomas walked to Jodie's side and placed his hand on her arm. She felt warm. He was startled at the heat from her body.

Jodie's chart indicated she had a low-grade fever during the night, but this was more than low-grade. He checked the monitors. Her heart rate was up some, yet not significantly. Thomas made a few notes and left the room to give instructions to the Charge Nurse, Ashley.

Ashley met Thomas in the hallway outside Jodie's room. They discussed the incident briefly, and then he asked her if she had noticed the change in Jodie this morning.

"Actually, I did notice. I was on my way now to check on Jodie."

Thomas was relieved to know that Ashley had been keeping a close check on Jodie.

"Here is an order for blood work and a chest x-ray. Please make certain someone contacts me the minute the results are back. I have my pager and my cell. If she has infection, we need to hit it hard with antibiotics before it takes up residence."

Thomas continued his daily rounds all the while his heart heavy with prayer for Jodie Scever.

Chapter 18

Cleansing

Mabry Allen froze when she heard the knock on her apartment door. "Who in the world could that be? It is not time for Edee."

She had found Edee by calling the cell phone number Edee's husband gave her. She found Edee at the hospital. Edee promised to come over as soon as she could. Mabry doubted she would be here already. Mabry felt badly about pulling her away from Jodie, but after all this visit might help Jodie in the long-run.

Knowing that the knock at the door was probably not Edee, Mabry immediately felt fear gripping her soul. Slowly, and cautiously, Mabry walked toward the door and looked through the peephole. Detective Wilson was standing outside her door, patiently tapping his foot and looking around.

"No, I will not deal with you today," Mabry whispered beneath her breath. "I cannot open the door this morning and allow Detective Wilson to see me in this condition. I only plan to see one person today and that is Edee, Jodie Scever's sister." Mabry was almost in tears as she whispered the words.

The voices began mocking her, "No, No; you are not the one I need, No, go away!"

She backed away from the door carefully as to not make any undue noise. She fell into the softness of her sofa and began to let the tears flow. It was not long until the pain softened. Mabry soon fell into the abyss of sleep.

Edee could not get the phone call from Mabry Allen off her mind. Edee had concerns about leaving the hospital at such a critical time. Matilda seemed to be in good spirits despite the situation. Edee decided to stay with her Mother a little while longer and then figure out a way to leave. The more Edee waited, the heavier the intensity of the phone call weighed on Edee's emotions.

Finally, Edee revealed to Ms. Matilda that she had an errand she needed to take care of today. "I promise I won't be gone too long. This is something that I have to do today. Call my cell phone if anything changes."

Mabry gave a convincing argument to Edee, which made her more curious. Mabry told her it might help with Jodie's situation. When she mentioned Jodie, Edee knew she had to see Mabry.

Edee decided to pick up lunch for Mabry and herself from the local sandwich shop near the University. She thought that perhaps a conversation with Mabry would be easier if they had lunch together even though it was after two 'o clock. Edee picked up sandwiches, a couple of soft drinks and headed to Mabry

Allen's apartment. She was anxious to hear Mabry explain the urgency of this visit, especially what it had to do with Jodie!

As Edee pulled into the apartment complex, she noticed a man sitting in a silver sports car near the line of trees at the back of the apartments. Normally, Edee would have thought nothing of this, but the man seemed to be staring at her as she was getting out of the car. She thought to herself, "didn't Dr. Smith say something about a silver sports car?" The man appeared to be watching Edee's every move. She continued to Mabry's door without looking back at him and quickly knocked on the door.

Mabry opened the door with a welcoming smile which immediately turned into horror as Mabry looked past Edee's shoulders! Mabry grabbed Edee's arm and pulled her inside. She locked and bolted the door, then fell into a heap upon the floor at Edee's feet.

Edee quietly whispered, "Mabry, please tell me what is going on?"

Mabry began to sob as her body shook. Edee sat the lunches down on the kitchen counter and then got down onto the floor beside Mabry.

"Is there something I need to do for you right away?"

Mabry looked up at Edee and started to speak. She realized that Edee was looking at her with eyes that saw something more than Mabry Allen. There was something about those eyes. They seemed to be caring.

Mabry tried to talk but only cried. Edee pulled Mabry into her arms careful not to hurt her where she already appeared

166

bruised. They sat like this for a long time. Mabry finally found strength to sit up and speak.

"I know you must think I'm crazy for pulling you inside like that, but you don't realize what danger is out there. There is a person stalking me, and I had no idea he was back. I saw him when I opened the door for you, so my only thought was to pull you inside and lock the doors."

"I think I know who you are talking about," replied Edee as her mind raced to gather more information of a car that was seen leaving Saints Hospital last night.

"But how could you know?"

"When I pulled up, I noticed a man in a silver sports car. He seemed to be too interested in what I was doing. I also thought it odd to be a silver sports car."

"Oh Edee, I am so sorry! I never should have asked you to come." cried Mabry. "You probably think I am a horrible person. I will not blame you if you leave."

"Listen, whatever is going on, we can handle this together. For some reason, you called me. You may think it is coincidental, but believe me when I tell you that God works in mysterious ways. He has brought us together at this moment for a reason."

Mabry looked at Edee with a surprise showing on her face. "Do you really believe that stuff?" she asked,

"Oh yes, more than believe Mabry, I live it daily." Edee continued, "I never really understood peace until I accepted God's full pardon and love in my life. Surely, Jodie has shared something of God's love with you."

Mabry began laughing nervously! "Jodie! What makes you think Jodie shares anything about God?" she asked sarcastically.

"Mabry, I realize you and Jodie had some issues to come up between you. However, it does not change the fact that Jodie still cares about you. Jodie may have strayed, but the God who forgives, and gave Jodie eternal security will not leave her. It does not matter what Jodie has done, may be involved in, or is even contemplating. Once a person gives his or her life to God, there is no removing that life from God's realm of security."

"I don't understand. I could sure use some security right now. I am so afraid Edee!"

"Listen Mabry, there is security and peace for you, if you are willing to accept it. It is an assurance that only comes from knowing God in a personal relationship. It is a strength and hope for each day. Because of the sacrifice of God's Son, Jesus, this relationship is available to all, including you. Do you think this is something you would be willing to believe and accept?"

"Security, peace, and assurance are definitely what I am interested in, especially if some areas of pressure in my life would stop! I might be willing Edee, but I still do not understand how it all works. It seems so ludicrous."

"I understand Mabry. Faith is what helps a person gain understanding. It is only by faith in a God that loves us, which one is able to understand." You see Mabry; God looks at us through His son, Jesus Christ, the One who took all the sins of the world upon Himself and became the Sacrifice that was needed to remove those sins."

Edee continued to explain, "Think of it as a stain on your favorite dress. You would never think of discarding or throwing away that dress. The dress is important to you, and you still love wearing it. You feel special every time you put the dress on and look into the mirror. However; it has become stained. The stain is too deep to remove by yourself, and you need help. You look until you find the perfect cleaner that will take out the stain. Once the cleaner is applied, you wash the dress and to your surprise, the stain is gone and dress is like brand new. You feel so refreshed and happy."

Mabry, this is how God works. You are the dress. The cleaner is His Son. God sees you and loves you, even though you are stained. He wants you to become clean and new again. So with your acceptance, He applies the cleaner and washes you. You come out brand new without the guilt and stains that made you feel old and used. Mabry, you can be clean and new again."

Mabry was crying again. This time it was not the fearful sobbing but a gentle flow of tears that broke Edee's heart.

"Mabry, do you want to be clean?" Edee questioned.

"Yes, Yes, I do more than anything, but how and what should I do? I am amazed that God would be willing to do that for me after all I have done. I am a terrible person Edee!"

Edee was crying now. She tried to remain strong and focused. "Mabry, God has never stopped loving you, just as you never stopped loving the dress."

"That is so wonderful and yet so amazing," responded Mabry.

"Exactly Mabry, It is an Amazing Love."

"Edee, I really would like to accept God's cleansing. I feel so dirty, ugly and useless. How can God love me? You have no idea what I have done. Will you help me?"

"If you believe in your heart that God loves you, can forgive you and give you a fresh start, then you have already taken the first step Mabry. If you believe this, all you need to do is personally ask God for His cleansing and forgiveness. Then, you accept His forgiveness and all that He can do for you."

"What do I need to do to ask for forgiveness?"

"We can do that now, and I can help if you would like."

"Please do," responded Mabry.

"Let's hold hands and pray. We will ask God to cleanse you. I will pray a short prayer, and you can put the words into your own thoughts and pray aloud to God. Is that okay?"

"Yes, I am ready." responded Mabry.

Edee and Mabry remained huddled upon the floor. They began to pray with Edee leading the prayer. Mabry was able to find in herself a strength she did not know she had as she asked for God's cleansing and forgiveness on her life.

When the two finished praying, they sat in the floor and cried for a long while. Edee shared scriptures she thought would be helpful to Mabry. She also gave Mabry her personal bible to keep and use as long as she needed it, or until she had one of her own. Mabry promised to share more of her story with Edee if she could wait until she made a couple of phone calls.

Edee responded, "Yes, please do whatever you are feeling led to do. I can leave if necessary."

"No, I want you to stay. Do you have time?" Mabry begged. "I promise to only be a few minutes on the phone, and then we can have the lunch you brought. I also need to share some things with you Edee, like how I was feeling before I called you. I was going to end… oh my, Edee! I was going to end my life! My intention was to have you over, tell you everything that has happened and why it happened. Then, I planned to take my life before you or anyone had time to come back for me."

"I am so thankful that it turned out differently Mabry. I am concerned at what would make you want to take your life."

"My life has been a mess! It would take a long time to explain everything. Thank you so much for coming! Do you mind waiting while I call my Mother?"

"Of course not, you have wonderful news to share."

Mabry hugged Edee again and excused herself to the bedroom to make one of the most important calls she would ever make. Mabry took her cell phone into the bedroom and dialed Johnsonville Police Department. After a brief conversation with Detective Wilson, she dialed her Mother. She walked by the window as she was waiting and noticed that her Stepfather's car was gone.

"Hello," answered Mabry's Mother.

"Mom, this is Mabry. Listen, I do not have a lot of time to talk. You need to pack your things as soon as possible and go somewhere where you feel safe."

"But Mabry, I…"

"Mom, please let me finish. You do not know many things concerning Stephen. I have just experienced forgiveness and cleansing that is more phenomenal than I can understand. Even without understanding, it is giving me the courage to take a stand. You are going to be in harm's way. There is too much at stake for me to remain silent any longer. Please do this for me Mom. Tell Stephen you have a business trip. Better yet Mom, get out before he has time to find you."

"Mabry, I am not following you. Where will you be? What is happening? What do you mean about forgiveness and cleansing?"

"Please Mom, just trust me and do this. I have to go now. Please Mom, listen to me!"

Mabry stood silently for a few minutes after she finished the phone conversation with her Mother. She had a lot to be thankful for, yet still so much fear. She made her way back into the kitchen to find Edee had arranged their lunch on plates at the modest table.

They enjoyed the lunch together in a more pleasant atmosphere than when Edee arrived. Even Mabry noticed the difference. She continued to thank Edee for taking time to come over.

Mabry kept her promise to Edee and shared a small amount of what her life was like before she met Jodie. Edee was intrigued at all Mabry had been through, but she was still concerned about all the bruises on Mabry. The bruises were not mentioned, so

Edee decided to wait for the right time to bring them up. Edee also tried to bring up the events of the past few weeks including the incident at the hospital last night. Each time, Mabry seemed to dance around the questions. Edee felt maybe it best to wait until they had more information. She did not want to ruin what had just happened.

When the two finished lunch, Mabry hugged Edee and repeatedly thanked her for coming at a moment's notice.

"Edee, will you pray for me this afternoon?"

"Of course, I will be happy too. Do I need to pray for anything specific?"

"Yes," replied Mabry. "Please pray for my strength and for my Mother's protection. I have to take care of some things that I should have done before now. This may set off a chain of events that could place my Mother in grave danger."

Edee's expression told Mabry that Edee was confused.

Mabry continued, "I will be going to see Detective Wilson this afternoon. I have information to share with him concerning Johnny Ricks, Jodie and Roger Yaddinski. Please do not tell anyone about this and trust me to do the right thing. You need not worry about Jodie, and you can expect to know the truth soon. Edee, your family can rest assured that Jodie is free of any wrong doing in this situation."

Edee wanted to shout for joy, but in that moment was so confused with the situation taking place, she listened intently as Mabry went on with her explanation.

"As much as I trust your God and know things are going to be different now; you must be careful too. When I have finished with Detective Wilson, anyone who knows me may be in danger. Understand Edee, these are dark secrets that once revealed may unleash an avalanche of events. Please take care of Jodie, watch your back and don't stop praying for me!"

Edee was in such a confused state over all Mabry was sharing that she hardly knew what to say. However, she found words to comfort Mabry and promised to pray.

"You must promise to contact me often Mabry. I want to keep up with you and hear how you are getting along. If you think of anything else you need, all you have to do is call."

With final good-byes and hugs, Edee left Mabry's apartment with a bittersweet feeling and a mirage of emotions over what had taken place in that apartment today.

Chapter 19

Changes

Thanksgiving was just a little more than a week away. Thomas found himself wondering if Jodie would be out of the hospital by then. He had already been thinking ahead of visits with Jodie unhindered by a doctor – patient relationship. His Mother extended an invitation for Thomas to bring Jodie home for Thanksgiving.

Thomas shook himself back to reality. He needed to get on with the business of the day. He had to begin the formalities of changing his career path. This was a lot for him to be juggling now, but he had faith that it was all going to work out for the best. Thomas soon made his way to the Registrar's office at Johnsonville University. He felt at peace within, although he was having bittersweet emotions.

"The hard part of this is leaving Dr. Smith, and the hospital staff with whom I have come to think of as extended family," he thought as he walked in the bright morning sunshine.

Thomas had already contacted his Advisor and explained his situation. Evidently, Dr. Smith had spoken to the Department

Chair as well and conveyed the changes Thomas was feeling called to make. So far, everything was falling into place without many hassles. It was almost frightening at how easy this was turning out to be. He seemed to be on top of the world this morning after the news of Jodie's improvement. Nothing could dampen his spirits today!

Thomas did not have to wait long for his Advisor. When Dr. Thompson called for Thomas, he responded with a hesitancy he had not planned on. He would only have a few weeks left working at Saints Hospital. He suddenly had a knot in his stomach thinking of the changes that lie ahead. This was a new feeling that caught him unaware. He had spent more than six months in constant prayer searching out the direction he should go with his career choice. It was evident to Thomas he was being drawn into a pathway that could be more rewarding than seeing bodies healed, and that was one of seeing souls saved, and lives changed forever.

Thomas stood and greeted Dr. Thompson. "Good Morning Sir, I really appreciate you making time for me today."

"It is no problem; I had an open spot on my calendar today," chuckled Dr. Thompson.

With a few formalities out of the way, Thomas went into the details of why he felt the need to change career paths. "Dr. Thompson, I believe the training I have received thus far has only re-emphasized the calling for me to do greater things, and that is to help change lives before a crisis happens."

"This is a mighty big task Thomas. You are at a good place to make these changes. Actually, your partial internship will be a credit to the program. The experience you gained from working with patients and their families should give you a better perspective in Christian Counseling. My only concern is that you realize this new field has no concrete answers. With medicine, you have tangible resources at your disposal. In counseling, you may find yourself reaching for the tangible, when all you have to use are intangible measures."

"Yes, I do understand this Sir. This Call on my life for a greater purpose has been with me for as long as I can remember. I have always known my life would be directed into some type of service to others. If you will forgive my forwardness, I do have tangible resources to guide me, one being God's word and secondly knowing that God himself will be my guide."

"Very well spoken Thomas, with that attitude you will be fine. All your medical training and background will transfer nicely into the new program. Your resources are greater than any I could offer to you. I wish for you more fulfillment than you can imagine."

"Thank you, Sir."

"Now let's get down to the business of making these changes." Dr. Thompson began entering the new program into the registration system. Thomas could look at his student page sometime in the afternoon and see that his major was realigned. At that point, Thomas could begin the transition. January would bring new and exciting opportunities.

Thomas left the University in anticipation and excitement for his future. He was confident of the choices he was making. He walked in lighthearted strides to his car.

"Today is the beginning to a brand-new future. I thank you Father for allowing me to see Your direction."

Detective Wilson could hardly believe the events of the last few days. Just when he felt like they might be on the right trail, things changed. He was not surprised at the phone call from Mabry Allen, considering he had been trying to find her. What did surprise him was what Mabry acknowledged. He was still pondering her words and trying to make sense of it all. Mabry sounded stable and profound in her statement concerning Johnny Ricks. Detective Wilson's original opinion of Mabry lent her to be a conniving and flippant person, not caring for anyone but herself. This new information now left him wondering about his initial thoughts. He really wondered if this was another of her schemes to free herself of any suspicion. Wilson's thoughts were interrupted by Detective Minton's knock upon his office door.

"Hey Boss, what's up?"

"You will never believe who came to the department while you were off to make a statement in the Johnny Ricks' murder." replied Wilson.

"Ah, don't tell me! Jodie Scever became miraculously cured and walked to the Department!"

"Funny! No, it is not Jodie Scever, but someone very close to her." responded Wilson.

Minton sat down at the conference table and became serious as he asked, "Is it Mabry Allen?"

"How did you ever guess?" asked Wilson.

Minton sat quietly for a few minutes. "Very interesting indeed, do you think she is feeling pressured?"

Wilson replied, "I have just been wondering the same thing. All Mabry Allen made known concerning this case also intrigues me. It is not every day a suspect walks into our office with a confession."

After what seemed an eternity to Minton, Wilson finally allowed Minton to hear the recording of Mabry's visit to the department.

Wilson invited Mabry to take a seat as he read her rights to her. Mabry agreed she understood what she was doing.

"Now that we have our formalities out of the way, please tell us what is so urgent that you had to see me today."

"I will be most happy to tell you and am anxious to have this behind me so you gentlemen can carry on with your work."

Minton listened intently as Mabry began telling her sordid story. "I realize my actions may have given you the wrong impression of me. I truly loved Johnny Ricks. That love interfered with another person's attachment to me."

Mabry continued the details. She spilled everything from the beginning with her stepfather to the last incident with Jodie Scever. When the recording finished, Minton sat in amazement.

Jodie Scever was finishing her breakfast. Today was the first time since her accident she could remember eating more than a few bites. Everything seemed to taste so much better. She continued to amaze everyone with remarkable progress. Nurse Nikki and Dr. Smith were impressed this morning to find Jodie's fever staying down again during the night.

Jodie begged Dr. Smith until he promised to move her back onto the floor. He had reservations, but since Detective Wilson recently gave him the latest news on Jodie's incident, he felt comfortable for her safety at least.

Jodie was glad to be going back into a room without the machines and windows where her every move seemed to be monitored continuously. She even tried to convince Dr. Smith to let her asked take a shower!

Dr. Smith laughed at her confidence, "Jodie; I'm afraid you would be too weak to stand in the shower for more than a half minute."

Jodie let out a big sigh, "Well can someone at least bring me some really hot soapy water. I feel yucky!"

Dr. Smith promised as soon as she moved to her new room, someone would help her get a significant sponge bath.

"I will be most grateful."

Jodie rested until a couple of Nurse Assistants coming to assist her move back to a regular room awakened her.

"Miss Scever, we are here to move you back into a regular neuro room. Do you have any belongings?"

"Yes I do; you will find a bag in the chair that is mine," answered Jodie.

"Are you ready to ride?"

"Definitely, but take me to my home," exclaimed Jodie.

Jodie and the assistants chatted on the way to her new room. It was on the same hallway, but closer to the Nurse's station and outside the unit.

"I actually have a better view from this room than the other room I was in. Thank you for helping me."

"You are certainly welcome. We hope you will soon be able to ride home," one of the assistants said with a caring smile.

As the two assistants were leaving, Jodie remembered what Dr. Smith promised.

"Will you let my nurse know that I am in my room now? Someone is supposed to help me bathe, and I am so ready to feel clean!"

"Yes, we will be glad to. We have to report to your nurse anyway."

It was not long until Nurse Nikki came in to help Jodie with a bath. They talked about her rapid progress and about how much she longs to go home. Nikki assured Jodie she would get there soon enough.

"We want to keep you for a few more days. You are our favorite patient, so you know, we will hold onto you as long as possible."

"Gee, how nice," laughed Jodie.

"Okay Miss Scever, let me help you to the bathroom before we get you settled in bed. I am sure this bath and moving rooms has made you tired."

"Jodie?"

Jodie stopped at the bathroom door and answered, "Who is it?"

"It is Debbie! Don't tell me you've forgotten my voice."

"No, I'm sorry. I guess I was not thinking about anyone coming this morning." Jodie said as Nikki helped her toward the bathroom.

"Nurse Nikki has just finished helping me clean up. I really had my mind on taking a shower, but Dr. Smith responded negatively to my plea."

"Yes he did young lady and for a good reason," remarked Nurse Nikki as she helped Jodie get settled. "You will be able to shower soon enough."

Jodie snickered, "I guess I forgot that part! I'll be with you in just a minute Debbie."

Nurse Nikki cautioned Jodie, "Remember Jodie; you have recently been through added trauma to your system. You will probably need to rest a lot. If you need anything else, just call us."

"I will not stay long." Debbie added to the conversation.

"Very well, I will be back to check on you soon Jodie." responded Nikki.

Although Jodie did feel weak, she managed to converse with Debbie. They spent time talking of the recent events and how badly Jodie wanted to go home and forget everything.

"I know I have not been here long, but I better go now and let you rest. Your nurse seemed to indicate that I should not stay. I promise to keep praying for you that you will be home soon and that this situation will be resolved soon. I will pray for a positive outcome."

"Thank you Debbie. I need prayer, and I know without any doubt that you will be praying for me. You are a true friend." Jodie responded with tiny teardrops swelling in and around her eyes.

It was not long until Jodie was in a sweet restful sleep, a sleep that Thomas Wiley would not disturb even though he really hoped to talk with Jodie today. His talk would have to wait. He needed to finish his rounds for Dr. Smith and then make his way back to the University bookstore to purchase needed supplies and books.

Chapter 20

Thanksgiving Plans

"What a gorgeous fall afternoon," commented Thomas.

Thomas was feeling spunky and light-hearted as he entered the hospital through the staff doors. He could not help but think that soon he would not have the privilege of using this entrance. He went straight to the Neurology floor making his way to the desk. Nurse Nikki spotted him first and told him Miss Scever was having a very good day. Thomas thanked Nikki and pulled Jodie's chart. Everything was looking exceptionally well for Jodie, her vitals, her memory, her response time and so many other areas of concern. They were now discussing the question Jodie kept asking. When could she go home?

Thomas smiled and filed the chart back in its place. He made his way to Jodie's room. She was sitting in the recliner next to the window. Her face shone with the radiance of an angel. She looked up when he entered and flashed a huge smile his way. Thomas felt himself wink at her despite his efforts to behave. Jodie let out a shy giggle. The two stared at each other for several minutes when Thomas finally broke the silence and told her how nice she looked.

"Why thank you Dr. Wiley, how kind of you."

Thomas took her hand to check her pulse and held it a few seconds longer than needed. "Young Lady, I believe your heart is racing! Should we call a Doctor?"

"Oh, I'm not sure any Doctor can cure this heartbeat," replied Jodie as she giggled.

"Goodness!" sounded Nurse Nikki's voice behind them. "You two are pitiful. Listen, if you need me I will be at the desk, otherwise I will leave you alone."

Thomas felt his face warming and turning red. He had not realized Nikki had followed him into the room. Jodie was still smiling at Thomas as he sat on the edge of her hospital bed.

"Miss Scever, it seems Nurse Nikki might think we are behaving irrationally!"

"Well, you are the doctor. You just tell me and I will try to behave properly."

Thomas could not help but laugh. He had only dreamed that he and Jodie might be able to carry on a conversation outside the patient – doctor relationship.

"Miss Scever, I have a simple question to ask of you, and then we may be able to determine the proper behavior."

"Ask away Doctor!"

"Are you ready to leave the neurology unit once and for all?" asked Thomas.

"You're kidding me, right? Tell me you are serious."

"Yes, I am very serious. Dr. Smith is pleased with how your condition has improved. There are some stipulations though if you wish to be discharged from the hospital. These are Doctor's orders that must be obeyed." said Thomas very seriously.

"Oh? Will it be difficult? I know I have been through a lot, but I do feel much better."

Thomas wanted to laugh. Instead, he kept the serious doctor face on just a little longer. "Miss Scever, you are under strict orders to rest, eat properly, get a little exercise, and engage in social activities involving Thomas Wiley."

Jodie was silent. The room was so quiet that Thomas began doubting himself. He stood up and walked toward Jodie. He was quite uncertain if he should apologize and pretend he had been joking or just be honest.

Suddenly, Jodie's demeanor changed from one of surprise to a delightful smile that spread all over her face. She was glowing even more! She reached for Thomas' hand and held it tightly gazing into his eyes. Thomas almost came unglued for a brief moment. Jodie's eyes said everything he needed to hear.

"Miss Scever, may I interpret your response as one of compliance?"

"Thomas Wiley, I agree to follow the doctor's orders exactly as prescribed."

The unsettling feeling Thomas had felt just a moment before now turned to elation as he spoke gently to Jodie. "We will need to discuss your discharge and follow-up appointments. Dr. Smith states that you may go home Thanksgiving morning. We should be able to have you home in time for the Thanksgiving meal."

"Yay, I am so excited! Who is we, you are referring to?"

"Oh, well since you have to follow my advice, I will be driving you."

Jodie felt herself go weak inside. "Really Thomas, is that allowed? Will you get in trouble?"

Thomas smiled, "It is acceptable if you agree."

"It sounds like I will be in good hands."

"I will do my best to see you follow the doctor's orders."

Thomas stood to leave and Jodie intentionally cleared her throat. "Did you say you needed to share something with me today?" she asked.

"Yes, I had thought about sharing something with you, but it can wait until Thanksgiving Day. After-all, it is only the day-after tomorrow!"

"Oh, that is mean, but okay!" Jodie said in exasperation.

Thomas took Jodie's hand again, but this time brought it to his lips with a sweep of a tender kiss then laid it softly in her lap. He turned and left the room. Jodie shivered and kept smiling. Today was such a fabulous day. She was feeling so giddy inside yet so weak and sleepy. She suddenly wanted to do nothing but get back into the bed and sleep. If she did not get into bed soon she was afraid she would become nauseous.

"Maybe I can do this on my own." Jodie said to herself. Jodie felt proud as she managed to get back into the bed without calling for the nurses. What a day! Actually, what a week it had been! Jodie's thoughts soon led her to the sweet place of fulfilling dreams.

Edee drove to her Mother's house Wednesday morning. They were going to pick up fresh vegetables from the market for tomorrow's Thanksgiving Feast. Edee brought the Turkey along in her car to leave at her mother's for tomorrow. She knocked on the back door for her Mother, who opened it with a welcoming smile and helpful hands.

"My goodness Edee that is a big Turkey; I think we can feed the neighbors too."

"I learned from you, Mother," commented Edee.

They put the Turkey in the refrigerator and put away the Black Walnut Cake that Edee baked. Matilda was ready except for grabbing her jacket. As soon as they locked the door and headed out to the car, Matilda's phone began ringing, but they were already too far from the house to hear it. Edee and Matilda left without any idea Mabry Allen was trying to reach one of them.

On the way to the market, Edee and Matilda talked about all the food they would prepare for tomorrow. Jodie loved Edee's cornbread stuffing and her Mother's gravy. They both had a lot of cooking to do but that was not a problem since both women loved to cook. Matilda had always spent most of her time either in the kitchen or at the sewing machine.

Edee, having a Family and Consumer Sciences degree, was just like her Mother when it came to cooking and sewing. Edee could have her own cooking or home show. She once had an offer, but felt she did not have time for such frivolous things.

Edee chose to spend her time serving her community and church family. Many were aware of her care and concern for others, and knew the fame of Edee's cakes. The freedom to help others was recognition enough for Edee.

At the market, the two women chatted about the food prices, the quality of the vegetables, and how much they should prepare. Finally, with everything picked out, purchased and packed into the coolers Edee brought along, the two ladies headed back to Matilda's.

"It is such a nice day today, why don't we ride over to see Jodie and take her some fresh clothes to wear home tomorrow. Do you have the time Edee?"

"We should do that! I will make the time. I think some fresh clothes would make Jodie feel better."

They took time to unload the car and put everything away before they made the drive over to Saints Hospital for a quick visit. Matilda walked by the telephone on her way to get Jodie's overnight bag; however, Matilda did not notice the voice message blinking on the phone. She and Edee left soon after. They spent most of the afternoon with Jodie, who was very surprised to see them.

"What are you two doing here?"

"Our mother took a whim to bring you some fresh clothes for tomorrow," answered Edee.

"Thank you! I am so glad you did. Dr. Smith is going to let me take a shower this evening. I am so excited. Now I will have some regular clothes to wear tomorrow."

The ladies enjoyed their afternoon time together. Edee promised Jodie she and their Mother would have plenty of good food, fun and relaxation awaiting her when she arrived.

By the time Edee dropped Matilda off at home, it was going on eight 'o clock. Edee apologized for keeping her out so long. Matilda thanked Edee for taking the time to spend with her and for driving her to visit with Jodie. Matilda then went straight to her bedroom to prepare for bed. It never crossed her mind to see if there were any messages waiting for her. She was only concerned with getting her rest, so she could start preparing the feast first thing in the morning.

Mabry boarded the plane at nine-forty-five in the evening. She was flying to India to spend a few weeks with her Father's sister. Mabry's aunt had kept in touch with her throughout the years after her Father's death. As a matter of fact, it was Mabry's aunt who arranged most of Mabry's finances for College.

"It will be so good to get away and not have to look back over my shoulder at every corner." Mabry thought aloud.

She knew if she stayed in town, there would be reporters and gossipers to contend with, besides she felt good about the trip. Her Mother, Barbara, was at an undisclosed location and seemed to be doing just fine. Barbara was still a little anxious concerning the reason Mabry insisted she hide herself away, especially since Mabry was going to India and not taking her, even though she had declined the offer. It was also disconcerting to Barbara that

Mabry felt she had to leave. Mabry kept telling her Mother that she had to believe and trust her. She promised to keep in touch and to return soon.

Mabry thought back to the last news Detective Wilson told her concerning her Stepfather. He had been staying around his house since Mrs. Allen had gone on her trip. Mabry knew her mother left Stephen a note stating she was tired and needed a few days by herself for pampering. She and Mabry collaborated on what to say in the note. They were afraid he would try to find her, but it seemed he was content to be alone. When he was seen out in the community, it was mostly at the local bars or even driving through the apartment complex where Mabry lived.

Thinking again to herself, Mabry whispered through gritted teeth, "I knew he was driving by the apartment. It amazes me that he thinks I don't know or don't see him."

He tried to call her cell phone repeatedly that day. Detective Wilson promised to keep a couple of people assigned to Mr. Allen, in case he tried anything suspicious. Luckily, Mr. Allen still did not realize he was the prime suspect in the Rick's murder case or that Mabry was staying at an undisclosed location made possible by the JPD. Detective Wilson warned Mabry about staying away from her apartment, and any place that Stephen might expect to find her. Wilson knew the consequences would be enormous if Stephen found out Mabry had given them information before the department could follow through with their plan to arrest him. Mabry allowed herself to think back to the conversation concerning Stephen's arrest.

"Detective, will you please wait until Thanksgiving Day. I know it is a day off for most people, but I will be out of the country, and mother seems safe where she is hiding. I have heard that Jodie is doing better and may be with her family on Thanksgiving."

"I'm sure we can find some willing souls to work a light shift Thanksgiving Day. We always have someone who wants to earn a little extra money," Detective Wilson replied to Mabry's request.

She and Detective Wilson carefully considered the advantages and disadvantages of waiting. Wilson could see how worried and frightened Mabry was, so he agreed to her ideas.

Mabry's thoughts turned Edee and Matilda. "I wonder if either of them got my message." Mabry had tried one last time before she left to reach them with no luck. She left a message on both phones letting them know she would be gone for a while.

Soon, Mabry's thoughts were losing eminence as she was reaching an altitude in her mind and on the plane that allowed her to close her eyes in a peaceful sleep.

Nurse Nikki came to check on Jodie. "My goodness, you look like a million dollars today!" "Your face is glowing!"

"Thank you," replied Jodie. "I did take a little extra time since Mother was thoughtful enough to bring this outfit when she came yesterday."

"Ah, so you dressed to please your Mother?" said Nikki inquisitively.

"Nikki you are too smart!"

"Well, at any rate, young lady, you look stunning. Now, we need to get this paperwork out of the way so you can get out of here and enjoy yourself today. Let me explain this form. You will sign stating you understand the orders Dr. Smith gave you for your treatment and follow-up. You are releasing the hospital, and the doctors from any liability should you fail to follow the treatment plan. In addition to the release form, we need you to sign the medication plan and the release of information form."

Jodie hesitated as she took the clipboard and pen from Nikki. She laughingly said, "Wow, this is more complicated leaving the hospital than it is to be admitted!"

Nikki laughed with Jodie and stated, "It is because we like to keep our patients with us, especially those who are difficult to get along with like you have been."

The two laughed together. Jodie's fears surfaced as she thought of leaving the hospital. What would she do if she had another seizure? What if she was not ready to function on her own again? She really was feeling uneasy this morning but dared not say anything to jeopardize her release.

Nikki noticed the change in Jodie's demeanor and quickly bent down to give Jodie a hug. That was all it took for Jodie to release her tears.

"Nikki, I'm afraid! What will I do if I feel another seizure coming on? I just don't know if I am ready for this? I am even afraid that the detectives will find some reason to arrest me again!"

"Jodie, honey, I do not believe Dr. Smith would have considered releasing you, unless he felt you were physically able. Of course, you will need to have someone with you for a few days as he suggested. You do have that arranged I hope!"

"Yes, I do. Thomas or Dr. Wiley is driving me to my mother's house, where I will stay for several days."

Nikki smiled and patted Jodie on the shoulder. "Miss Scever, how can you question Dr. Wiley's care of you? I have no doubt but that he will be seeing you quite often to make sure you are doing well and following the Doctor's orders!"

With that, Jodie felt her face turning red as she let a smile slip through to her lips. She picked up the clipboard again and signed the release along with the other forms Nikki had given her to read.

"You have made your point Nurse! Seriously, I feel so blessed to have the doctors and nurses of Saints Hospital caring for me. Everyone has been wonderful. I will definitely miss seeing you every day."

"I will miss you too Jodie! Now let's get your tears dried."

At the Johnsonville Police Department, Detectives Wilson and Minton arrived shortly after eight a.m. They met with the officers who were lucky enough to draw the card for today's duty, since it was a holiday. Detective Wilson explained that Mr. Stephen Allen was now the prime suspect in the Ricks murder. They were briefed on the case with as little detail as needed. Several scenarios were presented as possibilities. Officers were given instructions for each scenario. Wilson and Minton would lead the way. The entourage left at nine o'clock with all intentions to return with their criminal by Noon, in order to spend Thanksgiving with their respective families.

Thomas was up and dressed early. He was excited and anxious at the same time. Jodie's family was depending on him to pick her up at Saints Hospital and drive her to Cherry Hill where she would stay for a few days. It was not that he was not willing to do this; he was just apprehensive for the possibilities that awaited this relationship.

Thomas left his apartment at nine a.m. He was getting ready to pull onto the highway when he noticed emergency lights. He put on the brakes just in time as more than one police vehicle sped by his driveway. He shuddered to think that he may not have seen them coming. There were no sirens just the lights! "Man! That was close. I do hope no one is injured." Thomas made his way to the hospital taking time to phone Matilda.

"Good Morning Ms. Matilda. You sound chipper this morning."

"Yes, it is a good day. I am so thrilled Jodie is getting to come home. Now, you take your time getting here safely!"

"Yes Ma'am. I understand and promise to drive carefully. I am in the parking lot of the hospital now so I'll let you go. We will be seeing you before too long."

"See you soon," replied Matilda.

Matilda hung the phone up and walked toward the kitchen window. There she watched the leaves swirling around on the ground. Fall of the year always brought thoughts of family to her mind. Thanksgiving was probably her favorite holiday, and she certainly had a lot to be thankful for today.

Chapter 21

Cautious Expectations

Matilda gently shook Jodie from her sleep. The evening shadows were falling, and the wind was beginning to whip around the corner of the house. Jodie awoke in a confused state.

"Where am I?" she asked.

"You are in your own room at home, honey," replied Matilda.

"Oh goodness, how long have I slept? Where is Thomas? Is Dinner ready?"

Matilda softly rubbed Jodie's brow to calm her. "You have slept for a few hours. Shelton and Henry came while you were sleeping. We have all been playing Monopoly and working on a puzzle while becoming more acquainted with Thomas."

"What do you think Mom? Is he as nice as he seemed in the hospital?"

"Oh yes honey. I believe he is the nicest young man you have ever brought home! If you are ready to get up, Dinner is prepared and everyone is waiting with anticipation to see you. Everyone, including Pastor Rayford and his wife are here."

"Goodness Mother, you should have invited a few people!"

Jodie managed to get up, but with every move, she could feel the strength leaving her body. It was almost frightening. Matilda must have sensed something and called for Thomas. He came quickly, followed by Edee. Thomas reached Jodie, just as she began to fall. They were able to get her back onto the bed.

"I didn't realize I was so weak!" Jodie stated.

"You have been through a lot Jodie. It is okay." replied Edee.

"Please don't tell anyone. I want to enjoy this evening and dinner with all of you. I have so looked forward to this day." Jodie remarked with tears welling up in her eyes.

Thomas placed his hand on Matilda's shoulder to calm her. "Matilda, if you and Edee want to get the dinner ready for everyone; I will take care of Jodie. I assure you she will be fine. This is probably all the excitement of coming home, not to mention the strain on her physical body."

"If you are sure she is okay."

"I promise you that I will be right here with Jodie." Thomas assured Matilda.

Thomas turned his attention to Jodie leaving Matilda and Edee to decide their next move. Edee put her arm around Matilda and motioned for them to go back into the Kitchen. Matilda hesitated but with Edee's encouragement, they left Jodie in Thomas' care.

"Hey!"

"Hey," replied Jodie.

"I am here for you, just as I told you I would be."

"I know. I appreciate you so much. I am just unsure of why you have taken an interest in me."

"Dr. Smith's orders, it was the last order he gave me," replied Thomas.

The evening ended in an upbeat mood. Jodie managed to find enough strength to make it through the meal and some good family conversation. Thomas was amazed at how everyone "doted" on Jodie. Anything Jodie needed, one of the family immediately saw that she was accommodated.

Pastor Rayford and his wife took quite an interest in Thomas and his work. He was intrigued at the young man's determination to follow God's call for his life. Pastor Rayford invited Thomas to visit their church sometime.

"Young man, I believe it would do our congregation good to hear a testimony from you as to how God is working in your life. Mostly, it might help someone who is struggling to submit to God's will for his or her life."

Thomas was humbled. "I would love to do that Pastor. Although I am no one special, I am definitely willing to share God's blessing on me."

"It is settled then. I will call you when I get back to the office and check our calendar."

Soon after the meal, Pastor Rayford and his wife excused themselves. Shelton, Henry and the rest made their way to the living room. They were all engaged in conversation when the newscast came on. Jodie was the one who first heard the news.

The news anchor reported; "An arrest was made today in the murder of Johnny Ricks. Officers arrived at the home of Stephen Allen early this morning. Mr. Allen managed to barricade himself inside his home avoiding arrest. Area officers were called in to assist at the scene. After a heated round of gunfire late this afternoon, officers finally nabbed murder suspect Stephen Allen."

Jodie called for everyone to be quiet and called her mother and Edee to come listen. The news anchor continued.

"The officers went to the home on Briardale Drive around nine this morning. We are told that when Mr. Allen realized officers were at his door; he barricaded himself inside the home, threatening the officers. After almost an eight-hour standoff, Mr. Allen surrendered. Unfortunately, in the midst of the gunfire, a would-be passerby was wounded. It is now known that this person was none other than Mr. Allen's wife, Barbara Allen, who was returning from vacation. Mrs. Allen is in critical condition at this hour in Saints Hospital. Further news concerning this epic development in the murder case of Johnny Ricks will be aired tomorrow during our morning newscast."

"Well, I sure am glad to hear they found the murderer, instead of trying to pin it all on baby Sis," exclaimed Shelton. Silence ensued. Thomas sat on the edge of the sofa in amazement. Edee was crying. Matilda sat back in her recliner with her eyes closed. Jodie sat motionless.

Miles away, Mabry's plane began the descent to the runway at the Indira Gandhi International Airport. Mabry would be so happy to be off the plane, and in a country where no one could find her. She desperately needed time to process all that had happened in the last few weeks and try to make some sense of it all. She brought along the bible Edee let her borrow. She was hoping to find some answers she needed. Mabry expected her Aunt's home to be a safe-haven for her.

Sicillia Bharti was Mabry's birth father's only sibling. Sicillia had kept in touch with Mabry since her father's death. Sicillia always sent presents for her birthday and visited with them often whenever she came to the States on business. If not for Sicillia, Mabry may never have been afforded the many opportunities she had been presented.

Mabry considered the fact that she barely knew her Aunt and definitely knew nothing about the living conditions she would be going into. The few details she knew about her Aunt was that she had met her husband during a semester of study abroad sponsored by the University Sicillia attended. Sicillia returned to India after graduation and soon married into a family who owned a generational Carpet business. From all accounts, Sicillia married well.

"Mabry, is that you?"

Mabry looked up from the luggage carousel to see her aunt walking toward her. She had some gentleman with her. When Sicillia reached Mabry, she embraced her as if she was truly glad to see her.

"I am so happy to be off the plane Aunt Sicillia. My legs are stiff from the flight."

Sicillia motioned for the gentleman to take Mabry's luggage.

"We are certainly happy to have you here Mabry! It has been too long since we saw each other. We will get you home where you can stretch your weary legs and get some rest. Then we will catch up on our lives," stated Scillia.

"That sounds wonderful," replied Mabry.

They arrived at her Aunt's home to be greeted by servants and a young girl who introduced herself as Panita.

"Hello, Ms. Mabry. I will be your personal assistant during your stay with us."

Mabry was taken aback by all the material possessions and servants it appeared her aunt was fortunate to have. Mabry knew her aunt had married into a wealthy family, but she had no idea how wealthy the family was until now. The massive home was bigger than any Mabry had ever personally seen. She thought to herself that she could probably fit six of her house into Sicilia's one home!

Mabry obediently followed Panita, the young girl who could not be more than sixteen, as she escorted Mabry to her suite. Panita stayed and helped Mabry sort her things and showed her where to find toiletries, towels and other items Mabry might need.

"Is there anything else I may do for you Miss?"

"I do not believe so Panita. Thank you very much. You have been a great help."

"Would Miss like a cup of tea to help soothe your body?"

"Yes, that does sound good. Then perhaps I could just rest for a while if that is agreeable."

Panita responded; "Yes Miss, I will return with your tea."

Panita delivered the tea to Mabry and told her she would wake her in time for Dinner. Panita left Mabry's room to search for Mrs. Sicilia Bharti. She found Sicillia on the garden terrace taking her afternoon tea. Panita disclosed her interaction with Mabry. Mrs. Bharti gave Panita further instructions.

"Panita, let's try to keep Mabry comfortable and withhold from her any form of communication out of the States for a few days. Hold any calls she may receive, take a message, and I will decide if it is one Mabry needs to be disturbed for a response."

"Yes Mother Bharti."

"I believe Mabry needs a chance to rid her mind of the evils and strongholds she may have brought with her from home." Mrs. Bharti knew that Panita would understand the importance of her statement.

"I understand Mother Bharti. I know about evil."

Sicillia thought back to the day she and her husband took Panita into their home. The young girl cried at night for her "mommy." Sometimes, Sicillia would cry with her as she rocked her to sleep, wondering what this child may have been exposed to already in her young life. It was not too many weeks until the child began to refer to Sicillia as 'mommy." Sicillia continued to raise Panita as her own child and treated her with the utmost devotion.

"Is that fine with you Mother?" repeated Panita.

"I'm sorry Panita. I must have been day-dreaming."

Panita asked once again. "If it is well with you, I will take my afternoon tea and respite. Is that fine with you?"

"Yes dear, that is fine. I may go check on our Miss Mabry."

In the suite provided for her, Mabry pulled back the silk curtains and gazed out across the beautifully manicured lawn to a large grove of mango trees just beyond the walled estate. There appeared to be several varieties, but she had little knowledge of growing mangoes. She would have to question Aunt Sicillia concerning this. As she studied the estate from her guest suite, it occurred to her that she had not spoken with her Mother for three days. If she took into account the time difference between the States and India, it was actually almost four days. Her Mother would not have been able to reach Mabry personally since she had turned in her cell phone before leaving. She would check with Sicillia later to see if her Mother had called and if not, she would try to reach her before the day was over. Just then she heard a knock upon her door.

"Yes, who is it?"

"It is Sicillia. May I come in?"

"Yes!" answered Mabry as she hurriedly moved toward the door. "Please, come in. I have been admiring the estate from my windows. Mother would love it here."

"Sweet Mabry, I hope we can have her here soon."

"You are too kind to us Aunt Sicillia."

"Nonsense, it is what any Aunt would do. You are family dear. I wish we could spend more time together. Now, tell me, have you everything you need?"

"I believe so. Panita was most helpful. She is beautiful."

"Thank you; my husband and I are very proud of her."

Mabry thought for a minute wondering if she missed a comment or was supposed to know about Panita. Sicillia noticed the confused look on Mabry's face.

"Mr. Bharti and I took Panita in as a toddler after the murder of her parents. They were killed in a political uprising that left many wounded and dead. Panita's parents worked for my husband in the Carpet business. They helped me learn the ways and customs of New Delhi."

"I did not realize…"

"I should have explained. Panita knows her heritage. She is like our own daughter. Panita chooses to assist with the duties in honor to her parents for our taking her in as our child. Rather than argue with her continually, we agreed to tutor Panita in the ways of an exquisite hostess."

"She seems quite capable."

"I imagine I should let you rest before the afternoon is gone. Panita will call you for dinner; however, please make yourself at home."

"Thank you. I am ready to take a nap after the long flight."

Mabry changed into comfortable clothes and lay down upon the bed. It was not long at all until she fell fast asleep.

Chapter 22

Frightening Dreams

Matilda and Jodie were so upset by the news of Mabry's Stepfather and Mother that Thomas agreed to Matilda's plea for him to stay with them through the weekend. Matilda fixed him a bed on the sofa and made sure he was comfortable before she turned in for the night. Thomas felt as though he barely dozed off to sleep when he heard a blood-curdling scream. He shook himself awake and listened carefully. He heard Matilda call out to Jodie, and then he heard footsteps in the hallway. Realizing that he was a guest in Matilda's home, he waited patiently for any sign that he was needed. It was not long until Matilda came to the family room and asked Thomas to talk to Jodie. He made his way down the hall with Matilda leading the way to Jodie's room. Jodie was sitting up in bed holding her arms to her chest and rocking back and forth.

"Jodie? What happened?"

"It was her Thomas. It was Mabry," replied Jodie.

"Mabry is away on a trip according to your sister. She is not here," explained Thomas in a calm voice.

"No not here, Thomas. I have been having dreams of a woman in black clothing standing over me with a knife, but I always wake up before I see her face. This time I saw it. It was Mabry!"

Thomas sat on the edge of Jodie's bed, while Matilda rubbed Jodie's head. This revelation surprised Thomas so he began to ask Jodie a few questions.

"How often have you had this dream?"

"I guess I have had them for a week now, at least."

"Does this dream seem like you are an active participant?"

"Yes, it does."

"You believe it is real and not something you believe happened because of the conflict between you and Mabry?"

Jodie looked at Thomas oddly and remained in quiet thought. She soon responded. "It honestly felt real."

Thomas chose his words carefully. "You appeared so frightened. Do you have any real fear of Mabry Allen?"

Jodie appeared in thought again as Thomas waited. "I have not felt fearful of Mabry in the past – but this dream?"

Thomas looked at Matilda with a deep concern in his eyes. He felt torn as to what he should do next.

Matilda broke the silence. "Let me fix us all a cup of hot cocoa. Maybe it will help us calm down so we can get some rest." After Matilda left Jodie's room, Thomas made the decision to disclose some of the hospital events to Jodie.

"Jodie, do you recall anything out of the ordinary the night you had to be placed back into the unit?"

"I am really not sure Thomas. So many things have happened. It seems I can't keep it all straight in my head anymore."

Thomas began by explaining the events caught on the Security Cameras at Saints Hospital. He told Jodie of the woman in black clothing seen leaving her hospital room on the night of her last seizure, the one that sent her back to the Critical Care Unit. Thomas went on to explain all the details of that night.

"Thomas! I do not remember any of that. I just remember waking up in the unit feeling like I had been hit by a Semi Tractor and Trailer, not knowing why I was back there again," responded Jodie as Thomas finished.

"We know or at least that is what we thought, because you never mentioned the situation anymore. Dr. Smith would not let the detectives question you a second time. For some reason, they did not call and ask, which we thought very strange considering how they had hounded Dr. Smith for information. Of course, now we know why they never came back."

"Thomas… do you think it was Mabry?"

"We could not get a good picture from the security cameras of the woman's face when she was in the hospital. There was a decent side view as she got into the silver sports car that was waiting for her, but the lighting was too dark."

"Silver Sports Car?" said Jodie in an astonished tone.

"Yes, does that mean something to you?" asked Thomas.

"Oh Thomas, Mabry's stepfather drives a silver Sports Car. He has a history of making Mabry do things against her will. I wonder if he was with her that night; poor Mabry!"

"Why do you say poor Mabry?"

"Because she has lived such a life of turmoil at the hands of her stepfather," replied Jodie.

Thomas questioned her again, "Tell me how all this relates to you feeling sorry for Mabry when she may have tried to harm or even kill you?"

"Let me finish," she answered. "Mabry is a victim of abuse both physically and emotionally. There are things she has lived through that not even her mother knows!"

"So, I still do not understand how you can feel sorry for her after what you have just been through." Thomas replied in an angry voice.

"Thomas, she was my best friend. I understand what kind of life she lived and what her Stepfather did and is capable of doing. He may have threatened and forced her to come to the hospital. He is really a strange man. Mabry needs help to free herself from his hold, but I am not sure she even realizes that. It was so bad that at one time Mabry was hearing multiple voices telling her to do this or to do another thing. I have seen first-hand what that man has done to her. It would not surprise me to learn that he made her come into my room. I might even dare to speculate that she could not follow through because she still feels a bond between us!"

Thomas leaned against the wall and watched Jodie's face as she spoke compassionately about Mabry Allen. He had no doubt now, after hearing of Jodie's dreams that the perpetrator caught on camera was Mabry. What he did not understand, was why Jodie was taking up for Mabry and what the dream had to do with the actual visit that night. He needed to find out if Mabry threatened or tried to stab Jodie and was spooked away. With Jodie's memory lapse, and the way she was protecting Mabry, Thomas was uncertain how he would get this information.

Thomas realized that Jodie was asking him a question while he was letting his mind wander. "I'm sorry, Jodie. What do you mean?" he asked trying to cover up the fact he had not been listening.

Jodie asked Thomas again, "Do you think I will ever be able to remember that night to know if it really was Mabry in my room? I also asked you if you thought I would be able to remember what happened to Johnny."

Thomas looked at his watch as he prepared his answer in his mind. "Yes, I do believe you will remember at some point. However, with Mr. Allen's arrest, it may not be as urgent as before."

Matilda returned with a tray of hot cocoa for the three of them. It did seem to help calm Jodie down and allowed them to have some quiet conversation before going back to sleep.

"Edee seemed to be terribly upset at the news story tonight," commented Jodie.

"Yes, she was honey. It seems Edee knows the family. I guess it is from you and Mabry being roommates."

"But how does Edee know Mr. Allen," asked Jodie. "She has only met Mrs. Allen."

"Edee mentioned something about meeting Mr. Allen at Mabry's apartment the other day," replied Matilda.

"Why did my sister go to Mabry's apartment? I hope she did not go over there to start something or to give Mabry a hard time about our situation."

"She did not offer many details as to why she was at Mabry's. You know how your sister is Jodie. She may have taken her a basket of cookies or something. I know she remarked that she spent time witnessing to Mabry and now was praying for Mabry and her family," said Matilda.

"Wow! I'm not sure what to think of Edee and Mabry."

"There is nothing more either of us can do tonight. We will have to wait to resolve this situation. We will just have to ask Edee about the new friendship with Mabry. I believe we need to try to go back to sleep, and maybe things will be clearer in the morning," suggested Thomas.

"Yes doctor, if you say so." Jodie replied with a slight grin.

Matilda caught herself smiling as well. Thomas was the first one of Jodie's male friends she ever felt comfortable being around. He was definitely the first she ever allowed to stay the night in her home. Somehow, she had a peaceful feeling with having Thomas around.

Chapter 23

Buck Valley

"What do you mean; Mr. Allen is demanding his rights?" Detective Wilson asked of the Jailer on the phone. "Mr. Allen has made his phone calls, spoken with his Attorney and he has been fed. In fact, we have treated him very well. What else does he think he deserves?"

Minton was watching the frustration on Wilson's face as he discussed the latest demands of Mr. Allen with the Jailer. Minton could gather that Mr. Allen was demanding to see someone and although Wilson had not mentioned a name, Minton wondered if it was Mabry.

"Can you believe the nerve of that guy?" said Wilson as he slammed the phone onto the receiver. "He expects us to find and bring his stepdaughter to the jail to see him before the day is over."

"What have they told him concerning Mabry?" asked Minton

"Only that we have not been able to locate her," replied Wilson. "It will be best if no one knows any differently."

"I am going to head over to the hospital to check on her mother, Mrs. Allen. Can I bring you anything on my way back?"

"How about a Grande Irish Crème Latte with a double shot of espresso from Starbucks… I believe I need a strong drink this morning. It is bad enough to be here on Sunday, let alone listening to the demands of a prisoner!"

"Sure thing Boss," replied Minton as he left the Department.

Minton arrived at Saints Hospital's Intensive Care Unit at the same time a Code Blue was called to ICU, room eleven. Staff was rushing past him, and one nurse stopped to ask him to leave the unit until an all-clear was sounded. He agreed, but asked the nurse to page Dr. Thomas Wiley for him.

She quickly responded; "I'm sorry but Dr. Wiley is off and is even out-of-town this weekend."

"Do you know how I can reach him?"

"He has gone to his hometown of Buck Valley. Now, if you will excuse me, I am needed."

Minton watched as the nurse made her way to room eleven. He did not know which room Mabry's' mother was in, but from his viewpoint, there was a woman in eleven. He would try to find a way to reach Thomas Wiley.

The air was crisp and fresh. The drive to Buck Valley was very pleasant and refreshing to Jodie. This was her first real trip since the drive home from Saints Hospital. The sunshine through the passenger window felt wonderful on her face. Thomas invited her to go to his family get-together today. It seems Thomas' mother put off the Thanksgiving meal until today to accommodate Thomas.

They arrived at the Wiley's home shortly before noon. They pulled into the driveway just as Mrs. Wiley was getting out of her car. It was evident she had been to church services. Jodie realized that today was Sunday! It seemed she had a difficult time remembering something as simple as what day it was. So much had taken place in the last few days. Matilda managed to get Thomas to stay at the house with them. Between Thomas and her Mother, they kept her busy.

Thomas was already out of the car and opening Jodie's door for her. He gently assisted her from the car and led her toward his Mother.

"Mother, I would like for you to meet Jodie Scever."

Nancy gave Jodie a quick hug. "Hi Jodie, we have heard so much about you from Thomas. I am very glad you could be with us today. Welcome to Buck Valley and to our modest home."

"It is exciting for me to be here and get to meet Thomas' family!"

"Mom, let me carry your things. We can talk inside," offered Thomas.

It was not long until all the family arrived, including Paw and Maw Wiley. Thomas introduced Jodie to each one with a little remark about their personality. Jodie was impressed at how thoughtful Thomas was. She knew he was adding those extra remarks to help her remember each one. The trauma she had experienced still caused her problems processing a lot of information. With the introductions over, Thomas and his sister, whom they call Sissie, went to the Kitchen to help Nancy finish the meal. His other siblings were playing a game of checkers. Jodie stood by enjoying the interaction between the siblings.

Suddenly, Thomas' brother, let out a cry of defeat! "Whoa, where did that come from?"

Jodie jumped. Thomas' sister, Makayla, laughed until she was in tears. She pulled a "fast one" on her brother by quickly winning the game. Thomas' Dad snickered at the two siblings. Jodie was soaking up every minute.

Nancy called from the kitchen. "Okay everyone, it is ready!" Thomas helped Jodie to the table as if she were so delicate she would break. After everyone took a seat, Nancy asked Thomas to bless the meal.

In his own thoughtful way, Thomas prayed, "Father, we thank you for this food and the hands who prepared it. I pray your blessings upon this home and family. Bless this food to our bodies and allow us to be your hand extended. Be with those who are in need today, and those who do not have as we. Amen."

Time passed so quickly, Jodie could hardly believe when the meal was finished. All the food was delicious. Nancy had prepared turkey and country ham, gravy, mashed potatoes, green beans, creamed corn and the biggest biscuits she had ever seen. Thomas called them "cathead biscuits"! He explained to Jodie that Maw Wiley had made them, as he complimented Maw on her biscuits. Jodie ate more than she had in weeks.

The conversation around the table was lively and entertaining. Jodie could not remember having this much fun in a long time. When the meal was over, Nancy insisted they leave the dishes for later. She wanted everyone to relax and enjoy time together.

Nancy exclaimed, "I will have the rest of the day to wash dishes after the house is quiet! Let's enjoy each other while we can!"

After an afternoon of fielding all sorts of questions from his family, Thomas announced that he should be getting Jodie home. Obviously, Thomas could tell that Nancy had kept her promise not to mention his career change until he was ready to let everyone know. He was praying the ride back to Matilda's house would give him a chance to talk seriously to Jodie.

"Jodie, we are so glad you could be with us today. I hope you will come back again very soon." Nancy said as she reached to give Jodie a hug.

The rest of Thomas' family expressed how thankful they were that Jodie was able to be with them for Thanksgiving. They all invited her to come back when she regained her strength, and they would play cards or go bowling. The good-byes took longer than usual, but Thomas and Jodie were soon on their way back to Cherry Hill.

Jodie began telling Thomas how much she enjoyed the afternoon with his family. They talked a little about each family member, and Jodie tried to make comparisons to her own family.

When everything fell quiet, Jodie could feel herself getting nervous. She wanted to ask Thomas about something he said this afternoon, but she did not know how to begin. She started to question Thomas when he asked her if she felt like listening for a few minutes.

"Certainly" answered Jodie.

"This is something I have wanted to say to you since you first indicated an interest in talking to me. The more time I spent as your doctor, the more I wanted the relationship to become something special. I feel comfortable with you, as if we have known each other for years."

"You make it easy for me to be myself," interjected Jodie.

"So, I would like to ask you to think about seeing me on a regular basis?"

"Really, Do you mean that?" asked Jodie in surprise.

"Yes, I certainly do. You don't have to answer me now. Give it some time if you need to be sure."

Jodie turned toward Thomas and very confidently replied, "Thomas Wiley, I would be the happiest girl in the world if we could see each other regularly."

"Well Miss Scever, you have just made me a happy man. We will be two happy people together! Now that we have the formalities out of the way, let me tell you a little more about myself."

"That sounds good. I would love to hear!"

"Well, you just met most of my family. I am the oldest and of course the smartest and most handsome!" Thomas said jokingly. "I have always had a passion for serving and helping people. I thought I could accomplish that as a doctor, but I am realizing that I am not fulfilled being a doctor. Oh, that is with the exception of meeting you!" he added as he touched Jodie's hand. Thomas proceeded to explain to Jodie the recent change in his career path.

"It was during my many conversations with Matilda when I came to realize this was more than a passion, but must be the call I have felt on my life for a long time. Your Mother is a fine Christian lady. The accident and your involvement with Johnny left Matilda with lots of questions. I thoroughly relished in helping your Mother come into a place where she was comfortable accepting the situation. Am I boring you yet?" Thomas asked as he paused for a moment.

"No, I am enjoying most of this. Please continue."

Thomas continued explaining; "I didn't mean to bring up your situation. For a long time I have felt the conviction to go into Christian Counseling. It was my intent when I first met you to give you some subtle life advice. However, that part of my plan failed became I became attracted to you. Dr. Smith reminded me of my duty to you as a Doctor."

Jodie looked with surprise at Thomas. "I didn't know I caused a problem for you with your job!"

Thomas smiled and continued. "I have turned in my notice to Dr. Smith, that I will be leaving the internship at the end of the semester."

"I didn't know, why?"

"I wanted to tell you, but you were too sick."

"What will you do now?" Jodie asked.

"I have already changed my graduate program to Christian Counseling at the University. I begin in January."

The conversation continued until they reached Cherry Hill, which was only thirty minutes from Thomas' hometown of Buck Valley. By the time they arrived, Jodie was aware of Thomas' plan to complete his doctorate as already begun, except in Christian Counseling instead of Neurology.

Jodie teased him, "It is all a matter of the head anyway!"

"You think so? I will find a way to counsel you too young lady and we'll see how connected your heart is with your head!" Thomas replied laughingly.

Thomas knew in his soul she needed healing, not physically but spiritually and emotionally. He prayed silently for God to help him show Jodie Scever the way home.

Chapter 24

Unwelcomed News

Mabry could not remember when she had felt as rested as she did today. She slept most of the day Friday after her arrival in New Delhi. The flight and the nine plus hours difference in the time from when she left New York, found her even more exhausted than she realized. Panita attended to her every need since her arrival, pampering Mabry in every way possible.

It was now Monday afternoon. Mabry took time to consider how lucky she was, having an escape as nice as her Aunt's to give her a respite from all the turmoil she was going through. She had enjoyed the solitude of her guest suite and found the balcony off her suite to be her favorite place. She felt as though she could sit there for hours. She enjoyed retreating to the balcony to read from the Bible Edee gave her. Edee had marked several scriptures in the bible to give Mabry a way to begin to understand. Mabry tried to go through each scripture as many times as she could. She had already picked out her favorite scripture. It was a passage from Jeremiah, chapter one that read,

"Before I formed thee in the belly I knew thee; and before thou camest forth out of the womb I sanctified thee...."

There was one other from the book of John that she really liked. It was the one Edee shared with her that day on the floor of her kitchen. The verse read,

"For God so loved the world that He gave his only-begotten Son, that whosoever believeth in him should not perish, but have everlasting life."

Mabry recalled Edee explaining the verse. She said it meant she could live forever without any condemnation of her past, if she only believed in Christ and what He did for her on the cross. Mabry knew she would never forget that moment.

"Edee, you will never know how much I appreciate you. Where would I be if you had not had compassion and shared with me concerning Christ?" Mabry thought aloud.

It was on the balcony that Sicillia found Mabry. Sicillia sat with her for a time as they caught up on each other's lives. Mabry asked her aunt if she had heard from her mother.

"Good Afternoon Ladies!" Panita offered as she entered the balcony from Mabry's suite.

"Is there anything I might do for you… would you like some rice pudding?"

Sicillia stood and embraced Panita as she warmly explained to her that she and Mabry had been catching up on their lives and enjoying the afternoon.

"How would you like to show Mabry the estate? I remember how much Mabry's Mother loves roses. Perhaps you could take her to the rooftop terrace and show her all our roses."

"Oh yes! That sounds like a great idea," Mabry exclaimed.

"Very well, I will be most happy to show you around," replied Panita as she took Mabry's hand.

The two left Sicillia to her thoughts as Panita took Mabry on a personal tour of the vast estate. Mabry had never seen such beauty and could not wait to tell her Mother about the gorgeous roses.

After the interesting tour, Panita and Mabry made their way back to the rooftop terrace. Mabry wanted to take a few pictures of the roses for her mother.

The minute she stepped into the open air she gasped at the array of colors in the sky. It would soon be sunset. "How can anything be so beautiful? I am beginning to realize what a truly wonderful God exists!"

"Did you say something?" asked Panita as she came from the far corner.

"I'm sorry Panita. I was just admiring the beautiful sunset and thinking about our amazing God."

"God?" asked Panita.

"Yes, do you know Him?" asked Mabry.

"We have many Gods." replied Panita.

Suddenly, Mabry found herself scrambling to find the words to say. She realized that Panita probably had no conception of religious views in America.

"That is interesting Panita. As large as America is, we pretty much believe in one God."

"Yes, Mother Sicillia has tried to explain that to me, but I am afraid I get confused," responded Panita.

Mabry giggled to ease the tension and responded that she too got confused at times.

"Panita, I have a friend who took time to tell me about God and helped me to understand. Perhaps you and I can discuss Him sometime."

"That will be fine, Miss. We will need to be careful though."

"Why do you say that?" asked Mabry.

"Many servants live here. Many servants believe in many Gods. They become angry when Mother Sicillia speaks of one God."

Mabry became silent and studied Panita's face. She appeared to be frightened. After a moment, she replied.

"Panita, I will not mention it again unless we know we are alone."

"Thank you, Miss. Now, if you have no further need of me, I must draw Mother Sicillia's bath water."

Mabry watched Panita as she gracefully walked away and disappeared down the stairway. It was an interesting story that Sicillia had shared concerning Panita. Mabry felt it was almost a comparison to her being accepted by Christ. Mabry studied the sky as she felt inner turmoil over the conversation that had just taken place. Soon words of a prayer escaped her lips in the quietness of the evening air, a prayer for Panita, Aunt Sicillia and for an opportunity to share with Panita concerning

223

forgiveness and acceptance! Two of the most beautiful things she could ever imagine. Now, if she could learn to forgive the past and learn to accept that which took place in her life, even daily.

It had been a long day for Wilson when he should have been home relaxing on his back porch, reading the paper and drinking his coffee. The weather had been more pleasant and unseasonal as of late. Wilson felt the fever to get out on the Golf Course. However, as anyone in his field knows, when duty calls - you answer. It had been days since he had heard from Mabry Allen. He knew she was in New Delhi at her aunt's house. He called repeatedly only to get a servant who promised to give Mabry a message to call him. The Chief said they had waited as long as they could. Wilson could not believe Mabry had not tried to contact them or her Mother. Mrs. Allen's cell phone had been given to him after the incident. He had kept it charged in case Mabry tried to call. It now appeared he would have to contact the authorities in New Delhi to reach Mabry. As much as he hated to be the one to tell her, it was imperative to talk with Mabry concerning her Mother. Arrangements for her care needed to be discussed. Perhaps they would hear something tomorrow morning.

Monday Night-New Delhi

It was after eleven when Mabry went to her suite for the night. She and Sicillia spent the evening discussing her plans for the future. Sicillia insisted that Mabry accept her assistance financially through graduation, and until she could find employment. Sicillia also offered for her to come live with them in New Delhi, as long as she wanted. The offer was very enticing, but Mabry did not want to be that far from her mother. She felt that they were going to need each other now, more than ever.

Mabry was almost asleep when she heard the knock upon her bedroom door.

"Who is it?"

"It is Sicillia. May I please come in?" she asked.

"Sure, come on in. Is Mother on the phone?"

"Unfortunately, I have not heard from your Mother, but I believe we may have some news of her now. There is a gentleman in the foyer who wishes to speak to you concerning your Mother."

"Someone is here? Who is it? How do they know Mother?" Mabry asked in surprise.

"I am sure the gentleman will explain himself. We will wait for you in the Library," explained Sicillia as she left Mabry in silence.

Mabry's mind was spinning thoughts. She did not know whether to be concerned or happy. Something just did not feel right though, Mother knew how to get in touch with them. She reached for her robe and soon found her way to the Library. Aunt Sicillia introduced her to the gentleman.

Mabry heard the voices again for the first time since she had given her life to Christ!

"They have found you out, Miss Mabry! They know all the lies you told them, and now they have come for you!" Mabry felt sick to her stomach. She closed her mind to the voices, but she still had an uneasy feeling as she walked over to her Aunt's side.

The man stood to shake Mabry's hand, but she slid past him behind Sicillia. He sat back down in the armchair and took a deep breath.

Sicillia broke the silence by asking Frederic, of the New Delhi police, to explain his reason for coming.

"Mrs. Bharti and Miss Allen, allow me to thank you for your allowing me to disturb you at this late hour. I have information of urgency that I have been instructed to deliver to you tonight. Miss Allen, would you like to sit down?" Frederic asked out of concern.

"Why? Why do you think I need to sit? Is something wrong with my Mother?" asked Mabry in a panic stricken voice.

"Ma'am, I can only give you the information that I have been given," replied Frederic.

"Then please do so right away."

"Yes Ma'am. If you are certain you will not sit down, then let me explain. We received a fax at the department around nine-thirty tonight requesting we contact Miss Mabry Allen, supposedly spending time with her Aunt. The fax came from Johnsonville Police Department in the States. They had your Aunt's name spelled incorrectly, so you can see it took us a while to determine where you were staying. However, we found you and I am here to give you the message from Detective Wilson. He is requesting that you contact him immediately. He states it is an urgent family matter."

"Is that it, no details?" Mabry asked.

"I am sorry Ma'am but that is all. I can only stress that the Detective said it is an urgent matter."

Sicillia stood and thanked Frederic for delivering the message. She told him they would be certain to contact the detective immediately. Frederic let himself out as Sicillia watched in prayer from the library door.

Mabry was now sitting down with her head in her hands. Sicillia placed her hand under Mabry's chin to lift it up, so she could see Mabry's face. Mabry was crying. Sicillia kneeled beside Mabry and held onto her quietly.

Mabry soon responded to her Aunt's tenderness. "Aunt Sicillia, do you know anymore?"

"Not really honey, I think it is best for you to call the detective, and then we will know for certain what is going on." Sicillia answered.

"Do you mind if I call from in here?" Mabry asked.

"That will be just fine. I will wait outside the door until you need me."

"No, please stay here with me, I am frightened." urged Mabry.

"Very well," replied Sicillia.

Mabry walked to the large mahogany desk situated in front of a sizeable picture window. It seemed all the views from the home overlooked a well-lit garden. She thought about her Mother and her love for roses. She would never believe Mabry whenever she had a chance to tell her of the gardens. For now, she must pick up the phone and dial the Johnsonville Police Department. She placed her hand on the phone. She felt nauseous as she considered why they might need to talk to her. It had been days since she had heard from her Mother and really had not considered trying to call. The place her mother was staying was secure. Maybe it was minor. It could be she is worried about me and knew Detective Wilson might be able to reach me.

"Mabry dear, are you going to be able to call?" Sicillia asked. Mabry stood in silence, her hand resting on the phone cradle.

"Yes, I'm sorry Aunt. I was just thinking about Mother. She would love your gardens here. She has always loved roses."

Mabry picked up the phone and keyed in the number for the JPD using the secure calling card she had purchased prior to leaving the States. Her voice became shaky as she requested to speak with Detective Wilson. There was a brief pause, and then she heard Wilson's voice.

"Wilson here, may I help you."

"Detective Wilson, this is Mabry Allen."

"Thank God! It is about time you called. We have been trying to reach you for days. Did your servant girl not give you the message?" Wilson questioned.

"No, I did not receive any message." She answered as she cast a questioning look toward her Aunt Sicillia.

"At any rate, there is a matter of urgent business I need to speak to you concerning your Mother. Are you at a place where you can listen and is there someone with you?" asked Wilson.

"Yes, it is midnight here and I am not alone. My Aunt is in the room with me. If you do not mind, I will place you on speaker. Please tell me why you need me so urgently. This is very distressing!"

"Forgive me. Let me just go ahead and tell you there is no easy way to explain this to you, so I will get straight to the point. The Department carried out the arrest of your stepfather; however, during the process, there was a stand-off. Your mother returned and took us all by surprise. When she found out what was happening, she begged us to let her through to talk with Mr. Allen. She was certain he would listen to her and surrender. Are you still with me Miss Allen?"

"Yes, please hurry."

"We advised your mother to retreat to one of the patrol cars for safety. The next thing we knew, she had managed to get through our barrier. Mr. Allen began firing and shouting for her to stay away. We could not reach her before she was shot."

"No!" screamed Mabry with such a shrill voice that it frightened Sicillia and awakened one of the servants.

Mabry fell to the floor in a curled-up heap. She was helpless as the voices began tormenting her. They spoke to Mabry through their heinous laughter.

"Now, you have killed your Mother! You are so smart Miss Mabry! Don't worry; we will go with you to Prison!"

By this time, Panita was awakened and slipped downstairs to see what was happening. She saw Mabry in the floor with Sicillia bending over her. Without hesitation, Panita came to Sicilia's aid in helping get Mabry onto the sofa. Sicillia could hear Detective Wilson from the phone, "Hello, is anyone there?"

"Panita, sit here with Mabry while I talk with the detective on the phone."

"Detective Wilson, this is Sicillia Bharti. It seems Mabry is overwhelmed with this revelation."

"Ma'am I do apologize. I would offer to call back, but we need Mabry's instructions for her mother's care. It seems you and Mabry, are Mrs. Allen's closest relatives."

Sicillia acknowledged the importance of the situation. "I understand Detective. Please continue with what we need to know, and I will relay this to Mabry. Any decisions you need, we will make while you are on the phone with us."

"Very well," replied Wilson. "Mabry's Stepfather, Stephen Allen, was finally apprehended. Mrs. Allen received a bullet wound to the chest. Mrs. Allen is in Intensive Care at Saints Hospital. She is in critical condition. Mabry is needed to make decisions for Mrs. Allen's continued treatment."

Sicillia could not imagine how much more Mabry could take. Sicillia gently answered the detective. "I will see that Mabry makes it back to the States as soon as possible. What else may I do to help?"

"Ma'am, it is good to know Miss Allen has someone there to help. You may decide when to let Mabry know her Mother's condition. She is showing very little if any improvement. The doctors fear the worst as the outcome."

"Thank you Detective. I will let Mabry know this as gently as possible. May I call you when we arrive?"

"Yes, please call me. If you send me the details of your flight, I will have a car waiting for you at the airport. In the meantime, the doctors require permission to continue with necessary treatment as needed until Mabry returns to make decisions for Mrs. Allen's care."

"Yes, of course. Please ask them to do whatever is necessary. Mabry and I agree. We will do what we can to be on our way very soon. I will be in touch."

Wilson heard the phone disconnect. He felt tired and mentally exhausted. He thought to himself that he might just go back home and crawl into bed until he heard from Sicillia!

Sicillia placed the phone back into the cradle. Mabry looked at her Aunt with questioning eyes.

"Mabry, your mother is in critical condition at Saints Hospital. We need to arrange for you to get home. You are needed to make decisions and be by Barbara's side."

"I can't believe this is happening! Mother was going away until I told her it was safe to come back. I should have brought her here with me, and none of this would have happened."

"Now honey, we do not know that. All things happen for a reason whether we understand or not. It is up to us to trust and let God lead us to accept the circumstances."

"Sicillia, do you believe in prayer?"

"Absolutely, I do believe."

"Can you pray with me for Mother?"

"Let's hold hands and we will petition God on behalf of your Mother and my sister-in-law. Panita, come join us."

Chapter 25

Going Home

Jodie woke up with excitement running through her veins. She was going home to her apartment today. She could not wait to get back into a routine. Even though she was leaving her Mother's earlier than Dr. Smith advised, she had a peaceful feeling that everything would turn out fine. Actually, this was probably the first time in the last ten years; Jodie was not guilt-ridden about a decision.

Jodie got up, bathed, and dressed before her mother had breakfast ready! When she walked into the kitchen, Matilda poured her a big class of orange juice.

"Well young lady, are we in a hurry this morning?" Matilda asked jokingly.

Jodie laughed as she took the glass of juice. She looked her mother in the eyes and from somewhere deep within Jodie replied, "Yes, in a hurry to get back to school, but not to leave you Mother."

Jodie's reply stunned Matilda for just a moment. She reached out and gave Jodie a big hug trying to keep from crying. Something changed in Jodie. She noticed it Thanksgiving Day, but was apprehensive to hope for more than possible.

"Breakfast is almost ready if you feel like setting the table for us. Edee will be here shortly."

Jodie let go of her mother's embrace. She was surprised at how she welcomed the hug more than before. For some reason, she had never been fond of hugging her mother.

Matilda served breakfast as soon as Edee arrived. The three ladies enjoyed pleasant conversation as they discussed Jodie's immediate plans to return to school. They discussed how Jodie would take care of herself until Matilda seemed satisfied with the plan.

"Jodie, you know we are here for you if anything comes up you do not feel comfortable with or feel capable of handling. All you need to do is call one of us." Edee commented.

"I know, you and Mother have always been there for me, even when I was too stubborn to notice. I do appreciate all you both have done for me. I promise to call if I have any problem."

Suddenly, with tears in her eyes, Matilda moved away from the table and stated, "Goodness, look at the time. I do not want to rush you, but if Edee gets you home before Noon, we need to get you on your way!"

After some tearful hugs with her Mother, Jodie and Edee headed to the car for the ride back to Jodie's world. Ms. Matilda watched them drive away knowing in her heart that God was working in Jodie's life.

The sunshine was bright on Jodie's face and felt more wonderful that she could remember. She commented that the sky looked like a freshly washed blue sheet with billows of soft pockets beckoning her.

"I believe a person could lie down on those clouds and have a very peaceful rest. They look so inviting."

The drive back to Johnsonville was uneventful. Edee pulled up directly in front of the apartment. Much to Jodie's surprise, Thomas was waiting and immediately came to assist her into her apartment. Thomas shared a knowing look with Edee, as he almost carried Jodie into the apartment. He soon re-appeared to help Edee carry Jodie's luggage inside the apartment.

Thomas kidded with Jodie after he took her things to her bedroom. "Did you bring half of your Mother's house back with you?"

Jodie just gave him a quick look as he turned away from her timid attempt to slap his arm.

"Well Edee, I believe that will do it for now. I will come back later and check on her. See if you can make her behave."

"I will see what I can do Thomas," replied Edee.

It was apparent that Debbie had taken good care of things for Jodie while she was sick. She had obviously been baking. There were cookies cooling on a baking rack, and a pound cake sat on the bar with serving plates and utensils. Jodie smelled the coffee over all the other aromas. She loved coffee. They had not allowed her to have anything but decaf while she was in the hospital. Dr. Smith explained the caffeine could trigger a seizure.

Debbie opened the front door and entered with a vase of fresh flowers in her hands. "I saw Edee's car out front. I was hoping to get back before you arrived." Debbie noticed Jodie looking at the coffee pot. "I made decaf just for you Jodie."

"Thank you Debbie, that sounds wonderful."

Edee helped Debbie with the flowers and offered to fix Jodie some coffee and cake. Jodie replied that she was still full from breakfast but would take some before long.

"Edee, will you help me get situated on this sofa. It is not nearly as comfortable as Mom's sofa!"

"Do tell! It always seems Mom's house is the best place around," Edee remarked as she assisted Jodie to a better resting position. Once Jodie seemed comfortable, Edee sat with her until she fell asleep.

Mabry and Sicillia arrived at Johnsonville airport Tuesday night not long after Detective Wilson had retired for the evening. He was comfortable knowing he had arranged for a car to be at the airport thirty minutes prior to the scheduled flight arrival. The officer had instructions to wait for Mabry inside and assist with the luggage. Wilson also contacted Mrs. Allen's doctors with the approximate arrival time. Sicillia told Mabry they were fortunate to find a flight out so soon. For the first time since she left for India, Mabry had a sick feeling in her stomach. She feared the condition in which she might find her Mother. She also feared hearing from Mr. Allen, if that was a possibility.

The officer easily picked Mabry out of the line of people exiting the gate based on the description Detective Minton gave him. He waited patiently until the two ladies were out of the flow of people exiting and then immediately introduced himself.

"Ladies, I am from Johnsonville Police Department. I have been sent to assist you. My name is Matthew Downing. If you care to follow me, the car is waiting. Your bags will be sent directly to the hotel where Detective Wilson has arranged a room for you."

"Thank you Matthew. If it is suitable, we wish to go directly to the hospital before going to the hotel." replied Sicillia.

"Certainly Ma'am, we will do as you wish."

Officer Downing drove Sicillia and Mabry to the hospital, and then escorted them to the Intensive Care Unit. Once they arrived, the Charge Nurse met them and took them to a small consultation room outside the doors to the Intensive Care Unit. She explained that Dr. Overton was aware of their arrival and was now on his way to meet with them.

Officer Downing excused himself and noted that he would be in the hospital lobby when they needed to contact him. Mabry walked to the window facing downtown. She gazed into the lights of the city until she became dizzy. Sicillia had sensed the need to stand beside her.

"Mabry honey, let's sit back down. I'm sure the doctor will be here soon."

"I'm just so frightened Aunt Sicillia. I want to be strong and make the right decisions for Mother. My main goal, or at least what kept me going all this time was to take care of my mother. Stephen has been so cruel to both of us. I thought I had everything under control, but now…," Mabry trailed off as the tears came once again.

They heard someone knock on the door. Sicillia turned to see a doctor enter the small room. He introduced himself as Dr. Overton.

"I apologize for having you come at this hour doctor. We did the best we could getting a flight here." said Mabry.

"Do not let that concern you Miss. It is the least I can do for my patient and for your returning home on such short notice."

"Dr. Overton, I am Mabry Allen and this is my Aunt Sicillia. She will be helping me map out the plan for Mother's care. I hope that is not a problem."

Dr. Overton shook Sicillia's hand. "Miss Allen is lucky to have you here with her. Let's take a seat and I will go over the situation with you."

Mabry welcomed the seat offered her. A nurse appeared with some coffee. Dr. Overton took a moment to speak with the nurse although Mabry could not make out what they were saying.

"I trust you had an uneventful flight." Dr. Overton began. "We have Mrs. Barbara Allen in room eleven inside the Unit. She has a nurse with her at all times. At this point, she has improved slightly. After we go over everything, I will let you visit with her for a few minutes."

"Thank you Doctor. I think Mabry will feel much better after she sees her mother," offered Sicillia.

"As you have been made aware, Mrs. Allen was wounded by a bullet to the chest. Mrs. Allen arrived in the emergency room by ambulance. The paramedics had inserted an endotracheal tube to assist with her breathing. It was noted she was unconscious and her blood pressure was dropping. From that point, Mrs. Allen was immediately taken to surgery where the bullet was removed and the lower lobe of her right lung also removed."

Mabry was beginning to feel dizzy and sick again. She interrupted, "Doctor, could you have someone get me a soda? I do not feel so very well."

"Yes, by all means." Dr. Overton punched in a couple of digits on his cell phone and it was not long until the same nurse appeared in the room.

"Nurse Stanton, Miss Allen is not feeling well. Will you have someone bring her a ginger ale?"

The nurse nodded affirmatively and was gone as quickly as she entered. Dr. Overton checked Mabry's pulse. "Miss Allen, if you will, lean your head forward slightly and then rise up quickly when I instruct you to do so."

Mabry did as Dr. Overton requested and almost fell out into the floor. The doctor held onto her and asked Sicillia to stay with her while he checked on something.

"Here is your soda Miss Allen. Do you need anything else before I go?" asked Nurse Stanton.

"No, thank you. Wait! Do you know where Dr. Overton went? Is Mother okay?" asked Mabry.

"Your mother is resting. Dr. Overton is just checking on something for your comfort Miss Allen." Nurse Stanton left before Mabry could ask anything else.

It was not long until the doctor returned. "Miss Allen, I have made arrangements for you to have a mild sedative to help you relax and calm your nausea. I would like for you to go ahead and visit with your Mother if that is something you still wish to do tonight. After your visit, Nurse Stanton will give you a sedative and have Officer Downing take you directly to your hotel. If you find a need to be closer to the hospital, we may be able to arrange a room for you at Loman's Guest House across the street. The only other information you really need to know at this time is your mother is being treated with antibiotics to prevent lung and other infections, and of course we are giving her pain meds to keep her comfortable. We have been able to take her off the Ventilator and will be trying to move her in the bed as much as possible to help prevent pneumonia. Once you are rested, we can continue this discussion."

Mabry started to protest, but was interrupted by Sicillia. "Dr. Overton, thank you so much for your time tonight. If you don't mind, I think we will just take Mabry on to the hotel and see Barbara in the morning."

"Mrs. Bharti that is exactly what I would prescribe. I can arrange for a wheelchair and an escort in just a few minutes."

"Very well then, Mabry and I are very appreciative of your help."

"No! I really wanted to see Mother. Besides, I thought we needed to talk about her care and what needs to be done in making her well." cried Mabry.

"Miss Allen, there is really nothing more to be done tonight. You are definitely welcome to see your Mother, however; given your present condition I must insist that you get some rest."

Mabry tried to argue with both Dr. Overton and her Aunt but saw it was pointless. She realized just how tired and distraught she really was. It only took a few moments after getting in bed for the sedative to ease her weary body.

Not too far from the hospital, Jodie Scever was settling in at her apartment. It had been too long since she had been able to sleep in her own bed. Although she had concerns of a possible seizure with no one around, she soon fell into the sweet arms of restful sleep.

Mabry Allen shifted slightly in bed as the sedative took hold for the night.

In the tunnels of the mind live a million dreams; both lived and unlived; waiting to be caressed.

Chapter 26

New Developments

Roger Yaddinski returned to his apartment Wednesday morning to find it ransacked with most of his belongings scattered all over the floor. Things were in order before Thanksgiving break but now food was pulled from the pantry and lying on the counters. He walked into the bedroom and found it in dishevelment as well. He found his clothes thrown across the bed and shoes everywhere. Roger immediately picked up the phone and dialed the Johnsonville Police Department. He asked for Detective Minton in hopes the detective would remember him.

"Minton here, may I help you?"

"Hello Detective. This is Roger Yaddinski. I'm not sure you remember me, but I am in need of your assistance."

"Oh yes, I remember you Mr. Yaddinski. I spoke with you on campus one day, and I also investigated your unfortunate stabbing." Minton answered.

"You did. I did not realize that. At any rate, I have just returned here to my apartment to find that someone has broken in."

"Roger, are you in danger?"

"No, I do not believe so. I have been through the apartment, and it appears I am alone."

"I will be right over. Stay put and don't touch anything," said Minton as he placed the phone back on the hook. He grabbed his jacket and left without giving Roger a chance to reply.

Roger made his way back to the bedroom to check on his small stash of money he had put away. He opened the closet door and began searching. He was relieved to find his money safe where he left it. There was something over in the corner that caught his eye. It appeared to be a small black laptop under some shoes.

"What the heck is this?" Roger exclaimed aloud as he picked the laptop up. As soon as he did, he recalled Minton telling him not to touch anything. He put it back down. It must be Mabry's; she probably left it the last time she was here and with me being gone, she couldn't get in order to get it. How odd she would leave it in the closet though.

The doorbell rang, and Roger saw it was Detective Minton. "Goodness, you got here in record time!"

Detective Minton had another officer with him who began checking around the apartment. Minton asked Roger to concentrate on anything that could possibly be missing.

Although Roger did not feel anything was missing, he took a notepad and went through each section of the apartment making notes as he went. Detective Minton would make comment or ask a question as they went through everything. Roger finally stopped and asked what was on his mind.

"Why are you so concerned with the break-in? I thought you knew who stabbed me that day on the walking trail."

"We do have a statement from a reliable witness," replied Minton. "We need to examine all possibilities in case the break-in is related to the stabbing."

As the two continued talking, the assisting officer was gathering evidence from the bedroom. He called for Minton to come inside the room. Officer Luffman was in the closet where he explained to Minton what he had found. It was a laptop lying on the floor on top of some shoes and clothing. When he lifted the laptop, a picture of Johnny Ricks fell out of the side.

Minton took the laptop with the picture and walked back into the kitchen where Roger was. "Is this your laptop Roger?"

Roger saw Minton holding the laptop he had observed just moments before the officers arrived. "No, it must be Mabry's."

"If you don't mind, we will take it back to the station and have it inspected," replied Minton. "We have our information and appear to be through here. It may take a few days, but we will be in touch."

"That is fine. Why are you taking Mabry's laptop?" Roger questioned.

Minton walked over to the Kitchen and looked Roger directly in the eyes. "We are just collecting evidence, Roger. Considering Mabry Allen's situation and the Rick's murder, we will hold this laptop until it can be checked thoroughly."

"Yes sir, I understand."

"I do find it interesting that you referred to the laptop as Mabry's. When did she leave the laptop?" asked Minton.

"I really didn't know it was here until tonight. Mabry must have left it before the stabbing and could not get back in to get it."

"It is strange that Mabry would not miss the laptop or even try to find a way to get it."

"I'm sorry Detective; I don't have an answer," replied Roger.

"I understand. I have just a few questions for you."

"Go ahead," replied Roger.

"You stated you had just returned home. Where have you been?"

"I flew back home to Oregon for Thanksgiving."

"That's surprising, after the stabbing ordeal you went through." Minton remarked.

"Yes, I know. I was cleared for travel though."

"Do you have any idea who might want to break into your apartment, maybe an enemy?

"Oh, I'm sure I have an enemy or two, but I think they would come after me and not my apartment."

"You have been a very big help Roger. I believe we have enough from your apartment to piece some things together for you. We will be in touch. In the meantime, if you notice anything suspicious or find you are missing items, call the department and leave me a message."

Roger stood at the door watching Minton and the officer leave. He was puzzled over Mabry's laptop. Why indeed had Mabry not tried to reach him so she could get her laptop? Why did the Detective think he would lie about the laptop? At any rate, maybe they would find fingerprints to determine the culprit who did this to his apartment? He had other issues to deal with instead of worrying over this break in.

"Aunt Sicillia, why does mother have to suffer for what that "jerk'" has done?" asked Mabry as they were preparing to return to the hospital.

Sicillia reached out and held Mabry close. She gently replied, "Mabry, there are a lot of hurting people in this world. Yet, when it seems your situation is the worst possible scenario, you can always find someone in a more difficult circumstance than yourself. I know, that is not the answer you want, but unfortunately, honey there is not always a clear answer."

"Please don't leave me. I have no one else I can turn to. Will you stay until mother is better?" asked Mabry of her Aunt.

"Of course I will stay. You are my dear brother's only child. Just put all your worries on my shoulder, and I will help you carry them."

"Thank you Aunt Sicillia. I am so thankful I was with you when we received this news."

"You are welcome my dear. Now, why don't we find some breakfast before we visit with your Mother?"

"Breakfast does sound good," replied Mabry.

Sicillia found an information desk. The volunteer was very helpful in directing them to the hospital cafeteria. Mabry was hungrier than she realized. She ate eggs, bacon, toast and two muffins. It was amazing how she felt her strength returning as she ate her breakfast.

"You ate quite a bit of food my dear. That should give you some strength for what is ahead. Do you want anything else, maybe a coffee to go?"

"Oh no, I don't think I could hold anymore, even coffee," answered Mabry. "Besides, I am ready to see mother."

Sicillia and Mabry made their way to the hospital's Intensive Care Unit. Sicillia gave her an encouraging hug. "I will wait for you in the family waiting room so you can have some private time with Barbara."

"You are welcome to come with me Aunt Sicillia."

"I know that I am sweetie, but maybe you need a few minutes by yourself. If you are not back out in twenty minutes, I will look for you. Is that agreeable?"

"That sounds good. Say a prayer for me." And with that, Mabry disappeared behind the steel entry doors.

Mrs. Allen's nurse was in the room when Mabry walked in. The nurse explained all the monitors and equipment so Mabry would understand what was happening. She told Mabry that her Mother was stable and had actually had a good night. She encouraged Mabry to talk with her Mother. The nurse explained that Barbara might hear her; stating that a person's hearing was a powerful tool during the recovery process.

Mabry took her Mother's hand as the nurse left the room. Mabry wanted to cry, but she knew her mother might be able to sense her distress. Instead, she started telling her of Sicillia's beautiful roses and the rooftop terrace. She talked and talked of all she had experienced in the couple of days she was in India. Mabry promised her Mother they would both go back to visit Aunt Sicillia once she was healthy again. Mabry stayed with her mother for a good thirty minutes just holding her hand and silently praying in her heart.

"Mabry, are you there?"

Mabry turned to see Sicillia at the doorway to her mother's room.

"I am so sorry. The time got away with me. I am sure you were worried!"

"Well, maybe just a little," replied Sicillia with a smile. "Dr. Overton came by. He wants to meet with us again at Noon. Is that okay with you?"

"Yes, that will be fine. Here, you can sit and talk to momma for a few minutes? I have been telling her about your beautiful roses."

Chapter 27

The Vigil

The days since his arrest were unbearably long. Some days Stephen Allen was not sure he could continue. He knew he could be spending weeks in jail, not to mention a possible trial if it came to that. He thought to himself over and over how he should have killed Mabry while he was able. Now he had to devise a plan to ensure his freedom. That is what kept him going. He rehearsed the same scenario over and over, so that there were no loop-holes. Stephen could not afford any contradicting statements to indicate that he could be guilty, or even have knowledge of Johnny Rick's death until he heard the news reporting the murder. He really was not guilty anyway, although he was sure that devil, Mabry, had made-up tales to convince the police differently. Why, he would not be surprised if she had slept with the officers in order to get him arrested. She was nothing but trash he thought.

"Trash, Trash, Trash," he yelled as he threw his coffee cup across the jail cell and watched it break into a thousand pieces.

"That tramp has had it in for me since I married her Mother. We will see who has the last word this time!"

"Hey, you in there, stop yelling and quiet down, or we will have to put you in isolation again." called the guard.

"You bloody well can do whatever you want. If I want to yell, I will," responded Stephen.

"Listen buddy, you can calm down, or we will give you something to calm you down."

Stephen decided not to argue anymore. He knew if he had any chances for freedom that he would need to act with civility no matter how angry he was. Besides, he had another meeting today with his lawyer. Hopefully, an agreement had been reached for another bond hearing. He needed to be on the outside, so he could be certain Mabry did not do anything else to endanger his freedom or his marriage. She already caused him to shoot Barbara! He needed to go to Barbara and help her. He had heard she was hanging on for life. He was certain that she would want to live if he could be there to console her.

"She probably wonders where the heck I am anyway!" whispered Stephen. "This is all because of that blasted Mabry and her friends! One day, I will take care of little Miss Mabry for good. Perhaps, that nerd Roger will be close by and suffer the consequences as well. Besides, that nerd knows too much. The next thing you know, he'll have Mabry to himself." Stephen became louder once again as he allowed his mind to wander. "She is a slut! She is the cause of all this drama and the cause of my beautiful Barbara being shot! I need someone to let me out of here!" he yelled while shaking the cell doors.

"Hey Buddy! I told you to get quiet in there. This is your last warning, or you will find yourself in "la-la" land."

"Whatever," Stephen muttered as he sat down on the hard mattress. He would try to close his eyes. Maybe a little rest was all he needed.

Detectives Minton and Wilson were once again pouring over the evidence in the Ricks' murder case, the stabbing of Roger Yaddinski, the stranger in Jodie's hospital room and now the breaking and entering of Roger Yaddinski's apartment. They both had a gut feeling they were missing something. Wilson had a sneaking suspicion that all the incidents had to revolve around the same motive; they just could not put their finger on that key piece of evidence.

Wilson received the news that Stephen Allen's lawyer had won the argument for another bond hearing. The hearing would take place on December 10th, a few days away. He was determined to find something to keep that man in jail where he belonged. They were going to have to be diligent.

The conference table in Wilson's office was covered with information; a time line with pictures of people involved, the murder weapon, the hospital security video and now the laptop and from Roger Yaddinski's apartment. The lab had gone over the laptop with their expertise to reveal that it belonged not to Mabry Allen, but to none other than Jodie Scever!

Wilson had an uneasy feeling about Roger with no concrete evidence to justify his thinking. Wilson also knew his Chief was getting frustrated with the amount of time he was spending on the case. As far as the Chief was concerned, the suspect was in custody, and the other incidents were minor compared to all the cases that needed attention. He and Minton had been reprimanded for Minton's responding to the breaking and entering when it was not their section's responsibility. Wilson was able to argue their cause, considering how intertwined the incidents all seem to be with each other.

"Wilson! I think I have hit on something here," exclaimed Minton interrupting Wilson's thought pattern.

"Super, let's hear it."

"Remember when Mabry Allen called me to come to Roger's apartment? Listen to this scenario. Mabry and Jodie have a falling out with each other over Johnny Ricks. Roger Yaddinski enters the picture to console Mabry. Mabry allows him. Roger then becomes a target of Mabry, for some reason," explains Minton.

He continues, "Mabry needs to cover for someone or something and calls me to Roger's apartment to show you what she happened to find there. Do you think it is coincidence? No, I believe Mabry Allen planted Jodie's laptop in Roger's apartment, and she wanted me to find it. That would have pointed the finger at Roger."

"I'll buy that," said Wilson. "However; tell me why she turned her stepfather in and how she could make up such twisted tales of abuse? Also, why hasn't Jodie reported her laptop missing? Remember Minton, none of these people may be exonerated until we have all the evidence confirmed."

"True, I'm just trying to make sense of this entire twisted tale."

Jodie suddenly awakened. She had such a strange feeling, like one of those she had been having lately. At least the sun was peeking through the curtain, which gave her some consolation for facing the day.

"I need to shake this feeling and get up" she thought aloud. "Thomas will be here before I know it."

With that thought, Jodie jumped up to begin her day. It always amazed her how she could shake things off so easily. She had often been accused of being superficial and callous. In her heart however; she knew she was a very sensitive and caring person. She saw no reason to allow worries to control her life. After all, there was plenty of time to worry if the situation warranted the effort.

After a warm shower and a hot breakfast, Jodie felt much better. She studied her closet for an attractive outfit to wear. Finally settling on a slimming black pant outfit, Jodie was ready by eleven-thirty. She thought to herself, "I do look quite nice after having been hospitalized for so long. I wish I could do something for these dark circles under my eyes."

Jodie paced the floor waiting for Noon and Thomas to come around. She decided to call Edee and check on her while she waited.

"Hello," answered Edee.

"Hey, it's Jodie. I just wanted to let you know that I am going to lunch with Thomas."

"Wonderful. I am so glad to hear that. I like him Jodie. Of course, you know mother took to him from the very beginning," laughed Edee.

"Yes, I have heard as much!"

"Jodie… we all love you very much. We want you to be happy."

"Thanks Sis, I know you do. I will be just fine. Who knows, maybe God will reveal something to me today."

"Oh Jodie, please don't joke about that. He will speak to you if you are willing. Why don't you call me back tonight and let me know how your day goes?"

"Sure thing," replied Jodie and hung up the phone without even saying Good-bye.

Edee sat in her kitchen with tears streaming down her face. They all loved Jodie more than she realized, but since college, it seemed Jodie had left behind her Christian values and her love for the Lord. With a quick wipe of a tissue to dry her eyes, Edee whispered "Thank You Father for what you are going to do in Jodie's life. Thank You that she even bothered to call."

Thomas arrived a few minutes early. Jodie watched as he walked up the sidewalk to the front door. He had on navy slacks and a multi-colored shirt. He looked more handsome than she remembered, and it was just yesterday she saw him last!

Jodie opened the door to greet Thomas before he even made it up the walk. Her heart was so full of excitement every time she saw Thomas; it was as if she was meeting him again for the first time. As soon as Thomas saw Jodie, he gave her a wink that sent a tingling sensation through her body and soul. No one ever had this effect on her. It was all Jodie could do to keep from acting like a teenage schoolgirl.

"Good Morning Mister Wiley," Jodie said with a huge smile.

"Good Morning to you beautiful," responded Thomas. "My! You do look very nice in your black outfit."

"Thank you. You may compliment me anytime." Jodie said as she turned to go back inside the apartment. She would just grab her purse in case Thomas was in a hurry. She felt his hand on her shoulder as she began to turn. She stopped and was swept away as Thomas turned her back around to face him. He gently brushed a kiss across her lips and placed his hand under her chin.

"It was more than a compliment. It was from my heart. Now, I guess we better be going so we will not have to wait too long for a table. The Sandwich Shack gets pretty crowded at lunchtime."

Jodie slowly slipped from Thomas' embrace to find her purse and her wrap. The air was a little cool this morning, yet her heart was quite warm against the December chill. Thomas and Jodie drove by Saints Hospital on the way to lunch. Jodie could not help but wonder how Mabry's mother was doing. She wondered if Mabry was with her.

"Thomas, have you heard from Barbara Allen? Is she doing okay?"

"Yes, she is improving some. The last I heard, Mabry and her Aunt from India are here and sitting with Mrs. Allen."

"Bless her heart, I need to stop by and visit."

Thomas shook his head. "You amaze me Jodie Scever. After all you have been through with that family, and you still have empathy for them!"

Dr. Overton met Mabry and Sicillia at Noon in the same consultation room they had met in before. Dr. Overton asked if Mabry was taking care of herself.

"I am resting better. I appreciate your help and concern."

"Very well, let me update you. Your mother is improving slightly each day. I believe your being here may make all the difference in the world for her. I instructed the staff to let her know often that you are nearby. Each time you visit with her, continue talking as if she can hear you. Tell her current events and anything you want her to know concerning yourself or the family."

Mabry let out a cry, "What good news! Thank you so much. How long do you think it will be before she is conscious?"

"We would like to begin reducing some of the sedation to allow Barbara the opportunity to wake up. She may be confused at first and that is where you come in. I have arranged for you and your aunt to have access to Barbara's room at all times. It would be beneficial to have you at Barbara's side if she wakes up. The staff will be prepared in case of agitation. Once we know she can handle being awake, we can continue the plan to remove all sedation. Then, we can discuss a plan for Barbara's rehabilitation and release home."

Mabry questioned, "What is the plan, Doctor?"

"It will involve physical and occupational therapy for a few days. Your mother's body has undergone major trauma. The loss of blood and oxygen can sometimes leave a person very confused and lethargic. We will incorporate the therapy to strengthen her physically and mentally."

Sicillia commented her affirmation of Dr. Overton's plan for Barbara. She thanked him again for his time, his care and his concern for Barbara.

Mabry chimed in, "Yes, thank you Dr. Overton. I especially appreciate you taking care of mother when we were not available to consult."

"You are quite welcome Mabry. I hope you ladies have a good day today. I will be in touch with you later."

The three left the consultation room. Mabry returned to her mother's room full of hope and trust in Dr. Overton. Sicillia made herself comfortable in the waiting room where Mabry knew to find her if she needed a break.

Chapter 28

An Old Friend

"Service went very well today, agreed?" Thomas asked Jodie, who seemed much quieter than usual. Jodie enjoyed the Pastor's message and especially the choir. She thought about the older ladies throwing compliments at Thomas and asking him fifty questions about the young lady he had with him. She was almost embarrassed by all their questions and was so worried they would connect her name with the death of Johnny Ricks. Jodie realized this was the first time in a long time that she was concerned over what people thought of her. As she pondered these things in her mind, she realized Thomas was talking to her.

"Thomas, I'm sorry. Did you say something?"

"Well yes, I did. I said – I am starved, how about you?" asked Thomas.

"I am a little hungry! This looks like an interesting place to eat. The Dodge House... where is this anyway?"

"I didn't think you were with me," laughed Thomas. "We are about half-way between Johnsonville and Buck Valley. I thought we might get a good lunch and then visit with my family this afternoon; that is, if you are feeling okay."

"Sure, that would be great! I really like your family. Everyone seems so close."

"We are, of course, my Mother has a lot to do with keeping our family close," replied Thomas.

"She seems like a special lady."

"She sure is, but I know another special lady that needs to eat!" Thomas replied as he parked the car in front of the restaurant. Thomas got out of the car and was at Jodie's door to assist her before she even had her purse in hand.

Thomas and Jodie entered the restaurant to be greeted by the hostess.

"Thomas Wiley, is it really you? My goodness, I have not seen you in such a long time!"

"It has been a few years," replied Thomas.

"Will it just be the two of you for lunch?" the hostess questioned.

"Yes, it is just the two of us."

The hostess seated them in a booth next to the window. Jodie sat for a minute staring out at the trees when she felt tears welling up in her eyes. She was so fortunate to be alive, not only alive, but blessed to have someone like Thomas taking an interest in her. Today was the first time she had been to church since – well probably before college.

"Hey!" Thomas said as he touched her hand with his. "Are you here with me? You seem to be in a distant place since we left service."

"I am so sorry Thomas. I have been thinking how fortunate I am to have someone like you take an interest in me." Jodie replied as she touched her eyes to keep a tear from falling.

She definitely did not want Thomas to see her cry. She was afraid she would not be able to explain how she was feeling and furthermore afraid Thomas would not understand. She felt such comfort being with him, yet she felt so insecure. The minister's sermon spoke to her heart as well. She was overwhelmed at the moment with diverse emotions.

"Jodie, how could I not take an interest in you? You are a beautiful person inside and out. I am not sure you even realize that. Besides, I need an interesting project for my classes!" Thomas said teasingly.

Jodie smiled and could not help but to give him a gentle slap on the hand. The next thing she knew, the waitress was standing at their booth.

"So are you two lovebirds ready to order?" she asked. Jodie felt herself turning red from the tip of her toes to the top of her head. Lovebirds! Do we really appear that way? Thomas already answered and was engaging in conversation with the waitress. He asked her to give them a couple more minutes. They both turned their attention to the menu.

"What are you going to have?" Jodie asked.

"I normally order the flounder here. It is always delicious."

"I have never eaten flounder before. Momma doesn't like fish, so we do not have it at home. I have never had the nerve to order any."

Thomas smiled and took a minute to go over the menu with Jodie. He finally convinced her to try the flounder.

As they waited for their food, the waitress made conversation with Thomas. Jodie was a little annoyed with the waitress for taking Thomas' attention. Thomas noticed Jodie's demeanor and changed the conversation to focus on Jodie.

"Cathy, I don't believe I introduced you to Jodie. Cathy, this is Jodie Scever. Jodie, this is Cathy Bridges. Cathy and I went to High School together. She also dated my brother until she became wise!" Thomas laughingly remarked.

"Yes, I realized Thomas was a better catch, but he was too busy studying to notice me," answered Cathy. "Hopefully, you will have better luck with Thomas than I did. It is good to meet you. Now, if you will excuse me, I had better go check on everyone's food." Cathy said and took off in an instant.

"Well, that was just a little awkward!" Thomas commented.

"Yes, it was," replied Jodie.

Cathy returned with the couple's meal. Jodie watched Cathy constantly as she waited on them. Cathy seemed to take extra care in Thomas' direction. Jodie was glad when the meal was over.

Once they were inside the car, Thomas reached for Jodie's hand. "Hey, you handled yourself very well with Cathy."

"Oh? I really was not sure what to say. Cathy seems to be quite taken with you. I must be on my guard if we come back here anytime soon."

"Let me say, Miss Scever, that you do not have anything to fret your pretty self about concerning Cathy. She has no hold on my attention."

"Hum, if you say so!"

Thomas leaned toward Jodie, placed a kiss on her lips and replied; "I say so!"

Thomas put the car in gear. He turned toward his parent's house. As they rode in the quiet, Jodie took advantage of the time to think back over the last few weeks and how her life had changed. She wondered if she would have better luck with Thomas. Jodie also wondered if this was what she really wanted. She had never been tied down for more than a few months with any one particular person. Jodie made a mental note to call Edee before she went to bed that night. Perhaps Edee would have some advice.

Thomas pulled into the drive at his parent's home. He made mention to Jodie to look above the house at the smoke from the chimney.

"I have always been fascinated at the smoke swirling from the chimney. If you watch long enough, you will see many different patterns."

"You notice everything, Thomas Wiley. I would never think of watching smoke!"

"I guess that is another one of my quirks," laughed Thomas.

"Kind of like your friendship with Cathy?"

"Ah-ha; I knew that was bothering you. I told you that you have nothing to worry about!" Thomas reached for Jodie's hand and squeezed it to show his affection.

"Keep telling me that. I like what goes along with your convincing words," grinned Jodie mischievously.

Thomas noticed his Mother standing in the doorway.

"I guess we need to go inside. Mother is at the door. Meanwhile, you can put Cathy out of your head. You are who I am interested in Miss Scever."

"Yes Doctor. I will follow your orders."

Thomas took Jodie by the hand to lead her down the sidewalk. Nancy met them at the door. Jodie knew this was going to be an enjoyable afternoon.

Chapter 29

Catching Up

Mabry spent every day of the last week and half at her Mother's side. She remained in constant prayer to the Father whom she had recently trusted. Edee promised her that the Father would listen and give His children what they needed. Mabry was new at this praying thing; but if God was willing to help her, she was definitely agreeable to asking Him. Mabry rarely left her Mother's side. She only left to eat or freshen up. Leaving the hospital was not an option as long as her Mother was critical.

Mabry just finished eating lunch in the hospital cafeteria, when her cell phone rang. Sicillia had been kind enough to open a new mobile plan for her. Mabry now had a phone that did everything imaginable. The caller ID showed the number to be coming from the hospital.

"Hello?"

"Miss Allen, this is Dr. Overton. I would like you to return to your Mother's room if you can. I believe we have some good news for you."

"Really, I will be right there!" Mabry responded as she ended the call abruptly.

Mabry almost ran to dispose of her food tray. She caught the elevator and then hurried down the hallway to her Mother's room. Her heart was pounding in her chest, fearing what the news might be, even though the doctor said it was good. Her Mother's door was opened wide. Mabry could see a couple of nurses in the room. She stopped to catch her breath as she whispered a silent prayer for her Mother.

Mabry slowly entered the room. It was difficult to see around the nurses and the Doctor at her Mother's bed. She stood in silence waiting for the will to move closer. Dr. Overton must have sensed her presence in the room. He turned smiling at her, motioning her closer. Mabry slowly moved toward the bed. She suddenly felt faint! Could it be? Yes! Her Mother was looking around! When her eyes found Mabry, you could instantly see the change. Her Mother's eyes softened as she locked her gaze upon her only daughter.

"Mom, I cannot believe it. You are awake. I have prayed and prayed. This is so wonderful. Oh my goodness mother, I feel like running and telling everyone you are awake!"

Dr. Overton put his hand on Mabry's shoulder. "Young lady, your prayers have been answered."

"Thank you so much Dr. Overton. I know you have been diligent in taking care of her needs. I have prayed for you as well. God really does listen," said Mabry. "Oh, I need to call Aunt Sicillia and tell her the good news. Momma, you will never believe all I have to tell you. Aunt Sicillia is here with me. She has been wonderful to stay with me by your side."

Dr. Overton cautioned Mabry not to try and catch up on everything too quickly. Mrs. Allen was still very weak and ill. She could be overwhelmed easily.

"My suggestion is for a short visit now. Afterwards, I believe you need to take a break from the hospital young lady. Your mother will be in good hands. We will contact you if anything changes."

"It has been over a week since I have been outside the hospital. Maybe Aunt Sicillia will relieve me for a couple of hours. I really want to sit with Mother right now though."

"Good enough" replied Dr. Overton. He gave Mabry one last pat on the shoulder and proceeded to leave the room giving further instructions to the nurses.

Mabry moved closer to her Mother's side as she took hold of her hand. Mrs. Allen smiled as she mumbled the words, "I love you." Mabry felt the tears well up in her eyes. She had no intention of crying but this was so overwhelming. Mabry was exhausted from sitting by her Mother's side day and night. The fear of not knowing if her mother could regain consciousness was disturbing. Now her Mother was awake and trying to talk! The pool of tears found their way down Mabry's cheeks. It was all she could do to hold herself up.

"I love you too Mother. It is more wonderful than you know to hear your voice again. I have been so afraid."

Mrs. Allen squeezed her daughter's hand and nodded affirmatively. A knock sounded on the door. Mabry looked up to see her aunt Sicillia standing in the doorway. She had tears streaming down her face.

"Aunt Sicillia, come see what God has done!"

Mabry reached for Sicillia's hand. Mabry and Sicillia both stood in amazement watching as Barbara moved her hands to reach for them. Sicillia responded by grasping Mrs. Allen's hand.

"Barbara, it is so wonderful to see you awake. We have been concerned about you. Mabry has barely left your side," cried Sicillia.

Mabry suddenly became overwhelmed with emotion. She choked back her tears, as she hugged Barbara.

"Mom, I am going to leave the hospital for a couple of hours, while Aunt Sicillia is here. Dr. Overton says you are doing fine. Sicillia will stay until I can get back. I feel I need to rest a while so I can be strong for both of us."

Barbara squeezed Mabry's hand in approval. Mabry gave Barbara one last hug and left the room before she burst into tears.

Detective Wilson reflected as he considered the Ricks' murder case. He and Minton continued to make progress in the case. Stephen Allen entered a guilty plea in order to obtain a lighter sentence. He however; contended that all the acts he may have committed were done in self-defense. He stated he knew nothing of the break-in at Roger's apartment nor any of the other events the detectives kept hounding him about for answers.

Stephen continued to demand that he be given a chance to visit Mrs. Allen in the hospital, his request consistently denied. Considering all the events Mabry had confided in them was true; Wilson would see Stephen "rot" in jail. However, Stephen's lawyer was pursuing an opportunity for Stephen to visit with Barbara. Wilson knew Stephen would be a lucky man if the judge granted this permission prior to the bond hearing.

The initial arraignment hearing was scheduled for January 8th. This was the earliest date they could get with the holidays upon them. Wilson was actually glad it was after Christmas. He did not think he could enjoy the holidays if he had to listen to testimony this close to Christmas. He had already heard enough to make his blood boil.

Detective Wilson assigned Minton to keep up with Mabry Allen. Wilson thought something or someone else might come to light by following Mabry. Wilson gave Minton permission to use the department's expense account to keep up with Mabry and her Aunt.

Mabry stopped in the Ladies room before she exited the hospital. Now, with her tears dried and her face washed, Mabry headed downstairs, her emotions still consuming her. The next thing Mabry knew, she was looking directly at Detective Minton.

"Whoa here, Miss Allen; I was just on my way to check on you and your Mother. I didn't expect to actually run into you," Minton said jokingly.

"Accept my apologies, detective. I guess my mind is elsewhere."

"I understand. I hope all is well with your mother. We have been hearing of her progress."

"Mother is doing very well. In fact, she is not unconscious any longer. We have just been talking to her," replied Mabry, still trying to hold back tears.

"That is wonderful for you and your Mother. Are you going to her room?"

"I was on my way out for a while. You are welcome to visit with her though."

"If you don't think she would mind, I would just like to speak and give her my regards. Do you have time to walk me to her room?"

"Well, I guess I could. I am not sure Mother is up to answering any questions yet."

"That is not my purpose for being here. I promise not to ask any questions. Is that a deal?" asked Minton.

"Well, I guess that is okay if you are comfortable being with me."

"Why would I not be comfortable with you Mabry?"

"The last time we met, remember? When you came to Roger's apartment, you were not comfortable with me asking you to come inside."

"Oh, I had forgotten all about that encounter. I was just doing my job Mabry. I am off-duty today so you do not have to be concerned with any formalities." smiled Minton.

"Okay, I'm sorry I mentioned it. I think I am just an emotional bundle right now, so you will need to overlook any off-the-wall comments."

"No problem and no apology necessary. Say, do you think your mother might like some flowers? I mean, we are standing right in front of the gift shop. I would love to take her some."

"That would be very nice, detective."

Mabry walked with Minton into the gift shop. She stopped at the magazine rack.

"I will wait here for you. I may pick out a magazine to occupy my time when I return later."

Minton made his way to the flower case. There he picked out a nice bouquet for Barbara and one single pink rose for Mabry. He was able to make his purchase before Mabry realized he was ready. He walked over to the magazine rack.

"Those are pretty flowers you have," remarked Mabry.

"I am hoping your mother will like them also. Maybe these flowers will give her spirits a lift!"

"I am sure she will. I found a magazine I am going to get for mother. Let me pay for it, and I will take you to her room."

Minton and Mabry left the gift shop headed for Barbara's room. While waiting for the elevator, Minton brought his left arm from behind his back. He gently cleared his throat, "I was also wondering if Miss Mabry likes roses?" He held out the pink rose to Mabry for her acceptance.

"Oh, it is beautiful and I do like roses, but you did not need to get me anything, detective."

"It is just a simple gesture, Miss Allen. I know you have been through a lot of unsettling events. I just want you to know you have a friend in me, anytime you need to talk to someone."

Mabry was stunned for a moment. She finally allowed a smile to escape her lips. "Thank you. I really appreciate that."

Minton and Mabry made their way back to the elevator and up to Barbara's room. Barbara was surprised to see Mabry back so soon and with a visitor. Mabry introduced Detective Minton to her mother.

"This is Detective Minton, mom. He is from the Johnsonville Police Department. They have been investigating Johnny's murder."

Detective Minton spoke quickly before Barbara became confused as to his motive.

"It is certainly a pleasure to meet you Mrs. Allen. We have become fond of Mabry at the department. All of us at JPD want you to know, we are thinking of you. These flowers are a small token of our thoughts and prayers."

Barbara smiled in acknowledgement of the gift. After a brief conversation, Minton was soon gone. Mabry once again hugged her mother as she tried to leave for a short respite. She was soon on her way to the hotel, although with strange feelings of loneliness. Minton's visit allowed Mabry's thoughts to take her to a place she thought she had closed the door on.

Chapter 30

Leaving Town

Johnson Scever was gearing up for the final days of the Christmas festivities in Sugar Falls. The new visitor's center was bustling with activity. Johnson was looking forward to Jodie spending a couple of days with him as she had promised earlier. He had deposited a large sum of money in her savings account the last time he visited in Johnsonville. Johnson knew he should not give her the money so readily and that Susan would not approve, but his guilt over the wasted years gnawed at his conscience. He hoped the money would ease Jodie's pain and his as well.

The local playmakers of Sugar Falls were in full production of "The Wizard of Oz" which had always been one of Jodie's favorites. Johnson silently prayed that the gift of money and the production would be enough to lure Jodie into spending a little time with them.

It had been a little more than two weeks since Jodie had been to church with Thomas. He asked her to go the last two Sundays, but she just could not talk herself into going back. She enjoyed the service. She especially enjoyed the afternoon spent with Thomas and his family. She had no answer as to why she was avoiding Thomas. Her own mother had even questioned her as to why she wanted to avoid the "nicest man she had ever met." Jodie's mother had seen Thomas recently and conveyed her feelings concerning her daughter's lack of interest in a "good man" such as Thomas. Jodie was furious when she found out about the little conversation. Edee happened to let it slip when they talked on the phone one day. Now, with everyone trying to tell Jodie what to do again, she wanted to run away and hide! If she knew why she was having these feelings, she would do something about them herself. The uneasy, restless feelings were toying with her emotions until she thought she was being smothered.

Her suitcase was packed! The college was on Semester break. Jodie knew she was taking a risk driving out of town. Dr. Smith had advised her to only drive in close proximity to the University and her apartment for the next few weeks. Somehow, she just had to trust God to guide her driving. She would be back in time for Christmas which was only a few days away. Her destination was unknown. Her plans were still to be determined. She would let the road determine where she ended up.

With the money, her Dad had given her and suitcase in hand; she left her apartment, Johnsonville and Thomas Wiley behind! She really needed to clear her mind and make some life-changing decisions. Jodie drove south not having any idea where she might end up.

After a few hours, she found herself in the coastal town of Charleston, SC, a place she had always wanted to visit, but never had the opportunity. Even though she felt guilty for going against Dr. Smith's orders, she found the driving got easier with each passing mile. Her soon to be former doctor, Thomas Wiley, would be terribly upset with her traveling that far alone. She knew Dr. Smith would be angry, but she was willing to face the consequences.

"I just can't think about them now! No one understands what I'm going through. Lord, I know I am not supposed to be driving but thank you so much for helping me."

Jodie found a hotel along the river. It appeared peaceful to her, so that is where she decided to take a room. After unpacking the necessary items, Jodie set out to explore the historic town. She made her way to the Market with her Christmas list in hand. Hopefully, she would find some great bargains and unique gifts for the ones on her list.

Christmas music was playing throughout the town. It was enough to lift anyone's spirits. Jodie strolled through the market bantering with the vendors and happy with herself for being away on her own. When she finished, she was pleased at the progress she had made in filling the Christmas list. Admittedly, she even enjoyed the chitchat, the mocking compliments and the squabbling for prices. The vendors were good at striking up a conversation with you unawares. Even with so many of them vying for her attention, she managed to find a beautiful silk scarf for Edee; a gemstone broach for her mother; a handsome, straw hat for her dad and the big purchase of the day – a Coach pocketbook for herself!

Back at the hotel with the gifts packed away, Jodie lay down for an afternoon nap. No sooner than Jodie dozed off, the haunting dreams returned. Jodie tossed and turned, moaning as if in pain. Suddenly, she awoke with a scream.

"Dear God! It really is Mabry! She is who I keep seeing in my dreams – but why?"

Jodie sat up on the edge of the bed. She was so tired. Now she was shaking in her skin. Is this why Thomas kept asking her questions about Mabry? Does Thomas know something I do not know? Why? Jodie kept voicing these questions over and over to herself. Thirty minutes passed before Jodie felt stable enough to get up from the bed. She made her way to the room refrigerator for something to drink. All she found was water, which was probably best anyway. She stood, starring out the window at the river. Jodie had the strangest feeling that Mabry really had tried to kill her.

"Why Mabry, do you think I killed Johnny?"

Jodie pondered her dream a few minutes more, and then made her way to the bathroom for a shower. She decided she would dress up and stroll through the city. Perhaps she would have a delicious dinner, and then take in a movie or some other entertainment. The hotel desk clerk told her there was nightly music in the city park.

Leaving the hotel room, Jodie locked each of the locks on the door, although she was sure no one knew her whereabouts. She took the Hotel Shuttle downtown and made her way to a Seafood Restaurant she had heard great things about. Jodie was taken upstairs to a table by the window. As she studied the menu, she kept thinking about the last time she was with Thomas. That day, was the first time she ever tried to eat flounder. Thinking to herself, she decided she could not order flounder and allow even more memories to creep into her miserable soul. When the waitress came back, she explained the menu to Jodie. Jodie then made up her mind to be brave and try a meal of Crab Cakes. She also, against her better judgment, ordered a regular Dr. Pepper. Another rule broken, she thought.

"Oh well Dr. Smith, if you are going to be upset with me, I may as well break all the rules!"

She was glad there were only a few people in the dining room with her. It seemed to make her feel secure in her adventure. Jodie settled back in her chair and gazed out the window, deep in thought, watching the people below. Her eyes were moist when the waitress returned.

Jodie ate everything on her plate. She was finding out that she loved seafood. The crab cakes were scrumptious. Just the novelty of being in the restaurant, watching the world go by on the streets below her brought Jodie a nice change of pace. The waitress came by to check on her and caught her off-guard.

"Ma'am, Is there something else you need?"

"Oh! No I am fine. I guess I was thinking out loud," replied Jodie.

"No problem. Just let me know if I can get you anything else."

"Thank you. I believe I will just finish my drink, and then I will be ready for the check."

"Yes Ma'am that is fine. I will also bring you a "to-go" cup. Take all the time you need."

Jodie slowly sipped her Dr. Pepper as she thought about Mabry, Johnny and Thomas. What really happened and how much did Thomas know? Was he keeping things from her? That seemed silly though, considering she could not even remember. How would Thomas know what happened the night of the wreck or how Johnny was wounded, when I don't even know?

"Oh God, what is happening to me? Please help me remember?" Jodie whispered a prayer toward the heavens.

"Here you go – your Dr. Pepper and your check. Let me know when you are ready."

"Thank you. I am ready – here is my card." Jodie said as she pulled her credit card from her wallet.

Jodie left the restaurant with no immediate plans other than to stroll through the streets. She was so confused. The emotions running through her heart and mind were enough to create havoc in the healthiest body.

Hours later a distraught and disheveled Jodie Scever returned to her hotel room. The night clerk could not help but notice Jodie's appearance. Her eyes were swollen and red. Her hair was a total mess and she was hugging herself as if she was freezing. Jodie realized the clerk was watching her, so she hurriedly made her way to the elevator. Soon Jodie was in the darkness of her hotel room praying the headache would go away.

"Hello," said Matilda as she answered the house phone.

"Good Evening, Matilda. This is Thomas."

"Yes, I recognized your voice. I am sure you are looking for Jodie. We are too! That girl has no idea how she is worrying her mother. You are a good man Thomas. I hope she will call one of us soon," said Matilda.

"Thank you for your kindness. I am concerned about her also. I miss her terribly, but I am more worried about her physical and emotional state. It really has not been long enough for Jodie to be driving alone. I have checked with everyone I know, that could possibly know where she is, but to no avail. Her roommate Debbie only knew that Jodie wanted to have a few days by herself to think about things."

"That is all I know too Thomas. Her Father thought she was coming to spend a few days with him, but he has not heard from her either."

"I will keep looking for her and will call you the minute I hear anything."

"That would be great Thomas. I will do the same."

"Goodnight. Try not to worry too much."

"Goodnight Thomas and I will do my best not to worry."

Chapter 31

Missing

It was Friday morning, exactly three days before Christmas. Everyone at Johnsonville Police Department seemed to be in a good mood. Even Wilson and Minton were jollier than usual. Thomas sat in the office Wilson called his home away from home and explained his concerns for Jodie. He apologized for bothering the detectives, but considering the trauma Jodie had been through and her involvement in the Rick's murder case; he felt the detectives needed to know that no one had seen or heard from Jodie in three days.

"You say she has been missing since Monday?" Wilson asked.

"No, Monday is the last time anyone spoke with her," corrected Thomas.

"What was the exact time and what was the conversation?"

"Well, I called her Monday morning. I believe she also spoke to her mother on Monday morning. It was Monday night that Jodie told her roommate, Debbie; she would be gone for a few days," explained Thomas.

"Did she give any indication of where she was headed?" Minton continued with questions.

"She only mentioned visiting her Dad, but he has not heard from her either. We are all quite concerned."

"We will send out a message to all units within a one-hundred-mile radius. We will include a picture of Jodie. If she has been spotted, they will contact us. Do you have her license tag number? Do you or the family know if she had cash, or if she planned to use credit?"

Thomas thought for a moment on Wilson's questions, "No, I am afraid I do not know. I will need to check with Debbie."

"Great, just let us know and keep us posted on any new developments." Wilson responded as he walked Thomas out through the department.

Jodie awoke Friday morning with the worst headache she had experienced since being in the hospital. She tried to find her cell phone, but accidentally knocked it off the nightstand onto the floor. When she tried to rise up to reach for the phone, the room began spinning, as waves of nausea found their way through her body. Jodie fell back onto the bed in a cold sweat. Crying would not help. Screaming was out of the question – it would hurt too badly, if only she could reach the hotel phone. I will try again in a few minutes she thought. The darkness soon enveloped the room as Jodie drifted into an anguished sleep.

Thomas was beside himself with worry. He knew the detectives were doing all they could, but he had a terrible feeling that Jodie was in trouble. He called Debbie again and questioned her repeatedly concerning the last conversation she had with Jodie. Did she mention any place she wanted to visit? Did she take cash? How many clothes did she pack?

"Thomas, I have honestly given you all the information I know. Other than saying she might visit her Dad, there is nothing more."

"I'm sorry Debbie. I just need to find her. Has she ever mentioned a place she would like to go?"

Silence ensued for what seemed like an eternity to Thomas. Finally, Debbie answered. "She has always talked about Savannah, GA and Charleston, SC. She has a secret love of the south, especially the Civil War era. Maybe she has ended up in one of those cities."

"Thank you Debbie! You are an angel. I'll keep in touch," Thomas said as he quickly ended the call. He wheeled his car around in the middle of the street and headed back to the Johnsonville Police Department.

Thomas found Wilson in his office. He presented the new information to Wilson along with his own thoughts. He explained that Sugar Falls, where Johnson Scever lived, was between Johnsonville and either of the towns. Jodie would actually have to pass through Sugar Falls to get to either place. It might be possible that she traveled to Savannah or to Charleston with the intent to stop at Johnson's on her way back home.

"Interesting," replied Wilson. "Did you find out if she is using cash or credit?"

"No, I'm afraid not."

"Let me call her bank and see if we can get them to cooperate without an order. It seems I have that information on file from the accident."

"We can call Matilda if we need to, but I would prefer to wait until we know a little more," said Thomas.

"Sure, let me see what we have. Just sit tight and let me make a few calls."

Jodie tried once again to reach her cell phone in the floor. Finally, she had it in her hand. She knew she needed help and was actually beginning to be afraid. If she called her Mother, there was little she could do. Thomas was out of the question. After all, she is running from Thomas. Edee would never understand and would be no help. Maybe she could call Debbie.

She entered the name Debbie and held the phone to her ear as it rang. Soon a voice came on, "Hi, this is Debbie. I am sorry I cannot take your call at this time but if you leave me a message, I will get back to you." Jodie ended the call without leaving a message. She let the phone drop to the floor again.

Thomas left the Johnsonville Police Department in a run. Wilson's faxed authorization to have the bank trace Jodie's recent account activity proved beneficial. She withdrew five hundred dollars from her savings account on Tuesday. There was a credit card transaction for gas at a station in Rock Hill, SC. The break-though was a credit card transaction at a seafood restaurant in Charleston, SC. Thomas became very excited!

Wilson tried to talk Thomas into waiting for further investigation, but he would not hear of waiting. He knew he needed to be on the road. Thomas had a burdened feeling that Jodie was in trouble. Wilson promised to call Thomas as soon as he found any more information. For now, Thomas was on the way to Charleston, SC.

Jodie heard a knock at the door. She tried to get up but could not. As hard as she tried, she could not even call out to whoever was at the door. She heard the knock again - this time a voice – "Housekeeping." Jodie reached for the lamp and ended up knocking over a glass of water and also causing the lamp to fall onto the floor.

"Hello, this is Housekeeping." Jodie finally managed to get her feet to the floor. When she stood, the room began spinning. Nausea swept through her entire body sending her to the floor. She fell in a heap beside the bed. It seemed she could still hear someone knocking on the door but she was too weak to care.

Luckily, the housekeeper realized something was not right on the opposite side of the door. She went downstairs to her manager and explained what had just taken place. The two of them returned with keys to open all the locks. When they returned, the manager tried knocking again a few times before opening the door. When it was obvious, no one was going to come to the door; he unlocked all the locks and slowly opened the door. He called out again, but no one answered. He finally opened the door wide to find Jodie lying on the floor. He instructed the housekeeper to call "911" immediately while he looked up information on their guest.

An unconscious Jodie arrived by ambulance at the nearest hospital. Doctors immediately began working with Jodie upon her arrival. The hotel manager printed off all the information they had in the computer system on Jodie to send with the ambulance workers.

Thomas knew he needed to be careful, or he was going to get a speeding ticket. He did not have any intention of stopping until he reached Charleston. Who knew what Jodie was thinking or where she may be by now? He would take the picture he had of her and question the restaurant workers. He prayed Jodie made mention to someone of why she was there or gave some indication of her plans.

Thomas phoned Matilda to let her know what was happening. He explained he was on the way to try to find Jodie. Matilda cried and thanked Thomas for all he was doing and for being such a wonderful person. Thomas just smiled to himself as he ended the conversation. He thought it ironic that Jodie's mother thought so much more of him than Jodie seemed to show. He resolved to himself to break through the prison walls Jodie had built around herself and her heart. Thomas prayed insistently as he drove down the interstate.

Jodie awakened in the emergency room. She began questioning where she was and how she got there. The nurse explained all she knew, and that now they were working with her to stabilize and re-hydrate her body. The nurse asked Jodie if they needed to contact someone for her – anyone who might be worried about her.

"Yes, I am sure my mother is sick with worry, but I do not want you to frighten her."

"Would you like us to give her a call?"

"Yes, please. If you will, just tell her that I was visiting in Charleston and developed a bad headache. I came to you for some medication and that I am fine. You will find her number in my bag... if it is here. Did my belongings arrive with me?"

"I will relay your request to the doctor. He may have your information by now. The hotel sent along your registration information. Our secretary is working to retrieve more of your personal information. I will have her check on your personal belongings as well."

"Oh," cried Jodie.

"Is something wrong?"

"No, I just wish you could have waited until I awakened to search for my information," said Jodie in anguish.

The nurse turned and left the treatment room. Jodie had a sneaking suspicion that the nurse knew more than she pretended and would probably say too much.

It was not long until a doctor entered the room. He introduced himself and explained to Jodie what had apparently taken place. They were treating her for a migraine but he added that they would be admitting her overnight for observation. They hoped to rule out any seizure activity. She needed fluids since she had become dehydrated.

"So you do have my information?" Jodie questioned.

"Yes, we were able to obtain your medical records as soon as we found out your date of birth and a few other important facts," the doctor replied.

"Have you called my mother?"

"Our staff is making that call as we speak. Is there anyone else we need to contact?"

"No, mother will know what to do," replied Jodie.

"Very well then, you just try to relax. We will have your room ready in a few minutes. Someone will come for you and help you get settled. We will also be continuing the pain medications in your I.V. to help you rest. If you have need of anything else, please do not hesitate to ask."

Jodie thanked the doctor and turned away so he would not see the tears welling in her eyes. She knew exactly what her Mother would do! Besides contacting Edee, Jodie knew her mother would call Thomas before she tried anyone else. Was there not enough going on in her mind without bringing Thomas back into the picture? Jodie let the tears spill as she heard the door close behind the doctor. She closed her eyes and prayed for peace to fill her heart, even though the revelation of her traumatic night was still pounding in her heart.

Thomas' phone rang. It was Matilda calling again. "Hello," answered Thomas.

"Where are you?" Matilda inquired.

"I just turned onto I26 outside of Columbia, which will take me directly into Charleston."

"Jodie IS there! She is in Charleston. I just heard from the hospital," cried Matilda.

"Wait! Why did a hospital call you?" Thomas asked.

"Jodie became sick. The hotel housekeeper found her and they took her by ambulance to the hospital in Charleston. She is okay, but they have admitted her for observation. Edee is coming to pick me up, and we will be there as soon as possible."

"What hospital called you?"

"Oh Thomas, I think they said University. Is there more than one?"

"Yes, there is more than one but that is okay. I have contacts in Charleston and can find out. I will call Edee and let her know where to bring you."

"Thank you Thomas. Please tell Jodie we are on our way," said Matilda.

"I will do that. You take care of yourself and let me do the worrying. I am sure Jodie will be fine."

"I will try." Matilda responded with a weak voice.

Thomas said a quick prayer as he closed his cell phone. He then set the cruise control as high as he was comfortable driving. He would call his friend from college who now lived in

Charleston. He would have to stop for gas anyway and would take time to call then. He was sure his friend, Jake, could find out the necessary information he needed.

Chapter 32

Sordid Truth

"Dr. Overton, you have been such a wonderful doctor. We do not know how to thank you for all you have done," said Mabry. She and Sicillia met with the doctor to go over the details of Mrs. Allen's release from the hospital.

"It is all part of my duty. I do try to take my patient's health as seriously as I would have my own family members. Your mother should do fine once she regains her strength. She will still need help from someone for a few weeks, and then I would say she will be able to be alone again. I will have my office to schedule a return visit for two weeks. We will see then how she is progressing."

Sicillia stood and took the doctor's hand in a firm handshake. "Thank you again Doctor. We will see to it that Barbara gets her rest, plenty of nourishment, and whatever else she might need."

Sicillia and Mabry made their way back to Mrs. Allen's room to find her dressed and ready to go. Mabry could hardly contain her excitement.

Once in the bright sunlight, Barbara glowed with excitement to be leaving the hospital. They would go back to the hotel where

Sicillia had leased the best suite the hotel had to offer. Mabry was concerned about her Mother returning home so until the three ladies had some time to discuss the matter, Sicillia suggested they stay in the hotel. Mabry and her Mother decided to accept Sicillia's generosity. Mabry had plans to visit with Detective Wilson after Christmas to determine the safety of her Mother returning home. Mabry was also uncertain whether she would be comfortable back at home, once she knew the whole story.

"Mabry, will you get the suitcase while I help Barbara into the car?"

Barbara leaned heavily on Sicillia. Soon they were in the car, on the way to the hotel. Mabry tried to start a conversation.

"I hear there will be additional local events during Christmas this year. I think the University has a couple of events open to the public. Maybe we could all go if mother is up to it."

"That sounds lovely," answered Sicillia.

Barbara nodded and smiled as Sicillia turned into the hotel parking lot. Mabry was thankful for the quick arrival. She could occupy her mind now by getting her Mother inside and settled.

"Here we are Barbara. I hope you will be comfortable with this arrangement until you are well again. The hotel offers a lot of amenities, so we should be properly cared for during our stay."

"Sicillia, it is a very nice of you to arrange this for us. You have already done too much."

"It is what I wanted to do. Please enjoy yourself and take advantage of this time."

Mabry excitedly mentioned, "I will be happy to use the room service, laundry and anything else we need to try."

Sicillia laughed. "That sounds like an idea, Mabry. Let's get you and Barbara settled inside and in the largest bedroom. I will take this one right across the hall. Then, you might just go ahead and order room service for us!"

"That sounds great to me. I would love to have something to eat. I believe my excitement has made me feel famished."

Mabry knew they were so fortunate to have Sicillia with them during this ordeal. She made a promise to herself that one day she would repay all the kindness of her aunt Sicillia. Once they had their belongings in the proper place, Mabry assisted Barbara into a change of lounging clothes. She and Sicillia had gone to the old house to get some of their clothes and personal items while Barbara was in the hospital. Barbara instructed Mabry where to put a few of belongings when they heard Sicillia.

"Ladies, I will fix us tea and coffee," called Sicillia from the kitchenette. "I picked up some extra goodies we can eat after our meal."

Mabry smiled to herself as she helped her mother put on her house shoes.

"Mom, we really are going to be alright. I believe God put Sicillia back into our lives for a reason. She has been so good to me and now both of us."

"I believe you are right Mabry," said Barbara with tears in her eyes. Your father would be pleased.

Barbara's comment of her father surprised Mabry. She was not sure whether she should acknowledge her mother or let it pass.

"Mom, were you and my father happy?"

"Why of course, we were happy Mabry. He was the best husband and father. I think of him often and know he would be so proud of you."

Mabry smiled at her mother. She really did not know what else to do or say. She had not thought of her father lately.

"Let's get you in the living room, and I will call room service with our lunch order."

Once Barbara was comfortable, Mabry called in their lunch order. It was not long until the food arrived. The three ladies sat down and enjoyed lunch over much-needed conversation. Barbara was the first to bring up the avoided topic.

"Mabry, I know you are trying to put off discussing what happened to me, but I really need to know. I am still confused as to why you insisted I go away, and now I find that your stepfather is in jail, and I have been seriously ill. I only remember coming home to find police cars all around the house. When I got out of the car and started into the house, I heard officers "yelling" at me to stop. That is the last I remember until I woke up in the hospital."

Mabry exchanged a quick glance with Sicillia who turned her head away. Mabry noticed tears pooling in Sicillia's eyes.

"Mother, I promise I will tell you everything. Let's just finish up our lunch. Sicillia has some great-looking cookies she bought at the Bakery. I promise Mom, please."

Barbara nodded her head in silence. Sicillia got up from her chair and busied herself refilling Barbara's glass. She came back with tears dried.

Sicillia finally patted Mabry on the leg and encouraged her to begin telling her Mother what was taking place.

"Perhaps it is time to give your Mother the details sweetie. I believe she is stronger than we think. I will be in the Kitchen cleaning the dishes if you need me."

"You do not have to leave Aunt Sicillia. You may need to hear some of this as well. Actually, Mother and I may both need your support."

"Very well, let me put away the tea, and I will be right back. You go ahead and begin so Barbara does not have to wonder any longer," replied Sicillia.

Mabry drew a deep breath as she began. "Goodness! Mother, I hardly know where to start. I guess I should begin from the phone call I made to you asking you to leave town."

"That sounds like a good place to start Mabry."

"Are you sure you are up to this Mother? You have been through a lot at the hospital."

Barbara nodded affirmatively, "Yes; I need to know!"

"Okay, here goes. Mother, I know you have had a hard life with Stephen, and you did your best to keep a consistent home-life for us. Stephen just never was good enough to you in my eyes. That is one reason I asked you a moment ago about father. I am very glad to know you were happy once.

A series of events leading up to the phone call I made asking you to leave, caused me to realize that you and I both were in a trap. The only way we could be freed from that trap, was for me to tell the truth, which I had in fear suppressed for so many years."

Mabry stopped for a moment to survey her Mother's expression. She said a quick silent prayer for strength and wisdom to tell her Mother the horrific details.

"So, with a new resolve and God helping me, I went to the Johnsonville Police Department. Once I began telling the truth, it was as if I could not stop telling all that had happened in our home. I also shared the whole story of what happened between me and Johnny. I thought I could handle the trauma the rest of my life, but when I gave my heart to Christ, I realized I did not have to face this alone."

Barbara appeared very puzzled. Sicillia returned by this time and sat on the sofa with Barbara. Sicillia took Barbara's hand and held it as she asked Mabry to continue.

"I think I told you about my confession and acceptance of Christ. If I didn't, please remind me to share that with you later. Anyway, Stephen did not like Johnny. I am not sure if you knew that or not. Stephen was very jealous of Johnny. When I brought Johnny home to visit during break, the stage was already being set for our relationship to fall apart. Johnny did not like that I never shared with him about my family. He learned a few things while he was with us that I prayed would never become known to anyone, including you mother."

Mabry stopped and took a Kleenex from the box of tissues. She hung her head to wipe the tears and slowly began again.

"Things began happening to me early, after I started middle school. Stephen started acting strangely toward me. I did not understand his attention, but he told me it was how all fathers treated their daughters. He apologized for not being a better father and had me believing this was normal... (Oh God, I need your strength)... Mother; I am so sorry!"

Mabry ran from the room.

Barbara sat stunned looking at Sicillia. Sicillia reassured her that Mabry would be okay. "Give her a few minutes, and she will be back. We need to let her gather her strength."

Mabry did soon return. She took a chair to the side of her mother, so she could hold her hand.

"If you do not want me to continue, I can wait mother."

"No, Mabry; we all need to know the truth."

"Mother, I am sorry, but Stephen took advantage of me. He abused me physically, emotionally and well, I guess you have already figured out the rest."

It was all Mabry could do to stop the barricade of voices she so feared. Barbara was wiping tears from her own eyes and staring upward at the ceiling.

"I wanted so badly to talk to you mother, but once I realized this was NOT normal, Stephen threatened to kill you if I said anything. I knew he meant it, so I endured. When I had the opportunity to go to college, Stephen told me I had better not leave town, or I knew what would happen. So, I enrolled at Johnsonville University in order to be close to you. Just getting away from home and Stephen's constant presence was a relief. Things changed when I met Johnny. Mother, are you sure you want me to continue? Maybe you have heard enough for now."

"Please continue Mabry. I thought for years that things were not right between you and your stepfather. I had no idea or actually, maybe I did not want to believe anything was going on in my own home. This is so sickening, my precious daughter; why didn't I realize?" cried Barbara.

"No Mother, stop; please do not say that. You were my angel, my strength and stability. Without you, I could never have survived!"

Sicillia stood and took Mabry's hand. "Dear, I think perhaps you both need a little break. We have all three been tense since we walked in the door from the hospital. Why don't you walk downstairs and see if I have received any mail? It will do you good to walk it off."

At her Aunt's suggestion, Mabry nodded in agreement. She checked herself in the mirror and left the room. Barbara began crying uncontrollably. Sicillia sat down beside her again and pulled Barbara to her chest like a Mother would hold a child. The two sat like this until Mabry returned.

It was almost thirty minutes before Mabry returned. Barbara began to worry and was thankful when the door opened to reveal Mabry with her arms full of flowers, mail and magazines.

"My goodness, did you decide to go shopping?"

"You will never believe who was at the front desk!"

"Well tell us dear," replied Sicillia.

"It was Detective Minton! He stopped by to see how we were doing. He had this large bouquet of flowers in his hand for Mother, and these magazines for us all. We started talking and before I realized, I had been gone too long. He wanted me to tell you both 'Hello' for him."

"Interesting – he is a true gentleman," said Sicillia.

"He is a nice man. I never thought that one of the detectives who pressured me so heavily could be nice enough to bring flowers to my Mother. After all, He hardly knows her except for the hospital visits."

"He must really admire Barbara."

For the first time in days, Barbara chuckled softly and winked at Sicillia.

Chapter 33

Salvation

Mabry, Sicillia and Barbara took a brief time to rest after they finished their conversation dealing with Stephen. Barbara kept apologizing to which Mabry insisted that it was not her fault. Mabry indicated her hatred for Stephen. She also explained to Barbara and Sicillia about the day she was in crisis, and Edee came to her apartment. In the end, Mabry was relieved her mother now knew the truth. She just prayed that God would help her mother deal with the situation.

Mabry now lay with her eyes wide open. It seemed she could not close her eyes for thinking about Detective Minton. Until the day he paid them a visit in the hospital, their relationship was of a professional nature and mere acquaintance. What was she to think now since he had been to visit twice while off-duty? The odd part was he brought gifts of flowers both times. Mabry mulled over in her mind that perhaps Detective Minton was just trying to be kind, yet she felt a little something different in the way he looked at her. It was similar to the feeling of how she felt when Johnny used to look at her.

"Dear Lord, will I ever get over Johnny?" Mabry looked to the ceiling as she questioned.

"You will, Honey. It will just take time;" said Barbara, startling Mabry with her presence.

"I didn't hear you come in Mother. I thought you were on the sofa asleep."

"I'm sorry if I startled you. I was getting restless and decided to look about the suite when I saw you were awake. Did you rest well?"

Mabry laughed, "If lying here thinking a million thoughts count, then yes!"

"What is on your mind?"

Mabry was silent in thought. She finally answered, "Detective Minton was on my mind. I was thinking of the way that he has started visiting us. I thought of Johnny and that a part of my life is completely over. I am afraid, fearful of never being happy and never feeling safe again. I do not know who to trust. I do not even know how to be open and honest most of the time."

Barbara sat down on the edge of Mabry's bed. "Sweetheart, life has been difficult for you. If only I had known how hard, maybe I could have changed things for us. Just know that from this day on, I will try to be open and listen to all that is going on around me."

"Mother, I really do not know how I would have made it without you! You have always been there for me, even if you did not realize why. You are my hero! Don't ever forget that."

"Thank you Mabry," replied Barbara. "I believe I will go to the kitchen now to find something to drink. Can I fix you anything?"

"No, I will get up too. We can sit together and talk some more."

"I would like that," said Barbara. "There is so much yet that I do not know and so much I would like to help you with."

"Mother, are you certain you want me to continue telling you about Stephen? You look really tired and weary."

"I am not sure Mabry. I must know at some point, but perhaps I have heard enough for today. You said you wanted to talk more about your confession and Christ. I believe you also mentioned learning more of your father."

"Yes, I did. That would be excellent conversation," remarked Mabry. You go ahead and get comfortable. I will get us both something to drink and see if Sicillia wishes to join us."

The three ladies spent the remainder of the afternoon into the early evening discussing Mabry's salvation experience. Mabry explained thoughts of taking her own life, along with how Jodie's sister popped into her mind at that moment. Mabry told of Edee's simple explanation of cleansing. With tears streaming down her face, Mabry shared her modest prayer and the scriptures Edee wanted her to read. The one Barbara found most interesting was John 3:16; "For God so loved the world, that he gave his only begotten Son, that whosoever believeth in him should not perish, but have everlasting life."

Mabry promised to invite Edee over to share more with them as soon as things settled down with Jodie. They all knew the news of Jodie's disappearance and even though Mabry tried to forgive and forget, she still had a plethora of mixed emotions whenever Jodie's name was mentioned.

Jake delivered just as Thomas thought. It only took him twenty minutes until he called Thomas back with the needed information. Thomas would soon be at University Hospital. He called Edee and gave her the directions. He expected to arrive at the hospital within the hour, which should give him at least four to five hours with Jodie before Matilda and Edee arrived. He began praying for God to give him the right words to say to her. Never before had someone captured his heart the way Jodie had. He did not understand why she was shutting him out. He asked God for wisdom and patience in his own heart while praying for God to touch Jodie's heart.

The drive finally ended. Thomas felt he had worked as hard driving to Charleston as if he had just finished an eight-hour surgery. Once he found his way to the information desk and had Jodie's room number in hand, he took time to locate the hospital cafeteria. There he bought a much-needed soft drink to refresh himself. From the cafeteria dining area, Thomas noticed a wall of windows. Beyond the hospital wall, across a busy highway and out a few hundred yards, he saw a massive bridge across the river. As he stood looking through the window finishing his soft drink, Thomas could not help but think of the bridge as what

Jodie needed in a figurative way of thinking. In his mind gathered a prayer that needed praying. In the middle of the dining area, Thomas whispered.

"Heavenly Father, God. I have a deep sense of urgency for Jodie Scever. Lord, will you open Jodie's eyes to the bridge of forgiveness and mercy that lies waiting at her feet. Give Jodie the courage to take that first step onto the bridge that can bring her back to You. Dear Lord, please heal Jodie's heart and give her understanding of Your infinite love and mercy. Amen!"

Thomas found his way to the floor of Jodie's room. He stopped to inquire of the nurses concerning Jodie's condition. The news was comforting. Jodie would be released in the morning. Thomas slowly walked to Jodie's room. He was about to knock when a nurse opened the door startling both of them. He apologized as she opened the door further for him to enter. Jodie must have heard his voice because he heard her call out, "Thomas?"

There she was looking at him with those big brown eyes that cut deep into his soul. He walked to her bedside and noticed she was crying. He hesitated to say anything for fear of causing her more distress, so he just stood there. She finally held her hand out for his. Everything inside him melted. He had been so afraid for her. The uncertainty of where she had disappeared to, hearing she was hospitalized and now finding her to be fairly unscathed left him totally exhausted.

"I am so relieved to find you unharmed! You have had us all so worried," said Thomas.

"I am so sorry; I had no intention of worrying everybody. It was just something I felt I had to do."

"It's okay. It is over now and you are safe. We do not have to talk about it at all unless you want too."

"Thank you Thomas, but I may need to talk if you are willing to listen".

"I'm all ears!" laughed Thomas as he moved his head a little closer to hers. "You can tell me anything you want, especially your deep dark secrets."

"Some secrets are meant to be kept," replied Jodie.

"Whatever you say," responded Thomas.

Jodie lifted her hand and placed it on Thomas' cheek. She let it linger for a moment as they stared into each other's eyes. Then she quickly let it fall as if she realized she had done something she should not do.

Thomas did not acknowledge the moment for fear of saying the wrong thing. Instead he sat down in the chair at Jodie's side.

"It seems as though we spend a lot of time together in hospitals." said Thomas. "We are going to have to stop meeting like this or people will talk."

Jodie laughed. Thomas felt like perhaps he had reclaimed the moment. They chit-chatted for a while and eventually got back onto the subject of Jodie's little escapade.

"I honestly did not mean for everybody to be so worried about me. I just felt like I had to get away to clear my mind of some things. The accident, Johnny's death, the hospital, meeting you and all that is going on with Mabry – I just felt like I was choking." explained Jodie.

"Did it help you?" asked Thomas.

"Yes, even though I became ill, it did help tremendously."

"Is there anything else you need? Do you need some more time?"

Jodie lay silently for a few moments and replied, "I think I have found my answer."

"Good, if that is what you needed. I am glad for you."

"Like I said, I did not mean to cause everyone to worry. I had no intention of being gone more than just one night. Things happened and here I am still in Charleston," said Jodie.

"I hear from reliable sources that you always wanted to come to Charleston."

"Oh yes, I love the history surrounding Charleston. The waterfront, the nostalgia, everything here is so intriguing. I have wanted to come for a long time. I was hoping to take a tour today!"

"Perhaps you can come back again soon. If you need an escort, I will be happy to accompany you," added Thomas.

"That sounds like a plan. I did get to see some of the town before I…" Jodie stammered.

"Explain before what to me Jodie?"

"Before this excruciating headache began. I did some shopping when I first arrived. I returned to the hotel for a quick nap before heading out for Dinner. That is when it all started."

"The shopping or the headache started?"

"Thomas Wiley, the headache and the revealing of the truth."

"Is there such a thing as truth?" Thomas asked yet again.

"You sure are full of questions, Mr. Wiley." Jodie responded, "Yes, truth! The afternoon nap turned into a nightmare. I dreamed of that woman again and this time I am positive it was Mabry Allen. The feelings from the dream would not leave me alone. All through dinner, she was all I could think about. Thomas, she really did try to kill me, didn't she?"

"We should probably let the police decide that."

"She was the one at the hospital that night; I am sure of it, especially knowing her stepfather's car was spotted on camera. I just do not understand. I always thought our friendship would remain regardless of what happened with Johnny. The dreams have become too real Thomas. They are what led me to the park last night and probably what started this awful headache."

"Do you want to tell me about it?"

"There you go, questioning me again," said Jodie in a laughing tone. "Where should I start...?"

"How about you start at the beginning?"

"Oh you are so smart! Okay, let me see if I can start at the beginning! I had dinner at this great seafood restaurant. I really liked the flounder I tried when you and I last saw each other so; I decided that I wanted to try some more seafood. The hotel clerk recommended the restaurant to me. He said their crab cakes and the grits and shrimp are famous. I could not bring myself to order grits with shrimp in them! Instead, I tried the crab cakes, and they were scrumptious! I believe I could eat some more today! After dinner, I walked down to the park. I wanted to take a stroll through the park to try to clear my head. That is where I discovered more about the murder and also how foolish I have been."

"Let me make sure I understand. You found answers in a park and discovered you are foolish?"

"Yes Thomas Wiley, and yes, foolish! Stop mocking me and listen!"

"I'm sorry Jodie. Please continue."

"I have wasted several years of my life thinking I was in control. I realize that I locked myself in a prison of self-fulfillment and denial. Whatever Jodie wanted to do, see or be responsible for is what Jodie was going to do. I was afraid to trust anyone or allow myself to be dependent on anyone. I know that resolve stems from my family situation with my parents. I controlled my life; or at least I believed I was controlling my life. My main goal in life was to keep anyone from hurting me. I had no intention of being hurt like I was when my Father left Mother and me. I felt wounds so deep and so numerous, that I doubt anyone could count all the scars. It was then, as I wandered in the park, that I fell to the ground and began praying. Not only did I begin praying; I begged God to forgive me Thomas and to show me how to leave all the pain behind me for good. There I was all alone pouring out my heart and soul to God. I realized what I had become. Not only did I ask for forgiveness for my foolishness, but I asked for God to show me what really happened that night. I asked Him to restore my friendship with Mabry."

"That sounds good Jodie. I am happy for you. Have you had any further answers? What about Mabry?"

"Oh yes. I found out a lot more before I left the park. It was after nine o'clock before I left to go back to the hotel. An officer kept coming by to check on me. At first, I think he wondered if I was homeless, trying to find a place to sleep. I finally engaged him in conversation to explain that I was not loitering. I pleaded with him to allow me time for my thought process. I realize now God sent him to watch over me, else something terrible could have happened to me there in the Park alone."

"You could have been attacked or even killed Jodie!" Thomas exclaimed in anguish as he moved back to her bedside.

"I know, but at the time all I could think about was finding the truth. I needed to know how to change my life. I needed to find out what happened with Mabry and how Johnny died. I was a part of that terrible night Thomas! I had little to no clue to what or how it all happened!"

"I know."

"Anyway, as I prayed, my mind starting replaying the events leading up to the party. I actually started remembering the day of the party. Then, it was as if God opened the Heavens and began playing that night on a movie screen. I fell to the ground and watched in horrified amazement as everything became so clear. I saw myself standing at the back entrance to the clubhouse. There were glass windows and doors all along the back. I was enjoying the music and watching people mingle. Something caught my attention from the corner of my eye. When I looked out, I could not clearly determine what it was, so I stepped outside onto the patio. Someone was standing with their back to the clubhouse just a few yards down the back lawn leading to the Greens. It looked like Johnny. I started to walk toward him when I heard voices. I hid in the bushes so I could not be seen. It was Johnny and Mabry. They were arguing. Johnny kept asking why Mabry broke off the engagement to which Mabry kept saying she did not love him anymore. Johnny argued with her over and over. Mabry finally broke down crying and fell into Johnny's arms. They held each other and then began kissing. I felt like a used doll that had been torn and thrown aside."

"I am so sorry." Thomas replied as he rubbed Jodie's brow.

"Anyway, I turned away and was walking back inside when I heard a 'pop' and then Mabry's scream. I looked around and saw Mr. Allen standing over Johnny with Mabry's arm in his grip. Unsure of where he came from or what was going to happen, I hid again to watch. Mr. Allen had a pistol in his hand. He kept waving it around in the air and saying something to Mabry about "telling you to take care of this." Before I knew it, he left dragging Mabry by the arm. I was terrified. I did not know what to do. I knew Johnny would need help, so I ran to him as soon as I thought it was safe. He was still conscious. I had my cell phone ready to call "911" but Johnny begged me not to call. Johnny managed to stand up, and I helped him get to my car. I remember getting Johnny in the car and speeding off toward the hospital. I do not know where or how the wreck happened."

"I know this was terribly upsetting to you, but I do not understand why you didn't call for an ambulance or call 911, even though Johnny asked you not to call," inquired Thomas.

"Johnny was afraid it would create more problems for Mabry. He said we were to tell everyone that it was an accident. I had no idea we would not make it to the hospital."

"I understand, I guess. Are you confident in this revelation?"

"Yes, Thomas, I am; I feel as it is all coming together now."

"So, what happened to you after that? Did you get sick then?"

"Needless to say, recalling all that happened that evening was traumatic. I walked back through the park toward the city streets when the kind Officer came my way. He seemed to be very concerned for me and was as kind as he could be but was stern about my being alone. He told me I needed to go back to my hotel, unless I had someone to be with me at this time of night. I thanked him for all his help and asked if he could get a taxi for me. He hesitated and then offered to take me in the police car. By the time I made it back to the hotel and into my room, my head was pounding."

"Jodie, you are so lucky to be alive and here to tell me all this!"

"I realize that now. I am so sorry I had everyone worried."

"It is a miracle you were not attacked in the Park, a miracle for the guard watching you, and yet another miracle you did not have a full-blown seizure right there in the park." exclaimed Thomas.

"Thomas, I know. I said I'm sorry."

"The doctor states you will be fine. He said this was a classic migraine that went untreated for too long. It may very well have been brought on by the underlying injury you had along with the emotional stress you were experiencing. At any rate, I am not letting you out of my sight again!" Thomas said emphatically.

Jodie teared up and smiled at him from the pillow on the hospital bed. She gazed at Thomas for a long time until he became curious and said, "What?"

"I need to tell you something" said Jodie.

"Okay, you can…"

"I believe I have fallen in love with you, Thomas Wiley."

Thomas' critical attitude faded. His facial expression changed immediately to one no longer of concern, but one of pleasant surprise. Words were not needed as Thomas reached down and touched Jodie's face. He caressed her cheek for a moment then planted a soft kiss on her lips.

"Thomas, I have been so afraid. I have never felt this way before. I have kept my heart guarded for years. Your kindness and goodness frightened me. I have never allowed myself to be as open as I have been with you. This is all so new for me," continued Jodie.

"I was kind to you because I love you and I have since I first laid eyes on you."

Jodie began crying. "I am so undeserving of someone like you. It is still hard to believe this is happening. I am so happy!"

"Then why are you crying?" Thomas jokingly asked.

"Because!" said Jodie as she smacked his arm half laughing and half crying. "Besides, there is one more thing you need to know."

"Really, you mean you have not told me enough?"

"Thomas!"

"I'm sorry, go ahead."

"While the scene was playing for me, I kept having a strange feeling in my heart. And no, before you even ask, it was not heartburn!" Jodie continued. "I know that I have been in church since I can remember. Mother brought me up in the way a Christian should go. I know all the right answers, but I do not remember a time that I truly trusted God for anything. "

Thomas could feel his heart begin to pound!

"During the revelation of that night, I realized I have been a callous, inconsiderate, person. I know I was living only for myself. Not only that, but I realized I needed help to change."

Jodie surveyed Thomas' face. "Thomas, I have surrendered my life to Christ. I have received His gift of Salvation, Thomas!"

Thomas practically jumped straight up. The scene in Jodie's hospital room became one of rejoicing and laughter.

Chapter 34

Turning Pages

Christmas came with a bound and left just as quickly. The town of Johnsonville barely thought about the events of the past year. Everyone seemed in such a festive mood; the city was a Christmas light paradise. Johnson Scever spent time in Johnsonville with Jodie and Thomas. Johnson was very impressed by the decorations, and made note for his secretary to begin looking for creative ways to decorate Sugar Falls next year.

Thomas drove Jodie through town Christmas Eve as they enjoyed the snow falling all around. The lights made the snow more beautiful than anything Jodie could remember seeing in quite a while. Even the Johnsonville Police Department bore lavish decorations. Jodie thought the only kink in the decorations currently resided inside a cell at the Johnsonville City Jail.

Christmas Day dawned with a new snowfall on the ground. Children were out on sleds they received for Christmas, bundled in gifted scarves, gloves, and coats. Families and friends called out greetings to each other from streets and neighborhoods, wishing each one a Merry Christmas. The aroma of Turkeys, Hams, and pies filled the air. Smoke curled from chimneys. Yes indeed, Johnsonville had a very pleasant Christmas.

Thomas and Jodie had their first Christmas together as a couple. Thomas could not be more thankful for God's answer to his prayers. He had no doubt that God was now working in Jodie's heart and life. The future looked clearer and brighter to Thomas than it had in a long time.

As the old proverb goes, "all good things must come to an end" and 'end' is exactly what happened to the Christmas spirit. Once the New Year was upon the good citizens of Johnsonville, they began discussing the town's safety issues, financial issues, and the upcoming Ricks' murder trial, along with some of the town's juiciest gossip.

The top news story was the upcoming hearing for Stephen Allen, the man arrested for the murder of Johnny Ricks; rumors of University students requesting permission to hold rallies circulated in town. The students planned to march on the courthouse lawn all weekend prior to the hearing on Monday, January 8th. Talk of Jodie Scever being seen with former hospital intern Thomas Wiley, could be heard everywhere from the grocery to the beauty shops.

Gossipers even speculated that they were involved before Johnny Rick's death. The hot item of gossip, however, was the new rich lady in town who claimed to be Mabry Allen's Aunt. Some of the townspeople bragged of knowing Sicillia Bharti when she was just a girl in town - never mind that Sicillia did not even grow up in Johnsonville!

Mabry and Sicillia discussed how silly women can become when they place their envious eyes in other people's mirrors. Barbara Allen tried to take everything in stride considering her health issues. Barbara was about to become tired of the town, and the memories she would forever retain of recent events. Barbara's concern was for a full recovery and to be the loving supportive mother, she knew Mabry needed. It was still difficult to fathom what torment Mabry must have lived through. It made Barbara sick to her stomach.

Sicillia convinced Barbara and Mabry to stay with her at the Hotel Suite until after the hearing. Mabry was much relieved knowing they were safer at the hotel. She could leave when classes began January 4th, without worrying that her mother would be alone. The three ladies had even considered the idea of renting a town home on the opposite side of town until Barbara was comfortable going back to her own home.

Johnsonville definitely had a lot in store for the coming weeks.

Jodie tried to focus on her relationship with Thomas. She realized he was a very special person and hoped they would be able to stay together. She was also spending more time with her mother and sister.

"Hello, you have reached the Scever residence. Please leave a message."

"Drat, where is my momma? I have called several times in the last hour." Jodie said in a frustrated tone.

"Did you try calling Edee?" Debbie asked.

"No, I thought maybe she was just outside, in the shower or at the neighbor's house. I hate to bother Edee all the time. If I don't hear from her in another thirty minutes I will call Edee. It is just not like Momma to be gone this long without some of us knowing her whereabouts!"

"Hey Jodie, I checked the mail while I was out. It looks like you have something from your Mother, and some mail from that place where Thomas is from."

"You mean Buck Valley, Debbie."

"Yes, whatever the name of that place is. I wonder where that name came from anyway. Have you seen any deer when you visited?"

"Not that I recall. Of course, I have not really looked for any deer," replied Jodie.

Jodie laid aside the mail from her mother to open the envelope from Buck Valley. She studied the envelope, wondering if Thomas' Mother might have written her, so she hurriedly opened and read the hand-written letter. Jodie sat in amazement as she read. Thinking aloud she mumbled, "This must be a joke! There is no return address, just the postmark that shows it came from Buck Valley."

Jodie turned the letter over and over in her hands and finally said to Debbie, "You have got to listen to this; I can hardly believe what I am reading! This is a letter I will not soon forget."

Dear Miss Scever,

You have never met me, but I am a good friend of Thomas Wiley and his family. It greatly concerns me that you are constantly putting Thomas through un-settling circumstances. Thomas is a fine outstanding young man with a promising future ahead of him, or at least until he met you.

Now don't get me wrong, I'm sure you have your good qualities as well. We here in Buck Valley tend to take care of our own. Rest assured that I will be keeping up with your escapades and will not hesitate to speak to Thomas if I feel he is being mis-represented in any way!

Highly Concerned
Prominent Citizen - Buck Valley

Debbie looked at Jodie in amazement. "Are you kidding me? What are you going to do with that letter?"

"Well, I am certainly not going to let Thomas see it. Can you believe the nerve of this person, whoever he or she is?"

Jodie jumped when the phone started ringing. She was so taken in with the letter she just read that she was not expecting the telephone.

"Hello!"

"Hi Jodie, I see you have been trying to call me."

"Momma, yes I have. Where have you been? It is not like you to be gone so long unless you are at church or with Edee. I was getting worried."

"Really, I guess it is good for you to worry about your mother for a change," laughed Matilda.

"Hey, I'm being serious here. I really was worried."

"I understand. I am sure you were. I only went out for a little while with a friend."

"You only went out for a little while… with a friend… do you do this often, and I am just now finding out?" inquired Jodie half laughing yet serious.

"Why such sudden concern for my activity? I do go out occasionally with some of my friends."

"Sorry Mom! I am just used to you being at home. Who was it? Where did you go?"

"My, you sure are inquisitive. If you must know, it was my new next-door neighbor, Doris. She and I went to lunch at the Tastee-Freez."

"I didn't realize you had a new neighbor."

"Yes Jodie, now why did you call? Is there something you wanted?"

"Uh, uh… yes, but oh goodness, I don't even remember now! Who is your new neighbor?"

"Her name is Doris Stanley. She and I actually knew each other before you were born. We were so surprised to find out we are neighbors! Now, what do you need honey?"

"I was calling to see if you have plans for New Year's Eve."

"Well, as of now I do. If you had reached me earlier, I would have been free. "

"What do you mean, you would have been free?"

"Jodie, our conversation seems to be one-sided."

"I'm sorry, again! It's just that Thomas, and I wanted to take you out to eat. I should have called sooner, and I should not be asking you so many questions. I'll let you go. Maybe we can drive over on New Year's Day for a visit."

"I would really like that. My wish is for you to take care of yourself, Jodie. You do not need to worry about me. I love you and hope the rest of your day is good."

"Thanks, I love you too." Jodie held the phone to her face. She could not believe what had just happened.

"What happened, Jodie, I could tell you were arguing with your mother."

"Arguing? Did it sound that way? I really wasn't."

"Do you want to talk about it?" Debbie asked.

"Not right now – it was just a weird conversation. Would you believe that my own mother does not want me to visit? Then on top of it all, I receive his letter from Buck Valley! Maybe sleep will change my mood."

Thomas rearranged his desk. His bedroom doubled as an area for study. The desk was neatly tucked in between bookcases on either side. This made it easier to reach whatever he needed. He had decided he should go through all his books soon since he had been accumulating from the beginning of college. "Some of these books may no longer be needed. I will pack these up and donate them to the Thrift Store."

Finally pleased with the organization of his workspace, Thomas sat down on the bed to remove his shoes and socks. He could see the city park from his bedroom window. There were several families out enjoying the sunshine.

"One day, I will have my own family to take walks and enjoy our time in the park!"

Thomas walked to the window and watched for several minutes. A young mother was pushing a stroller with a small baby inside. A couple of small children were playing on the slides. Thomas found himself thinking what it might be like to have children around. He knew he wanted a family and now with Jodie in his life; he wanted nothing more than to show her his love and intentions to make her a part of his future.

Thomas had an amazing visit this afternoon with Matilda and her friend Doris. They had lunch together at a local diner called the "Tastee-Freez. Matilda was very gracious to him when he asked her blessing on his relationship with Jodie. He found Matilda to be such a humble caring lady. It was a wonder they could meet without Jodie finding out. Thomas was excited for his future.

Chapter 35

Rendezvous

Detective Minton waited for Mabry Allen at the "VillaPasta" restaurant on the corner of Spruce and 9th streets. He thought this would be an out-of-the-way place, where they could relax and have some private conversation. Wilson had overheard his phone conversation with Mabry and questioned him about the meeting. Minton covered himself by attributing the meeting to obtaining more background information on Mabry's stepfather.

"I think we should leave that information to the lawyers and the court, don't you? After all, we have gathered and presented the evidence that has Mr. Allen in custody."

"I just don't want any of this to backfire on us. Allow me to go through with this one meeting and then if you think it is not necessary, I'll back off. After all, I am just following through with your directions to keep an eye on Miss Mabry."

Minton had put Wilson on the spot with his last remark.

"Alright, but you be careful. You have an expected code of conduct to live up to as an officer."

Minton shrugged his shoulders. "Whoever came up with such an idea anyway. We signed our contracts and the officer's code which say nothing about escorting a lady out for dinner."

Minton left the office without any other word to Wilson. He soon arrived at the VillaPasta where had a corner table reserved off the main dining area. He did not want to take any chances for townsfolk who might be interested in seeing Miss Allen. He already knew he was taking a chance, but he wished Wilson had not rubbed it in. Maybe he was getting too comfortable being with Mabry.

It was the evening before New Year's Eve. Minton felt if they went out tonight, they would not encounter as much risk of nosey people. Mabry arrived just as Minton was getting concerned she might not show up. He could not help but watch her as she walked toward him from the Bus stop. Her hair was swaying in curly wisps around her face as she walked. She had on a black skirt with a multi-colored sweater that fit her perfectly. Minton swore to himself as he thought about Mabry and those long beautiful legs of hers, "Keep your head on straight pal or Wilson will have your head."

"Good Evening Miss Allen. It is good to see you. I believe our table is ready."

They went inside the restaurant to be greeted by the hostess. She escorted them to their table all the while studying Mabry as she explained the menu to them.

"I believe the hostess is quite taken with you Miss Allen," said Minton.

"Yes, I noticed that. I thought she was going to ask for my autograph!"

"Let's pretend we are not here and ignore her," replied Minton.

From out of nowhere came the whooshing sound of voices in Mabry's head; "Miss Mabry is in trouble; she can't be ignored. Miss Mabry will be caught." Mabry shook her head slightly in an attempt to stop the voice. She focused on her dinner date, while closing her mind to any interference from the horrid voices that had been absent for so long.

"Thank you for inviting me out tonight Detective Minton. It has been a while since I've had an evening without having to look over my shoulder."

Minton nodded, "It is my pleasure to be here with you Miss Allen. I am glad you could make it. I am also happy you like Italian since it is one of my favorite cuisines."

"Mine too; Mother fixed Italian at home when Stephen was not around. My stepfather was not particularly fond of Italian food. I enjoy every opportunity I get to have Italian!"

"Then you must order your favorite item tonight. I insist!" declared Minton.

"What is your favorite dish?"

"I would have to say the Sicilian Scampi. What is yours?"

"I guess either the Chicken Parmigianino or the Manicotti."

"I believe any item from the menu will be delicious," observed Minton.

"Good evening, Detective Minton and Miss Allen. My name is Blanco; I will be your waiter today. May I start you with something to drink, perhaps a glass of wine?

Mabry looked at Minton with a surprised and puzzled look on her face. She moved her mouth enough for Minton to know she was asking how this waiter knew them by name. Minton was a little taken aback as well. Even though he frequented the restaurant, this was unnerving since he was trying to get Mabry out of the limelight.

"Blanco, I'm sorry, do I know you?" Minton asked.

"No sir, but I have seen you in the restaurant on occasion."

"Forgive me for sounding like a Detective – how did you know Miss Allen?"

"Detective, surely, you have seen this evening's newspaper."

"I am afraid that I haven't. Look, regardless of the paper or how you know who we are; let me politely ask that you allow us a little privacy. You see; this is all a part of the investigation, and I am sure you would not want to interfere. I must request that you not acknowledge to anyone that we were here this evening as it could hamper the evidence. Do you understand?"

"Yes sir, I understand." Blanco answered with a smirk. "I will never speak a word of this. Let me get you some complimentary wine while I see what we can do to make this area a little more private for the investigation." With that, Blanco turned on one foot and disappeared through the back of the restaurant. He could not wait to make a telephone call.

Mabry sat in disbelief. Minton could tell that she was about to lose her composure.

"Mabry, do you mind if I call you Mabry?"

"That's fine," she half-heartedly answered.

"We can leave if you are not comfortable here. Just say the word and we can go."

"I'm fine. I guess this is something I will have to get used to with the hearing coming up. It was just such a surprise that anyone knew me, and a surprise that this dinner is part of the investigation!"

"I understand Mabry. I should have given this evening a little more thought. I only mentioned the investigation to encourage Blanco to give us some privacy. You are not being questioned, at least not about the investigation," said Minton with a smile.

"I see. I am quite uncertain then why you asked me out."

"Honestly, I wanted to learn a little more about you Miss Allen. When I first met you, it was just part of the job. Recently, I find you more intriguing. I do apologize for false pretenses."

"I see. Then, I will just have to get used to the stares."

The two sat in silence for a moment. Mabry was unsure of her own feelings. She was the one to break the silence. "So, do you think the Judge will rule that there is enough evidence to charge my stepfather with the murder?"

Just then, Blanco appeared with two glasses in one hand and bottle of wine in the other. Behind him were two other waiters with a privacy screen and a basket of bread. They set up the screen, poured the wine and even served the bread! Blanco thanked the two men who assisted and then turned his attention back to his dinner guests.

"Does the lady need anything else?"

Mabry hesitated as she spoke, "Yes, I would; I would like a glass of sweet tea if it is not too much trouble."

"No trouble at all. Is La Mia Bella Donna not pleased with the choice of wine?"

"No, I am sure the wine will be fine. I am not a wine drinker by choice if you please."

"No problem, I will have your tea for you. Detective, may I get you anything at the moment?"

"I am fine, thank you."

"I will return shortly," replied Blanco.

To Mabry's astonishment the voices crept back to mock her, "I'm not a wine drinker!!!" She heard them say with heinous laughter.

"Detective, I would like to apologize again for my behavior toward you at the onset of this investigation. I allowed circumstances and emotions to control me. Hopefully, I am past that now and am trying to begin afresh."

"No apologies necessary but accepted!"

Aside from the brief mishap at the onset of Dinner, Minton felt very good about the evening and his time with Mabry. Of course, they discussed the upcoming hearing and the chain of events that could possibly trigger further protests. Minton reassured Mabry that she was doing the right thing by letting go of the past and moving forward with a clear conscience. Outside the restaurant, Mabry shook Minton's hand and thanked him for a very enjoyable evening.

"I have to admit I was uncertain about having dinner with you, but you made me feel very comfortable and at ease with conversation," commented Mabry.

She started to walk away, but Minton reached out for her arm to stop her.

"Look, I'm not sure what is in the evening paper, but it might be a good idea for me to drive you home."

"Are you sure you don't mind. I can take the bus."

"I insist. Besides, you are our key witness, and the department would be furious with me if I let something happen to you."

"Oh." Mabry uttered with a small degree of disappointment.

"Mabry, I didn't mean, well – I didn't mean that is the only reason. I would be highly upset with myself also if something happened to you." Minton said as he moved closer to Mabry.

"Let me drive you home," He said as he slipped his arm around Mabry.

Mabry felt a chill unlike what she had ever felt from anyone touching her. She locked eyes with Minton, and saw in his eyes a soft glowing look of concern. She nodded affirmatively as Minton lightly touched her lips with his.

Flash, Minton heard the snap of the camera. The bright lights stunned both Minton and Mabry as they drew apart to see what had just happened. They saw the back of a woman retreating into the Villa Pasta.

"Mercy, I am so sorry. Let's get out of here." Minton grabbed Mabry's hand and led her to his car. They sped away in stunned silence with the exception of the voices in Mabry's head.

Chapter 36

Chance Meeting

Thomas was up and ready to go before eight o'clock on New Year's Day. He planned to pick Jodie up at nine, and they were heading to Buck Valley to have lunch with his family. He was looking forward to spending the day with his siblings and watching Jodie interact with his family. They would then have to leave in time to go by Matilda's on the way home. Jodie seemed angry toward her mother, for some reason. He had tried to get enough information out of her to find out what was going on, but Jodie would not talk about whatever happened. It was unbecoming of Jodie and very disconcerting to Thomas that Jodie could act this way. This was the first time he had seen this side of her.

Thomas walked out to pick up the morning paper. He had just enough time for another cup of coffee and the paper. Back inside, he unfolded the paper to reveal the headlines for today.

The headline story was the New Year's Baby born to a Hatterfield couple just after midnight. The picture of the couple with their newborn was the center top page. An article about the Johnsonville New Year's Day Parade was just below the headline story and then in the bottom right corner a picture caught Thomas' eye. It was – no it couldn't be.

Thomas looked closer at the picture. He threw the paper down in disgust. How could this be? Where had he missed the connection?

Thomas sipped his coffee as he studied the picture. It was un-mistakenly the two of them as the paper stated. Right there on the printed page was a picture of Detective Minton kissing none other than Mabry Allen! He read the article:

"Recently, Detective Chase Minton of the Johnsonville Police Department has been rumored to be having secret meetings with Miss Mabry Allen, stepdaughter of Stephen Allen who is in custody for the murder of Miss Allen's former fiancé, Johnny Ricks.

The rumors began a few weeks ago when Detective Minton was seen walking into the hotel Clifton where Miss Allen is staying with her wealthy aunt and her ailing mother. Detective Minton was carrying a vase of fresh flowers. Sources indicate the two have been seeing each other regularly since the hotel sighting. Detective Minton and Miss Allen were seen with each other at VillaPasta, where they spent the evening together over dinner. This picture was taken outside the restaurant after their private dinner.

The two deny any romance. Whatever truth is seen in the picture; one has to wonder what effect the relationship will have on the investigation of Johnny Ricks' murder."

Thomas read the story once again to be certain he had all the facts. This is crazy he thought to himself. He knew he had to keep quiet about this until after the day was over. He was certain it would upset Jodie even more, and since she hardly ever read the paper, he was certain he could wait to tell her about the article. Although, one-day Jodie was making excuses for Mabry and the next day, she was upset with her.

Thomas realized the time was getting away from him. He could finish the paper later. He gathered his things and left to pick up Jodie Scever.

Sissie was waiting when Thomas and Jodie arrived in Buck Valley. She met them at the door with a big grin.

"Hey brother, guess who is here to have dinner with us? I bet you'll never guess."

"Now don't go bothering your brother with my presence here. He might not be as glad to see me as you are Sissie," sounded a familiar voice from inside the home.

"Is that you Mrs. Stella?"

Thomas led Jodie inside and saw Stella sitting in the living room. Mrs. Stella is one of his favorite people from Buck Valley. He immediately went to her and gave her a big hug. Thomas then grabbed Jodie's hand to introduce the two.

"Jodie, I want you to meet Mrs. Stella Carson. She is one of our dear friends."

"How nice to meet you," Jodie responded shyly.

"Well young Lady, it is definitely nice to meet you. Why, when Thomas' mammy here told me ya'll was coming; I just had to pay me a visit. Thomas is like my own young'un. Nancy and I have been friends for going on nigh thirty years," proclaimed Mrs. Stella.

"Mrs. Stella, it is good that you are having lunch with us today. It will be nice to catch up on everyone," remarked Thomas.

"Yes, Nancy talked me into staying. You know how I love your mammy's cooking, especially her coconut pies!"

Thomas took a seat in between Sissie and Mrs. Stella. Jodie just stood there awkwardly for a minute then walked into the kitchen where Nancy was setting the table.

"Hi Nancy, may I help you?"

"Well honey, it is ready. I just need to fix the drinks, if you want to help me with finding out what everyone will have to drink."

Soon, they were all crowded around the kitchen table, at the bar and in the living room enjoying each other's company. The television was on so Thomas' Dad could watch the Bowl Games.

The chatter and laughter were catching, yet Jodie kept watching and listening for every word that Mrs. Stella had to say. There was something about Stella that bothered Jodie, although she wasn't sure what it was. She kept thinking to herself that she could not let her defenses down until she knew more about Mrs. Stella.

Thomas offered to help his mother clean up after the meal was over, but she insisted that he spend time with his family. Jodie decided not to ask or offer, but just to stay in the kitchen with Nancy so to avoid Mrs. Stella. She was sure Nancy would appreciate the help. Jodie and Nancy worked well together. Jodie was very comfortable around Nancy and felt as if she belonged when she was with her. When they finished the clean-up, Jodie made her way to the living room. Thomas made a place for her to sit beside him. Jodie readily took the seat. This was the closest she had been to Thomas since their arrival. Somehow being near Thomas gave her security to be herself.

Mrs. Stella seemed to dominate the conversation talking about this community event or church happenings and "little Thomas!" Stella was talking about a new family that was coming to church. It seemed they were less fortunate than most. The church fell in love with them according to Stella. It was the next comment that Stella made, which caused Jodie to turn sick on her stomach.

"You know that toddler boy of theirs reminds me of Thomas when he was little. He is just as friendly and smart in Sunday School as Thomas was when I taught him. When the church council asked me my opinion of giving them assistance, well, you know what my reply was! We here at Buck Valley Baptist Church take care of our own." Mrs. Stella stated emphatically. *We take care of our own…* Jodie thought. She rolled that statement over in her mind wondering where she had heard it before. Suddenly, the words came back to her like a knife thrown directly into her heart. *"We here in Buck Valley tend to take care of our own."* It was her! It had to be her. This was too strange for it to coincidental. Jodie felt the color drain from her face.

She began fidgeting. When Thomas noticed, he laid his hand on her knee.

Mrs. Stella just kept on talking. Everyone but Jodie seemed to be enjoying the conversation. Only Thomas' Dad would make a sound occasionally indicating they were too loud for him to hear the television. Thomas's hand on Jodie's knee made her feel trapped. She finally stood up abruptly and walked down the hall to find the bathroom.

Once in the bathroom, she locked the door and turned on the cold water. Jodie found the washcloths and took one from the linen closet. She let the cold water soak into the cloth and then placed the cloth gently over her face. "Why did I come here?" she thought to herself. "Thomas is too good for me, and his family evidently wants someone better for him than me. After-all, who would want their son to be involved with an apparent murderer! I was crazy to think that I could be a part of someone's life as good as Thomas." Jodie realized she was crying. She wet the washcloth again and tried to cool her body with the cold water. She was hot all over.

Jodie heard the doorknob turn and then a knock on the door. Nancy called her name. "Jodie, are you okay? You've been in there so long Thomas is worried about you."

"I'm sorry to make everyone worry." Jodie replied. She then opened the door to Nancy, who could not help but notice Jodie's swollen blood shot eyes.

"I am sure that I look horrible now. I just became sick and needed to get away from everyone. I'm afraid I have another one of those horrible headaches coming on," commented Jodie when she saw how Nancy was looking at her.

"Let me get Thomas, and I am sure he will be glad to take you on home."

"Oh no, I don't want to interrupt his family time or his catching up with Mrs. Stella. Please do not bother Thomas. You know; I can just wait in the car and maybe even nap a little until this wears off."

"Nonsense, you'll do no such thing while you are at my house. You come on in here and lie down on my bed. Mrs. Stella just left, and we can all be quieter so you can rest. I would not think of you sleeping in the car!" Nancy replied.

Oh great, Jodie thought, now I have offended Thomas' mother. What else is going to happen today?

"Hey, what is going on in here?" Thomas asked, standing in the doorway.

"I think I am getting another bad headache," said Jodie, trying not to let her face show the truth.

"We can go now if you need to. I don't want you to get sick," said Thomas.

"Maybe we should." Jodie replied in almost a whisper. She felt like she was going to smother with the three of them closed up in that small bathroom. She may not have really been sick, but she knew she probably would be at any minute if she could not get away from here.

"Let me go start the car so it will be warm. I'll be right back, and we can go on to your mother's house." Thomas hugged his mother and thanked her for helping Jodie. He left the two in the small bathroom alone.

Nancy took the washcloth from Jodie's hand and looked her in the face. "Jodie, did something upset you today?"

"Why do you say that?"

"I just noticed you seemed uncomfortable around Mrs. Stella. She is a bit different but means no harm to anyone. She just has a colorful personality."

"She seemed very nice Nancy. I guess I am just not used to all the chatter. I hope you understand."

"Okay, well I think I hear Thomas. Let's get you back in the living room so you two can be on your way."

Thomas helped Jodie with her coat. They hugged everyone and said their good-byes. As Thomas pulled from the driveway, Jodie began.

"I am sorry for spoiling your family time and your time with Mrs. Stella. She is some character. All her chattering really got on my nerves."

Jodie's comments immediately upset Thomas. He did not respond, which caused Jodie to feel even more insecure with herself.

"So, tell me why Mrs. Stella is such a special person."

Thomas carefully chose his words. "Mrs. Stella is a long-time family friend. Our families have attended church together since I can remember. She does have a different way about her Jodie, but she means no harm. Once you get used to her, you will love her too."

"Well, she just got on my nerves. I think you should just take me home. I am up to going to my mother's today. I am going to need some quiet time and rest if I am to get over this headache."

Thomas made no answer, but set his mind to take Jodie home. The words left unsaid, and the feelings left untouched made for an enormous mountain that Jodie and Thomas would eventually have to climb.

Chapter 37

Reassigned

Detective Wilson was waiting for Chase Minton bright and early, January 2nd. Wilson had already consumed most of the coffee he made earlier. He paced the floor, wondering how his partner became so enamored with one of the persons involved in the murder case; not only just one of the persons but Mabry Allen herself!

Wilson was almost livid. They had worked so diligently on this case and now with the news of Minton's escapade, there would probably be more work to come. His only direction to Minton was to keep an eye on Mabry, not to have a fling with her! Wilson looked at the newspaper lying on the worktable and just shook his head.

Chase Minton finally showed up for work at eight–thirty. He entered the building ever so quietly and made his way to the second-floor office suite he, and Wilson shared. He knew that Wilson was probably pacing up and down waiting for him to arrive. Minton took a little more time this morning putting off the inevitable. He knew now he may as well go straight to Wilson's office and face what was coming.

Minton paused at Wilson's office door. He could see Wilson at the large window where he so often stood when pondering evidence or studying a case. Minton had an uneasy feeling about what was going to take place once he opened that door. Finally, he pulled himself together and plunged feet-first into Wilson's arena.

Wilson whipped around when he heard the door open. The two detectives stood looking at each other for what seemed an eternity. Wilson finally spoke.

"I guess you have already seen the newspaper!"

"Yes Sir, I have. I have seen the paper and believe me when I tell you that I have read it a 'million' times."

"Come, have a seat."

"Sir, if you don't mind, I think I would rather stand," responded Minton.

"Very well, Minton, I don't think I have to tell you what a predicament you have brought upon the department with your escapades."

"No Sir, you do not."

"What pains me most is that you claimed to be doing this in the name of the police department. If I had this to do over again, I would have never allowed you to call that dinner meeting, but what's done is done. We can't change it now. We are going to move forward. Unfortunately Son, we are going to move forward without you on the case. You have actually been re-assigned, pending investigation, to another unit up-state for an initial period of thirty days."

Wilson paused to study Minton's face. It was difficult to read him today. The two had always been close enough it seemed they could read each other's next move. Minton stood stone cold facing the window.

"It is with much hesitation and regret on my part that you are being re-assigned. However, your new duty is to Bristol County to assist an investigation of a possible cult ring in the area. An extravagant religious leader began a church there a few years back. Recently, there have been some reports of animal sacrifices and possible abuse of some young women. The Bristol Sheriff's Department requested some top-notch investigators to be sent their way by any State Law Enforcement Agency willing to release the person for up to six months. This will be your new home if you choose to accept. We will review the status of your work monthly. Depending upon your actions and the progression of the Ricks' murder trial, you may eventually be returned home to the good town of Johnsonville to resume your post. If you choose not to accept, then I am sorry to say that is the end."

"Thank you Sir. When do I report?"

"I'm glad to see you cooperating with this son. Your duty begins next Monday. Until then, you are placed on administrative leave with pay. You may go now."

Minton turned and left Wilson's office without a word. He did not even go to his office to gather any belongings. What did it matter now? They could do what they wanted with his personal effects. For the moment, he could not think of anything but Mabry Allen!

Minton sat in his car. He watched the people coming and going from the Johnsonville Police Department. He considered the recent months and how he had managed to get to this point. There were ten-thousand thoughts racing through his mind. What would he tell Mabry? Did she care about him the way he found himself feeling about her? Maybe it was just a desire in the beginning stages of meeting her, but now he had such a different feeling; a feeling of longing that was difficult to describe. It was almost as if his life would always be empty without Mabry. He knew the minute the flash snapped that their lives would be in turmoil. How could he be so careless? What would Mabry think when she found out the dinner meeting was planned? What a mess this was turning out to be, just because of a simple kiss!

Thomas had not heard from Jodie since New Year's Day. He dropped her off at her apartment that day and left her in Debbie's care. Jodie promised to call him as soon as she felt better. He had tried calling her cell phone, the apartment phone and had even gone by her apartment - knocking on her door with no results. Matilda told him not to worry that Jodie often pulled stunts like this when she did not get her way. Thomas just could not understand what was going on. There was no reason he could think of for Jodie to act this way.

It was a terrible week for Thomas. He was trying to get himself reorganized to begin his study in Counseling when the University opened again on Monday, January 8th. He spent time researching the courses he enrolled in, had purchased his books and materials, and had his study space set up the way he wanted it. Thomas liked organization. At the moment, all was organized except for his heart in the matter of Jodie Scever.

Today was Saturday, the day they usually spent together on some new adventure. Jodie called it "gomming around." It did not matter to her if they drove on new roads, ate at a new diner found a new spot to enjoy the scenery, or even window-shopped. She seemed to be happy just being with him. He really did not know how he could concentrate on anything when classes began if this was not soon resolved.

Minton was packed and ready to leave for Bristol County, his new assignment. He found out through his Bristol county commanding officer that he had room and board at a local Bed and Breakfast for the next thirty days. He was taking only what he thought he might need for the time he planned to be away. He could always drive back if necessary.

Minton drove by the hotel one more time where Mabry was staying on his way out of town. He had thought about calling her, but decided to leave well enough alone. He decided he had already caused enough trouble and doubtless would be an un-welcomed visitor. He would just leave without any word. Maybe Mabry would forget him anyway.

On the outskirts of town, Mabry, her mother, and aunt Sicillia were moving into a rented townhouse directly on the road Minton would be taking to get to the Interstate.

Chapter 38

Hearing

The courthouse lawn was full of bystanders. There were some University students picketing on the lawn. The signs read with statements such as, "Justice for Johnny", "Keep Our Town Safe" and other such remarks. Sicillia had employed a driver to take Barbara and Mabry wherever they needed to go in the safety of a rented black SUV with tinted windows. The driver, Sam, made himself available with only a short notice to drive Mabry to the hearing.

Mabry saw the crowd on the courthouse lawn and suddenly had a lump in her throat the size of a golf ball. She wished Sicillia or her mother were with her. Barbara was still not up to facing the man who shot her after years of living as husband and wife. Minton had obviously deserted Mabry after the newspaper ran the article with their juicy picture. Siciliia had gone back to India to take care of some business, so Mabry was truly alone.

"Ma'am, do you need me to accompany you into the courthouse?" Sam, her driver inquired.

Mabry sat up and answered, "That might be a good idea Sam if you don't mind."

"That is not a problem for me Miss Allen. I am here to serve you. It will be my pleasure to accompany you."

Sam proceeded around to the back of the courthouse where the officer motioned for him to go. Sam spoke to the parking attendant explaining why they were there. The attendant pointed them in the direction of a private back entrance into the courtroom so Mabry could stay as much out of the limelight as possible.

Sam held onto Mabry's arm as he escorted her to the courtroom. There they found the clerk, who assisted them with where they needed to be seated. The clerk explained just a little of what they could expect. Mabry was very nervous. She was feeling vulnerable and scared. She noticed the bailiff moving toward the back door. When he opened the door, Mabry's heart sank. Her stepfather entered the courtroom followed by a guard. He looked as if he had aged twenty years. His face was drawn and unshaven. His once shiny dark hair was disheveled and showing gray streaks.

Stephen glanced in Mabry's direction and gave her one of his quirky smiles she had always hated! She felt the room going dark! Sam felt Mabry's head on his shoulder and realized she was fainting. Mabry's speech became garbled as she tried to whisper to Sam. He was unable to understand what she was saying, but realized she was going to fall if he did not catch her. Sam gently shook Mabry and held her by the arm as tightly as possible. Finally, Mabry came back to reality before more than a few people noticed them. Sam helped Mabry sit up just as the Judge was announced.

"All rise for the Honorable Judge Whitaker."
Judge Whitaker entered, took his seat, and announced, "Please be seated."

"Baliff, what is our first case?"

"Your Honor, the case is the preliminary hearing of Stephen James Allen vs. the Citizens of Johnsonville."

"Very well, does the prosecution have a witness?"

The District Attorney stood. "Yes your Honor. The prosecution calls Miss Mabry Allen to the stand.

Mabry stood very slowly, her knees as weak as water, yet she made her way to the witness stand. She answered questions she never expected. She tried to maintain her composure all the while trying to keep from looking at Stephen. After a long intimate and too personal an interrogation, the prosecution began wrapping up the questioning. Mabry acknowledged the demands of her stepfather and admitted this is why she came forth. She knew someone else would be hurt if he continued his tirades.

"Miss Allen, from what you have told us today, your stepfather had malice and jealously toward Johnny Ricks for his intentions of marrying you. Is that correct?" The District Attorney asked.

"Yes sir, that is correct."

"Do you believe your stepfather is capable of murder?"

"Yes sir, I do."

"Thank you, that is all."

After Mabry finished, the D.A. called the investigating Trooper from the night of the accident. The Trooper described what he found when arriving at the accident scene. He stated that Johnny Ricks had an apparent gunshot wound to the chest area.

Also called to the stand to Mabry's surprise, was Roger Yaddinski, who testified to Mabry's fear of her stepfather and of her devotion to Johnny Ricks.

Finally, the prosecution called Jodie Scever to the witness stand.

"Miss Scever, you heard the Trooper who investigated your accident. He gave us the information that Johnny Ricks had a gunshot wound. Do you happen to know how Mr. Ricks received this wound?"

"Yes, I do," replied Jodie in a soft whisper.

The entire courtroom erupted in expectation. Up to this point, Jodie Scever had sworn that she had no knowledge of the wound.

"Miss Scever, for the record, will you please repeat your answer in an audible voice?"

Jodie raised her head and looked directly into the district attorney's eyes.

"Yes sir, I do know how Johnny Ricks was wounded."

Everyone in the courtroom became so quiet you could hear a mouse squeak. Mabry was as surprised as the people in the courtroom.

"Miss Scever, will you please explain to us how you know this?"

"Sir, I have recently been blessed to regain much of my memory. I recall listening and watching an argument between Johnny and Mabry outside on the lawn at the Country Club. They had no idea I was there. I turned to go back inside when I heard the gunshot. When I turned around, I saw Stephen Allen with a pistol in his hand and holding Mabry by the arm."

"How is it Miss Scever that Johnny Ricks ended up in your vehicle?"

"Mr. Allen dragged Mabry away from Johnny. When I was certain they were gone, I ran to Johnny's side. He was still conscious. He would not let me call 911. He did not want to cause Mabry anymore trouble, so I helped him to my car. We were on our way to the Emergency Room. Johnny planned to tell them it was an accident. That is all I remember sir."

"Thank you Miss Scever."

Judge Whitaker asked for further questioning to which, Mr. Allen's attorney approached the witness stand.

"Miss Scever, is there any chance the trauma of your accident caused your memory to be inaccurate?"

"No sir, you see..."

"Now, Miss Scever, do you think it is possible you may have shot Johnny Ricks while driving - causing your vehicle accident?

"No sir, I did not shoot Johnny!"

"Thank you that will be all."

"But, I..."

"Miss Scever that is all, you may step down."

Mabry held on tightly to Sam's arm in disbelief.

The Judge dismissed the courtroom for a brief recess. It seemed to Mabry to be an eternity before the court was re-convened. She was more fidgety now than ever.

Judge Whitaker made the following statements. "We are here to determine whether there is sufficient evidence to support the charges against you, Stephen Allen. Considering what we have just heard and based on the Coroner's report, it is determined that there is sufficient evidence to support the case against you in the murder of Johnny Ricks."

"Furthermore, Mr. Allen, in light of your arrest, additional charges of attempted murder, resisting arrest and endangering a community are filed against you today. Bail will remain denied as set forth at the Arraignment."

"Be it known to all, the case will be bound over to Superior Court for trial; date will be set forthwith. Mr. Allen, you are advised to secure an attorney to represent you. If you do not obtain defense council prior to your arraignment in Superior Court, you will be represented by the court-appointed attorney."

"Miss Scever and Miss Allen, please approach the bench."

Jodie and Mabry looked at each other in shock. They moved slowly at the judge's order.

"Ladies, in light of the involvement the two of you play in this case; you are required to maintain contact with the courts of your whereabouts. You will report to the clerk's office once a week on Mondays at eight o'clock am. If at any time, you leave the state, you may be arrested. Is this understood?"

"Yes, your honor," replied Jodie.

"Yes, your honor," replied Mabry.

The judge sounded, "This Court is now dismissed."

The Bailiff stands and states, "All rise."

Mabry watched Judge Whitaker leave the bench and then found she could not help glancing in the direction of her stepfather. He held his head high and moved along in front of the officer as required. Mabry thought he looked pale and slimmer than before. She then glanced at Jodie Scever standing beside her with an ashen look on her face. For a brief moment, their eyes met; Mabry shook her head and moved toward Sam as quickly as the Judge and defendant left the room.

"Are you feeling okay, Miss?"

"No Sam, I feel terribly sick. Get me out of here!"

As soon as Sam could get Mabry to the SUV, they sped away back toward the townhouse. Mabry turned her thoughts away from what had just happened in an effort to free her mind. Instead, she became consumed by her loneliness. She thought about losing Johnny, her best friend and fiancé. Jodie came to mind and she wondered if they could ever be reconciled after all that had happened between them. She had no idea Jodie had been watching at the clubhouse that night! Finally, Mabry allowed herself to think about Chase Minton.

Chapter 39

Burning Hurts

Thomas met with both his scheduled classes. The morning flew by faster than he thought. He was successful in keeping his mind focused on the instruction and not worrying over Jodie. As soon as he left the main hall and stepped out onto the University lawn, he caught a glimpse of Jodie. He had no idea what her schedule was or where she was headed, but he knew he needed to catch up with her. He moved faster. He followed her weaving in and out between students. He was gaining on her when she turned and disappeared into the Athletic Building. Thomas stopped in his tracks. What was Jodie doing? Why would she be entering the Athletic building? Thomas had no intention of competing with a dead man. He thought about all the negative things Matilda and Edee had said concerning Jodie. Perhaps his mother and Mrs. Stella were right. He may have jumped into this relationship too fast.

Thomas decided to walk away. He started toward the parking lot where his car was when he found himself arguing with his heart. He passed a few benches outside the Library and chose to sit down to sort things out. He hung his head. The thought entered his mind that he should just kneel at the bench and pray when he heard someone say his name. It was Debbie, Jodie's roommate.

"Thomas, how are you doing? It has been a while since you have been around to see Jodie."

The words hit Thomas like a ton of bricks. Did she just say what he thought she had said? He could only look at Debbie in disbelief.

"Thomas, did I say something wrong?"

"Debbie, I have not been around because Jodie is avoiding me. She will not answer my calls, my e-mails or answer the door."

"Oh I see now. Jodie has played it as if you did not want to see her. Thomas, I hate to say anything bad about Jodie, but I have seen her do this before. Anytime she gets close to someone; she breaks it off. It is as if she loses all interest or something. I have not been able to figure her out!"

"Yes, I've heard that same story from others. I guess I thought this time would be different."

"I take it you two are talking about me behind my back," said Jodie as she accidentally walked up on Thomas and Debbie.

Debbie stood. "Jodie, you know better than that. I will see you back at the car."

"Sorry if I interrupted your conversation. I knew if I didn't speak, you would both think I was being rude," replied Jodie. Debbie gave Jodie a stern look and walked away. Thomas then stood to face Jodie. If looks could tell all the soul was feeling, Jodie's would be speaking volumes.

"Jodie, I think you and I need to talk."

"Why? I really don't have anything to say," replied Jodie.

"Jodie! Please stop trying to hide your hurt. I know that I must have done something for you to stop taking my calls."

Thomas took Jodie's hand in his. "Jodie, look at me and tell me you want me to leave you alone."

"Thomas, I just finished testifying in court this morning, and I don't think I'm ready for this."

"You are not ready for what? Have I pressured you into doing anything that made you feel uncomfortable? Jodie, I did not know you had to testify. Do you not think that I would have been there to support you if only you had told me?"

"Please Thomas, not now."

"Yes, Jodie. We must talk about this now! You are hurt, and I am hurt. We can't go on not talking to each other."

Jodie turned her head away but not before Thomas noticed tears pooling in her eyes.

"Jodie, call Debbie and tell her not to wait for you or at least let me call her."

Jodie would not look back at Thomas nor acknowledge his request. Thomas dialed Debbie's number himself. He explained to her that he and Jodie were going to spend some time together, and he would bring her home later.

Thomas put his hand on Jodie's shoulder and turned her toward him. She was definitely crying. Thomas knew she still cared. He pulled her into his arms. As he did, he could feel her releasing herself into his caress. Thomas held her for a few minutes then gently lifted her chin up to his. No words had to be spoken. The kiss said it all.

Thomas led Jodie to his car. He drove away not really knowing where they would end up. He just knew they had to have some quiet time to talk. It was not too long until Thomas turned onto the road leading to the lake. He drove to their favorite picnic spot. Thomas parked and they both got out and made their way to the picnic table they always sat at. It was really odd that no longer than they had known each other that they both knew where to go without saying anything.

Thomas spread out the old towel he carried in his car on the bench for Jodie. He sat down beside her. The sun was warm on their faces. They sat in silence, hand in hand, watching one lone fisherman out on his boat. After about fifteen minutes, Thomas began.

"Jodie. I want you to know that I love you with all my heart. If I have done anything to cause you doubt or concern, please forgive me. It is not my intention to hurt you."

Thomas could tell Jodie was crying again. He put his arm around her and pulled her close. He let her cry. Another thirty minutes passed before Jodie had the courage to speak.

"Thomas, this is hard for me. I have no clue why I shut you out, except I am afraid of being hurt. You are the kindest, most gentle person I have ever met. You are almost too good to be true. It has always been my fear of being hurt worse than when my father left my mother."

"Jodie, I am not your father. I may not be perfect but at least give me a fighting chance. My heart has belonged to you since I first laid eyes on you."

"I know. Do you remember any of the conversation that took place at your mom's on New Year's Day?"

"Maybe, what do I need to remember?"

"It was something Mrs. Stella said. I doubt you thought anything about it, but I knew what she was inferring."

"I'm not following you Jodie."

"Do you remember when Mrs. Stella was bragging on you, and she brought up the new family in their church?"

"Yes."

"She was talking about the council and helping the family?"

"Yes, I remember."

"Well, she made a comment that I had heard her say before."

"What? How could you have heard her say anything prior to that day? You only just met her."

"True, I did just meet her, but I knew of her before," she replied as she reached into her purse and pulled out a folded piece of paper. "Here, take a look at this."

Thomas unfolded the paper and saw that it was a letter. He instantly noticed the signature at the bottom before he even read the letter. He drew his attention back and read aloud...

"Dear Miss Scever,

You have never met me, but I am a good friend of Thomas Wiley and his family.

It greatly concerns me that you are constantly putting Thomas through un-settling circumstances. Thomas is a fine outstanding young man with a promising future ahead of him, or at least until he met you.

Now don't get me wrong, I'm sure you have your good qualities as well. We here in Buck Valley tend to take care of our own. Rest assured that I will be keeping up with your escapades and will not hesitate to speak to Thomas if I feel he is being mis-represented in any way!

Highly Concerned
Prominent Citizen - Buck Valley"

Thomas became still as he sat with the letter dangling from his hand. It was unbearably quiet. Jodie was afraid that she had made the wrong choice by showing him the letter. She started to speak but Thomas put his finger to her lips. He pulled her close.

"That is when you got up and went into the bathroom, isn't it? I should have realized you were upset or at least tired of hearing Mrs. Stella go on and on. She is a family friend Jodie, but she does not control my life or yours. I will not subject you to that kind of ordeal again. If I had only known about the letter, maybe I could have done something about this situation. I thought you were being insensitive to Mrs. Stella."

"Don't Thomas. It is my fault for not showing the letter to you when it arrived. I thought it to be a jokester that was just messing with my mind. Then, I thought there was no need to bother you with it in case it was only a prank."

"If you don't mind, I am going to do with this letter what it deserves." Thomas commented.

Jodie just nodded as Thomas tore the letter into as many small pieces as possible. He placed them in the nearby fire pit and lit a match. He and Jodie watched Mrs. Stella's words go up in flames.

By the time Thomas drove Jodie home, they had a new understanding. They committed to each other that they would voice their feelings and share when or why they were upset. Thomas and Jodie promised to conquer the next battle together.

Chapter 40

Bristol County

Chase Minton found Bristol County to be a friendly place. He spent his first day there scoping out the town, meeting with his new commanding officer and filtering through the information thus far gathered about the "cult." The owner of the Bed and Breakfast was delighted to see him. She explained that the county had been in turmoil over some of the stories being circulated about the "cult' as she called it. Chase had actually found out the name of this religious organization to be "Jehovah's Redemption Church of the Last Days." The organization's information was in a folder for him when he arrived. Minton had poured over all the information before bed.

"Good Morning Detective Minton, I trust you had a good night's sleep last night."

"Morning Ma'am, I rested fairly well for a new place," replied Minton.

"Well, you just git yourself on in here to the dining table and fill up on some o' my good country cooking, then you'll be a raring to go! I've got salt-cured county ham fixed right out back in my own smokehouse, some homemade pork sausage, eggs, brown gravy, grits, homemade biscuits and any kind o' jelly or preserves you be a wantin'," boasted Ms. Mary Beth. You missed out on my cooking yesterday, and I'm going to see to it that you don't leave here this morning without your fuel for the day."

Chase wanted to thank Mary Beth and tell her he never ate more than a bagel for breakfast, but he noticed a couple of other men around the table. It appeared they were waiting for him to join them.

"I must say it all smells good. Maybe I can eat just a little. I am really not used to a big breakfast." Minton said as he smiled at Mary Beth.

"Aw Shucks! I've never seen me a man but what could put away a good breakfast! Come on in here. We are ready to say the blessing and eat. Then ya'll can be on your way. I reckon Charlie and James here are ready to get to the woods."

Breakfast conversation was nothing like Minton had ever been a part of before. It seemed Charlie and James came for the week to go "Duck Hunting." Mary Beth explained there was a lake just about a mile north that was plentiful this time 'a year with duck and other fowl.

Minton was in a hurry to get through so he could report to his new assignment. He was used to being early. He was shifting in his chair, getting ready to excuse himself when Charlie said something to Mary Beth that stopped him in his seat.

"How's that fine nephew of yours from over in Johnsonville, Mary Beth? Reckon I've not seen him for almost two years now."

"Oh, he is jest fine. He seems to stay too busy according to family. I talked to him jest last week when he was a figuring how to help us out with this here "cult" in the county. You're a looking at one of his finest detectives he sent up here to help us out," said Mary Beth as she winked at Minton."

"I'm sorry?" Minton started to ask.

"Oh now son, don't you be sorry. I know it would have been nice to have my nephew come do all the detecting, but seems he's sent us a good one in you. I'm sure you will be jest fine for the Job."

Minton had no clue what to say next. He stared at Mary Beth, and then looked at the two men who in turn seemed to be gazing back at him.

"Who is your Nephew?"

Mary Beth slapped the table and let out a roar of laughter, "why, none other than your boss Sonny boy. It's Willard Wilson! Don't tell me you didn't know you was a comin' up to stay with Aunt Mary Beth?"

Minton sat stunned! "No ma'am, I can't say that I knew."

"Well you jest relax. You go do all that detecting we need you to do and when you get back, Aunt Mary Beth will have you the best supper waitin' you ever did see!"

Minton could not find any words to respond to Mary Beth. He backed away from the table, excused himself, and made his way back upstairs to the bedroom. Once inside, he leaned back against the wooden door and voiced the thoughts swirling in his head.

"So this is how it's going to be until the trial is over.... I wonder what else Auntie and Wilson have not told me. Jest relax, right! I might need to sleep with the light on!"

Mabry dreaded starting classes at the University today. Last semester's grades were not finalized for her yet. She had concentrated on catching up over the Christmas and New Year's holidays. Not only did she start her new classes today, but also she would have to take the finals in last semester's courses before the end of January. It seemed she had more to deal with than she wanted to think about, if only Chase Minton would call.

Chapter 41

The Stranger

Classes were definitely back in session at the University. The student parking lot was full. Wilson had luckily found a visitor's parking place early this morning before everything filled up. He was dressed in khakis, a denim shirt, and tennis shoes. Wilson carried a bulky backpack and wore a Johnsonville University cap. He pulled the cap down over his forehead in his best effort to disguise himself.

Wilson had spent extra hours the last week reviewing the documents relating to the Rick's case. He did not have a good feeling about the case going to trial. Wilson felt like something was missing, something, or someone who held more information important to the case. His first priority today was to follow Mabry Allen and make note of all her contacts. Wilson had a feeling she had not told them all she knew, even with her sharing the unexpected revelation of Stephen Allen's involvement. Besides, if Minton was determined to have any relationship with Miss Allen, Wilson wanted to know she was legitimate and not a "con."

"I hate I had to send Minton away. One thing is for sure. I will not let this young lady use him and bring dishonor to his name."

So far this morning, he had managed to follow Mabry to her morning classes, to the library, and now he was sitting in the cafeteria across from where she was having lunch with a few other people. It appeared to be a casual lunch. Wilson finished his burger and was about to leave when he noticed a young man walk over and bend down toward Mabry's ear. His face was hidden by Mabry's thick wavy hair. Wilson got up and walked over to the dessert bar where he could get a closer look. As soon as he found a spot where he could get a good look at the young man, he turned and walked away from Mabry's table. Mabry was just staring into space, as though she was in shock.

Wilson left the cafeteria in pursuit of the young man. He was not sure what had just happened, but he was certain Mabry did not expect whatever had just taken place.

"Mabry, are you alone?"

Mabry looked around to see none other than Jodie Scever standing at her table.

"Yes, my friends just finished. I will be leaving soon too."

"If you don't mind, I would like to sit with you for a few minutes," said Jodie.

"Help yourself," replied Mabry.

Jodie took a seat, bowed her head for a minute, and then began to eat. Mabry noticed that Jodie had apparently prayed. This was something Mabry had not seen Jodie do in the past. Jodie was half finished with her tray before anything else was said between them.

Jodie decided it was now or never. "Mabry, I am really sorry about Johnny."

"Yeah sure, whatever!"

"I really am Mabry and not just because he and I had been seeing each other."

"Look Jodie. I am not sure what you want from me, but I am not up to this conversation."

"Mabry, if you will just let me talk. Please listen."

Mabry sat in silence. If only she had seen Jodie come in the door, she thought to herself.

"Mabry, I promise not to take a lot of your time, but I do have something that I must say to you."

"Shoot! Oh sorry, I guess that was a bad choice of words."

"Mabry, that night at the Country Club, I was hiding behind some bushes. I saw what happened. I want you to know that if I had it to do over again, I would have tried to intervene. I saw and heard you and Johnny arguing, and then kissing and the last thing was the gunshot. The rest is vague except for seeing your stepfather holding onto you and standing over Johnny's body," replied Jodie.

"Listen Jodie, I really do not know what you want, but I do not care to re-live any of the past. I heard your testimony at the hearing, and I honestly am not in the mood to hear anything else you have to say, Good-bye."

Jodie watched as Mabry hurriedly deposited her lunch tray and left the cafeteria. She could feel her eyes pooling tears as she tried to fight back the emotions. Thoughts of self-pity flooded her mind, "How will I ever be able to make things right? God is probably punishing me for all my years of foolishness."

Wilson caught up with the young man on the back part of the campus. He was headed to the walking trail. Wilson followed until he found a spot near the trail where he could sit and not be noticed. He took his position and watched hoping the young man would walk toward him, so he could get a glimpse of his face. There was something peculiarly familiar about this person. The young man stopped at one of the benches, sat his backpack on the bench, and began to take out several items. Before Wilson had a chance to see his face, the young man had put on a face toboggan, gloves, and was off on the trail in a run.

"Oh, great!" said Wilson under his breath. I must be getting slack he thought or just too dependent on Minton to do the undercover work. Wilson sat for a few minutes and decided to give it up for today. It was cold, and he was out of his element. He decided to go back to his vehicle and hope for a quick glance as he drove off around the trail. Wilson was missing Minton more than he wanted to admit.

"Jodie, why are you so quiet tonight?" Thomas asked as he and Jodie ate dinner together. Thomas picked Jodie up at her apartment for their planned evening. First, they were dining at the Lakehouse Restaurant and then taking in a movie.

"I had a difficult day today, I guess."

"Your classes, the instructors, who or what gave you such a hard time?"

"No, nothing like that Thomas, it was an encounter with Mabry."

"Was it an accidental meeting or by choice, Jodie?"

"Well, I saw her in the cafeteria sitting with some other people. I paid for my lunch tray and noticed the others' leaving which left Mabry alone. I had an impulse to go to her table."

Thomas waited... "and?"

"I asked if I could join her. She did not seem to mind, so I took a seat. I tried to talk to her. I just wanted to explain some things but Mabry was very cold. She told me she did not want to hear anything I had to say. It is like she still blames me for all that has happened."

"I don't know what else to do Thomas. I really want to make things right between us, but you and others think Mabry is out to get me. I am just so confused and frustrated."

"I understand Jodie. However, you will never be able to make Mabry listen to you until she is ready. Give it some more time. See what happens during the trial and then maybe she will warm up to you again."

"That's just it Thomas. I would like to be a support for Mabry as her stepfather goes to trial. I know what kind of life she had at home and how much she loved Johnny. It is so sad that things have ended up the way they have. If only I had tried harder to get those two back together instead of being Johnny's confidant."

"Do you believe you were in love with Johnny?"

"Why do you ask me that, Thomas?"

"If you still have feelings for Johnny, they could haunt our relationship, not to mention how difficult it will make the situation between you and Mabry for reconciliation."

"Oh," replied Jodie.

"So, is that a yes?"

"No, well maybe, oh Thomas; this is not what we should be talking about. I am spoiling our evening."

"You are not spoiling the evening, Jodie. These are things you and I need to discuss if we are going to have any kind of relationship together. I can accept that you had other interests prior to meeting me, but I am not sure I can share you with a ghost."

"Oh no, Thomas, I will not do that to you."

"Then, tell me whether you were in love with Johnny."

Jodie sat motionless with her eyes in a fixed gaze toward the lake. Thomas had reserved a seat by the window, so they could watch the water and any boats that might be about.
Finally, Jodie let out a sigh. She faced Thomas and began.

"Honestly, I don't believe I was in love with him. He was exciting, and had a fabulous career ahead of him. He and I were so much like brother and sister in the beginning that I could not have been comfortable with any serious relationship, even if he were still alive. I do think about him, but only because of the news that keeps bringing up the murder and the accident. I wonder what would have happened if I had just called "911" like my instincts told me to do. I cannot change what I did and what happened between Johnny and me. I can promise you, Thomas Wiley that Johnny will never come between us. Truly, I have not at any time before, known the feelings I have when I am with you. I used to wonder what love was like. Even when I was seeing Johnny, I questioned love. Those last days that you and I were apart were some of the worst days of my life. My heart ached so bad, longing to see you. The saying "sick in love" took on a new meaning for me."

Thomas reached for Jodie's hand. "Then I will never question you about Johnny again. Jodie Scever, I am totally in love with you!"

"I am totally in love with you also, Thomas Wiley!"

Jodie and Thomas both noticed the sparkle in the other's eyes. It was as a seal upon the relationship. They finished their dinner and left the Lakehouse arm in arm. They had no idea they were being watched during the entire meal. He hid himself well. It was coincidental that he ended up at the Lakehouse at the same time Miss Scever and Thomas Wiley were having dinner.

He waited until he saw Thomas drive off, and then he moved around the table where he could face the water. He had kept his back to them yet stayed close enough to hear some of their conversation. How interesting that Miss Scever wanted to be friends with Mabry again. He would see to it that Mabry was not bothered by Miss Scever anymore. He needed to finish his meal then set about the mission he planned to finish tonight. He had a lead on where Mabry was living now. He intended to check the place out.

Barbara was feeling much better now days. She had regained a lot of her strength and felt up to trying a few things around the house like folding towels and fixing a small meal. She just finished preparing some spaghetti for herself and Mabry for a late evening meal. It had been easy to fix, especially with Mabry there to help her. They were enjoying their time together as Mother and Daughter. Barbara knew she was blessed to be alive.

Barbara was noticing major changes in Mabry recently. At dinner, Barbara decided to approach this subject.

"Is your Spaghetti good Mabry?"

"It really is Mother. I didn't realize how much I missed your cooking!"

"Ah, that is always good for a Mother to hear. Mabry, I was wondering if you could read some to me tonight from the book you have been reading. It must really be interesting."

"I would love to read to you. The Bible is what I am reading," answered an excited Mabry.

"Oh, I didn't know it was still the Bible?"

"Yes, Mother it is. Edee marked several passages of scripture for me. Maybe I could start with those."

"That sounds lovely Mabry."

"Mom, I don't mean to change the subject, but Jodie Scever tried to have a conversation with me today. It really upset me. I can't tell you how badly I wanted to slap her face."

Barbara was surprised. "Goodness. I am surprised she spoke to you after what has happened."

"I know, and unfortunately, neither of you know the half of what has taken place. If Jodie really knew, she would never talk to me again. You see, that is what makes this so hard. Jodie seemed sincere, but I know all the secrets, and I do not know how I can ever be friends with her again. Then, I read the scriptures and feel guilty that I can't let this go!"

"Mabry honey, I know you still hurt from losing Johnny, but quite frankly, I don't understand what you mean when you talk about secrets. What else has happened that we don't know about?"

"I'm sorry. I never should have said that. It is just stuff that came between Jodie and myself. Some of it Jodie is aware of and some she is not."

"You may not want to hear this Mabry, but it sounds like you and Jodie should have a sincere talk with each other. I would hate to see the two of you enemies for the rest of your lives. Time passes too quickly honey. One day you may look back and wish you had the friend beside you that you once had in Jodie."

"I know. I have thought about that. Maybe I can make that my prayer time for the next few days. If God opens the door again for us to talk, then I can try to be more receptive and open."

"Good, Mabry. I am so proud of you. You have grown into a beautiful mature woman within the last year. I hate it had to be through tragedy, but I am certainly glad someone saw fit to keep you and I together."

The dinner conversation took a lighter turn as Barbara and Mabry discussed some changes they might make in the townhouse decorations. They both enjoyed the location and the convenience to the university and shopping. Perhaps, once everything settled, Barbara could make this her new home.

Mabry helped her Mother clear the table. As she placed the dishes in the dishwasher, she happened to notice a dim light at the back of the townhouse, but quickly dismissed it as her imagination. No one really knew where she was living now anyway. Mabry finished up in the kitchen. The last thing she did was to close the blinds and turn out the kitchen light before she went back to the living room to be with her mother.

He felt himself swell with pride as he walked away in satisfaction that he had found Miss Mabry's new hiding place.

Chapter 42

Headlines

The paper headlines were bold in the morning's paper with two top stories competing for front-page priority. The first headline read, "Johnsonville Detective Solves the Mystery of the "Jehovah's Redemption Church of the Last Days."

Just to the side of this headliner was the other big news story of the day. "Ricks Murder Trial Slated To Begin March 4th."

Thomas bought two newspapers. He took one back to his car and threw it into the back seat. He took the other with him into the coffee shop. Thomas ordered his usual black coffee and blueberry muffin. He noticed others were reading the paper and talking amongst themselves about the stories.

Thomas was anxious to see what the headlines meant. He began reading about the Johnsonville detective first.

"Yesterday, in a press release from Bristol County, the Johnsonville Herald learned that one of Johnsonville's own has been working undercover to help solve the mystery surrounding a religious sect in the county. Detective Chase Minton was recently recommended to Bristol County Sheriff's

department as one of the finest and sharpest detectives in the tri-county area. Detective Minton's supervisor, Willard Wilson, having kin folks in Bristol County was willing to share Detective Minton in hopes to help his family and our neighboring county with an urgent case.

The religious sect had been growing in supporters and believers over the past several months. It was not until November of last year that complaints surfaced of livestock missing from local farms. In a search for some of the animals, deputies stumbled upon a wooded area in the vicinity of the church where evidence lent itself to animal sacrifice. After increasing complaints and more animals reported stolen or missing, the Sheriff issued a bulletin offering room and board, a ten-thousand dollar reward and an honorary induction as a Bristol County Deputy to anyone willing to assist the department in solving this mystery. The townsfolk were highly pleased to find out that one of their own was sending a detective to help out.

Detective Chase Minton made himself known to the leaders of the religious sect as a newcomer looking for a good place to build a house and start a cattle ranch. Minton was soon accepted in the inner circle of the sect's leaders. Authorities will not say what directly led to the arrest of the leaders but did state that it was all due to the diligent and efficient work of Detective Minton.

Thomas finished reading the article which elaborated more on the inner workings of the religious sect. It was amazing how many followers the sect had drawn. Unfortunately, animal sacrifice was only one of the vices practiced by this sect. Thomas was almost sick at his stomach after he read the entire article. It was amazing to him that people could be caught up in that type worship.

Thomas checked his watch. He probably had enough time to finish the paper before his first class. He continued on to the next headline story about the trial.

"Stephen Allen, being held as the prime suspect in the murder case of Johnny Ricks, learned yesterday that the trial has been set to begin March 4th. Johnny Ricks, a senior at Johnsonville University, was in the prime of his life. Unfortunately, that life was cut short by a bullet to his chest.

The article continued to recap the murder and the accident Jodie was involved in. The last line of the article read: *Jury selection will begin soon according to the District Attorney's office.*

Thomas hung his head and prayed for all who had been and would still be touched by this murder trial. He prayed for Jodie. He prayed for Mabry. Before Thomas finished his prayer, he had thanked the Lord for good detectives like Chase Minton willing to assist others in bringing answers and peace to a community.

As Thomas arose to head out for class, he noticed a small picture and caption on the bottom of the page. At a closer glance, he knew it was the "talked-about" picture of Chase Minton and Mabry Allen. The caption read: *"Will Detective Minton come back to Johnsonville to continue his romance?"*

Thomas thought again of all the people that could be affected by today's top news stories. As he got in his car, he paused once again to whisper a prayer for all involved.

The headlines seemed to drive the University gossip for the week. By Friday, the rumors were flying that Mabry was now engaged to Chase Minton. Jodie was upset by another ardent rumor stating she had actually been in bed with Johnny when he was murdered. It took Thomas hours to calm her down after hearing this rumor going around campus. Jodie became obsessed with Mabry more than ever. She began having anxiety attacks thinking about the rumor and Mabry's dislike of her.

Jodie was very happy to see Friday come. She intended to stay at home and study. Hopefully, studying for the two tests she had coming up would keep her mind off Mabry and the trial.

Late Friday afternoon, the doorbell rang at Jodie and Debbie's apartment. Debbie answered the door to find one of their college friends. He asked to see Jodie.

Jodie was in the kitchen and heard him ask to see her. Debbie asked him in by this time. Jodie offered him a soft drink, but he refused.

"I am here for one reason Jodie."

"Okay Roger, would you care to sit down."

"No, I won't be long. I am here to ask you to stay away from Mabry. She has had enough trouble from you. We want you to leave her alone."

"Roger, I don't mean to be a bother to Mabry. I only want to make things right between us. Mabry was once my best friend!"

"She doesn't need your friendship any longer. I am serious when I tell you to stay away. You especially need to stay away from her when the trial starts. She does not need you there to add to her misery! Take this any way you choose, but you will be sorry if you don't stay away from Mabry."

"Roger?"

"I am not kidding Jodie. Stay away!"

Roger turned and let himself out. Jodie and Debbie stood staring at each other.

"Well Jodie, I believe you have just been threatened," said Debbie in disbelief.

Jodie was stunned. She immediately picked up her phone to call Thomas. She knew he would know what to say to calm her down. Thomas phone rang several times with his voice message coming on. Jodie became even more frustrated.

What Jodie did not know was that Thomas was engaged in a conversation with her own sister, Edee.

"Thomas, this is Edee."

"Yes, how are you today?"

"I'm fine Thomas as I hope you are. Listen, I have just had a phone call from Mabry's Mother, Barbara. I am not sure how she got my number or what she wants, but she has asked me to visit with her tomorrow."

"Okay, are you going?"

"I don't know what to do. That is why I called you. Are Jodie and Mabry talking again? I know the rumors this week have upset Jodie terribly."

"No, Edee, they are not. Jodie has tried to talk with Mabry and make amends but to no avail. These rumors have re-opened the wound for Jodie. She just will not let it go!"

"Well, I know they had a major falling-out over Johnny; I didn't know if they had ever reconciled. I haven't seen Mabry since the day she asked me to her apartment."

"What? When was that?" Thomas questioned with surprise in his voice.

"Oh that was back in November when Jodie was still in the hospital."

"What did she want? Does Jodie know about this?"

"Well, it is a long story Thomas. I don't know if Jodie knows or not. I figured it was Mabry's place to tell why she called me. Listen, let me think about this. I may call you and ask you to go with me over to Barbara's if I decide to go. I told Barbara I would let her know first thing tomorrow morning."

"Okay, but tell me about..."

"Thanks Thomas, good-bye!"

Thomas pulled into the driveway at his apartment. He sat in the car reflecting on the phone conversation he just had with Edee. What did Edee have to do with Mabry Allen? Why did she go to Mabry's apartment? Now, Barbara Allen wants to see Edee. He could not imagine why either of the Allen ladies needed to see Edee.

The weekend went by in a blur for Thomas. He accompanied Edee to Barbara Allen's house. In retrospect, he should have allowed Edee to go alone. Barbara asked Edee to explain salvation to her. It seems Barbara had been reading the bible with Mabry and was under conviction. Thomas was shocked to find out that Mabry owned a bible.

Much to his surprise, he learned the reason Edee had gone to see Mabry last year as well. Mabry had asked God to forgive her and now Barbara wanted to do the same.

Thomas was in awe and yet confused. On the ride back to his Apartment, Thomas asked Edee to explain what happened the day she visited Mabry.

"Thomas, it was during the time Jodie had the night visitor. We were all so concerned for her safety. When Mabry called I could tell she was very distraught. I almost told her that I could not come. I really was torn. Here Jodie was fighting for her life once again and possibly, in harm's way, yet my heart was led to oblige Mabry's request. I am happy now that I followed my heart."

"I'm sorry but what day exactly did you go to Mabry's?"

"Well, I think it was the day after the night visitor. Why does that matter?"

"Edee, you may not know but it is possible the night visitor actually was Mabry Allen. That is why I am so interested in the day and what happened when you were with her."

"No, Thomas, it could not have been Mabry! She seemed so sincere and so afraid. When I arrived, she actually fell in a fetal position at my feet."

Thomas studied carefully how to respond without discouraging Edee.

"I am sure Mabry was upset and that whatever happened while you were there was meant to be. It is just curious that all this took place on that particular day."

"Thomas, I really believe Mabry made a life-changing decision that day, and you know yourself we are all "Babes'" in Christ. It takes time learning and listening to God's word for any maturity."

"You leave me speechless Edee. I apologize for doubting Mabry."

"I understand. Coming from your perspective, I can see where you would have questions. Let us just wait and watch to see how Mabry responds. I believe she will do the right thing when all of this is over. We need to pray for her just as much as we pray for Jodie."

Thomas remained quiet even though he was left wondering how odd the timing of Mabry's cry for help seemed to be. He trusted Edee and knew her to be a very devoted and spiritual lady. Inwardly, he was embarrassed to admit his prayers for Mabry were definitely lacking.

Edee broke the silence. "What do you think of the Mabry and Chase Minton rumors?"

Thomas had inquired as to Mabry's whereabouts. Barbara explained to them that Chase Minton showed up around Noon. He and Mabry had a heated conversation with Minton leaving abruptly. Mabry left shortly after Minton, and Barbara had not heard from her since.

"I'm not sure what to think Edee. The papers and rumors make it all sound convincing, although I know they are exaggerated. It is possible for them to have fallen for each other."

"I know. I was thinking the same, especially after Barbara told us what happened today. It almost sounded like a lover's quarrel."

"True! Well, here we are Edee. I am truly glad you asked me to accompany you today. I've learned by watching. You are a great asset to your family and friends."

"Nonsense, I am just doing what I feel God would have me do Thomas. Besides, I must be the one to thank you for going with me."

Thomas assisted Edee into her car and watched in silent wonder of the day as Edee drove away.

Monday morning came as usual for Willard Wilson drinking his third cup of coffee since arriving at the office a short time ago. It was difficult for him to get started this morning, for some reason. He had many things pressing upon his mind. One issue was the person he had followed last week at the University. There was still no indication as to who he might be. The other issue was Chase Minton. He had been pleased to see Chase Minton on Saturday. More than anything, he was proud of Minton and told him so with as many words as he could find. Giving flattery was not one of Wilson's traits.

He almost wanted to take back his compliments when Minton surprised him with a resignation letter. Wilson recalled the conversation.

"Sir, I have been offered a permanent position with the Bristol County Sheriff's Department. I know it was originally planned for me to stay until the Rick's murder trial was over. However; this seems to be a good opportunity for me, and it would remove me from any publicity during the trial."

"What position have you been offered?"

"I would be taking over the Supervisory Detective's position. The person currently in this position is retiring March 1st."

"Have you given this plenty of thought? You have only been gone a few weeks."

"Yes Sir, I believe that I have. It does seem sudden, but considering the situation here in Johnsonville and my feelings toward Mabry; this would not only give me a new start, but will be a challenge that I feel I need," replied Minton.

"I see. Well, I am certainly going to miss you in the department. You have been my right arm. Bristol County is very fortunate!"

Wilson was definitely going to miss having Chase Minton in the department. He gave Chase his blessing and offered assistance if ever needed in his new position. They spent about thirty minutes reminiscing and talking of the future. Chase left with intentions of stopping to visit Mabry. If she was not too upset with him, he intended to ask her to begin seeing him regularly.

Wilson once again gave Minton his blessings and asked him to keep in touch. Now, Wilson seemed to be regretting that he ever let Minton leave Johnsonville. At the time, it was the best decision for the department and for Johnsonville.
Wilson's phone rang and interrupted his thoughts.

"Hello, Wilson here."

"Detective Wilson, this is Mabry Allen. I was hoping I could stop in to see you this morning before my first class."

"Well yes, that should be fine. Actually, I just had you on my mind. What time do you need to come?"

"I can be there in about fifteen minutes if that is okay?"

"Certainly, I will be waiting."

"Thank you Detective. I will not trouble you long."

Sam was already on the way to the Johnsonville Police Department with Miss Mabry in the vehicle. Mabry had been terribly upset over the weekend, and Sam did not like to see her so discouraged. Sam overheard the intense argument between Chase Minton and Mabry. It left him uncertain of who to be upset with, Chase Minton or Willard Wilson!

Sam pulled into the JPD and assisted Miss Mabry out of the car. He offered to wait inside with her, but she declined.

"I will not be long Sam. Just wait for me."

The receptionist appeared to be arriving as Mabry entered the building. Mabry explained that Detective Wilson was expecting her. She soon heard Wilson greet her "good morning" and explain to the receptionist to hold his calls.

"Miss Allen, have a seat. Would you like a cup of coffee?" Wilson asked as they made their way into his office.

"Yes, a cup of coffee would be nice. I take a little cream with my coffee."

Wilson took a cup from the cabinet and fixed Mabry a cup of coffee. He allowed her to sip for a moment then he asked the question.

"Miss Allen, you wanted to talk to me about something, in particular, or do you have concerns about the trial?"

"Detective Wilson, if it is possible, I would like to know all you can tell me concerning Chase Minton. You already know that Chase, and I were becoming close friends when suddenly he disappeared from my life. Then, I recently have learned he has been working undercover in another county. Chase came by to visit me on Saturday unexpectedly. We ended up arguing. I am afraid I let him get away without knowing how to get in touch with him."

Wilson took a minute to gather his thoughts. He could tell Mabry was sincere. She had an almost hollow look in her eyes. Wilson took that to be a sign she really missed Minton.

"Miss Allen, Chase Minton was reassigned to Bristol County several weeks ago to help investigate a religious sect. If you have seen the papers recently, no doubt you have read about the operation."

"Yes, I did read the article. Please tell me when Minton was sent away. Was it after our picture from the restaurant was in the paper?"

"Yes, Miss Allen, it was after the picture ran in the paper. The department has to weigh anything that could become an obstacle in our investigations or that might hamper an upcoming trial. We felt the incident posed a possible problem for the trial. Minton was reassigned to Bristol County until after the trial. It was not Minton's decision."

"Thank you Detective. You have told me what I needed to hear. I now understand what Chase tried to tell me."

"Miss Allen, I am happy to shed light on the situation for you. Is there anything else on your mind?"

"Yes, as a matter of fact. I am afraid that I need to take out a restraining order against someone while I am here."

"It is not Jodie Scever again I hope."

"No, but if it were I hope you would be of assistance. Actually, it is Roger Yaddinski."

"Roger, whom was your friend, and the one who was stabbed on the walking trail during the time Jodie Scever was hospitalized?"

"Yes, that is the one."

"You know you will have to explain your reasons."

"Yes sir. I do know that. Roger has been a good friend, but somehow I feel he is becoming possessive of my time, has demanded my attention, and lately I feel he may be stalking me."

"Interesting, isn't it odd how one day we think we know someone, and then you turn around and find they are someone entirely different than you imagined." Wilson stated as he slid some paperwork toward Mabry.

Mabry considered Wilson's remarks as he was explaining to her. "If you will complete your part of these forms which are highlighted, then we will take them over to the clerk's office to file them. The order should be served today."

"I can't thank you enough for all your help today. You have given me the answers I needed."

Chapter 43

Matilda

It was Wednesday, and Matilda had not heard from Jodie in several days. She decided to call and invite Jodie and Thomas to dinner Friday night. She would invite the other children to stop by and visit with them.

"Hello, you have reached Jodie and Debbie. If you will leave a brief message and your number, we will return your call. Thank you."

"Hi Jodie, this is your Mother. I thought it would be nice to see you and Thomas. Will you and Thomas come to dinner this Friday night? Call me back. Love you!"

"Jodie must already be in class this morning."

"I am sure she will call you back soon." Edee replied. "Now, we best get going if we make it to Adenville in time for the Noon play."

"Let me get my wrap."

Edee and Matilda had tickets for the play, "The Phantom of The Opera," at a Theatre about three hours away. As fate would have it, Jodie tried to call not long after the two left for the Theatre. Jodie tried to call until it was time for her to leave for class. She would try again this afternoon when she returned.

Only, Jodie would still not reach her Mother. Matilda had found a new way to enjoy life. Matilda and Edee were meeting a group of newfound friends at the Theatre.

"I thoroughly enjoyed the play today. I have never been to the Theatre and have always wanted to see a play. The closest I've ever been was to see the church plays and the ones the children were in at their schools."

"I am sure those were good plays too," replied Doris.

"Yes, they were. I will have to admit that I was a little unsure how to act at the Theatre."

"You seemed to make out just fine," laughed Doris.

Doris and Matilda had become close friends again even though they had been apart for years. Doris moving nearby to Matilda was a blessing. Doris and the friends she met recently at the weekly bible study brought fresh life to Matilda.

The three ladies discussed the play several times during the ride back to Cherry Hill. They enjoyed the play and the time with friends. They finally arrived back at Matilda's around seven o'clock that evening after a full day. Matilda found several messages left by Jodie on her answering machine. She started to call her back but decided to wait for surely Jodie would be calling again! Matilda laughed under her breath thinking how odd it was for Jodie to be searching for her. "The tables have turned on us Jodie!"

Jodie called Thomas several times complaining to him about her mother. She had tried to call Edee too, but only got Charles, whom she evidently awakened from sleep. He was probably resting before his next trip. He sleepily told Jodie not to worry that Matilda and Edee had gone with friends to see a play. Jodie was exasperated. "Why all of a sudden is my Mother not letting me know what is going on in her life and Edee too!" Finally, Jodie reached Matilda before going to bed. Contrary to Jodie's fears, her Mother seemed fine and was in a lively talkative mood. Their conversation lasted for more than thirty minutes.

Jodie was excited that Matilda wanted her to come for dinner and bring Thomas. "It will be nice to have some time with my family."

Matilda seemed to want a quiet dinner with just the two of them. She explained that the others might stop by to visit later. Nonetheless, Jodie was looking forward to spending an evening at home.

Thomas and Jodie left Friday right after classes. The sun was shining beautifully and felt warm on Jodie's skin. She opened the sunroof on Thomas's Solara. With the sun on her face and the air blowing through the car, Jodie settled in for the ride home.

"You look like you are enjoying yourself," commented Thomas.

"Somewhat, I guess" replied Jodie with a huge smile on her face.

"The sun makes you look radiant, Miss Scever."

"Ah, you're just saying that!" teased Jodie.

"Whatever you think, my dear!"

"It is nice being with you Thomas. You make me feel special, and I am always comfortable around you. I feel I can be myself, and not try to make you like me or act a certain way to please you."

"I feel the same way Miss Scever. It is so easy to spend time with you."

"I wonder what mama is fixing us for dinner. I would love to have some good homemade lasagna!"

Thomas curled up his nose at Jodie's dinner choice. "I think some meat and potatoes would be fine."

"What is wrong with lasagna?"

Thomas thought carefully and replied, "It is just not one of my favorites."

Jodie studied Thomas' face and realized there are many things they have never discussed. "Oh. I guess we have not really talked about our favorite foods, have we?"

"It hasn't been necessary. I am not hard to please as long as you don't ask me to eat Mexican food!"

Jodie laughed at the way Thomas answered. "Shucks! I planned to take you to the local Mexican diner for lunch tomorrow. We are friends with the owner – some of the best Mexican fare around Cherry Hill."

"Well, if that is what you want to do, I can try," answered Thomas.

"You would not do that! Seriously, Thomas, we should discuss some of our likes and dislikes, so we are not caught at the last minute making a bad decision."

"I agree. My most favorite thing is spending time with you Miss Scever." Thomas replied as he reached for Jodie's hand.

"You sure know how to change the conversation, don't you? That is sweet though. You too are my favorite to spend time with."

Jodie relaxed her hand in Thomas' hand and laid her head back against the headrest. She felt like a queen in the presence of Thomas Wiley. They carried on simple conversation until soon they were in sight of Jodie's home in Cherry Hill. Jodie seemed anxious to get there, stretching to look beyond Thomas as they circled the roundabout to reach the road leading to Matilda's driveway.

As soon as Thomas stopped the car in Matilda's driveway, the back door flew open and Matilda stood there waving to Thomas and Jodie.

Jodie almost ran to greet her Mother. Thomas felt something different today in the way Jodie was acting. It was a pleasant feeling. He wondered what changes might be taking place for them soon.

"Come on in you two, you are a sight for sore eyes. Look at you both; you look like you have been up to something. Hurry on in and tell me what's going on in your lives."

Thomas and Jodie exchanged looks, "talk about us. You seem to be in a mighty good mood," commented Jodie.

"Oh yes I am Jodie. Life is good. God is good and I have the two of you here to keep me company tonight. It is just a blessed day!"

They continued toward the house. Thomas took a glass of water from Matilda. He felt parched all of a sudden. Jodie immediately went to her bedroom to put away her things. Matilda told Thomas he could use Edee's old room. Before he could finish his glass of water, Matilda was already carrying his bag to Edee's room.

"Hey now, I don't expect you to wait on me Matilda. Let me take my bag."

She obliged and led him into Edee's old room, which looked like it probably did ten years ago when Edee was still at home. At least, the bed looked comfortable. Thomas placed his bag on the bed and returned to the living area to wait for Matilda and Jodie. He sat down in Matilda's recliner. As he reached for a magazine on the side table, a piece of paper fell out of the magazine. Thomas reached to pick it up. It was not just a piece of paper but was a ticket stub. Thomas read, "Phantom of The Opera." Just as Thomas began to look at the ticket, Matilda returned.

"I see you found my ticket stub."

"I'm sorry. It fell out of this theatre magazine when I reached for it."

"Theatre Magazine, since when did you start reading theatre magazines?' asked Jodie coming into the room.

"It is quite a long story, honey, but certainly a good one. We'll talk about it over supper. Thomas, you make yourself at home, watch TV, read, whatever you like. Jodie can help me finish the meal and set the table."

Jodie felt a sense of obligation to follow her mother into the Kitchen. Even so, Jodie could not remember when she had seen her mother act so strangely. Jodie helped Matilda get the food into various serving dishes and to the table. Jodie placed the dinnerware exactly as Matilda instructed. Soon they were all seated and ready for Thomas to ask the blessing. Thomas, Jodie, and Matilda were enjoying small talk over dinner. Matilda had prepared a beef brisket, mashed potatoes, green beans, candied carrots, and a black walnut cake with chocolate icing. Thomas carried on with Matilda about how delicious everything was and how he sure hoped Jodie could cook like she did.

Matilda gently cleared her throat. "Jodie used to help me cook all the time. I am sure she will be able to fix some tasty meals when the time comes."

"Mama, what do you mean… when the time comes?"

"Oh you know. Whenever you have someone special to cook for, which reminds me, you wanted to know about the theatre."

"I do want to know your sudden interest for the theatre, but I am serious about your comment. Are you sick? Do you plan to stop cooking?"

Matilda laid her fork on the table and folded her hands in her lap. Her demeanor gave Jodie even more concern until Matilda suddenly started smiling.

"No, I am not sick, and I have no plans to stop cooking. To the contrary, I may be cooking even more. It gives me pleasure to do things for those I care about."

"Mama, I know you think highly of Thomas, but you don't have to cook for us all the time. Besides, with our schedules, it is hard to come as often as I would like."

Things were uncomfortably quiet for Thomas. He felt rather awkward for a moment. He did not know if he should say something or let Jodie and Matilda talk while he continued to eat. Luckily, for him, Matilda stood and began cutting the cake.

"Thomas, are you ready for a slice of cake? This is Jodie's favorite!"

"Sure, I'll have some," replied Thomas with relief.

"Here you go Thomas and here you are Jodie. Now, let's have some serious conversation. I have something I need to share with you Jodie and Thomas I would like you to hear this too. Please enjoy your cake and just let me talk for a few minutes."

Matilda waited until Jodie nodded her head, then she began. "My recent interest in theatre came about because of my interest in a certain group of new friends. Jodie, you remember my old friend Doris, I told you about."

Jodie nodded affirmatively.

"Doris invited Edee and me to a weekly Bible Study at her home. We have been going for several weeks now. I must say I was hesitant at first because I have felt like a loner since your Father, and I divorced. At any rate, I have met several new friends and have been able to catch up with some of our neighbors."

"That sounds like a good thing for you to do Ms. Matilda," interjected Thomas.

"So what does Bible Study have to do with the Theatre?" Jodie questioned.

"The group decided to do some things together outside of the study. That is where the Theatre comes in. We went to see "Phantom of The Opera" in Ardenville on Wednesday. I must say I enjoyed the day immensely!"

Thomas rubbed Jodie's shoulder. "I am happy for you Matilda. It is wonderful that you have found some friends to do things with and enjoy life."

Matilda smiled and continued, "Thank you Thomas. It really helps not to sit in this house all the time. Doris moving back is such a blessing!"

"Tell us about Doris. I don't remember her."

"Well Jodie, she and I became friends long before you were born. After she married her now-deceased husband, Martin, they moved to California. We tried to keep in touch, but life happens."

Thomas noticed Matilda take a deep breathe. "Matilda, I think that is wonderful. Everyone needs special friends in his or her life."

"Just don't go finding too many friends," exclaimed Jodie. "I might never be able to make contact with you!"

"I understand, Jodie, but I have been lonely for some type of life outside of my church. Don't take me wrong. I love my church family, but sometimes with them, I find myself trying or pretending to be someone I am not. Doris and I share a lot of memories. Even though we were apart for years, it seems like she has only been gone for a little while. That is what happens with true friendships. It really doesn't matter how long you are separated or how many miles are between you. The heart of the friendship never dies."

"It sounds like God knew exactly what you needed." Thomas remarked.

"I believe so too Thomas."

Jodie sat in deep thought at what her Mother had imparted to them. "It would be nice to think that Mabry, and I could be close again one day."

"It is always a possibility. Be patient, pray, and never stop believing."

"I will Mother and I really do want you to be happy. It is just I was worried and afraid something could have happened to you. I am not sure I could handle that right now, or anytime as a matter of fact."

Thomas noticed Jodie the remainder of the evening. She seemed to be trying harder to please her mother. There were no stabbing comments or any smart remarks expecting her mother to laugh with her. Maybe Jodie really can change; Thomas thought.

The next morning, Matilda had coffee, juice, donuts and bagels ready for them. She told them they would have a light breakfast because Doris had invited them to have lunch with her and some friends before they had to go back to Johnsonville. Thomas held his breath waiting for Jodie to make a sharp comment about having to share her time. Instead, Thomas was relieved to hear Jodie remark casually.

"That would be nice. Thomas and I would have to eat anyway. I would love to meet your friends," Jodie exclaimed and raised her glass of Orange Juice in her Mother's direction.

Thomas continued to be amazed at the apparent change in Jodie's attitude.

Chapter 44

Bed & Breakfast

Mabry knew what she had to do to make things right with Chase. She called the number Wilson had given to her. Some woman answered the phone, and after an interrogation by Mabry, called Chase to the phone. It took a few minutes for Chase to answer. When Chase heard Mabry's voice, he hardly knew how to respond.

"Hi Chase, Detective Wilson told me how to reach you. I probably gave the woman who answered the phone a hard time. I just didn't expect a female voice."

"I'm sure Mary Beth will recover."

"She didn't tell me her name, just that she owned the Bed and Breakfast where you are staying."

"I must say I am surprised to hear from you Mabry. I figured you had written me out of your life after last weekend."

"Chase, I really would like to try that conversation again. Do you think we could get together sometime soon?"

"Well, I am on call this weekend. It will be next weekend before I would be able to come see you."

"Maybe I could come to you if you don't mind."

"I don't mind at all Mabry. Tomorrow will work for me if you don't mind my taking calls when necessary."

"That will not be a problem. What time should I come?"

"Well, it will take you a couple of hours to drive here and then your drive back home. Maybe you could plan to arrive around one o' clock tomorrow afternoon. You can see where I am staying and meet Mary Beth. We can talk as long as you want," replied Chase.

"That sounds fine Chase. I will see you tomorrow then."

"I will be waiting."

Chase placed he phone back in the cradle and allowed his mind to wander back to the VillaPasta. He was so happy to hear from Mabry after their argument. Tomorrow could not come soon enough!

Sam drove to the front door of the townhouse to pick up Mabry. He had only been with the family a few weeks, yet he was becoming protective of both Mabry and Barbara. Sicillia left him specific instructions that he should take good care of them while she was gone. Sam knew that Chase Minton had upset Mabry last weekend. He would not let that happen again if he could help it. Mabry promised Sam she would be fine if he would let her drive alone, but Sam refused. After much discussion, Mabry agreed to let Sam drive her and drop her off at Chase's place. Sam would find something to do while in town, but would be close enough to come to Mabry's rescue.

The door to the townhouse opened and not only did Mabry appear, but Barbara was coming toward the SUV, as though she were going with them. Sam immediately jumped to attention and was at the vehicle doors waiting for them.

"Good Evening. Shall I be escorting both of the lovely ladies?"

"Yes Sam. Mother has decided she needs to get out of the house for a while. She is riding with us. Perhaps you can take her to eat and to shop while I spend some time with Chase."

"My pleasure, Ma'am," replied Sam politely although annoyed by the situation.

With Mabry and Barbara in the back seat of the SUV, Sam pulled out of the driveway and turned in the direction of the Interstate. It would take them a couple of hours to reach Bristol County based on the directions Detective Wilson gave Mabry. Sam's cell phone rang as soon as they were on the interstate. He checked the number and realized it was Sicillia calling.

"Sam here, may I help you?"

"Sam, I just wanted to let you know that I will be arriving back in the States next week. How are Mabry and Barbara doing?"

Sam took a few minutes to update Sicillia. "They seem to be doing fine Mrs. Bharti. I am driving them now. They both wanted to have an afternoon out of the house."

He gave her as much information as he felt she would need to be satisfied. He did not want her to worry. Sicillia seemed happy with the report. They ended the call with Sam expecting Sicillia's arrival details in the next forty-eight hours.

Sam used the vehicle's intercom to alert Mabry and Barbara that Sicillia had called and would be returning next week.

"Ladies, excuse me, Mrs. Bharti just called, and she states her plans are to return here next week. She sends her love."

"Thank you Sam," replied Barbara.

Barbara and Mabry engaged in conversation for the next several miles of the trip. They discussed what a blessing Sicillia had been to them during their difficult time. Barbara was enjoying all the pampering and attention Scillia was making sure she, and Mabry received, but they both really wanted the trial to be finished. Barbara hoped for justice and for her and Mabry to be able to have their lives back. The two of them talked about Jodie and about Mabry's issues with Roger Yaddinski. Although they reached no solutions, they were both relieved at being able to talk about these problems. Mabry rested her head on her Mother's shoulder for the last part of their trip to Bristol County.

"We are almost at the Bed and Breakfast Mabry. Wake up so you will not be groggy when we get there."

"I didn't intend to fall asleep."

Mabry checked her eyes and her make-up. Soon they were driving up a long winding paved road. There were Apple Trees lining the fence along the road. Barbara pointed out some horses in the field. Mabry wondered if all this was part of the same property of the Bed and Breakfast. She soon found out as they saw a sign ahead that read,

"Destiny's Horse Farm; Hunting Reserve; & Bed and Breakfast "

Sam spoke into the Intercom again. "It looks like we are here ladies."

Sam parked the SUV and opened the doors for Mabry and Barbara. Mabry instructed Sam to wait until they made sure Chase was here. Barbara also needed a few minutes to rest before going anywhere else. Sam decided to stay outside until he was needed.

Mabry realized they were a little early, but she knocked on the door anyway. It was not long until a tall lanky woman answered the door. Mabry immediately recognized the voice.

"Well hello there! You must be Mabry Allen. Have I heard about you or what? That is all that Chase has talked about since that call last night. Whew! I am sure glad ta see ya Mabry Allen! Come on in and make yourself at home. By the way, I'm Mary Beth."

Mabry stepped inside and introduced her mother to Mary Beth. "This is my Mother, Barbara Allen. She just needs to freshen up and rest for a little while. Our driver is outside waiting for her."

"Well now, it is sure nice to meet you too Mrs. Barbara Allen. You jest help yourself to anything you need. I'll have Mattie come show you around." Mary Beth walked away.

Barbara looked a little overwhelmed. Mabry took her Mother's arm and led her over to the sitting area. They both sat down and waited for Mattie.

"Hello, I'm Mattie. Mary Beth asked me to give you the tour around our farm. She also said to let you know that Detective Minton should be back soon. He had to run over to the office for a few minutes."

"Thank you! I am Mabry Allen and this is my Mother, Barbara Allen."

"It is good to meet you both. Mary Beth asked that I show you to the Ladies room. You will find plenty of toiletries there, please feel free to use whatever you wish. I will get you ladies some refreshments and meet you back here."

Mary Beth came back downstairs to help Mattie with the refreshments for Mabry and her mother. It was actually time to place refreshments in the Parlor for the guests anyway. Mattie took a tray of snacks and iced tea to the sitting area for Mabry and Barbara. She stayed with Mabry and Barbara to give them a little history of the farm. The history of the family and the reason for the name of the farm touched Barbara's heart deeply.

"Mary Beth's parents owned the land and a small house which now serves as worker's quarters. Mary Beth was an only child so of course she inherited all her parents owned. Mary Beth married a local boy. The two of them were sweethearts since seventh grade. They were married right out of high school, and it was not long until they had a little girl, they named Destiny. Destiny was born with a heart defect but grew and was as active as any child around. Destiny loved animals with her favorite being horses. Mary Beth and her husband, Tony scraped enough money to buy a horse and not long after, they bought another. Soon, everyone around the area knew the farm as Destiny's horse farm. At age sixteen, doctors felt Destiny needed some surgery to keep her from having future complications from her heart defect. An unfortunate mistake occurred in the operating room, which resulted in Destiny's kidneys failing. Destiny only lived three days after the surgery."

Mattie paused for a moment as if she could not go on. She released a sigh and continued.

"Eventually, Tony and Mary Beth won a settlement for more than one million dollars. Tony could not get over Destiny's death even after the satisfaction of proving the doctors contributed to her death. One of the workers found Tony out in the horse pasture after he failed to show up for supper. Tony had committed suicide."

"And the rest is history!" Mary Beth stated as she walked up behind Mattie.

Barbara stood to offer gratitude for the hospitality and to show her concern for all the tragedy Mary Beth had witnessed.

"Destiny would love what we've done to the place. I imagine her out there riding and grooming those horses all the time but living on memories will "git ta" a person at times! That is enough reminiscing! Chase called and is on his way back. We are not far from the Sheriff's office, so he should walk through that door nigh on any minute."

"I should be going too. Sam will wonder if I am staying all night!" said Barbara.

Just then, they heard the door open and in walked Chase. He stopped inside and looked at everyone. "I see you have all met."

"Yes, we have son. I was telling them you would be here any minute," replied Mary Beth.

"Hi Chase," said Barbara. "I was just leaving. Sam is waiting for me. We are going to grab something to eat and do a little shopping, maybe some sight-seeing."

"You are welcome to stay, I'm sure. There is plenty to do around here." Chase remarked.

Mary Beth chimed in until they talked Barbara into staying at the farm. They had Sam to come inside as well. Mary Beth took Barbara and Sam to the enclosed back porch where she had a fire going in the outside fireplace. She explained she needed to finish a few chores and she would be back.

Mattie, Chase, and Mabry were still in the sitting room. After answering a few of Mabry's questions, Mattie removed the refreshment tray and headed back to the kitchen leaving Mabry and Chase alone.

"Well, here we are," said Chase.

"Yes, here we are." Mabry replied.

"I see you have already had an afternoon snack."

"Yes, Mattie brought us some tea and some mini-cakes."

"Mabry, you look wonderful."

"Thank you Chase," replied Mabry. She was feeling very awkward. She had never felt this way before. Part of her wanted to run into Chase's arms yet she was afraid of what he might think. Luckily, for Mabry, she did not have to make the decision.

Chase dropped his briefcase to the floor and intently walked to Mabry not taking his eyes away from hers for a moment. Once he reached her, he immediately pulled her into his embrace.

"I am so happy to see you Mabry. I have been miserable without you." Chase whispered in her ear and then kissed her with a passion and hunger from deep inside his heart.

When Chase released Mabry, he saw she had tears in her eyes. She was shivering. Chase took his coat off, wrapped it around Mabry, and held her tight a few more minutes. He knew it would soon be afternoon parlor time, and guests would be coming in and out for refreshment. He did not want Mabry to be any more uncomfortable than she already was.

Chase took Mabry's hand and led her outside to a swing by the Creek. The weather had been pleasant for this time of year, but the afternoon air was beginning to get a slight chill. Chase was glad he had given Mabry his coat. He helped her into the swing first then took a seat beside Mabry. Chase pulled her close to him as they sat silently watching the water rippling over the rocks.

"I love to sit here when I need some quiet time. It helps me to listen to the sound of the water and think how easily the water makes its way over each rock. To me, I see the rocks as obstacles. Each rock the water flows over is another hurdle or trial conquered."

"Chase, I am so sorry for not listening to you. I need to explain my being upset with you and ask your forgiveness. Please forgive me."

"I already have Mabry. As for explanations, none is necessary. The only thing that matters to me now is that you are here. I truly love you and look forward to us spending more time together."

"I look forward to time with you, but…"

"But what, what is it, Mabry?"

"Well, this is going to be difficult after all the problems, I have had trusting men. I want to have a relationship free of guilt, fear, and condemnation. We know little of each other except you probably know more of me than I want you to know."

"That does not change the way I feel."

"That is nice to hear Chase. Let us just take this slow and see how we feel when the trial is over. I have already caused you enough trouble."

"Nonsense! You have not caused me any trouble that I did not deserve. "

"If I had left the dinner and not been so vulnerable to your affection, maybe you would still be in Johnsonville."

"Oh Mabry… I guess I need to confess."

"Confess, what are you confessing?"

"Where do I start? Before I say anything Mabry, you really must believe that I care deeply for you."

"Chase, what are you doing to me?"

Chase stood from the swing, moving in front of Mabry. He bent down on his knees in front of her taking both her hands gently in his.

"Mabry, I thought I was only doing my job. Wilson and I conspired for me to keep an eye on you."

"Keep an eye on me - why?"

"Wilson felt that if we followed you, we might find other evidence. I offered because I... well, because I liked your looks."

"Stop!" Mabry jerked her hands free of his and tried to get up. Chase managed to keep her from knocking him down the embankment.

"Please Mabry, it is not like you are thinking…I promise, let me finish."

"Do you not see that my life is already in turmoil? You are just like all the others."

"Mabry, please, you have to hear me out."

"I have to leave here is what I have to do Chase. It was a mistake for me to think this could work. I am so blind and stupid."

Mabry ran back to the house, leaving Chase on his knees with his head in his hands. Soon, she and Barbara were on their way back to Johnsonville.

Chapter 45

Snow

Valentine's Day came to Johnsonville with one of the fiercest snowstorms the town had seen in a while. The Public Schools had to close; the University closed early, as did most of the businesses in town. The storm caught everyone by surprise. Even the local weather station exclaimed they were not expecting the storm to swing as low as Johnson County. The storm was really going to hurt the town's business and profit from the expected Valentine's Day activities. The local florist had to call in extra help to make all their deliveries before nightfall.

When the florist van pulled into the driveway at Mabry's townhouse, she could not help but wonder if she was receiving flowers from Chase. She started for the door when the bell rang but heard Sam behind her.

"Miss Mabry, I will answer the door for you."

Mabry stood still where she was thinking to herself how glad she would be when Sicillia came back. Sam was just taking his orders too seriously. She sat down on the sofa by the fireplace and anxiously waited to see what the florist had delivered. The fire felt wonderful to her. She had been cold all day and was glad to be back at the townhouse where they could stay warm.

Sam entered the room with a huge vase of roses. They were a beautiful deep red color. It was hard to see Sam's face for the roses! Mabry jumped up to help him. He handed them off to her as he said, "there are more in the entryway. I will be right back with them."

"More," exclaimed Mabry as Sam walked away leaving her wondering. While she waited for Sam, she opened the card on the roses she just placed on the coffee table.

"Oh how sweet," She read the card, "To my beautiful Niece and my precious Sister-In-Law on this special day. I look forward to seeing you on Friday, With Much Love, Sicillia."

"Goodness! What do you have, Mabry?" asked her Mother. Barbara was upstairs resting when the doorbell rang. She made her way down to see who could possibly be calling in this weather.

"They are from Sicillia! She states she is coming in tomorrow!" Mabry handed the card to her Mother. Just then, Sam came back with two more vases of flowers.

"Gracious Sam. How many more do we have?" Mabry asked.

"There are two more, Miss Allen. I will be right back."

"You are kidding!"

Mabry stood there holding the two vases Sam had just deposited with her. Barbara placed the card beside the roses and took one of the latest vases from Mabry.

"Honey, are you just going to stand there?"

"I'm sorry Mom. Can you believe this?"

Sam came back with a huge potted plant that Barbara called a Peace Lily. Mabry fell back onto the sofa knowing Sam was going back to get another vase, pot or something the florist had delivered. He soon returned with another large vase of roses that were peach in color. Mabry just sat on the sofa staring at all the flowers – her eyes wide with surprise.

"Sam, are you certain the florist left all these for us or were they just afraid to drive any further to deliver them to the rightful owner?" Barbara said in a teasing voice.

"Yes Ma'am, they all belong to this address. If you will excuse me now, I will wash my hands and see to dinner."

"Well Mabry, do you want to see who all these are for or do you want me to do that?"

"Wow, I am just amazed. I have never seen this many flowers at one time in my life," answered Mabry. "I can't wait to see who sent all these flowers!"

Mabry stood up to help Barbara, who handed her the small vase of flowers with Mabry's name on the card.

"These other roses are for you as well. The Peace Lily has both our names on the card, and this last plant has my name on it. Go ahead and see who the fresh flowers are from first."

Mabry opened the card and read it aloud. "To My Friend Mabry; I hope you may find it in your heart to forgive me. Jodie." Mabry sat in silence looking at the flowers. She almost teared up, but could not allow herself to think about Jodie.

Barbara then carried the vase of peach roses over and sat them before Mabry. "That was nice of Jodie to send flowers. Now, see who these are from."

The card from the peach roses read: "I am lost without you! Love, Chase."

"How sweet," said Barbara.

Mabry gave her Mother a very stern look as she picked up the vase and carried it to the farthest corner of the room. "I think you should open the last card now Mother."

"Your name is actually first on the card. Are you sure you want me to read it?"

"You open this one mother since your name is on it too, or maybe you should open the one with just your name."

"Oh no, we can do this one now, and I will look at that other one last." Barbara was thankful Sam had placed the plant on the sofa table since it appeared to be heavy. She really did not feel like lifting anything. She was feeling a little weak today. Barbara took the card from the plant and read it aloud.

"Mabry, your peace will soon end. Bar...Barb..." Barbara's voice trailed off as she slowly fell to the floor.

"Mom! Mom! Oh, Sam, come quick, hurry!"

Sam came at a hurried pace to the living room to find Mabry kneeling over Barbara. Sam immediately checked Barbara for a pulse, which he found. She was breathing okay. Sam surmised that she only fainted. However, to be certain and not receive any backlash from Sicillia, he told Mabry to dial "911."

Mabry did as Sam asked. She came back and told Sam they said it would be a few minutes due to the road conditions. The 911 operator said she would send a first responder as soon as possible.

"Miss Allen, what happened?" Sam questioned.

"I am not really sure. She was reading the card from the Peace Lily when she quit talking and just fell to the floor."

"What did the card have on it?"

"Oh, let me get it. I don't even remember now."

Mabry found the card a few inches away from where Barbara fell. She picked it up and read it. She looked up at Sam with eyes full of fear.

"What is it Miss Allen?"

"Oh Sam, this is awful! Do you have any idea who sent this?"

"What does it say Miss Allen?"

"Here, you read it. I can't." Mabry handed the card to Sam and closed her eyes.

Sam took the card and read to himself. "Mabry, your peace will soon end. Barbara, may you find peace once your Mabry is gone."

The doorbell rang several times. Sam placed the card inside his jacket pocket and rose to go open the door. He left a distraught Mabry with Barbara.

Two first responders came back in the room with Sam. They took over caring for Barbara. Sam helped Mabry to the sofa and stayed by her side.

Mabry watched the first responders work with her Mother. It appeared that Barbara was trying to wake up. One of the men noticed Mabry. She started rocking back and forth on the sofa. He also noticed that she was moving her lips as if she were talking to someone.

"Miss, can you hear me? Are you okay?" One of the men questioned Mabry as he continued working with Barbara. He then motioned to Sam, "will you help the lady until we can look at her? You may need to help her lie back on the sofa."

Sam held onto Mabry and tried to steady her. He also noticed the way she was moving her lips. Sam tried to talk to her but she seemed to be in another place or time.

"Just keep talking to her and hold onto her. As soon as we get this lady stable we can take a look at her."

As soon as the first responder had finished his instructions to Sam, Barbara opened her eyes. She seemed confused as she looked around at the two men working with her.

"Ma'am, my name is Danny. I am a first responder. You evidently blacked out and we were called to come help you."

"Where's Mabry?" Barbara asked in a soft whisper.
The two men looked at Sam. He nodded toward Mabry.

"Ma'am, she is on the sofa and is fine. Now, tell us how you are feeling." replied Danny.

"I think I will be okay. I just felt sick and that is all I remember."

Sam motioned for the other first responder to come over to him. Sam reached into his jacket pocket and pulled out the card he had placed there earlier.

"Here, Mrs. Allen was reading this when she fainted."

"I see." He then handed the card to Danny for him to read.

Danny read the card and placed it in his pocket. At that point, someone was calling on Danny's radio. Danny answered. Danny got up and walked back out to the entry door. Sam heard the door close, which seemed to startle Mabry.

"What was that? Did someone come in?" Mabry asked in a shaky voice.

"It's okay Ma'am that was Danny. We are first responders here to help your Mother. I assume this is your Mother?" Sam nodded affirmatively.

Mabry saw that Barbara had opened her eyes. Mabry went to her side.

"Mom, I was so worried about you. Are you okay, please tell me you are okay?"

"I am sweetie, don't worry I will be just fine."

Danny came back into the room. He knelt beside Barbara. "I'm afraid the ambulance is stuck in the snow about one mile down the road. We are going to have to take you to meet them. The roads are in fair condition from that point into town. They should be able to get you to Saints Hospital."

Barbara tried to argue but was too weak. Sam encouraged Barbara to let the first responders take her on to the emergency room for precaution.

"It would be in your best interest Mrs. Allen to do as the gentlemen suggest. I will bring Mabry along in the SUV."

They were all soon on the way to Saints Hospital.

Thomas had driven Jodie and Debbie back to their apartment. He had sent Jodie a text to wait for him after classes. Jodie laughed when she saw the text. Thomas had no idea how long she had been doing things for herself. She and her Mother had no man around to help them. Jodie was the one that the manager of Eagles always called to come in to work when it snowed. She always made it in just fine and returned home without any problem. She started to text Thomas back and tell him she would be fine, but something kept her from sending the message. For whatever reason, Jodie allowed Thomas to drive them home.

"Ladies, you fixed a fine meal. I am stuffed," remarked Thomas.

"It was the least we could do for a gentleman who offered to drive us home," said Jodie. Debbie added her agreement.

"Actually, I should have cooked for you two. You know it is Valentine's Day!"

Jodie stopped getting up the dishes, put her hand on her hip and remarked… "Well sir; we just may take you up on that meal before long. It doesn't have to be a special occasion!"

Thomas laughed, "I'll do it!"

Thomas helped Jodie and Debbie clear the table. He made sure they had everything they might need for a couple of days, in case they could not get out.

"I guess I had better be going before it gets too bad for me to get home. Jodie, do you mind walking to the car with me?"

"Sure, let me get my coat."

Thomas led Jodie to his Solara. He opened the door for her to get inside out of the weather. Jodie watched as Thomas opened the trunk and took out a long box and a gift bag. She turned quickly so he would not see her watching. Thomas opened his door and laid the long box over into the back seat. He shook the snow off his coat and managed to get into the car with the gift bag still intact.

"Wow, it is cold out there. Let me start the car so it will warm up some in here. I will not keep you long. With this weather, I was not sure if you and I would have any time together for a day or two. This is not how I wanted to do this, but I want you to have these gifts today!"

"Thomas, they can wait if you want to wait. I don't mind."

"No, I want you to have them now. It is a good thing I parked under this streetlight, so we can see. Here, let me get the box for you to open first."

Thomas reached into the back seat and pulled the long box forward hitting Jodie in the head. They both laughed at the situation, sitting in a cold car, snow falling all around and Thomas hitting her while trying to make the evening perfect.

Thomas and Jodie spent a few more minutes talking and making plans for the weekend hoping the snow would stop. Thomas was opening Jodie's door to walk her back into the apartment when they heard the sirens.

"What a terrible, cold and snowy night for someone to need an ambulance," commented Jodie.

Thomas agreed with Jodie wondering himself who was in need. He left Jodie at her door with her roses, with a promise and a date for Saturday.

Detective Wilson made it into the office around ten the following morning. There seemed to be a skeleton crew of workers and officers who had made it in. A few of the officers spent the night at the department to keep the phones answered and to respond to any emergencies.

Wilson was making his coffee when his phone rang. He recognized the number as Mabry Allen's.

"JPD, Detective Wilson speaking."

"Detective Wilson, this is Mabry Allen. I seem to be calling you a lot anymore. Is there any possible way you could come to Saints Hospital to see me and my Mother?"

"Why are you at Saints Hospital?"

"That is the reason why we need to talk to you. We are okay but mother was admitted last night. Do you mind?"

"No, I don't mind. I will be over within the hour."

Wilson checked his calendar. He made a few notes and left them on his Secretary's desk in case someone needed to make contact with him. The coffee was ready, so he took time for a cup and filled it again for the road.

When Wilson arrived at the hospital, he spotted Roger Yaddinski leaving from the front entrance. He wondered why Roger was at the hospital. He would have to keep that in mind for later. He had his pick of parking spaces this morning. There were very few cars in the parking lot. He could tell that some of them had been there since the snow started. Wilson stopped at the front desk where a hospital security officer was sitting.

"I see they have you doing double duty," remarked Wilson.

"Yes sir. The volunteers are encouraged not to come in if the weather is dangerous."

"That is a smart move on the hospital's part. Listen, have you been sitting here long?"

"I have been. I arrived here about seven this morning."

Wilson pulled out his badge and showed the security officer. He then asked his question. "That young man that walked out just a couple of minutes ago... did you happen to help him or give him any information?"

"Yes, he stopped and asked for Mabry Allen's room. I explained to him that we did not have a Mabry Allen, only a Barbara Allen. He said he must be mistaken, thanked me, and left."

"Interesting, I appreciate your sharing that information. I have someone expecting me, so I will be on my way. Just one more thing, if you notice the young man come back will you give me a call?"

Wilson gave his card to the Security Officer and left through the front door the same way he came in. Luckily, for him, Mabry had given him Barbara's room number. Wilson left the hospital parking lot hoping to throw anyone off who might be watching him. He pulled away from the hospital, circled the block, returned going to the Emergency Room entrance, and parked there. He used his Officer's hospital clearance to enter the secured doors.

Barbara was sitting up in bed when Wilson arrived at her room. Mabry was asleep in the chair beside her bed. Barbara motioned for Wilson to come in but placed a finger on her lips for him to be quiet not to wake Mabry.

"Thank you for coming detective. We had quite a night last night."

"I'm sure it must have been or Mabry would not have called me, and I take it your being in the hospital has something to do with why I am here."

"Yes, unfortunately it does detective," replied Barbara. Barbara explained how the florist had delivered the many vases of flowers and the plant. She gave him as many details as she could remember and then gave Wilson the card that had the threatening typewritten message. She had to question Sam when they arrived at the hospital to find out what happened to the card. Barbara was able to retrieve the card from Danny before he left the hospital, promising him that they had connections at the JPD who would handle the situation.

Wilson studied the card and questioned Barbara concerning the time the plant arrived, and whether they noticed anyone in the area that did not belong. Barbara explained she, and Mabry had both stayed inside while Sam took care of the person delivering the flowers. Wilson asked how and when he could see Sam.

"I'm afraid Sam has gone to Charlotte to pick up Sicillia from the airport. His plan was to leave early this morning, so he could take his time on the roads. Sicillia's flight is scheduled to arrive at three this afternoon, if there are no delays."

Mabry stirred in the chair. She opened her eyes and realized Detective Wilson had arrived. She sat up suddenly and apologized for sleeping.

"Nonsense! It sounds like you probably need some rest after your ordeal last night."

Wilson asked Mabry some of the same questions. He also asked if she had any idea who might be threatening her.

"I wonder if it is Roger. You know we just completed the Restraining Order on him. He is the only one I can think of now that Stephen is incarcerated."

"Actually, he was the first person I thought of as well. Do you know his schedule this semester?"

"No, I'm afraid I don't. I have tried to stay clear of him as much as possible."

"I know you explained how he seemed to be following and becoming obsessed with you. Do you have any recollection as to when this relationship began changing from friendship to obsession?

"I have thought about that Detective. Roger really helped me after my breakup with Johnny. He knew I was struggling, and he knew I was afraid of my Stepfather. As I told you the other day, he was a big help to me initially. It seems that right before Stephen was arrested things began changing between us, and I haven't had much to do with him since Thanksgiving."

"Thank you Mabry. This will help me fit the pieces together." Wilson turned to Barbara. "How long will you have to stay in the hospital?"

"We think they will let me go home tomorrow. So far, the tests have come back negative for everything they have checked except for my blood. They are giving me shots for that so hopefully I can return home sometime tomorrow."

"Very good, I am glad it was nothing more. I will be in touch. Do not hesitate to call me or the department if anything comes up to cause you concern or to make you feel unsafe."

"We will. Thank you for coming." Mabry stood and walked Wilson to the door.

Mabry hesitated, "Detective? I – I really do appreciate you, and all your department has done for my mother. Please accept my apologies for any trouble I may have caused for you or the investigation."

Detective Wilson reached out to shake Mabry's hand – "You are forgiven, young lady."

Chapter 46

Revelation

Roger Yaddinski got up early in order to make his visit to the Johnsonville Jail before the town started to wake up. He needed to deliver one last message before he could finish his work. So far, his plan was working out well.

It was quiet inside the jail. Only one guard was at the front desk. Roger asked to see Stephen Allen. The guard began questioning Roger as to his purpose, asked for ID, and explained to Roger, he would need to complete some paperwork. Roger felt angry at the questioning, but knew he had to remain calm. He took the papers from the guard and found a chair to sit in while he filled out the forms.

The first section of course was name and address. Roger listed himself as Roger Allen with an address he had used previously without being caught. Hopefully, it would work again since he did have a registered driver's license with the same name and address thanks to a friend who had a side business. Roger completed all the information and received clearance to visit with Stephen. He felt satisfied with himself as he followed the guard into a waiting area.

After a wait of about fifteen minutes, another guard came out from behind a steel door and led Roger to a part of the jail used for visitation. Roger had to pass through a metal detector and then had to empty his pockets. The guard placed his belongings in a locked cabinet before taking Roger into one of the visitation booths. There were five booths that looked like something Roger had seen in old gangster movies. The guard directed Roger to the last booth. While Roger waited for Stephen to be brought out he surveyed his surroundings. The booth was small with heavy-duty iron bars on the window in front of him. A small opening was at the bottom of the window, which appeared to be about nine inches by twelve inches and about three inches in height. It appeared to be large enough to place a hand inside but not much more. Roger saw an inner door open and the same guard following an older looking Stephen stepped into the room.

The guard seated Stephen and explained to them both that they had twenty minutes and no more. Security cameras could capture their every move, and each would be searched again when the visit ended. The guard left.

"What are you doing here?" Stephen growled at Roger as soon as the guard was gone.

"I wanted to deliver some news and watch you squirm a little more." answered Roger with a hint of sarcasm.

"Look son, you, and I are history. Now unless you have something important to say to me, get yourself out of my face!"

"You will never be rid of seeing my face. When you are rotting away in prison, I can guarantee you it will be my face you see daily, and you can thank me for putting you away since you will no longer be able to have Mabry for yourself."

"You have a peculiar way of getting under my skin son, now, what do you want?"

Roger leaned forward toward the window. He placed his hand through the cut-away in the window and released a camera memory card. "You will find what you need to know on this and don't worry about losing it because I have a copy stored in a safe place."

"Just get to the reason you are tormenting me Roger, tell me what's on here and what you want."

"I want to know that you are put away for life. I want to know that you are miserable for as long as you live. As for what is on the card, you should know. It is a picture story of how you hurt Mabry and how you kept me from her."

"You are an idiot son; guard!"

"Oh don't call the guard yet. You have not heard the juicy news I brought to you. Your precious Mabry is living out the last days of her life. Soon you will hear the news of her demise."

"Listen, I may be in jail now, but I will be out one day soon and when I am you better watch your back son, because if you hurt one hair on Mabry's head you will pay with your life."

"Oh, are you threatening me Stephen? You might want to look at the pictures on the card before you make big threats. You will find lots of evidence that can put you away for life."

"You don't have anything on me," laughed Stephen.

"I was there when you dragged Mabry through the woods; I was there when you shot Johnny; I was there when you broke into my apartment both times; and I was there when you bought the knife you used to stab me."

"I know you're an idiot now. Get out of my face; I have had enough of you, guard!"

Roger continued, "Go ahead, and call the guard. Maybe he wants to hear what I have to say. He might want to see your pictures too! You have caused me more misery than you know. When I had a chance with Mabry, you ruined it. Everyone will soon know what a hellish life Mabry had to endure at your hands. They will know how you treated her and how you used her Mother in order to have Mabry. I think Mabry has suffered enough. If I cannot have her, no one will. Do you hear me? No one will have Mabry. She and I will soon be together forever!"

"Son, you are a lunatic. I am through listening to you." Stephen started to get up.

"I will leave but you just remember when you hear about your precious Mabry, that you are the one who caused all the pain." Roger stood and left as Stephen verbalized a string of cursing.

It had been a week since Edee sent flowers to Barbara Allen. She decided to call Barbara just to check up on her. It was not important that Barbara acknowledged the flowers, but Edee did want to know if they were delivered or not.

Barbara answered the phone in a voice that Edee felt sounded very weak.

"Hello Barbara, this is Edee Spencer. How are you feeling today?"

"Oh Hello Edee, I have seen better days, but I am making it."

"I am sorry to hear that. It has been a while since I have talked to you, and I just felt the need to check on you. Would you like me to come for a visit?"

"You know Edee that would be nice. Sicillia is planning to take Mabry to look for some things at our old house. I expect they will be there for a while since it is the first-time Mabry has been back at the house since Thanksgiving."

"I can be there in an hour or so. Could I bring you anything?"

"No, just having your company will be fine," answered Barbara.

"That sounds good to me too. I will come on over."

Edee tidied up and grabbed a pound cake from the freezer to take with her. Edee always had a cake or two in the freezer, just in case she needed to take one to a friend. She placed the Chocolate Pound Cake on a plate and added a fancy ribbon to the top. I hope that the cake will thaw enough by the time I get to Barbara's to serve her a piece thought Edee.

When Roger left the jail, he made his way to the townhouse where Mabry was now living. He had already scoped out the area and knew where to park so to watch the house unnoticed. To Roger's delight, he did not have to watch long at all until the door opened, and Mabry came out followed by her aunt Sicillia. They got into the SUV without the man Roger had seen driving them around town. "This is perfect," he said and laughed heinously.

Mabry appeared to be driving. Roger waited and fell in the traffic flow following Mabry and Sicillia to the Allen's house. He was already planning to pay a surprise visit to Mabry this morning but things seemed to be playing fully into his hands. Roger was quite pleased with himself.

Roger circled the block and parked nearby where he could watch the SUV. After waiting about fifteen minutes, Roger walked quietly up the sidewalk to the door of the Allen house. It still had a yellow crime-scene tape around the doorknob. Sudden memories of that day rushed back into his mind. Stephen had warned him to stay away, but they were in this too deep, so he had knocked on Stephen's door bright and early that November morning. Neither of them anticipated what would take place later that day. Roger let himself dwell upon the memories for just a few minutes until he realized the neighbor across the street was walking in his direction. Roger started down the walk, smiled and spoke a good morning to the gentleman.

"Good Morning. May I help you? I'm afraid you will not find anyone at home here," stated the middle-aged man as he approached Roger.

"I see, sorry I bothered you. I have just been trying to watch the place for them. A person can't be too careful under the circumstances."

"Not a problem, it is good to have neighbors who will watch out for you. I am certain that Barbara and Mabry appreciate what you are doing."

"Yes, I'm sure they do. Well, I will be on my way. Please let Mrs. Allen know she has been in our prayers."

"I certainly will. Thank you again." Roger said politely. Roger proceeded to ring the doorbell. He waited, and then rang it again. Finally, he saw the blinds move as though someone had peeped out to see who was there. He rang the bell again repeatedly! The door slowly opened and Roger saw Mabry standing there with a puzzled look on her face.

"Hey Mabe! I was on my way to your townhouse for a visit this morning and saw you pulling from your driveway. I hope you don't mind that I followed you. Is there anything I can do to help out?"

"Uhh, no not really, my Aunt and I just came to gather a few things."

Roger jerked the door from Mabry's hand. "Nonsense, I want to come in and help. I've never met a woman yet that couldn't use a little manly muscle!"

Roger forced his way into the house and put his right arm around Mabry, so he could move her along. He had already wasted enough time for the neighbor to become suspicious.

"Mabry, who was at the door?" Sicillia questioned from upstairs.

Roger leaned into Mabry's ear, "You had better make up a good lie!"

"Just someone trying to sell me something Aunt Sicillia," answered Mabry.

"Oh, okay. I'm glad you got rid of them."

Roger gripped his hand tightly onto Mabry's wrist and whispered in her ear again. "Stall somehow so she doesn't come downstairs!"

Mabry called out to her Aunt, "I will be back up in a minute. I need a glass of water."

"Good girl," said Roger as he led Mabry to the staircase.

"Now, as long as you do what I say, your Aunt will live, but one wrong move and she dies too!"

"So it was you?" Mabry questioned with fear in her eyes.

"Well of course Darling. Who else did you think it would be...Stephen maybe?"

"You Jerk! Let me go or I will scream for my Aunt to call the police."

"Oh that would not be very wise unless you want the pleasure of watching her die right in front of your eyes!"

Roger took some rope from his jacket and began tying Mabry to the stairwell. He stuffed a handkerchief in her mouth and pulled up a chair from the foyer to sit in while he talked to Mabry. He also took a pistol from his pocket and held it in his lap.

"Now that we are comfy, let's talk; what's that? You have nothing to say! I'll go first then!" Roger said with a sneer as he rubbed Mabry's cheek.

"Do you remember all those times you ran to me for help? I thought you really cared for me! Then when you broke up with Johnny, I knew you would run to me! Guess what? You did, but you were too fickle to see what you had right in front of you! I loved you Mabry Allen! What did you do in return? You walked all over my heart! It was not until I ran up with Stephen that I knew what I had to do."

Mabry began squirming and trying to talk.

Roger slapped her across the face! "Shut-Up! You will listen to me!"

Roger got close enough to Mabry that his breath was heavy on her face. He began to nibble at her ear as she struggled to move away. Roger then grabbed her face.

"Oh Mabry sweetheart, let's not fight."

Mabry managed to kick Roger in the ankle with what little force she could muster.

"You keep trying to fight me, and you will get what's been coming to you sooner than you think, you tramp," Roger yelled.

About that time, Roger heard footsteps. He looked up to see Sicillia standing at the top of the stairs with her mouth open and her eyes wide with horror.

"Hello, Aunt Sicillia. It is a pleasure to meet you. Why don't you come on down and join our little chat?" Roger remarked as he stood pointing the pistol in Sicillia's direction. Mabry saw the pistol and winced. Roger realized she was looking directly at the pistol in his hand.

Roger laughed, "Do you recognize the pistol Mabry? It looks just like yours, doesn't it? Don't worry, it is not, but I am proud of myself for finding one just like yours."

"What is it, you want?" asked Sicillia.

"When you get down here, I will tell you both. Now come on before I come after you!" demanded Roger.

Sicillia thought about running into one of the bedrooms and calling "911" but she was unsure what he might do to Mabry.

"Let me turn the iron off and I'll be down, I don't want it to catch fire." Sicillia quickly turned away from the stairs and managed to dial "911" from her cell phone.

"Where did you go Auntie? You had better get your sweet self-down here before I come after you."

Sicillia quietly laid the cell phone down on the floor as close to the stairwell as possible. "I'm coming. I honestly needed to turn the iron off. Here I am." She finally started to descend the stairs all the while trying to think of how to distract the man, so she might get the gun away from him. Sicillia took a chance and pretended to lose one of her shoes as she let it roll down the stairs.

"What's the matter Aunt Sicillia? Are you too clumsy to come down the stairs in your shoes?" Roger sneered as he picked up her shoe and threw it aside.

Sicillia took the moment when Roger stooped down to speak as loudly as possible. "No, I'm not clumsy. I am not used to Barbara and Mabry's stairs!"

Roger turned his attention back to Sicillia as she slowly descended the stairs. By the time she made it to the bottom step, Roger immediately grabbed her and pushed her down on the stairwell floor beside Mabry. He proceeded to tie the women together and reinforced his work with a long chain that he seemed to pull from out of thin air. He weaved the chain between them and locked it to the stairwell. He left Sicillia's mouth unbound.

"Now, let's see, where was I? Oh yes, I was about to tell you how I met Stephen. It was this past summer. You thought I was in Oregon, but I was actually right here in town. I got a job at the Country Club for the summer as one of the Grounds and Greens Crew. Stephen and I became best friends since we both had you in common, Mabry darling! After spending time working for him, I somehow figured out that it was really Stephen, who you were afraid of so I confronted him. He had just a little too much to drink that night, so he told me everything! What's that you say Aunt Sicillia?"

"Please, let us go. What do you want with us?"

Roger threw his head back and let out a big heinous laugh! "Mabry of course, don't all the men? Just look at those long striking legs. Too bad Stephen is the only one to go there, unless that Detective you hung out with had the pleasure. I might have to take her on before I kill her just to rub it in ole Stephen's face!"

Mabry was so frightened; Sicillia felt her body shaking uncontrollably against hers. "I am serious whoever you are! You

432

need to let us go, and get on with your life. We did not ask you to come here. You need to get off Mabry's property," yelled Sicillia.

To Sicillia's surprise, Roger fired a shot at the ceiling out of his frustration.

"I think you need to shut-up too!" as he stuffed her mouth with Kleenex he found on the foyer table. "Now we are going to have to hurry in case your nosey neighbor heard that shot!"

"Where was I? Yes, well when I found out what was going on with Mabry and Stephen, I realized how I could win Mabry's heart, or at least I thought. I disclosed the next day to Stephen that he had told me his dirty little secret and that if he wanted to keep seeing Mabry, he would have to answer to me! Ladies, you are looking at Mabry's hero. I am the one who shot Johnny. I am the one who Stephen knows will kill him if he ever hurts Mabry again although Stephen tried to get rid of me by stabbing me. I am too tough to die without Mabry or maybe my love for Mabry is too tough. Stephen will take the rap for killing Johnny since I switched guns with him before, and again after without either of you knowing. He will take all the punishment for his sins and ours! Stephen and I did a lot of planning. He of course knows the consequences if he squeals. As for me and Mabry, we will spend eternity together!"

Roger stood waving the pistol into the air. "Which one wants to be first?"

Suddenly, there was a knock at the door. Roger froze in his tracks.

433

He looked at Sicillia, then at Mabry. "Mabry, you call out and ask who it is?"

Roger removed the handkerchief from her mouth as he held the pistol to her temple. Mabry was so frightened but managed to do as commanded.

"Who is it?"

"This is Mason from across the road. Is everything okay in there, I thought I heard a shot fired?"

"Yes, we're fine. I accidentally let my pistol fire when I was showing it to my Aunt," replied Mabry.

"I would feel better if you opened the door, so I can see that you are fine!"

"Thank you Mason, but we really are fine and are actually about ready to leave."

Roger noticed something at the window to his left. He swore he saw someone looking in. All this was making him entirely too nervous! He stuffed the handkerchief back into Mabry's mouth and kissed her cheek.

"Mabry, my love, I will give you the honor of being first!"

Sicillia somehow managed to push all the Kleenex forward with her tongue. She was waiting for the right moment and it was now! Sicillia spit the Kleenex with all the force she could manage directly into Roger's face as she let out a blood-curdling scream.

The wet Kleenex and spittle threw Roger off guard as he felt it hit his face. The wet stuff along with Sicilia's scream startled

Roger so that he stumbled backward dropping the pistol causing it to discharge.

All of a sudden, the front door came crashing in and more than one police officer entered to find the gruesome scene.

Wilson stood in amazement, watching the blood that was pooling around Roger Yaddinski's head.

The kind neighbor, Mason, turned and ran from the house at the gruesome picture in front of him.

Chapter 47

Choices

"Well Ladies, it looks like we have the murder case of Johnny Ricks all wrapped up. Sicillia's quick thinking to dial 911 from her cell phone made the process a lot easier than it could have been. Most of Roger's confession is on the 911-dispatch recording. What we do not have recorded, we have witnesses who were standing by the window. We might still be questioning Roger had things turned out differently."

"Scillia always seems to be coming to my rescue! She did so much for us during the last year. You have too Detective. We are very appreciative of you and the department for your work, and for coming whenever we needed you." Barbara stated.

"Will Stephen remain in custody?" asked Mabry.

"Yes, we plan to keep him. Since the murder charges are no longer pending, the trial date will be re-set, but I think we have enough on him that the Judge will not set bond. I am sure he will be charged as an accomplice to the murder of Johnny Ricks. The only thing left that concerns me now is how you will handle the trial if you are called to testify?" Wilson remarked with concern on his brow.

"I know." said Mabry. "I will just have to wait and see if that happens, and if it does I will pray for God to give me the needed strength."

"You are a determined young lady! We will do all we can to keep Stephen in custody. What are your plans now that the murder is behind you?" asked Wilson.

Barbara spoke before Mabry had the chance. "We are going to see that Mabry finishes college, and then we are going to take a long vacation to India to visit with Sicillia. I can't wait to see all the roses Mabry described to me! We will take the next step as we feel directed."

"Yes, we will!" injected Mabry. "Detective Wilson, I am sorry to keep bringing this up but tell me again what charges are being brought against Stephen?"

"That is not a problem Mabry. Stephen will be charged with: assault with a deadly weapon, attempted murder, accomplice to murder, and with sexual assault and rape unless you drop those charges."

"Do you think the evidence is great enough to convict him on the other charges and put him away for a long time?"

"I wish I could answer that Mabry. It does seem we have enough, but it will be in the hands of a jury." Wilson answered.

"Let me pray about it. I hate what he did to me, but I am not sure about participating in that trial after all we have already been through even though I know God will help me."

The doorbell rang, and Sam appeared from the Kitchen to answer the door. Mabry heard him exclaim, "Well hello Mrs.

437

Edee; it is so good to see you again this soon. You and your friend come on in. The Detective is here, but I am sure Mrs. Barbara will want to see you."

Barbara heard Sam and went into the foyer to greet Edee. Detective Wilson stood and made his way toward Mabry.

"I will make my way back to the Department now. If you have any more questions or want to discuss this further just let me know."

"Thank you!" replied Mabry. "I may call you in a few days after I recuperate."

Mabry stood and walked with Wilson toward the door. She was startled when she saw who the friend was with Edee.

"Hi Mabry," said Jodie.

"Hi," replied a somber Mabry.

"Well let's don't just stand here. Everyone come on in and have a seat. Sam, will you get us some tea or coffee, whichever they would like. You know how I like my tea." said Barbara.

"If you don't mind, I would like to speak to Mabry alone if she is willing," responded Jodie.

"Certainly!" Barbara replied not giving Mabry a chance again to speak. "Edee you come on in. We will go into the Kitchen and see what Sam is working on for Dinner."

"Do you want to come in and sit down?" asked Mabry of Jodie.

"Sure, if you don't mind."

Jodie and Mabry took opposite seats in the Living Room. Jodie began to express how sorry she was for all Mabry had to experience recently.

"Edee told me what happened at your home. I know you were frightened beyond words. I am really thankful you were not harmed."

"Thank you. Hopefully, this nightmare is over for good, and I can go on with my life." Mabry replied.

"I would like for us to start our friendship all over again. Do you think you can forgive me for all my actions I took without considering your feelings? I would be most grateful," said Jodie.

Mabry laughed and turned her head away. Jodie was taken by surprise at Mabry's reaction. She almost felt hurt all over again until she noticed that Mabry was no longer laughing but was now crying.

Mabry slowly turned back to face Jodie. "You have no idea how many times I have needed to say the same thing to you. If you only knew what all went on, you would hate me."

"I doubt that." Jodie said.

"Listen, I may as well tell you everything, so I can feel freedom from all this guilt. When you saw me at the Country Club arguing with Johnny, I was there to see you! Stephen had forced me to come. At the time, I thought it was him all along pressuring me, but we know now it was both he and Roger. Anyway, I was there to single you out so Stephen could "take care of you." You know what happened next, and I guess you know now that it was Roger, who fired the fatal shot."

"I do know about Roger."

"That was not the only time Jodie. The night in the hospital, that someone visited you in a dark coat – that was me! I was threatened by Stephen to kill you. I was still under bondage to myself, Stephen and those horrid voices."

"But you didn't kill me?"

"No, I could not bring myself to do such a thing. I was still upset with you but something deep inside stopped me. I think I know what it was," remarked Mabry.

Mabry continued, "I believe now, that it was God working on me. The next morning I called your sister Edee. I had never felt as low as I did that morning. I even thought – thought about ending my own life."

Jodie moved from the side chair to sit on the floor in front of Mabry.

"Anyway, Edee came and told me about God and Jesus and how I could be cleansed of all my wrong-doing. It was amazing to hear that God could love someone like me, but I am so glad He did and He still does Jodie. Because of Him, I have already forgiven you. However; I need your forgiveness!"

Jodie was crying now. She reached up to take Mabry's hands and in between her tears, she whispered her forgiveness of Mabry, her Mother's words clearly ringing in her mind; "the heart of the friendship never dies."

Mabry slipped into the floor beside Jodie. The two reunited friends sat together crying and talking until they heard Barbara call them to Dinner. Mabry, Jodie, Barbara, and Edee spent a wonderful evening with each other. It was great to be together with friends.

"Please promise you will come visit us again soon Edee."

"Yes I will Barbara. I have really enjoyed the evening." I really do want you and Mabry to be happy. I am available anytime you need to talk."

On the way home to her apartment, Jodie asked Edee to drive her by the jail.

Edee was quite surprised at the request. It was getting late and Edee really wanted to get back home.

"Why do we need to go by the jail?" asked Edee.

"Just trust me Edee. I really need a few minutes outside the jail. The jail is well-lit, and we should be fine," replied Jodie.

"Okay, I guess. Please don't be long."

Edee pulled into the parking lot at the Johnsonville Jail. She started to get out with Jodie but Jodie asked her to remain inside the car. Edee watched Jodie walk toward the flower garden at the front of the jail. Jodie sat on the small concrete bench in the middle of the garden. Cars were whipping by, but Jodie did not care who saw her. She bowed her head. Jodie's prayer was so intimate that not even the guard who walked out to check on her could interrupt Jodie.

Edee promised the guard that Jodie would be leaving soon. Edee decided to get out of the car and check on Jodie regardless of Jodie's wishes. She walked slowly to the bench and sat down putting her arm around Jodie.

"Edee, God forgave me when I was in Charleston. He cleansed me and I now belong to Him. I had to come back here tonight to thank Him for this prison, and for allowing me to not only be free from the physical facility, but also now free from my own prison I built around myself. I am so excited about the future. God has sent me a wonderful person in Thomas Wiley. He has allowed forgiveness between Mabry and me. I know now that God is in control and will see me through!"

Edee felt more rejoicing in her soul than she thought she could contain. "Yes, He will Jodie, I do believe He will. He brought you this far, and I can see Him using you in ways we have never dreamed!"

ABOUT THE AUTHOR

D.J. Lambert uses a blend of romance, suspense, and life situations to bring about a sense of involvement and identity with her characters.

Readers will find themselves sharing the experiences of each character as they delve deeper into the commonalities faced by each of us at various times in our lives.

Having written for years as a hobby, D.J. has turned her hobby into a reality. Beginning with her first novel, Freedom's Choice, D.J. plans to continue with a second book in the Freedom series

www.ingramcontent.com/pod-product-compliance
Lightning Source LLC
Chambersburg PA
CBHW070345260626
47161CB00001B/27